The Darkly Luminous Fight for Persephone Parker

LEANNA RENEE HIEBER

LOVE SPELL NEW YORK CITY

To Ronan Harris, VNV Nation,
For encouraging us all to "Remain where there is light."

LOVE SPELL®

May 2010

Published by

Dorchester Publishing Co., Inc.
200 Madison Avenue
New York, NY 10016

ISBN 10: 0-8439-6297-6
ISBN 13: 978-0-8439-6297-0
E-ISBN: 978-1-4285-0860-6

The name "Love Spell" and its logo are trademarks of Dorchester Publishing Co., Inc.

Printed in the United States of America.

10 9 8 7 6 5 4 3 2

Visit us online at www.dorchesterpub.com.

Other books by Leanna Renee Hieber:

***THE STRANGELY BEAUTIFUL TALE OF MISS
PERCY PARKER***

The Enemy Triumphant

"It started with my bride—she whom I took rightfully for my own. She was made of feminine joy, loyalty and youth. She was a creature of light. We were meant to be. We make the necessary pair, she, the light to my shadow!" Darkness's beautiful face looked pained before it again became a skull. The skull grimaced. "She already had a lover, stupid girl. I burned him to a crisp. But he lived on in human pawns, and her damnable heart would never surrender."

Percy didn't bother to hide her disturbed expression. "What happened?"

"Muses followed what was left of him, seeing themselves as his votaries. They jumped into human flesh to form a rather troublesome cult. My sustenance is the sorrow and misery gathered unto me by restless minions I send to mortal earth. But the blasted Guard sends them back empty, starving me, while they live on! But in the end, all human flesh must come through here. Even they."

Percy gulped. "And then?"

"I'm supposed to let any who wish move on to Peace." He waved his hand in disgust. "Not them. I've collected them all into woe."

ACKNOWLEDGMENTS

Thank you friends, family, and Marcos for supporting Miss Percy above and beyond what I could have hoped.

Thank you Marijo and Mom for being the first to read this book.

Thank you to True-Blood.Net and to the many wonderful book bloggers and reviewers who championed Miss Percy and told the world; you are my heroes and I appreciate you more than I can say.

Thank you to McGuffey Foundation School, Edgewood High School and Miami University for not only being wonderful foundations but for the wonderful homecoming.

Thank you to the readers who have fallen for *Strangely Beautiful*; I am so blessed to have you along on this weird and wonderful journey.

Thank you Dorchester for your enthusiasm, and to my editor Chris Keeslar for continuing to make me a better writer.

The Darkly Luminous Fight for Persephone Parker

PROLOGUE

A most critical evening in the Year of Our Lord 1888

Beatrice Tipton knew a few things as she stood with her eyes closed at the edge of the undiscovered country: She knew that her life had been sacrificed to what she hoped would indeed prove to be a greater good. She knew her corset was laced too tight beneath the sensible layers of her dress—she should've thought to bring a traveling cloak, for the Whisper-world was colder than she'd expected. And she knew she was now something like what she'd once fought as the leader of The Guard. She would not be surprised when she opened her eyes and saw other ghosts; they had been something of a profession. What she hadn't expected so soon was to hear the scream of her husband.

They had gone into the Whisper-world side by side, hand in hand, to face the next grim adventure. They couldn't be separated so soon, not again . . . Her eyes shot open. She stood at one end of a long grey corridor of stone. The ceiling was impenetrable darkness, its peak unseen—perhaps it had no rafters—with charcoal clouds heavy in periodic intervals, like trembling chandeliers of mist. These roiled with subtle, unsettling shapes, hissing with soft sighs and eternal regrets. Water lapped at the toe of her sturdy boot; an impossibly black, onyx liquid as unwelcoming and seemingly alive as the mist.

At the other end of the dripping corridor was Ibrahim, wearing the fine tunic in which he died. Once full of the rich honey brown hues of his native Cairo, he was now fitted with the greyscale palette of a ghost, yet even in death Beatrice was struck by his handsome, distinguished figure. She glanced down to find that the gathered folds of her linen dress and its cloth-covered buttons, once beige, were also grey. Her skin was solidly, sickly white. Death had dulled once-bright colours, replacing them with a wash of grim hues that only darkened as the corridor drove inward toward the bosom of the Whisper-world.

"Bea," Ibrahim murmured. The water between their ghostly forms began to spread and deepen. Though it was perhaps the depth of a wide puddle, it felt like an ocean now separated them, and an absurd fear gurgled in Beatrice's ghostly veins, a fear reflected on Ibrahim's face.

"Come back across, love," Beatrice said brightly, swallowing sudden terror, gesturing to her side of the water. "Our Lady said the doors are to be knit here from the periphery and I'll need your help. I cannot do without my Intuition—my second," she said with a rallying smile. "Come take my hand, it's only a bit of water."

Ibrahim had no time to agree, or to join her. And it was no mere water. The Whisper-world was bent on separating, on isolating, and it would do its job. The water rose unnaturally and beat him back: horrific horse heads capping waves, fanged and red-eyed. Beatrice would close the distance, but the water whispered things. Shaking off the soul-chilling misery it wished to impart, she darted forward and flung out her hand. A trickle of blue flame, the only spot of colour in this grey purgatory, leaped forth but died quickly. She might once have been the leader of The Guard, but her power had long since gone to another.

She cursed herself. The Guard had been warned they might be attacked entering the Whisper-world and made captive to Darkness; she should have been prepared. Powerless, they would likely be imprisoned someplace beyond imagining.

Prophecy's war was yet to be waged. Had the goddess left them entirely helpless?

"Ibra—" she started to cry out, steeling herself to wade through the nightmare, but a hand clamped over her mouth and she was pressed into the shadows and against a wall where insidious moisture seeped through her lace collar, past her pinned-up locks to kiss her neck. A strong man held her fast, and while Beatrice prided herself on being a spirited fighter, she struggled in vain.

Ibrahim did not again call her name as he was driven into darkening depths. As frightened as he seemed, perhaps he intended subtlety, keeping her safe by not alerting the agents of Darkness to her presence. The cresting waves of horse heads gnashed around him, nipping bits of his death grey flesh. He ducked beneath his arms and blurted out a familiar stanza, in Arabic: "'To us a different language has been given, and a place besides heaven and hell. Those whose hearts are free have a different soul, a pure jewel excavated from a different mine.'" Oft used by him, her Guard's Intuition, the ancient Sufi words ever confounded misery's minions. The monstrous forms hesitated.

"I'll see you again, my love," Ibrahim called. "I choose to trust in you, Our Lady and in Prophecy!" He turned and fled farther into the labyrinth, leading the terrors on a desperate chase.

Beatrice sobbed against the palm of her unseen captor, her lover's words ringing in her ears. How odd for Ibrahim to have found faith in this terrible transition. Or perhaps he said those words—once her Guard's favourite verse—only for her, as a reminder to keep faith in the tasks to come.

"Let him go, leader, we cannot help him here alone," her captor said. His voice was gruff and heavily accented. Beatrice dimly recognized it as old Irish or Scots. Gaelic. "Help London's Guard and they can help him. You know what to do."

The man spun out into the dim light of the corridor, kept her pinned in his grasp but away from the wall. Immediately she could breathe more easily. Whisper-world moisture, it would seem, was a potent poison. Beatrice stared into the grey eyes of a rugged spirit once as handsome as a warrior god, fabric draped over his firm, bare chest, metal bands and leather thongs encircling his arms. His hair was a grey mane down his back. He took his hand from her mouth.

"Who are you and what do you know about The Guard?" Beatrice hissed.

The man held up a pendant. It was a plain locket that sparked a familiar blue at the edges. His palm glowed with warm, pale light before fading, an echo of his power lingering in faint traces. Beatrice gritted her teeth. "So you were a Healer. One of us. What does that mean to me now? I gave up the Grand Work years ago—to the very London set you mention. Can't you just leave me to aid my comrade?" She made to follow Ibrahim.

The man held her fast. "Hardly. My name is Aodhan, and Our Lady said to watch for you, Beatrice Tipton. Your work is far from done."

Beatrice scowled. "Yes, the doors and all that. Don't you think I knew she would be of age, don't you think, even without powers, we sensed it was time, that our mortal coils failed and we stepped into this despicable place, sacrificed to the Work once more? Ibrahim can help—"

"He'll be corralled with the others. For now, you must go and make sure of Prophecy. Otherwise none of us will ever be free. Take this. Our Lady saved it for you. It holds power you'll need."

The man clasped the plain locket around her neck. She didn't need it opened to know its contents: some part of the ash of Phoenix, held aside from his burial chamber. Its hazy blue nimbus was indication enough. A sparkling, dancing tendril of fire snaked out from the pendant and kissed her throat. She opened her palm. An orb of cerulean flame appeared, steady, hers again to command. It was a comfort.

Beatrice furrowed her brow and looked again at Aodhan. "How is it you weren't imprisoned like the others?"

"Impossible love opens doors and frees souls," Aodhan murmured, and gestured behind him.

She turned and her heart seized. There was an open portal to England. Beatrice could have recognized her native country anywhere, the patchwork sounds of London's cluttered brick lanes, the gritty smell of industry hanging thick in the grey air. She loved and hated it all at once, but it was colourful, scented and alive, and she'd had no idea how much she could yearn for it in death. In view was a tall, modestly dressed woman in long wool skirts, a cloak and dark blonde hair tucked haphazardly beneath a plain bonnet, walking along cobblestones in Bloomsbury, turning down an unmarked street toward a Romanesque fortress of red sandstone that Beatrice knew well: Athens Academy. The woman hesitated, her fair face troubled, before lifting her skirts and trotting up the stairs.

"I've long been tied to Jane and her world," Aodhan continued. "Tied more to her there than myself here." Jane, the woman Beatrice recognized as the Healer of the modern Guard, heaved open the hefty doors of Athens and vanished within. "And so must you be tied to her world, and to Our Lady, until the vendetta ends."

Beatrice held up a hand. She hated being reminded of duty. "I know I've no choice in this, so I'll not fight you. I'll fight for Ibrahim, and for the hope that Our Lady of Perpetual Trouble will have found her destined love." Muttering, she took a step toward London. She turned back, her hard face softening. "But how is she? Our Lady? Is she with the good professor, well and happy, as they both should be?"

Aodhan's chiseled face darkened. "You've not seen her?"

"Foundations in place, our Guard returned to Cairo,

retired until in death our services would be once more called upon. Our Lady didn't want us to interfere once the course was set; we were to leave them to it. Isn't the girl at the academy?"

"I don't know. I don't think The Guard has found her. All I see is a darkening sky, and if they fail"—he gestured behind him, toward the terrible labyrinth of darkness—"misery will bleed with no suture to stop it. The pins loosened, the veil thin . . . we're about to split open. Not just London, but everywhere. And you know we can't part the veil until *we're* ready, when the doors belong to Light and—"

Beatrice sighed. "Indeed. It seems Our Lady left me all the responsibility. Keep an eye on Ibrahim, will you?" She choked, her emotions getting the better of her. "We fought too hard for too long to be separated again."

Aodhan interjected with sincere empathy, "The Grand Work has never been easy for anyone."

Beatrice nodded a curt good-bye and turned toward England. She closed her eyes, and the shadows receded. The incessant murmurings of misery shifted into a cacophony of clattering city sounds; a whiff of roasted chestnuts from a vendor down a bustling lane was followed by a passing factory-borne mist that tasted slightly sulfuric. The air was warmer. Late fall was turning cold in London, but anything felt warmer than the world of the dead. Opening her eyes, she saw the formidable red sandstone edifice that was her destination.

She looked down and frowned. Her feet floated above the cobblestones. Mundane particulars she'd taken for granted: the firm, solid press and the sound of her boots against stone. And while still greyscale, she was now transparent—invisible to most.

Floating up the sandstone stairs, Beatrice braced herself. She wafted through the hefty front door of Athens Academy, a building that the goddess and her Guard helped secure years ago. "Hmm," she breathed, looking back at the door. "At least that didn't hurt."

Wandering the stately halls, down marble floors and through Romanesque arches, passing in front of oblivious students, Beatrice sought familiar faces. She wondered if she'd recognize the current Guard. None of them had known her. None of them were supposed to. She assumed, however, she'd recognize their leader, Professor Alexi Rychman, and wondered if he'd grown into the intense and formidable man his youthful self had foreshadowed. Beatrice's own Guard had served an unprecedented short time before Alexi's took over. Her personal service, however, had been extended. Not that the deathly-pale mortal girl who now embodied her Lady, one Persephone Parker, would remember anything. The goddess was dead. Young Miss Percy Parker, however, should be very much alive.

It was alarming, then, when Beatrice swept through the infirmary to find the girl in question. Beatrice had only seen her as a snowy-skinned baby, but she'd grown into an eerily beautiful young woman, her white hair splayed like glistening spider silk about her moist face. She lay unconscious, draped in sheets as white as her skin, too much like a lovely marble statue laid atop a tomb.

"Oh dear," Beatrice murmured, floating near. The girl's eyes shot startlingly open, bright white orbs centred with sparkling sapphire. Beatrice retreated to watch and ascertain. She'd only interfere if she must. Fate and Prophecy could only be manipulated so much. Mortals had to make choices, else their destined paths would never take. But this was not a good sign.

A nurse fussed over her, but the girl would not be dissuaded from rising.

"I need a breath of air," Percy murmured, trotting awkwardly to the terrace doors.

Beatrice followed but stopped as the girl choked. A man strolled below, and Percy had seized upon him. Beatrice recognized him, too. Tall and striking, with tousled black locks that brushed his shoulders in the wind that buffeted his sharp features, Alexi Rychman had grown only more compelling through the years. His black robe billowed about him, a crimson cravat tight around his throat, his presence utterly magnetic, though his dark eyes were murky with conflict. Beatrice wasn't worried that Percy stared at him with what was obviously a yearning, aching heart. That was as expected: she should love and ache for him. The problem was the woman who strolled beside Alexi, her arm in his. The woman was a paragon of beauty—save for the fact that her head was wreathed in serpents.

As powerful as he was, Professor Alexi Rychman didn't seem to realize he was courting mythic disaster. The ghosts hovering about the courtyard were murmuring to beware. "You've got it all wrong," Beatrice called out. But Alexi could not hear her, just as she herself could not hear spirits until death, and Percy was too absorbed in the sight below to notice. The confused and stricken look on the girl's face was heartbreaking.

The Gorgon's head of snakes turned their flaming red eyes and forked tongues up at the terrace. Percy loosed a heartrending wail and ran back into the room. "Miss Parker?" The nurse rushed over and returned Percy to her bed. "Poor dear, your friend said she would return to sit with you soon."

"Yes," Beatrice murmured, "you need a friend. You need people to fight with and fight for. You're a target if you're all alone, my lady—The Guard should be at your side!"

Percy's eyes rolled and her breath hitched. "All the creatures of the Old World, and nothing to protect me! The spirits are crying out, but he can't hear the warning . . ." She fainted. The nurse murmured benedictions, pressing a cool cloth to her chalky forehead.

Beatrice bit her lip and flew to the edge of the bed, her panic mounting. "My lady, wake up! Don't you understand what's about to happen? Every Guard that's ever been is in peril, your world is about to be overrun! Fly to that professor of yours and make it right, or all our love will be in vain, in this world *and* the next!" She tried to float down, to shake the death-pale girl, but her transparent hands gained no purchase. Cursing, she flew from the room.

Floating was quite useful in getting places quickly, and in a mere moment she arrived in the grand, colonnaded upstairs foyer of Promethe Hall, staring down at a mosaic eagle and an inscription. "'So knowledge bears the Power and the Light . . .'" Beatrice closed her eyes and hoped whatever was left of Phoenix was listening. Clutching the locket she begged the stones, "Please help! She needs your help; she doesn't know the power she wields. It's eating her alive not rousing her to action. *None of us has ever needed you more!*"

She felt something tickle her hand, and she opened her eyes. A wispy feather of blue flame floated before her. It sparkled, and power enervated her. "Oh, that does feel good," she breathed. Rich life force surged through her body, and she hadn't realized until that moment the extent to which death had limited her senses. While the mortal incarnation of their goddess might not be faring well down the hall, the hallowed fire of The Guard was alive and well in the bricks of Athens.

The feather bobbed off toward the infirmary. It had a mission to complete, and Beatrice trusted it would bring the appropriate parties together. It was his vendetta, after all—Phoenix's, and that of his goddess. Her mind began to wander. Perhaps that's how it was as a ghost; a mind grew restless. Before she knew it, Beatrice wandered the halls she'd strolled years prior, pining for Ibrahim a world away in Cairo while completing her duties in England. It was a bitter irony to return to such a state, still separated from her unlikely soul mate.

Pining felt all the keener as a shade. She had no concept how long she haunted the halls, but she looked out the window and it was dark. Time was different in death, and suddenly she empathized with the goddess, unable to quite grasp the rigours of mortal time—the reason the poor professor had been a bachelor for far longer, surely, than he'd have liked.

Beatrice floated out onto the square cobblestone courtyard near the wide-winged angel fountain dimly illuminated by perimeter gas lamps. Glancing up, she was alarmed to find that the sky had a split layer: the protection her Lady had put around Athens was cracked. "Your shield is broken! The guard dog might find you—Oh, why am I not at the chapel?" She batted at her head, trying to clear the fog of death from a cobwebbed mind.

The chapel at Athens appeared much like any other: a white room with stained-glass angels and a modest altar. Except, this chapel served as a portal to the London Guard's secret meeting space. A black maw of a door currently floated where the altar should have been, a door that led past time and reality into a space where great things could be wrought.

Grim sounds erupted from within. The door belched out the sort of spirits The Guard was meant to fight. Restless and malevolent, they poured free like rioting prisoners. The pins were loose. The veil was lifting on Darkness's terms, not theirs.

Beatrice flew into the portal, down the stairs and into utter chaos. The interior of this sacred space looked much like hers had in Cairo; for all she knew it was the same. The same as The Guard of Rome. Moscow. New Amsterdam; any locations previous Guard had known.

One difference: the current Guard was facing a horror they'd unwittingly invited into their nest, and they were dying. Six middle-aged Londoners who might have otherwise led ordinary lives were being strangled by elongated snakes attached to a Gorgon's head; the woman's beautiful face was now a nightmare. Fire licked the circular room. Insects crawled over petticoats and shirtsleeves. The powerful form of Alexi struggled most heartily against the monster. Patrolling the circle was a chimerical hellhound, the likes of which Beatrice had only seen in fable but was all too real, its gruesome head morphing from one into thirty, all with blood-drenched maws.

However ineffectual their powers, she recognized this Guard, or at least its respective energies: Healer, Memory, Heart, Artist, Intuition and Power—the Power manifesting in their Leader, who guided them all. She compared them to herself, her own power and her own Guard. Would her friends have fared any better? She trembled in fear. What could she do? Where was the essence of Phoenix she'd roused to help them? What would happen if this Guard was killed? What if the restless dead won free reign over the whole mortal world? She'd had a taste of that nightmare and wanted none of it.

Prophecy, as it was called, this daring plan to buck Darkness with mortality, was new territory. While planned to the best of their abilities, the venture was untried and unpredictable, particularly as the girl the goddess had become knew nothing about it. Perhaps they'd gone about it all wrong . . . What if the divinity fondest of the name Persephone had indeed failed, what if her mortal incarnation, this death white, sweet yet fragile Percy Parker, was no match for this fearsome calling?

The Gorgon spoke, taunting. "What a pity your lover never did find you! Maybe it was that unfortunate Miss Parker after all. I wish she were here. I'd have liked to show her this final end to your nauseating, epic drama once and for all. I did think that once I brought you to your knees she'd come running. Ah well. She's a coward after all. Mortal arbiters between life and death, fool romantics, sorry remnants of a charred, dead god—your end has come! It's time for *you* to cross the river!"

"NO."

A voice boomed behind them, and an amazing, blinding white form burst from above. When her bare white feet stepped across the threshold, the altar door snapped shut with a thunderclap. Eyes blazing like stars, hair wild and raging, snowy arms outstretched and glistening with light as her thin white gown whipped in the wind of her own power, nineteen-year-old Persephone Parker descended through fire and entered the circle where the Gorgon stood staring, dumbstruck and quizzical. The spiders scattered and the hellhound squealed; tucking countless incorporeal tails.

Lifting a hand, every muscle taut with energy, Percy Parker spoke and her words cast a marvelous echo. "Demon, you'll not destroy my world!"

No one had ever, including Beatrice, found themselves in such awe. The serpents retracted and The Guard fell limp upon the floor. Lucille scowled. Alexi gaped at Percy transformed by power. Beatrice could see in his eyes, in the way his stern face was lit with wonder, that no matter if he had been led astray, he clearly adored this strangely beautiful creature. Her panicked heart eased; their love was the key to victory. London's Guard began to rouse to their tasks.

Percy considered the spirits madly careening about the space. She frowned. "Go home!" Her upraised hand closed into a firm fist. The pin between worlds, loosened and removed by the Gorgon's call, now had a new mistress. That gritty stone cylinder ground loudly against the floor. It lifted, shedding debris as it began to screw itself back into place.

Everything reacted. The spirits shrieked, though the disquieting noise was audible only to Percy and the ghosts themselves. Beatrice winced. As if pulled by strings, the horde was drawn back through the black hole to the netherworld. Clawing and screaming, unable to shake London loose as they wished, all were absorbed. Beatrice, too, was unable to fight her new form. The eddying force would not be denied, and she like hundreds of others was cast back into the Whisper-world, back into the dank, eternal corridor.

The assembling dead were jostled by a blast—Miss Parker's vanquishing blow. There was a terrible shriek and the stones before them exploded, the seal between worlds molten with power. Ash was everywhere. A squealing, hissing snake head rolled past Beatrice's foot. She stepped on it, and it crunched sickeningly but satisfyingly beneath her boot. Then she took refuge in the anonymity of the mad horde and hoped to elude the grasp of Darkness.

It wasn't long before Aodhan sought Beatrice out, his broad grey form sidling up beside her at the edge of the labyrinthine set of corridors. She answered him before he could even ask. "It's done. She is with them and they are safe."

"Good work," the man said.

Beatrice nodded. "I hope the dear girl's game for the next match."

CHAPTER ONE

"He's nearing," Headmistress Rebecca Thompson said quietly, carefully setting down her teacup lest her trembling hands overturn the saucer. A flurry of action began around her.

The lights were trimmed at their highest, to banish the evening's terrors. The best guest room, readied for their important charge, was again inspected. Private stores of clean clothing and toiletries were seized and prepared. A clatter from the kitchen below signaled that the maid rushed to prepare a fresh pot of tea.

Rebecca remained still, sitting stiff in a high-backed chair, her trembling hand stilled on the knee of a grey wool dress that was quite the worse for wear. Absently she reached up to touch the bruise around her throat where a snake from the head of a Gorgon had nearly choked her to death. In the sumptuous drawing room of the grand Withersby estate, where Lord Elijah held more sway than a second son of the marquess should, such a thing as a Gorgon seemed impossible. But those called The Guard knew better.

"He's here," announced the beauteous Josephine Belledoux, anxiety heightening her French accent. Only two shocking streaks of silver hair might have indicated her age, had the frosty locks not been there since youth. Her typically immaculate coiffure was anything but—a barometer of the night's difficulties. Olive skin flushed, dark eyes wide, she threw open the door. Lifting her torn, doubled skirts, she ran outside, leaving the entrance open in welcome behind her.

Beneath the sheltering stone arches of the portico, a striking figure descended from a carriage and gave Josephine a brief nod of greeting. He placed a finger to his lips. "Keep everyone quiet." Professor Alexi Rychman's rich, low murmur carried like thunder, preceding the storm of his presence. "She's fast asleep, and I dare not wake her."

The professor's usual ensemble was smeared with ash. His finely tailored black frock coat and vest showed stress at the seams; one cuff of his white shirtsleeves was in tatters, his crimson cravat open and lopsided around his neck, the purpling bruise of the Gorgon's embrace gruesomely offsetting his sharply elegant features. But his dark eyes were focused. He'd smoothed his hair into some semblance of order. His pale face, while weary, was relieved.

He reached carefully into the cab, lifting an unconscious woman into his arms. Her petite body wrapped tightly in the folds of his cloak, it was as if Alexi Rychman held the moon swaddled in black, and the warm affection with which he stared at the girl made Josephine gape before she recovered herself. "We're overeager and filled with questions, desperate to know Miss Parker is well . . . and desperate for your forgiveness."

Alexi pursed his lips. "What, must I bless you all with oil and take you into a confessional?"

"Perhaps," Josephine murmured, guiding him up the walk. "I assume, since you're not driven to utter distraction, that she's resting?" He nodded. "And you've . . . made up?"

"As much as a few moments allowed."

"I can only imagine how weary she must be."

"God, yes—think of it," Alexi muttered in awe. "The poor girl woke from fever to find the man who shunned her half strangled while the bowels of hell poured out, rescuing us with entirely foreign powers bursting from her body. Perhaps a trying evening for a heretofore meek young lady."

"Bless her sweet, brave young heart." Josephine held the door as Alexi edged through with the white body in his arms. "Speaking of which . . . how old is she, Alexi?"

"Nineteen," Alexi replied. "Older than the other students at Athens by far," he added carefully, trying to cast in a favourable light the fact that he had been her teacher. "She was only there because her convent didn't know what to do with her."

"Nineteen," Josephine murmured, peering at the crease on Alexi's oft-furrowed brow and the lines near his eyes that placed him at nearly twice that number. "Won't you just be the envy of all?"

A smirk pulled the corner of his chiseled lips. He hesitated in the foyer, eyeing a small door to the right of him that was designed for a lady at a finer engagement, should she wish to dart upstairs and into a washroom to make herself presentable before descending the grand staircase for a perfect entrance. Tonight was no such engagement, but he did wish to bypass ceremony at the front door.

Josephine slipped off ahead. "I'll hold them back," she promised. "The best guest room has been made up; you may take her there directly. One moment."

Alexi heard The Guard murmuring inquiries about Miss Parker's health and his own state of mind. He waited while Josephine shuffled them into the withdrawing room and returned to open the interior door. Passing her without a word, he glanced at the pallid face of their prophecy fulfilled, the seventh member of their exclusive Guard of six and the long-missing piece of his lonely heart. With only the creak of his boots on the stairs, the slow breathing of his beloved and the pounding of his own heart to accompany him, Alexi allowed his mind to wander to the sensual delights that would await him in the coming days.

A vague uncertainty, a creeping shadow of inexperience

damped his desire. What incredible power his dear Percy had shown and wielded, throwing herself into harm's way to save him and his fellows. But had she, inadvertently, escalated the dangers of the Whisper-world? He knew that she didn't understand the magic that burst from within her, or how to use it. He hoped this evening wasn't a further call to arms. There was much of vagary about his calling, and it frustrated him to be so oft cast into the grey areas of divine mystery.

The guest room door was open, the lamps trimmed low, giving the gilt bedposts, fine tapestries and paneled mahogany wood a resonant warmth. The head of the bed was turned down, and Alexi slid Percy, cloak and all, under the covers. She stirred only slightly: a small, aching pout when released. Alexi nearly climbed in beside her to indulge her with a continuing embrace . . . But Percy remained in sleep's hold, and Alexi reminded himself he was a gentleman. Tucking the covers to her bosom, he stepped back. A thousand sentiments were on his lips but he could only stare at her body, with hardly a distinction between the colour of her skin and the crisp white linens save the shadows the graceful lines of her face provided. How could she not think herself beautiful?

He sensed a presence and turned to see Vicar Michael Carroll just beyond the threshold. Bushy haired and ruddy cheeked, an affable man of the cloth, Michael had bright eyes and a smile Merlin would have coveted for its power; his capability for joy was The Guard's most potent balm throughout the years. But even Michael had seen unprecedented strain these past days, noticeable in the deepening circles beneath his eyes.

Alexi walked to the door and closed it quietly behind him, curtly addressing the vicar. "Mr. Carroll?"

"I know." Michael held up his hands in acquiescence. "I've been told to leave you alone, but I know you'll never sleep at this rate, and you need to rest. Your heart's been shut from my powers since our youth. Until now." If it were any other hand placed on his shoulder, Alexi would have shirked it. "You've broken open, my good man. I feel your anxiety and confusion, fear that she'll wake up and want nothing to do with this destiny. She might even question whether she loves you."

Alexi opened his mouth to protest and found he couldn't.

"Love makes a man mad. So allow me to perform a little magic. It's the least I can do." Michael's eyes sparkled strangely.

Alexi stared at his friend, whose gift was knowing hearts, and a looming, burning question sprang to his lips. "What *is* she?"

Michael blinked. "Does it matter? She's Prophecy."

"But if she truly is her namesake, *Persephone,* then is she mortal at all? Will the Whisper-world keep coming to steal her away?" Mounting tension turned Alexi's mouth into a grimace. "If she's a goddess, is she doomed to watch me age and die while she lives on—?"

"Alexi. Whatever powers she may possess, I'm convinced Percy Parker is mortal, albeit a great channel for great deeds. Need I remind you she nearly died in your arms? If there's something of a goddess in her, divinity was forsaken to live a mortal life. It wouldn't be the first time in the history of mankind that—"

"Yes, thank you, Vicar, the comparison's not lost on me," Alexi muttered. His friend was staring at him with knowing amusement. Alexi found himself, to his chagrin, confessing. "I'm . . . addled. I feel . . . oddly full."

"Welcome to *emotions,* Professor." Michael grinned.

"I couldn't . . . Before, I—"

"If you'll permit me?" Michael held his hand up over Alexi's heart, inhaled, exhaled and bestowed his gift. Alexi felt his tension ease. His careening thoughts calmed to love's clarion focus: his desire to be by Percy's side, to be the strength that she needed, to let her passionate nature delight him and ease his weary soul. Indeed, nothing else mattered. For now.

"Thank you," Alexi said, furrowing his brow and puzzling over the complication that was Man.

"My pleasure."

"Now, for the sake of safety, I shall spend the night in this room. But if I hear one word of gossip against Miss Parker's honour—"

"You'll not be suspect, have no fear." Michael moved to the stairs. He stopped, a wistful smile on his lips. "One last thing, Professor. She *adores* you. Don't question that. The girl couldn't close her heart to me if she tried. It's too big, too radiant. A time may come for future worry, but for now, do enjoy true love. Not all of us can." A melancholy look crossed his face before he descended.

Alexi turned back to open the door. His eyes sought Percy's peaceful face, framed by its halo of shimmering spider-silk hair. She was as pale as the ghosts they both could see, yet more alive than anyone he'd known. And she made *him* feel alive. She was his. Not a god's, not destiny's, not The Guard's, not England's but *his*. He'd fight to death and beyond to keep it that way.

CHAPTER TWO

The Whisper-world was in a state of unprecedented chaos. Not that Darkness didn't like a certain amount; he thrived in it, enjoyed creating it. But everything has a scale, and every scale must have a fulcrum. Darkness fancied chaos of his own making, carefully orchestrated and meticulously controlled, with crafted conflicts, builds and climaxes, a well-made play that he, as director, could change at will. There was an art to chaos. Not this. This was not his, and this was not art.

The battle cries of his sworn enemies echoed down the endless halls, they having escaped their prison tower. He would, of course, round them all up again. But it was surely *her* fault.

He glided through the careening forms of once-human energy, spirits too agitated to obey him or offer appropriate deference. His shadow reached out as he passed, black phantom limbs that lengthened to shove spirits out of his way while his body remained gracefully still and erect, tossing spirits toward the river to drown, smashing their fragile heads against stone. His jaw ground with pleasure as he heard each satisfying crunch of bone and gorgeous keening that was the last of a humanity draining away, a pathetic cry of pain and dust, its owner never to plunge from these purgatorial shadows deeper into hell, or even to cross into the mysterious Beyond.

He glided toward a rectangular slate door that hissed, molten liquid bubbling around its edges. The haste and force with which the portal had been closed was evidenced by a few finger bones caught in the corners. Ash was everywhere. It filled what served as Darkness's nostrils as he moved to touch the door still rumbling with residual tremors.

The Groundskeeper appeared, cursing the mess everyone was making of his riverbank, his gravestone gardens, his fountains of mist and trellises of bones. At the mouth of the corridor, he paused, staring into the inscrutable shadows that rose tall and smothering: the lord of the land, himself. The Groundskeeper bowed and scraped, his long coat brushing the wet ground. "Ah, hello, Master," he sputtered. "The crash sent me runnin'. Something dreadful's gone . . ." He stopped and bent down to examine a heap before him, some of which became discernable as body parts made of ash, still hissing with vanquished heat. He cried out, voice cracking, and raked hands through his shock of calico hair.

"Oh, no! My sweetie-snaky-lassy, my Gorgon-girl. What's this? What've you gone and done?" His voice shifted accents as he spoke.

Darkness stepped back, repulsed. This pile of ash was what remained of the Gorgon that had been his spy, his emissary and best soldier. And where was the *dog?* If the dog were in pieces, this place had not yet seen his anger.

"I'll put you together again, my lovely," the Groundskeeper crowed. "You'll be as good as new, just let me just bottle you up! Indeed, Master?"

"Indeed," Darkness replied. "But you'll have to commence another Undoing. The seals must be open. Pour the restless onto the earth until they drag her back!"

"But, Master." The Groundskeeper trembled. "The pins between worlds are sealed fast again." He held up fingers blackened with blood.

"*Undo.* Them. Again," Darkness growled. "As often as it takes."

"But Master, my lovely needs me! The longer she's in pieces, the less of her I can—"

Darkness's shadow arms pounced, twisting the Groundskeeper's wrist and binding with his royal crimson cloak the creature congealed from a hundred spirits who'd once served human masters. Clutching the bloody and sore patches of his servant's hands with one preternatural grip, he held a razorlike nail to his throat with the other. The Groundskeeper squealed like an animal as the nail cut deep, and the sound was caught up in the vast stone chambers and amplified, a warning that the Master was not in a mood to be trifled with.

"Why do you punish those loyal to you?" the Groundskeeper gasped, pleading.

"Because I can't get my hands on who dearly deserves it," Darkness growled. He threw his servant to the floor and kicked his pathetic form for good measure. "Put my best soldier back together. Then. Undo. The. Seals!"

"Yes, Master, of course," the Groundskeeper sniveled, crawling off to procure supplies. As he did, he began an awkward singsong rhyme: "Lucy-Ducy wore a nice dress, Lucy-Ducy made a great mess . . ."

Darkness stared at the sealed door. Anger stung his narrowed eyes and scarlet fire leaped from them. A sharp female voice scolded, "It won't do to light up the whole Whisper-world in one of your tantrums."

Growling, Darkness whirled to face a tall woman wearing the greyscale of death. Her clothes were the sort of layered, stiff Western fashion that his assistant had taken upon her mission to England, along with the name Miss Linden.

"Who. Are. You?" he demanded, keeping himself cloaked in shadow so only the red light of his eyes could be seen. The woman set her jaw, and her eyes, perhaps once a magnificent blue, flashed with pride. If she were terrified she did not look it, but he caught a whiff of fear off her freshly deceased flesh, and the scent of it was tantalizing, delicious. He wanted more.

"My name is Beatrice Tipton, and I led The Guard until the post was ably taken up by my successor. It is my duty to tell you, sir, that all this nonsense between you and my lady *will* come to its inevitable, blessed end, and you will free the noble souls you've taken hostage—"

Darkness roared, and the ghost winced. "You and that damned Guard! I will wage war for her, you know."

"Indeed," Beatrice breathed, trying to sound confident, but again he caught the intoxicating perfume of her fear. The ghost continued, narrowing her eyes: "Pity you can't cross over to the living realm to find her yourself. Perhaps a higher power indeed gave us that advantage. The doors have been blown wide, and your enemy aches for a fight," she warned, nodding to the corridor behind them.

A sudden racket prevented Darkness from questioning her further; a host of separate battle cries in every tongue and custom coalesced into a thunderous shout. He turned to behold a mob of grey spirit bodies in all manner of dress, a tumbling, angry sea of Guard. While their service was long since spent, it seemed they remembered their pasts. They invoked their sacred rites against him as they'd done for eons, disparate cultures made one with a binding language. Music rose in the air. There was enough magic left in them yet to try a fight. But the fact remained that they were trapped in *his* territory.

Darkness chuckled. He raised a fist. Water and shadows leaped to life in the form of dread horses, dark with gnashing teeth. The beasts charged, stampeding, wet and chomping for scraps of dead flesh. The Guards' battle song was drowned by thunderous hooves. Their advance halted, the spirits were driven mercilessly back. Squeezing his fists, Darkness pressed forward the suffocating shadows until voices cried out in agony. This restored a momentary, soothing sense of control, and he reveled in it.

A tapping drew his attention back to the nearby spirit. Desperately chanting something foreign, she rapped upon the heart of the seal between mortal and spirit world. A circle of blue fire flashed against the stone. Looking over her shoulder with enough smug triumph to infuriate him, she stepped nearly through to the other side. With only her head remaining, she hissed, "If you'll excuse me, I've work to do. Have a lovely time cleaning up your mess." Then she vanished along with the fire she'd created.

Darkness whipped shadows forward in a vicious blow, but these fell uselessly against the stone. Damn them! Damn *her*. War, indeed. He'd make it all come undone—every last mortal mind—and bring his rebellious prize home screaming. He'd break her divine body to his eternal will for *every* season.

Beatrice Tipton forced her essence back into the colonnaded, circular room that she recognized well, this sacred space where everything had very nearly gone wrong just hours prior, and murmured thanks to the Phoenix fire for facilitating such coming and going. Free of the oppressive terror that was Darkness, grateful he could not follow, she prayed that Ibrahim would be spared pain if he were again taken hostage. Darkness would not punish him further, as they'd not been seen together, and for that she was grateful. Aodhan had been more help to her than she'd known. To have a friend in the daunting tasks ahead was a comfort she dared not take for granted.

She beheld the sacred space and scowled. "Good God, all of you made a right mess of it in here, didn't you?" There were cracks in the walls and ash in the stones; the stained-glass ceiling of the burning-heart bird showed hairline fissures in its beautiful panes.

At the centre of the floor, Beatrice bent over the great feather in the stone, blowing dust and grit aside. She touched her locket and opened her opposite hand. Blue fire leaped from her fingertips. Hurling it at the feather's tip, she saw a wisp of blue smoke curl up from a keyhole. "The groundwork is laid. The first key ready to reveal its mysteries. Now, to knit the worlds. Ibrahim, don't worry. We'll free you as soon as we've the advantage." Then she flew from the floor, heaving a sigh. Blue fire coursed over her body, invigorating her, inside and out. "I hadn't thought it would feel so refreshing to be at Work again! Come now, my lady. To war!"

CHAPTER THREE

Miss Persephone Parker lay deep in the honeyed thick of dreams, shifting between terrible vision and wonderful memory.

The terrible vision began beautiful but ended in horror,

she recalled. She was young and powerful, standing in an endless field of perfumed flowers. The sky was what she imagined of heaven. Eternal and wondrous, a beautiful black-haired man held her tightly in his arms, and his great wings encircled their clinch, grazing her satin skin, which ached for his touch. Phoenix was more than man or angel; he was a God, a being of sense and light, reason and truth. He was the perfect complement to her life force of beauty, kindness, sensibility and love. Their mutual fellowship of light was blinding. Never had two beings been so suited. They loved each other not because it was destined but merely because it was right and mutually joyous. Their respective divine forces fit together as a puzzle, interlocked and stronger for it.

But jealousy set the God aflame—literally. Darkness set Phoenix on fire, and her lover died before her heavenly eyes. Screams shook the earth. Tears enough to drown the world flooded the ground. His great form crumbled to dust, and the vendetta was born.

She turned back to the cave from whence came murder. Red eyes burned from the shadows. Vengeance flared in her heretofore peaceful breast, fueling a hallowed blue fire forged from the remnants of her one true love—and somehow the girl that was now Miss Parker knew that what she viewed here was a score she would unfortunately have to settle herself.

The scene shifted from nightmare to memory. Here she recognized herself and remembered that friends called her Percy. A distinguished professor held her in his arms. Her body was corseted, swathed in satin, wreathed in heather. He wore a fine frock coat and waltzed with her by moonlight. His black hair lustrous in shafts of silver light, his dark eyes bright and compelling, this was her one true love. Acutely aware of the press of his hand and the curve of his lips, here was her destiny, the man who understood her, who unlocked her eerie visions and made everything strange about her beautiful.

The handsome, stoic face of Professor Alexi Rychman suddenly shifted, and in its place flashed angry red eyes—fiery, terrible eyes—and she heard the all-too-familiar hissing of snakes. She bolted upright, launching herself toward consciousness before those eyes could seek her out.

Percy awoke in a large room she did not know. Upright in a strange bed, thin nightgown askew upon her shoulders, a black cloak that had been wrapped around her body was cast back against the sheets. Tiny flecks of ash remained lodged in the cuffs of her meagre sleeves. She squinted, her pale, sensitive eyes straining against bright light. French doors covered in lace curtains led onto a terrace. Beyond, a few trees and chimneys were visible in the dense morning fog. The room was full of rich furnishings, fresh flowers and finery. Percy had never set foot in a room so regal. All that she recognized in the moment was her own colourless flesh. That, she was sure, was uniquely of her own time and peculiar existence in the year she knew to be 1888.

A tall clock near the bed chimed eight in echoing tones. Works of gilt-framed art on the walls seemed illuminated by their own paint, the distinct style of Miss Josephine Belledoux, a friend of her dear prof—Her heart seized. Where was he?

"Alexi!" Percy gasped, batting locks of ivory white hair out of her eyes.

"Percy," came a rich voice from behind her.

With a rustle, the thick velvet duvet was tossed aside. Percy turned to behold a formidable man who was older than she, singularly breathtaking, and . . . sharing her bed. Her veins flooded with incapacitating heat.

Alexi groggily rose to a seated position at her side. His striking figure, ever clad in various fabrics of black and the occasional grey, was in a state of uncommon disarray. A delectable sound escaped him as he reached for her hand and brought it to his lips, kissing the ring that had so recently betrothed her to him. It wasn't a dream. True, they'd just survived a nightmare, but she'd emerged from the other side victorious—and *his*.

The line of his sternum, the graceful curve of his collarbone, was a fresh sight Percy glimpsed through the open neck of his clothing. This heretofore hidden treasure heightened her feverish temperature. The hem of his signature scarlet cravat clung limply to his collar like a stream of stage blood. The purpling bruise around his neck reminded her of the night's horrific events. She'd never seen him so disheveled, and she'd never allowed herself such an intense flood of emotion at the sight of him.

She choked, overcome. Mere months ago, she could never have imagined this strange fairy tale: to have gone from an awkward student, trembling in this man's presence, to waking beside him as his intended. She found her awkwardness now layered with smoldering heat, making her feel all the more constrained and breathless; delicious torture.

"Do forgive the bold act of lying next to you, Percy," her beloved murmured. "But after last night I was too exhausted to keep watch and, dare I say, too covetous to be out of reach."

"If I'd awoken alone, Alexi, I'd have screamed for you something terrible." She glanced about the room. "Where are we?"

"The grand estate of Lord Elijah Withersby."

"Ah. Are the others here? Your . . . *Guard?*"

"Yes."

"Oh, goodness." Percy felt her face flush a mottled pink. "They don't suppose you and I have . . . ?"

"No, dear." Alexi could not hold back a smirk. "They do not imagine your modesty in jeopardy, if that's what concerns you."

"Ah. I . . . well, I wasn't sure if I ought to be embarrassed before your friends." She gave a nervous laugh.

"No, but . . . As the pleasures of holding you close are such a recent revelation, might your fiancé indulge his newfound heaven again?" What started as a polite request finished more as a demand.

Percy bit her lip, hard. "Please," she breathed, and collapsed against him clumsily. He wrapped his arms around her, breathing slowly in as she relished his nearness. She dared to press her pale lips to the bared portion of his breast.

He shuddered in response, murmuring, "My love. As much as I'd like to forget recent terrible events, I must say it is The Guard who are embarrassed for having so courted danger. I did insist that Prophecy meant *you*. Please believe me. But they wanted none of it; instead, that horrid woman—"

Percy eased back to look up at him, stilling his mouth with her fingertips. "It's done, Alexi. While I barely survived the heartbreak, and *wouldn't* if it were to ever happen again"— Alexi started to make protest, but Percy continued—"we must move forward, you and I, and your Guard. Together." She grimaced and added, "You may apologize, however, for having been very cruel."

"I'm so sorry," he declared, cupping her white cheeks in his hands and staring unflinchingly into her eyes.

She was not inclined to doubt his sincerity. "Apology accepted," she murmured.

He drew her in, greedy. Her body thrilled everywhere at his touch, trembling deliciously in the throes of this foreign intimacy after so many years of thorough loneliness, an odd orphan hardly touched. Newfound heaven, indeed. But then her eyes clouded suddenly in the familiar onset of a vision: A large, black, open door. A long, stone corridor shimmered in the dim beyond. Beckoning. Demanding. The sound of a river . . .

The vision blinked away. "Damn," Percy muttered, rousing from it. More doors.

Alexi brought her eyes up to meet his. "You curse at my embrace?"

Percy shook her head, laughing nervously. "No, a vision. I assure you, I'll never tire of your embrace."

"Visions. I was hoping you'd be done with those. Unless it was a vision of us entwined . . . ? For I assure you, that's in your future," he purred, dragging a finger down her cheek and tracing the hollow of her throat.

"Alas," she sighed after a momentary shiver of anticipation. "It was a door."

Alexi pursed his lips. "I was hoping you'd be done with those, too."

A dreadful, high-pitched shriek that only Percy could hear came through a painting, splintering a pane of glass. A ghost dressed in seventeenth-century foppery swept into the room and lurched, as if hoping to fright them. Alexi, who shared Percy's ability to see the spirit, evaluated both her wincing reaction and the split windowpane; he grimaced.

"Shriekers," he muttered. "My least favourite spirits. Fitting, that a Withersby antecedent should be a noisemaker."

"Shh," Percy commanded. The spirit hung its head and, defeated, vanished through the closed terrace doors just as the bedroom door was flung wide and a boisterous French accent filled the room.

"Lord Withersby! You let them be!" Josephine stopped up short, realizing the spirit she chased was nowhere to be seen. Sheepishly, she turned to the couple who had tastefully disentangled themselves. "Forgive my intrusion, *mes amis,* I thought Great Uncle Withersby might have been after you. He likes to remove covers and do other unmentionable things, and I thought that might be a bit, well . . . Ah. Yes. Indeed. Hrm. Well, I'd better let you both dress for breakfast. All are assembled. Miss Parker, you'll find a change of clothes in the wardrobe. Alexi, you're far too tall for Elijah's clothes, so—"

"I'll continue to look like hell, Josie, thank you. We'll be down in a moment."

The woman nodded and disappeared.

"She seems awfully nervous," Percy noted, feeling her own unease.

"Our lives remain in your debt. If you hadn't come to the chapel, we would have died." Alexi looked away. "I'd have been the downfall of mortal civilization. Me, a *leader*," he spat.

Percy reached out and touched his cheek. "Whatever power lay dormant within me might never have woken without such cataclysm to bring it forth. And I'd have died if you hadn't been able to rouse me. Your light met mine and woke me from death's kiss. My God, though, Alexi . . . It was terrible in the making—all of it. It was as if something were eating me alive from the inside out."

"Your waking powers, surely, pressing against the limits of your mortality. Is that what drove you into the storm?" he asked.

"I tried to warn you," she murmured. "But I was burning up, maddened by whispers and fever, my body so weak."

Alexi glanced at her. "It wasn't just my . . . rejection that incapacitated you?"

Percy looked at him and raised an eyebrow. "Are you gauging the extent of your guilt or my womanly weakness?"

Alexi appeared surprised by her directness. "Perhaps both."

Percy set her jaw. "While you devastated me, Alexi, my condition was compounded by having vomited pomegranate seeds that I never ingested."

Alexi's eyes widened. "Oh, my."

"Perhaps your guilt and my weakness are each given a bit of credit in the face of such inexplicable supernatural phenomena."

"Indeed," he murmured. "You've accepted my apology. But do you forgive me?"

A mere month ago, she might have blurted a silly school-girl's words. But harrowing circumstances had tempered

Percy. He had been quite terrible while their destiny was misunderstood. But she stared at him now, at the love in his eyes, at the way his striking face was drawn with anxiety. She cherished the firm way he held her, and knew that he was unequivocally hers and helplessly under her spell—which was all she needed to know, for she'd long ago been under his.

"Yes," she murmured. He released a kept breath, and his body eased. "But I remain overwhelmed!" she continued. "I wake from fever only to find an entire other world accessible via the chapel of Athens Academy—a world from which such powers and terrors might come to hold court." She offered him a dazed smile. "I've much to learn."

"I've much to teach," Alexi murmured, his tone indicating not the Grand Work but instead something far more intimate. He seized her in an eager, questing kiss. Gasping with pleasure, she drew back. His eyes widened as her thin gown gaped open. The phoenix pendant around her neck dangled in the air between them, but the item of recent keen prophetic interest was overshadowed by bare skin.

His gaze might have set the room on fire—literally—had Percy not righted herself, her entire body flushing with rosy-patched colour. "P-perhaps I'd best dress myself."

"Yes, yes." He turned away, clenching his fists in the bed-clothes as she rose and moved to the side of the room. "But I've gone a lifetime waiting. I shan't wait much longer."

Percy turned to him, her hand on an ornate oriental dressing screen. She smiled, cultivating a never-before-used quality, the feminine wile. "I should hope it won't be long, *Professor,* else our tutorials in your office shall take an entirely distinct turn." His subsequent growl informed her she could well imagine it.

She dressed herself as Alexi attempted to straighten his appearance. The best he could do was retie his cravat, adjust his shirtsleeves and smooth his waistcoat and hair. She glanced over the top of the dressing screen to find him, to her delight, straining to catch a glimpse of her profile, his attempt to be a gentleman failing.

Emerging in a layered, lace-trimmed muslin dress of her favourite light blue, she felt positively regal but unfinished. "Would you clasp the buttons up my back? I'm not used to such elegant trappings that require aid," she admitted, breathless as he approached with smoldering eyes. Life with Alexi might make the mottled blush upon her cheeks a veritable tattoo.

He clasped each pearl button slowly. As his fingers fumbled over the last, at the nape of her neck, his hands trespassed up into her snowy hair. He pulled her against him and mused, "I wonder if Science is disappointed in me. Reason and moderation fly when my hand encounters you." Clearing his throat, he continued, affecting his instructor's voice surely as much for his sake as hers, "Miss Parker, now you must pull yourself together. My fellows expect much of you. And me. Hide your beguiling eyes, for if I show evidence of distraction Lord Elijah Withersby for one will never let the matter alone. I'm sure they're all heartily gossiping as we speak."

And yet they dallied and perhaps would have again lost track of time, reason and moderation, had Lord Withersby the Deceased not swept screaming again through the wall. Percy whirled to him with a firm look and a finger to her lips, shooing him off.

"To be insufferable, I see, runs in the Withersby bloodline," Alexi muttered, placing Percy's arm in his. "Shall we to breakfast, love?"

As they were about to leave the room, Percy noticed a colourful scarf upon a brass peg. She slid it through her fingers unconsciously, moving to wrap it around her head; such a habit it was, to hide her pearlescent hair and pallor from full view.

Alexi caught her hands in his. "Miss Parker." His voice was stern, as though she were in one of his tutorials again.

"Oh, you needn't be worried, Alexi," Elijah replied. "If there was ever a doubt about your omnipotence, your Royal Eeriness, rest assured that we'll never again question the throne. We have been soundly beaten, and bow to our great leader."

"Bow, rather, to my darling Miss Parker," Alexi said, guiding her forward a step.

Elijah's eyes nearly leaped from his skull and his hands rose in dramatic flourish. "My God, Alexi, who are you? Either it's love or a severe blow to the head—though that's one and the same. Doth the great Professor Rychman defer to another? I'm feeling faint." The man turned to Percy and groveled a bit.

Percy giggled and glanced at Alexi, whose sculpted lips were pursed in a familiar expression of irritation. "You may call me Percy, too, Alexi," she murmured, steering clear of what was clearly an ongoing verbal battle.

Her beloved turned next to a tall, hearty woman in a simple dress, sporting dark blonde hair flecked with a few strands of grey. "May I introduce Miss Lucretia Marie O'Shannon Connor, our Healer?"

The woman bounded forward. "Call me Jane, Miss Percy," she bubbled in an Irish brogue. "The rest is such a mouthful."

"None of us know whether that mouthful is her true name or, rather, a more romantic offering she dreamed up when we met." Rebecca smiled sardonically.

Jane's wide hazel eyes glittered. "The great mystery of our age."

"Last but certainly not least," Alexi stated, "Vicar Michael Carroll."

Michael came forward, his face amiable and ruddy cheeked, his bushy hair disheveled as if he'd been raking it in every direction all morning. Tears wet oceanic blue eyes. "My dear Miss Percy; radiant as moonlight, kind and gentle, with such a fierce, loyal heart. Oh, Alexi—if I'd met her, I'd have known she was the one in the instant. I am so sorry. My God, to think we might have lost you, dear girl."

"Vicar Carroll here, our sentimentalist," Alexi said. Michael reached out and clasped Percy's hands. Alexi continued. "He is the Heart—a most valuable asset against the forces of Darkness."

Percy looked into the clergyman's sorrowful gaze, unsure what to do other than offer a smile, releasing this earnest soul from any further guilt. He excused himself to wipe his face with a handkerchief.

"That concludes our number, Percy," Alexi murmured. "If you will have us, my dear, your family awaits."

Percy looked around the room, feeling her orphan's heart swell in her chest, a giddy rush of grateful blessing. "I've always wanted a family," she replied, and even the sharp Elijah could not help but be visibly moved.

Alexi leaned close, his long, aquiline nose brushing Percy's ear, causing her to shiver in delight. "Shall I announce our marriage in the Athens chapel tomorrow?"

"Tomorrow?" Percy blurted. She clapped a hand over her mouth, blushing.

"Is it too soon?" Alexi raised an eyebrow.

"No," Percy gasped, still incredulous at the idea of any husband, let alone this one.

"Good."

A maid entered and curtseyed. Surprisingly, she did not start at the sight of Percy's deathly pallor. Either she had been informed or, perhaps just as likely, had grown accustomed to the unusual company Lord Withersby kept.

"Master, breakfast is ready." She barely concealed an Irish brogue.

"Indeed, Molly, thank you." Elijah rose.

The maid nodded, her red hair bobbing, and Jane winked and smiled. "Always good to see you, Molly m'lass." Hearing her accent, the girl let loose a broad smile and swept away with additional bounce.

The dining room, off the main foyer, was a white room whose carved ceiling rounded cavernously over a sumptuously set table upon a red silk runner. The very latest in gaslit chandeliers blazed above, making the room nearly as bright as the day outside, hazily visible through fine lace curtains and valances drawn and tied with golden cords. Percy, raised in the Spartan atmosphere of a convent, was unaccustomed to such domestic grandeur. When Elijah made an offhand comment about the estate being fitted within the year for the new electric light, she wondered if her simplicity was too evidenced by her subsequent gasp.

As Molly and a second housekeeper cleared the warming trays and the company was bade sit, Alexi, after placing Percy to his right, smugly took the head of the table. Elijah eyed him from the other end.

Alexi patiently waited for the staff to slide the carved wooden door closed behind them before plucking a luminescent white feather from his pocket and tapping it soundlessly against his crystal goblet. Cued by this action, a sudden symphony filled the air. Percy started, looking around her with wide eyes. Alexi turned to her, schoolboy pride glistening in his eyes as he returned the feather to his breast pocket, and said, "A bit of atmospheric noise to discourage eavesdropping."

"How magical!"

"That's the *least* of our parlour tricks that may impress you." Alexi turned to his company. "Allow me to announce happy news. Miss Parker graciously agreed last night to become my wife. We shall return to Athens this evening, where we will be married on the morrow."

"Tomorrow? In a hurry, are we?" Elijah asked with smirk. He yelped when Josephine, seated nearby, tried to surreptitiously kick him under the table. "Why is it that, in the last few days, acts of actual physical violence directed toward my person have increased at an alarming rate?"

"Because," Rebecca was swift to clarify, "your capacity for the daft and the inappropriate has soared to such alarming heights as warrants a sound beating." Her upraised glass was clinked by a giggling Michael's.

"In my own house, no less," Elijah pouted.

"In Auntie's house," Josephine reminded him sweetly.

Alexi turned to his betrothed and Percy grinned; meals at the convent had never been this lively. "You see, Percy, around the age of fourteen we were overtaken by the powers that would forever change our lives. The happening also, however, stunted certain persons' intellectual growth. I believe some of us never actually matured further."

"And so did those born insufferably haughty and miserable remain similarly unaltered," Elijah replied, leveling eyes with Alexi as he took a sip of liqueur.

"But for reaping the benefits of an ever-expanding intellect," Alexi sallied. Elijah snorted. "And so my mind and my heart—the latter of which Miss Parker has taken upon herself to expand—shall be joined with hers in our chapel."

Percy, without the faintest idea of what to say, delicately sipped her glass of cordial, a blush burning her ears.

Jane smiled and gave a toast: "To the betrothed." It was eagerly met.

Percy, trembling, nodded thanks to all. She knew she ought to perhaps say something; they were all looking to her. She opened her mouth and wished her voice weren't so hard to find, but suddenly she didn't have to say a word. A black rectangle of a door popped to life behind Elijah, who whirled in alarm. A tall, middle-aged female spirit with intense features, tightly pinned hair and a piercing gaze, clad in a snugly buttoned traveling dress of contemporary vintage, stepped to the threshold. Alexi jumped to his feet, blue fire immediately in his hand.

The woman opened her mouth, staring intently at Alexi,

and said a word in a language Percy did not know and could not place, yet understood; uncanny facility with language was one of her many gifts. "Peace, friends."

Blue fire extended from Alexi's hands like water from a fountain. Headmistress Thompson rose, her head cocked to the side, her brow furrowed as if in recognition. Percy jumped also to her feet, realizing her ability as The Guard's new translator might never be more important.

"She says, *'Peace, friends,'*" Percy repeated the exact words the others had not heard. The Guard started, recognizing their particular language, and Jane's cup clattered to her saucer.

"You can hear ghosts, Percy?" Jane squeaked.

"Yes," Percy said, unsure why that should alarm the Irishwoman or turn her a sudden bright red. The spirit at what Percy could only assume was the threshold of death smirked, as if knowing Jane's secret, before turning to address the company. She was lovely, in an Amazonian sort of way, her nose a hard, long line with nostrils that flared with strength.

"You likely do not recognize me, but I was one of you," she began. "My name is Mrs. Beatrice Tipton. Born in London, raised in Cairo, I was the leader of The Guard that came before you. The Guard that put the seeds of Prophecy into place."

Percy repeated this and cringed as Alexi pounded his fist against the table. "Really? Well, then, you could've left us some bloody clues, Mrs. Tipton," he barked.

Beatrice raised an eyebrow. "Destiny cannot hold your hand; you must find and make it for yourselves, else it will not hold," she retorted. "Fate means nothing if you do nothing to embrace or honour it. You ended up here together. That's what matters." Percy translated, attempting to exchange the caustic tone for something more gentle, so as not to escalate Alexi's irritation. Her beloved sat, grumbling.

"But . . . I recognize you," Rebecca murmured, still standing.

Beatrice sized up the headmistress. "The vast mental catalogue that is your gift, Headmistress Intuition, serves you well. Indeed, you of all people must have seen me most. Though I tried to stay out of your way, I did work to make sure the sacred bricks of Athens Academy would fall under your capable auspices."

Rebecca's mouth opened at Percy's translation, and her body tensed as if there were a torrent of questions waiting to spring forth. But Beatrice continued. "Do you recall your first charge, the day you received this fate?" She looked at each one of them, evaluating them, and they nodded. "You served my circle that day. That woman in the hospital was our Healer."

"But why did none of you say?" Josephine murmured. "We could have helped each other—"

Beatrice held up a hand. "Our tongues were literally shackled. Our powers gone. Our work done. When you arrived, we were again normal citizens. You see, two Guard are never in the same city. It has never happened like this, there has never been a Prophecy as such, the goddess, Our Lady, never took such a chance as this. It is an unprecedented time. An unprecedented future is before us. And the next phase of battle is at hand." Percy's heart sank as she translated.

"Haven't we fought enough?" Michael murmured.

"It's just begun," the spirit replied. "The Whisper-world is a hazardous place, and war must be brought into your mortal hands to settle the score once and for all." Here Beatrice looked at Percy, which did not go unnoticed.

"And this secondary score commences when?" Alexi asked coolly. "And how may we avoid it? I'll not put my bride anywhere near further danger."

Beatrice fixed him with a deep stare, profound sadness on her face. "You know as well as I that there's no avoiding this. We were bound to serve vengeful gods." She turned with a look that was neither amenable nor even kind as Percy repeated her words, breathless, shrinking from that withering stare. "Tell me something, my lady." Beatrice leaned in, narrowing her eyes. "Do you remember anything of your former existence—the one you relinquished to become what you are now?"

"No," Percy answered, recalling that Alexi had once posited the same question. "I am no divinity. *Please,* I'm flesh and blood and don't understand what's happened to me or why, so please don't expect knowledge of a woman I never was, a woman I'm not," she blurted, visibly shaking as she clutched the tablecloth. Alexi stilled this by placing his hand atop hers.

Beatrice sighed, and her hard stare softened.

"Then you, too, are nothing more than a pawn." Her piercing gaze found the rest of The Guard. "But we've a duty, friends, to free your fellows overtaken by Darkness's vengeance. You've a call to arms. The sooner you take to it, the sooner this damnable business will end. My part will begin past purgatory's walls. When it's time, you'll do yours."

Percy tried to mitigate Beatrice's tone. It was familiar, though, a quality she recognized in her betrothed. Perhaps leaders shared a certain profile.

"And shall we simply intuit our parts?" Alexi hissed. "Query destiny until she unfolds herself, or deign you to give us a bit of direction, Mrs. Tipton?"

"Do what I tell you, when I tell you," the spirit replied, folding her arms.

As Percy repeated this, Alexi straightened in his chair. "Indeed? Well, to my knowledge, I remain the leader." Blue sparks crackled around him, a spire of blue flame in his palm. "And I'm going on a honeymoon, and neither you nor the Whisper-world can change that. I'll fight if I must, but good God give us a *moment's* peace."

Beatrice eyed Percy bitterly, then Alexi, but her voice belied profound emotion. "Of course," she murmured. "Marry her. Celebrate love while you have the chance. Treasure it, please, for life is oft gone before it's even begun."

Percy blushed and turned to Alexi. "We're to marry and celebrate love. Treasure it, even."

Alexi's hand tightened over hers, and he addressed their visitor. "Mrs. Tipton, that's the first sensible thing you've said."

Beatrice smirked, and for a moment the two leaders' expressions were oddly similar. "I've work to do, regardless," she replied, "so consider yourself lucky to gain that time. I must work from the inside out. But you mustn't be gone long." The spirit retreated into the shadows, that damp grey darkness stretching out behind her into what seemed eternity. There came a sound of weeping and water. It was not a place Percy wished to visit.

The ghost came forward again, weary, conflicted. "Lady Percy, don't repeat this: I know the importance of trusting the family fate gave you, but as you've seen, no one, not even these fine people, are infallible. *Our* Heart, Ahmed, was a torrent of visions. None of us could keep up with him, not even you—what you were then—so nobody knew if he spoke truth or madness. But, he warned of betrayals from people dearly close, so . . . do be careful. In the end, Miss Parker, you're the key to everything. It's your duty to protect yourself. No one here would intentionally harm you, but betrayals are always a part of great prophecies, aren't they?" She rallied a meek smile and murmured, "I'll see you soon. Try not to be afraid. Trust your heart. And don't refuse when called."

The ghost turned again to the darkness, lifted her shoulders as if steeling herself, took a deep breath and vanished. A lingering chill slid across the table as the portal shrank away.

Alexi was looking at Percy expectantly. "And?"

Percy stared at her companions, all of whom were looking at her with hope, warmth and anxiety. Of all the times in her life, she had never felt safer than here with her beloved among these new friends. She could choose fear and to anticipate danger around every corner, or she could choose to boldly trust the bonds her heart had so long yearned for. The choice was easy.

"She said not to fear, to trust my heart. And I tell you, this morning, that my heart is with all of you—and I hope you will entrust yours to me in return."

Everyone smiled brightly, especially Michael. Alexi bent close to graze her temple with his lips and, as no one knew what else to say, the conversation turned to the more cheerful talk of a wedding.

"Mrs. Rychman and I shall take time also," Alexi said, "to adjust her to the estate of which she will be mistress. I trust you all to keep order. I expect no communication until a week has passed, after which Percy and I would ask you dine at our estate."

The intimate isolation of which he spoke, the word "wife" and the thought of sharing an estate with him, sounded incredible to Percy's ears, one of her hazy classroom daydreams. Only the sound of her teacup against its saucer and the thrilling press of Alexi's hand upon her knee convinced her otherwise. She belonged to a peculiar destiny, and to this man seated next to her. She'd always wished to belong.

The group quit the table for coffee. Rebecca and Alexi rose in unison. She touched his elbow, and he immediately drew her into an adjoining, oak-paneled hallway. Percy stood frozen, blinking after the retreating figures, and she felt a sudden, surprising flare of jealousy. Would Alexi forever be at the bidding of Headmistress Thompson? Then she chided herself for being foolish. Alexi and the headmistress were her superiors, and she must respect stations established years before, regardless of the fact that Alexi was hers.

Her new friends were close at hand. Jane showed Percy into the withdrawing room and bade her sit on a sumptuously brocaded pouf. Josephine tossed a nonchalant nod toward Rebecca and Alexi and said, "You mustn't mind them. They're always sidling off into deep discussion, and have for years."

"Is that so?" Percy said.

"Without her and Alexi's strength," Jane assured, "we'd never outlast the spirits we battle."

"Of course." Percy nodded. "I have always admired the headmistress's obvious strength of character. In fact, I was always quite intimidated by her."

"We all have been," Josephine confided, taking up the role of hostess and passing out coffee from Molly's silver tray. "Between her and Alexi, we're never at a loss for intensity."

"Indeed," Percy murmured. "Oh! When I first met Alexi . . ."

"Terrify you, did he?" Jane smirked.

"Yes!"

Josephine laughed. "Don't tell him that, he'll take it as a compliment."

"Yes, he did." Percy grinned.

"When did it stop?" Josephine asked. "Your terror?"

Percy thought a moment. "I'd fled alone into a dark foyer at the academy ball, too nervous to be seen." Her voice dropped, and the women leaned closer. "But Alexi sought me out, waltzed with me in moonlight to an echo of music. I was lost to him forever." She blushed and looked at the floor. Jane sighed dreamily.

"Mon Dieu!" Josephine exclaimed. "We must procure you a wedding dress!"

"Oh!" Percy quaked. "What does one wear?"

"Leave that to me," Josephine assured her. "You'll have something fit for a goddess!"

Delight was reflected in Josephine's eyes, but Percy saw wistfulness, too. "Weddings," the Frenchwoman murmured. "They are beautiful things. Everyone should have one."

"You're very beautiful," Percy offered, when Jane reached out a hand and squeezed Josephine's, blushing. "I'm sure you'll have no trouble—"

"Oh, but Josephine likes trouble," Jane said, earning a sideways glance from the other woman. "Besides, this fate . . . limits our options."

Indeed, Percy thought, shifting awkwardly in her seat; none of these people were married. Because they were following the bidding of spirits and gods. And here she was, the young newcomer, up and marrying their leader, her professor. It was a lot to take in.

"Is there anyone we must not hesitate to invite?" Josephine asked, her melancholy gone.

Percy's hand flew to her mouth. "My God, my dearest Marianna! With no one to vouch for my whereabouts, heaven only knows what she'll think!"

"A matter for the headmistress." Josephine slipped into the hall and motioned for Rebecca to join them.

Alexi and Rebecca both rounded the corner, and Alexi's eyes went right to Percy, as if he'd known her exact location even through the wall. Jumping up, Percy offered him the seat by her side and darted to procure him coffee. He smiled broadly. She was unaccustomed to his smile, as he had always furrowed his brow at her before, scowling and brooding. So enthralling was the sight, she nearly spilled his cup. Alexi thanked her and bestowed a lingering kiss upon her cheek; Percy reddened, fell into her seat and nearly dumped both their coffees.

The headmistress darted to a writing desk in the corner. "Of course, I should've thought to send word to Miss Farelei—my apologies, Miss Parker." Procuring a fountain pen and paper, she began scrawling. "I shall say you are well in health and shall return to the grounds this afternoon. Elijah," she called as she went to the window. "May I open the casement for a bit of business?"

"Yes, dear," the other drawled over his coffee, moving to lock the room's sliding doors to prevent intruders.

Rebecca opened the beveled glass panel and loosed a low whistle. An impressive black raven with something glittering on its breast fluttered onto the windowsill. "Frederic, Athene Hall please," the headmistress said to the bird, who obediently opened its beak for the paper, emitted a muffled squawk and flew off.

Elijah unlocked the doors again, to allow passage of the house staff, who were clearly not privy to the less-than-ordinary aspects of the lives of The Guard. Percy herself had never dreamed the headmistress made pet of a raven, much less one who followed commands.

Jane leaned forward in her seat, grinning. "That's Frederic. I've a cat, Marlowe. They've been frightfully useful."

"I should say!"

Alexi patted her knee, enjoying her gaping astonishment.

It was then that the alarm sounded. Hands flew to temples and the company swayed on their feet. "Threadneedle Street. Luminous," Alexi and Rebecca chorused. The Guard rose obediently.

"Couldn't they give us a single day of respite?" Elijah muttered.

"Thank goodness, Percy," Jane exclaimed, taking her by the arm and leading her to the door. "I thought these niceties would never end. Now you get to see us as we truly are."

Josephine was clearly put out. "Could not they have waited until I was in less fine a dress?"

CHAPTER FOUR

Percy allowed the whirlwind to happen around her and watched. She didn't dare posit questions; it was clear that the practices of their odd calling were well established, and she didn't want to seem the intrusive novice. Elijah fussed over Percy at the door, procuring blankets and a traveling cloak, thinking her still delicate and recovering from the previous evening's exertions. Percy was gracious and, indeed, once she drew the curtains of the carriage so that the bright light didn't hurt her eyes, quite comfortable.

The fine carriages of the Withersby estate ushered them expediently southbound. Alexi held Percy as their cab jostled into the city that grew denser and darker with each passing street. He watched her squint out the window. "Are you ready for new wonders?"

Percy chuckled nervously, turning and looking up at him. "Truthfully, I'd rather talk about the wedding. What's happening at Threadneedle?"

He shrugged nonchalantly. "Not uncommon to find spiritual unrest in that general vicinity, centre of the city and all. There was a plague pit nearby."

Percy shuddered, then voiced a sudden worry. "Could I have done more harm than good? Perhaps it's that horrible woman coming for vengeance—"

"Hardly," Alexi scoffed. "You reduced her to ashes. You saved the day, my dear, and none of us shall forget it."

"You and the headmistress said 'Luminous.' What does that mean?"

"When something overtakes a human body—a possession with intent to harm—the bodies glow. When I first
beheld you in my classroom, I thought as much of you."

"Ah," Percy said, recalling that first meeting. "But,
Alexi . . . A possession requires exorcism."

He paused. "Admirable institution, the Catholic Church,"
he began, taking Percy's white hand in his. "And if for
some reason we were entirely indisposed, I imagine the rite
suffices. But the most permanent solution lies in what you
shall soon see."

Percy shook her head. "And no one knows of you? Not
the church? No one? How is this possible?"

"For that, you may in part thank Lord Withersby. He
does have his uses. You'll see." Alexi pointed to a fine Tudor-
style town house. "Here."

Percy turned her attention to the few random passersby.
Some gazed around curiously, as if sensing something was
wrong. All mortals had a certain capability to sense the unknowable, if few could actually see it. Six, it seemed, could
truly affect it.

Once The Guard alighted from their respective carriages
and the drivers were sent off, they linked hands on the street
below and stared at the town house in question. Pale blue
halos lit their bodies. When Alexi seized her hand, Percy felt
a surge of energy blaze up her arm and into the core of her
body. Elijah closed his eyes. He slipped a hand from Josephine's and snapped his fingers. All the lingering and curious citizens wandered off, as if they'd not seen a thing out
of the ordinary.

A fresh wind whipped the edges of Percy's skirt and billowed Alexi's cloak. The same bluish flame that had roused
her from the brink of death now surrounded them in a sapphire circle. A strange, ancient harmony rose, as if the breeze
had tuned strings for them. Alexi's voice cut above it all, in
a private command of peace. He then turned calmly to Rebecca.

"Third-floor den, top of the stairs," the headmistress said. "Young male, catatonic. Luminous."

"Thank you," Alexi said, turning to Percy. "You, my dear, will remain directly behind me." His fellows he told, "The rest as per custom."

The company broke into formation, Alexi at the head, Michael directly at his side, Jane at the other. Percy furrowed her brow as the Irishwoman tied a leather apron around her waist that appeared stained with a dark substance of indiscernible origin. Alexi's steady hand guided Percy behind him, Rebecca close beside. Josephine had slung a rectangular canvas bag over her shoulder and brought up the rear with Elijah, who was scouting for further passersby.

"Once more into the breach, dear friends, once more," Alexi stated.

The house was charged. At the bidding of Michael's upraised hand, doors swung open. They passed through the entrance foyer and up two grand sets of stairs, clearing befuddled maids with startled cries along the way. With calm waves, Elijah managed to send most lazing off with dumb expressions, lulling the tumult. The Guard tore into a fine room with carved cherry paneling from floor to ceiling. A long bar at one end, a wide hearth at the other, lush chairs and a few gaming tables sat sportingly in between. Ornate gaslight sconces burned low.

A pale young man lay crumpled and shuddering on the floor, in a disturbing state of disarray. Alexi directed a powerful gesture at him, and a cord of blue lightning shot forth. The twitching heap of a man groaned, rolling onto his back, and Percy heard a hiss the rest of the group could not.

Jane rushed forward, crossing herself. She lifted a hand glowing with healing light, her palm a small star. She touched the victim's ashen face. His features were revealed as blood magically faded from his cheeks, unmatting from the place upon his crown where a gash mended beneath Jane's fingertips. "Aren't you a pretty one," she murmured, having taken his head onto her lap. Percy grimly realized the dark stains upon her apron were from similarly supernatural wounds.

Josephine strode the room, examining each wall as if measuring space. Rebecca took notes in a small book. Michael moved about, peering at his comrades as if determining symptoms. Elijah approached the subject upon the floor.

"What *is* that suit you're wearing?" He bent over the body. "These nouveau riche. I can't bear it. Excuse me, Miss Connor." Making a face, Elijah bent closer and touched a fingertip to the gentleman's nose. An odd shudder worked him back to his feet.

"Name?" Rebecca asked.

"Matthew Van Courtland. Dutch merchant. Textiles." Elijah's apparent disdain deepened. He stared down at the supine body. "Whatever are you doing in England, sir? You see, it hasn't been amenable to you, has it? Why don't you leave colonialism to us, thank y—"

"Nature of possession?" Rebecca curtly interrupted.

"I broke free," the spirit cried. Percy winced, knowing she was the only one who could hear. "But there's a black dawn coming for you, just like the black plague—but for your mind! You'll ne'er be free. We'll turn the tables on you, just wait." Percy shuddered but said nothing.

Elijah slipped off one shoe and slid his foot beneath Van Courtland's knee.

"Lazy," Jane scoffed, batting at Elijah's foot.

Withersby's face twisted into something pale and helpless, and he wrested away with a growl. "Oh, and to waste such fine brandy!" He turned to face a long mahogany bar, where a decanter and tray of glasses lay broken on the floor in a pool of dark, pungent liquid.

"Well, our friend here seems to have escaped after last night's melee. Most of the offenders were driven back to their proper place, thanks to Miss Percy, but this one managed to indulge his fancy for Van Courtland's innards. He's right terrible, and took many a soul with him on his way to his mass black-death grave." Noticing Percy out of the corner of his eye, he said, "Why, my dear Miss Parker, are you all right?" Everyone turned to stare at her, sunk upon a nearby stool. She supposed she looked as ill as she felt.

"You just wait," the spirit gurgled, its voice wet from inside the mortal trappings of Van Courtland. "Wait and see what we'll do to you when you're dragged to the other side. Especially you who look just like us. I'm sure *special* treats await."

Percy flared with righteous indignation. She turned to Alexi and tried to speak calmly. "He's taunting, saying such things as would not befit a lady's repetition. Be thankful you have deaf ears tonight, friends." She waved a hand that they might not worry further over her.

Alexi turned. "In the presence of a lady? How dare you!" His hand issued a more powerful jolt, binding the victim in shackles of light. There was an immediate shift through Van Courtland's skin, the spirit within struggling to pull free.

The sight was revolting, but Percy watched. Alexi's sparking cords squeezed closer and closer, and she heard the spirit's tirade become struggling gasps. Josephine opened her bag to reveal its contents: a small shimmering painting of an angel. Lifted out to hang upon the opposite wall, the image filled Percy with peace and joy all at once, and she felt the warmth of the phoenix pendant around her neck, flying upon the ruffled folds of her fine dress. Glancing down, she could see her pendant glowing with an empathetic light similar to that in the air here.

Josephine squinted, adjusted the corner of the frame and turned to kneel beside Jane. "Van Courtland, *mon chéri*," she murmured near the man's ear. "Do look at that image. It will soothe you, ease your troubled mind." She had to force open his lids, but once he caught sight of the painting, his eyes ceased their rolling dance of panic. "*Oui,* Matthew, focus. Your guardian angels are by your side, helping you fight. Now, you mustn't remove this painting. It's your guardian angel for life." Her hand was stroking mousy brown hair from his temples. Percy couldn't help noticing Elijah make a face.

With a small flutter of her fingertips, Jane countered the man's convulsions, some of which brought either blood or bile trickling from his thin lips. His muscles unclenched and the fluids ceased, but the battle raged on within him. All the while, it was as if Alexi was drawing the slack from his illuminated threads of sapphire flame, binding his body partly like a weaver, partly like a conductor, constricting the terror with each deft movement, crushing the vehemence out of the terrible presence, light against the force of darkness.

Rebecca, secretarial duties sufficiently undertaken, returned pen and paper to her reticule. Her eyes closed then shot open, a pained breath escaping her. Michael was at once nearby, giving a soft, relaxing sigh. She gifted him with a genuine smile, all discomfort in her features vanishing.

"We must put it down as best we can, Alexi," she said, catching her breath. "There's nothing that it seeks in restlessness that it will not try to inflict by vengeance. It doesn't want peace and so we must dispel it."

"I couldn't agree more," Alexi replied, picking up the tempo of his conduction. The spirit shrieked in Percy's ears, and the fortitude of his vile proclamations was renewed.

"Bind," Alexi called. The group formed a circle, save Jane and Percy. Without taking his eyes from the victim, he knew precisely where his betrothed had sunk into a seat. He transferred one cord of light into the palm opposite, as if they were luminous reins, and his swift hand caught her arm and pulled her up and into the circle where a bond of bluish flame connected each heart in light. A woven star that for years had known six now had seven points.

Percy felt The Guard's power, but there was another sensation here, something else pressing in: the unwelcome and stifling dread of death. Then there came a laugh—Michael's soft laugh—and she could breathe again.

The moment all hands clasped, Alexi shouted in their unknowable tongue, *"Hark."* Music burst tangibly into the air, magic that this union alone created, called sharply into service by their leader. It was lovely, coming partly from the air and partly from their throats, drawing now into a sweet pianissimo.

For a moment the spirit writhing in Van Courtland seemed to listen. The possessed man then began to shake so violently that Jane could hardly control him. He flopped about, gasping for air in a hideous display. Jane swung her arm over him, now bending over his torso, her glowing, healing hand pressed directly to his heart. Maintaining life was a struggle, and she nearly had to pound upon his chest. He was hideous, his skin inhuman, flickering from pale to bruised to rotting before their eyes. Each horrific shift, Jane countered with a renewed healing burst. But she was tiring.

"Alexi," she called softly, and with a fierce cry he threw an arm toward the floor. There was a veritable explosion as he, in his rich and masterful voice, issued a powerful torrent of an otherworldly chant that Percy could compare only to an Old Testament proclamation from God. The possessor hissed as if scalded, and the nauseating metamorphoses of Van Courtland ceased.

The group heaved a huge communal breath, and their circle closed in. Rapt, Rebecca suddenly rattled off a philosophical admonishment that Percy believed was from Sophocles. The spirit growled and hurled unspeakable curses toward her, and Percy gasped until Alexi tossed a fireball down its throat, sufficiently garbling the sound.

"Thank you," Percy murmured.

"I wish you were as deaf as we tonight, dear," Alexi offered.

Van Courtland's body was now bound wholly by flame, and a peculiar chant Alexi named the Cantus of Disassembly flowed from The Guard, a music connected with wind, heartbeats and eternity, bequeathed to their minds and hearts many years ago upon the Grand Work's birth within them. Yet it was somehow familiar to Percy.

There came one last gruesome gasp. Dark fluid was rustling beneath Van Courtland's nearly transparent flesh, in patterns as if he were full of liquid marble. Whether this was blood or the spirit's vile, vaguely tangible essence, it could not be determined, but whatever purity and magic the assembled company had brought to the air, it was being fouled by noxious gases from the usurped body, slipping out every orifice and leaking from beneath his fingernails.

Percy felt her stomach heave. Jane was rotating the star of her palm in slow curves over Van Courtland's body, leaving traces of light hovering there, a misty shroud of a Celtic knot. Her healing white light and Alexi's blue light of purification now bound together over Van Courtland. A punctuation rose to each of their lips, Percy included, and their incredible benediction lulled into a final *"Shhh."*

In a puff of sour-smelling smoke and with a final damning curse, the spirit at last departed the ravaged body of its victim. The group saw their foe for what it was, so rotted and disintegrated that it was but shreds of skin and muscle. This decomposed form lifted up to hover before them, swiveling its horrible head to stare from putrid sockets.

"You should have disassembled," Alexi said angrily. The horror dodged a blast of fire.

"You fools, you fools!" Its jaw flapped as it spoke for Percy's ears alone. "There's no end in sight. It is war, you know, now that the bride is gone. Hell has broken loose. You won't last. We'll win you yet! That fight on the borderland was only the begin—"

"Shut your unholy mouth!" Percy spat. Everyone whirled. She glanced down to see that her bosom had begun to glow white, just like the night prior. Alexi was at her side immediately, embracing, trying to move her behind him, to keep her away from the spirit. But she stood her ground.

"Well, well, so we meet again," the phantasm mocked. "I take it you'll try and banish me like you did at the school? You're such an odd little thing, aren't you? Are you even human? What are—?"

Percy's eyes flashed. A tearing sound thundered through the room, and suddenly a dark rectangular portal opened. Spread out behind was a long dark corridor, and hazy forms floated there, seemingly unaware. Surely, the Whisper-world was at hand. Percy felt a churning power gather within her, but she remained unsure how to control it.

"Darling . . ." Alexi murmured warily, but her eyes stayed fixed on the doorway.

The spirit squealed. "You may banish me back, but I'll keep trying. We all will. Since the bitch fled, we're more resolved than ever."

It cried out as Percy threw her hand forward and, pieces of flesh trailing behind, shot backward as if dragged by invisible hands toward the portal. Beyond, Percy heard a slow singsong chant. "Lucy-Ducy wore a nice dress, Lucy-Ducy made a great mess." Her blood chilled. She dearly hoped the name was just a coincidence.

"Percy, what are you hearing?" Alexi murmured, a tinge of helplessness in his voice. "Tell me what you h—"

"It doesn't matter, love, just nonsense," she replied, forcing herself to remain calm. She took a step toward the portal, needing to clarify the eerie rhyme and yet sickened by it.

"Percy, no." Alexi took hold of her again.

A tall and glowing spirit stepped suddenly to the portal threshold, raising a firm hand in a command to halt. He was hard-featured and rugged, with fabric draped over a broad chest, metal bands and leather around strong arms, and a wild mane of hair. Jane gasped and clapped hands to her mouth. The spirit reached out a powerful hand, grabbed the pile of rot by the neck and tossed it to a heap at his feet where it smacked wetly with a grotesque cry.

Scanning them, the spirit found Jane. His eyes sparkled with fondness. "Oh, my dear Jane," he said in old Gaelic. "How I wish you could hear me and heed my warning."

"I can hear you," Percy replied in the same language. Jane whirled, half shocked and concerned. The rest of the group stared, wondering what new and surprising detail would follow.

"Oh!" the spirit declared. "Are you . . . ? Wait! Oh, pardon me, my lady, the power has awoken you." He fell to his knees.

"No." Percy blushed. "You needn't . . . Please, sir, do get up."

He beamed as he stood. "My name is Aodhan. I was a member of The Guard ages ago, and I guard still. There's a change comin', and I'll help be your guide, White Woman, but not now. This portal shouldn't be open long. It attracts the unwanted, and The Guard daren't enter." He tapped his temple with a transparent finger. "Isn't good for the minds."

Percy nodded. Her companions could do nothing but watch.

"Do me one favour," Aodhan continued. "I know my dearest Jane cannot hear me. Would you please tell her, in private, that I love her?"

"It would be my honour," Percy replied.

"Now, I don't rightly know how this opened. I don't suppose you know how to close it?" Aodhan asked.

Percy whirled to Alexi, who was clearly perturbed by the one-sided conversation. "How did I close the portal last night?"

"I . . . believe you . . . cast your arm out," he replied, his hand a vise upon her.

Percy reached up and closed her hand in a firm fist. With a popping sound, the door began to shrink. Aodhan waved good-bye, receded from view and the door was no more. All eyes fell upon her. She stared at her hand, and again at her body, whose light had faded, and shrugged with a nervous smile. "Well . . . it seems I do have control over the portals, though I've no idea how I opened it in the first place."

"You were angry," Michael stated. "You were feeling threatened."

"Who was that man?" Rebecca barked. "Jane, he kept looking at you."

The Irishwoman's face was a mixture of confusion and fear, so Percy cut in swiftly. "His name is Aodhan, a member of The Guard long ago, and he pledges his help." Jane offered Percy a furtive, grateful glance. There would be a discussion sometime soon, but a moan from Van Courtland recalled them all to their task.

Briefly, Percy caught Alexi's attention. His sculpted lips thinned, and the crease upon his brow deepened. His grip upon her arm did not relent, even when she shifted slightly and said, "It's all right, Alexi. For the moment, all is well."

"I certainly hope so," he said. Percy frowned as he released her, smoothing his dark clothes. He moved to examine the stains upon the floor left from the supernatural melee. Glancing up, he waved a hand and the dim room was suddenly well lit by tall gas flame.

With Jane's aid, Van Courtland again resembled a human being, if not much of one. Josephine tried to keep his gaze on her visual benediction, but his eyes would not stay open. His pulse was faint. He would not rouse. His breaths were shallow. When Elijah came over and examined him, they all shook their heads.

"It may take him a while to recover," Jane said sheepishly.

"If he shall," Rebecca remarked. "It's all right, Jane, it's not your fault. You did everything right. We all did."

Percy eyed Alexi in alarm. His stoic face betrayed nothing, yet Percy, who had spent so much time taking in his most minute details, saw sadness in his eyes. He addressed her evident concern. "We cannot save them all. But we . . . usually do, Percy. We usually do." When she nodded and took his hand, the pinched look around his eyes eased slightly.

Michael went to each member of the group and placed a thumb upon the centre of their back, imparting a frisson of comfort, offering a smile to rally them from the hopelessness they felt when such a vulgar and oppressive session ended thus. Elijah wandered off to soothe a few screaming maids who had somehow eluded his spell; after a wave of his fingers they would bob away, cleansed of all intrusion.

Michael and Alexi lifted Van Courtland and disappeared with him into the master bedroom. To his staff and family it would appear that he'd merely fallen ill, comatose, a mysterious ailment from which he would hopefully someday awake.

Rebecca, having catalogued the particulars of the room the moment of their arrival, rearranged its contents to their exact prior placement, save the broken decanter and glasses, which she gathered into a small leather bag that she cinched and hung at her side. She caught Percy staring and explained, "The less evidence of destruction of his property, the better hope for recovery."

Alexi and Michael returned, and without another word the entire group made its way through the dark and now-slumbering house. "I'll bring the carriage to you, Percy, wait here," Alexi commanded.

As he disappeared around the corner, Percy worried at his cool tone and the way he'd reacted to the portal. Things simply happened around her. It wasn't that she was trying to be trouble, but that spirit had been provoked by her, perhaps was more malevolent because of her. She heartily prayed for Van Courtland.

"Nicely done with the doors, Miss Parker, I think you're a quick study!" Michael exclaimed at her side.

She turned to him, grateful. "Thank you, Michael. I rather needed to hear that."

"Knowing hearts is my talent. Though, I wish my words were always perfect." He glanced unconsciously at Rebecca, who was taking more notes outside the town house door.

The carriage rounded the corner. "Now that you've seen the Grand Work, what do you think?" Alexi asked as he approached Percy, collecting her firmly against him.

"You were incredible to behold, my love. Truly, Alexi, The Guard is a wonder." She thought a moment. "Music to fight the spirits. How odd and incredible. It's like it comes from the very air."

Alexi shrugged. "It wasn't we who determined our weaponry; our talents were set long ago by men and women now forgotten. Inspired by Muses, tuned by the heavens—I suppose they thought every restless spirit needs a lullaby. A Greek chorus, the holiest of holies." He smirked. "Would you rather we shout at them?"

"No, no, there's enough noise as is." Percy chuckled.

"Alexi, old chap," Elijah called, gesturing grandly. "You and your fiancée—good God, how odd to say that—ride in the best carriage as guests of honour. Josie, you come, too. The rest of you divide up among yourselves en route to Athens."

Percy noted out of the corner of her eye that Rebecca's mouth thinned, masking a grimace. Perhaps, she thought, the headmistress was used to riding at Alexi's side; perhaps she had grown attached to little habits that Percy's presence would upset. The headmistress turned and began to walk away. Michael trotted after her with a tiny, "Wait, dear Rebecca. Wait for me."

Percy wondered if the headmistress didn't see, or refused to see.

CHAPTER FIVE

"Alexi," Josephine began as the carriage jolted off toward the centre of London, "I'll take charge of your lady's apparel."

"Ah, good. Spectres and phantasms mustn't derail us, we've a wedding to prepare." He glanced at Percy, who gave him a joyous smile. "Bring the bill for what you buy her, Josie, and I shall remit."

The Frenchwoman turned to Percy, beaming. "There's a woman in Covent Garden—not the most reputable part of town, but her work's swift and exquisite. She tailors for the royal all the time—"

"Josephine," Alexi interrupted. "Do not have my bride looking like an act in a halfpenny theatrical."

"And why not?" Elijah cried, giving a sharp-toothed grin. "You stalk about all day in sweeping black robes. Isn't it fitting to have your bride trailing iridescent textiles like a votaress of Diana on her way to the . . . well, the sacrificial altar? Oh, Miss Terry's Lady Macbeth at the Lyceum sports a gown of beetles' wings. Can you imagine? That would be quite fitting, Your Royal Eeriness."

"You didn't want to treat me to a ride in your carriage," Alexi accused. "You wished to torture me." Percy giggled.

"The sweet lady has to know what she's getting into. You must have worked mighty magic indeed to have her so moony-eyed."

"You mustn't tease Alexi so about his manner, Lord Withersby," Percy said. "I'm far more the misfit. As for moony-eyed—well, I am . . . naturally." She blinked her opalescent eyes.

"I suppose you have a point," Elijah allowed. "Goodness. Your union—simply terrifying. Children living near your estate will tell such tales."

Alexi chuckled, pleased by the concept, but Percy let loose an audible gasp. "But I know nothing of estates! I've no dowry, nothing to bring to this marriage. I haven't the faintest idea how to run a household. No one at the convent ever thought—"

"Darling," Alexi said. "We shan't be a couple who entertains or makes a show of things like many of our station. Our destiny isn't for such luxuries. I believe your peculiar talents far outstrip domestic economy."

"Oh. All right then." But Percy was not convinced. The thought of making a home was as overwhelming as any supernatural task that lay ahead.

Josephine beamed. "Don't worry, Percy, The Guard will come calling. Besides, the Wentworths have been silently running the place for years. They'll run it just as smoothly with you as an addition."

"And more happily." Elijah snorted. "To have something sweet and dainty to look after, rather than His Royal Eeriness, Minister of the Constant Sneer . . ."

Percy glanced at her betrothed. "You don't sneer. Do you?"

"See?" Alexi offered blandly to Elijah.

"Perhaps you've been spared, Miss Parker. So far. But, beware. Who knows what may happen now? My God. The bravery, my dear Miss Parker, the bravery of your young heart! Oh! Take note, Miss Parker—you see?" Elijah cried.

Percy turned. Alexi was indeed sneering. She laughed. "Why, I've never seen that look before, Lord Withersby. You must be its sole inspiration."

As Elijah folded his arms, Alexi changed topics. "Percy, we must discuss what's to become of you, as you cannot in good faith continue as a student. Athens is central to our work, and I want you near. We'll find a place."

"Thank you!" Percy exclaimed. Having only spent a quarter at Athens, she was quite fond of its stately Romanesque halls. It was the first public place imparting any measure of comfort, offered primarily by her friend Marianna and then Alexi.

"So much change," Josephine breathed. "We've been waiting for our seventh for so long, and now that you're here, Percy, everything can change." She glanced hopefully at Elijah, who shifted a bit and turned to stare out the window. Though she tried to mask her disappointment, her expressive face hid nothing from Percy. Alexi seemed oblivious, lost in thought.

The carriage stopped, and Alexi helped Percy from it. Tucked quietly into the middle of London, the surrounding buildings seeming to have turned their backs, a veritable castle of red sandstone rose before them. Percy shielded her eyes, gazing alternately at the familiar rough-hewn bricks, at her new friends and her new fiancé. Students milling about on the stairs stopped to stare. Percy, as Alexi ordered, hadn't draped a scarf around her head. Her tinted glasses remained somewhere in her room, and her white-blue eyes strained against the light. Alexi waved all the youngsters away, gliding smoothly into his role as professor even if his battered attire did not match.

The second carriage pulled up. As the others disembarked Alexi said, "Thank you for escorting us hence, we ask you to keep time until tomorrow morning's ceremony." Reaching out a hand for Percy, he led her up the stairs. Turning, he interrupted a burgeoning conversation between Michael and Elijah, discussing which club had the best cigars. "Mr. Carroll, my good vicar, may I beg a favor?"

"Anything at all," Michael replied, striding up to meet him.

"Would you be so kind as to fetch my sister? She would be furious with me if she missed tomorrow."

"Oh, yes, Alexi. Alexandra *must* be present!" Percy exclaimed. It was not long since a harried evening spent at Miss Rychman's quaint cottage, the home a welcome respite from the spectral hound whose jaws seemed bent on searching out Percy. She prayed it had indeed been put to rest.

Alexi fished in a coat pocket. "These notes ought to suffice for the distance. Tell the driver Nine Hampstead." Percy, glancing at the assembled Guard, noticed Jane was absent, but she was distracted when Josephine took her other hand and whispered conspiratorially, "Percy, you must meet your friend and tell her your news. Now, I'm off! You won't be disappointed." She strolled toward the theatre district, casting one final glance at Elijah.

"Rebecca, your office, in a moment," Alexi directed. The headmistress nodded and disappeared through the main doors. "Percy, my dear"—Alexi steered her, opening the door and gesturing her inside—"I'll escort you to your hall, but then I must discuss how we inform the faculty of our new . . . status. I'll leave you to your friend and come to call on you this evening to bid you good night. You'd best not take my arm until we've properly informed the faculty."

"Of course."

Alexi leaned in as they traversed the entryway. "Although, I wouldn't mind giving that dreary Mrs. Rathbine palpitations by seizing you in a kiss right here in the middle of the school."

Percy blushed and giggled, and nearby students stopped to stare. "You can't, Professor," she murmured. "All think you inhumanly cold and without humour. A glimpse of affection would destroy your fearsome reputation."

"Right you are, Miss Parker," he replied. "Right you are. Now, Percy, speak nothing of The Guard or recent phenomena—not even to your dear friend."

"Alexi, if I told anyone of last night's particulars, I'd be deemed mad. However, Marianna will insist—"

"Say that your fever worsened and I took your care upon myself. As for our marriage, it needs no explanation other than that you're madly in love with me. Wedlock was the only way to keep you from making a fool of yourself," he declared, a sporting light in his eye.

Percy stifled another giggle, and side by side they opened the glass-paneled doors to the small cobblestone courtyard between the Athens clerestories. Blinking from the light, she lost her smile to a sudden thought. "But, what of the institution at large? Privately the thought of scandal thrills me, but everyone will question a sudden marriage between professor and pup—"

Percy heard the squeal before she saw a figure fly at her. *"Mein Gott!"* cried a young German voice. Percy choked as arms flew around her neck. "Where in the whole"—she fumbled for a choice English declamation—*"bloody* whole world have you been? I thought you were dead!" Marianna, her fair cheeks blazing and her wide green eyes filled with tears, noticed Alexi. She whirled, breaking from Percy. "And you! You! What on earth did you do?" she cried, closing the distance to stare up at him, brandishing her fists and offering a few German curses for emphasis.

"Marianna, please." Percy blushed and tried to grab the petite blonde by the arm, but her friend stood her ground. Two female students sitting on the angel fountain fell into immediate gossip, and a few male students, eyebrows raised, thought it best to disappear into their dormitory hall.

Alexi, a full two heads taller, eyed this furious German who had taken to Percy on her first day, and whom his betrothed simply adored. He offered her a gracious expression, which only seemed to infuriate her further.

Percy finally pulled Marianna back and attempted to smooth her friend's disheveled scarf and russet vest. "Marianna, my sweet, hush! Professor Rychman has meant me no harm, I am well again and everything is wond—"

"No! When I last saw you, you were nearly dead. What on earth happened between yesterday and this morning . . . ?" She turned again upon Alexi. "What spell have you cast over her? She was heartbroken just the day before, and you—why you look like you were in a brawl!"

"Marianna, there was no magic!" Percy insisted. "There was a great misunderstanding. Calm yourself. I have news, happy news."

Alexi spoke gently. "Miss Farelei, I understand your confusion. Please accept my apologies for any wrongs you feel I have done Miss Parker. I do not presume to know the confidences you may have shared, but rest assured I have only Percy's interests in mind, and would stake my life on her welfare."

Marianna blinked at him, scowling.

"Marianna." Percy took hold of her friend's hands. "We are to be married. Tomorrow morning. Here at the chapel. Alexi Rychman is to be my husband!"

The blonde girl's jaw dropped, and it was a long moment before she could speak. "No. You jest."

Percy held up her ringed finger. Marianna turned to Alexi, gaping.

"It's true, Miss Farelei," he answered. "Please do us the honour of attending."

Marianna turned back to Percy, whose cheeks were scarlet, and screamed. She threw her arms around Percy and then, in turn, moved to throw her arms around the professor.

"There's no need to make a scene. Good God!" Alexi grimaced, awkwardly patting the girl's shoulder in an effort to extricate himself. Percy hid her face. Even she knew better than to embrace the stern Professor Rychman in the middle of the academy courtyard.

"I would have never dreamed it!" Marianna cried, and

Percy hushed her into a whisper. "I never thought I'd hear the end of her incessant pining over you."

"Marianna, honestly," Percy scolded. She noticed Alexi's mouth curve.

Her friend wore a wide grin. "How can you hush me? You cannot expect such exciting news to escape bold outbursts."

"Ladies, if you will excuse me, I will leave you to your blushes, giggles and other absurdities. I've much to attend. But, please, as we've yet to inform the rest of the institution, try not to get everyone in an uproar." The twitch of a smile remained on his lips, and Percy's blush persisted. Marianna giggled as he bowed slightly to Percy. "My dear, I shall come for you later this evening."

Marianna turned to Percy, who was drinking in the sight of her betrothed disappearing into Promethe Hall. Immediately they both screamed and embraced, creating a bit of a scene. "Come, come." Percy dragged Marianna into the next hall. "We must tell Mina, the Apollo librarian. She'll be so shocked! But she's fond of me and the professor, and I'd hate for her not to be included."

Marianna couldn't stop giggling. "I daresay shocked faces will abound when you waltz through Athens in a wedding dress."

The Whisper-world remained messy. Some of the spirits had torn themselves limb from limb; countless others had hurled themselves against Darkness. He'd grown weary of swatting them into pieces. Once he locked away his opposition once more, satisfied that they were appropriately wasting away, he glided in the form of shadows to the Groundskeeper's side. "Progress?"

"Slow," the Groundskeeper replied. He fussed with bottles and brooms along the corridor strewn with ash.

"Steady," Darkness said. "And keep undoing the seals. Be. Quick."

The Groundskeeper nodded, groveled and waited for the telling shadows to disappear. Then his singsong voice, a mixture of every lower-class accent throughout the far-flung reaches of all empires, echoed out: "Lucy-Ducy wore a nice dress. Lucy-Ducy made a great mess." He carefully swept up the ashes, pausing at points to fill a number of open glass jars using a garden trowel. He chanted at the piles of dust, "All the king's sweepers and all Ducy's ash, still will put Ducy together at last—"

A breeze swirled by, followed by a pack of wild spirits, and ashes tumbled off for what could be miles. The hollow-faced gentleman gave a pitiful howl and scrambled to catch the fleeing specks. The same spirits tore screaming down another corridor, inciting all those around them to lift up in banshee wails, and the Groundskeeper clapped his hands over his head in frustration, wiping his brow with his coat sleeve. "Why did this have to happen, my sweet Dussa-Do? Oh, look at you, you're all around me." He sighed and let loose a strange yearning sound. "Ashes, ashes, we all fall down!"

He fell to his knees, scattering the remains of his charge about him, picking up fistfuls of dust and massaging them with greedy hands. It was everything he could do to not roll about in the pieces. His breathing grew laboured before his mottled eyes closed with shame and he released his hold. He hung his head and began to weep. Locks of black and gold hair spilled from his tattered seaman's cap over drawn features almost too dirty to be seen. "If I can put you to-gether again, you'll tell me who did this to you. And you'll turn such eyes to them! But for now, I'll touch every piece of you. I'll track down every last speck. And when we put you together again, you'll turn such eyes, you will!"

He jumped up and tore off down a diagonal corridor. "West, east, north, south, another seal, another seal!" He sighed, putting his hand to his throat where the attack of his master still smarted. "So much work before war!"

* * *

Her office door flew open, scattering papers everywhere. "Alexi," Rebecca groused, "will you ever—?"

"Knock? You may yet teach me one day."

"A man about to be married ought to have better manners."

"Ah, but isn't there something devilishly charming about one who commands a room as he pleases? I do believe my betrothed is quite taken with the quality." Alexi smiled haughtily.

"Ask her once you've startled her in her boudoir. Once too often, it may grow tedious."

"Until then—"

"You shall remain a brute; yes, indeed. Now. What is to be done with your . . . fiancée?"

Alexi took the seat opposite. "We ought to have a linguistic department, considering Percy's uncanny ability with language. Athens could draw additional income from literary translation, fund a scholarship for women. She'd like that. She'll need an office. Perhaps eighty, Apollo Hall."

"Alexi, language is a humanity. Her place would be in *this* hall, not yours. You mustn't make it entirely obvious how close at hand you'd like your young wife."

Alexi raised an eyebrow. "Right, then. Well, the Bay Room . . ."

Rebecca raised a hand. "It's haunted."

Alexi blinked. "And that should bother her?"

Pursing her lips, Rebecca moved to a cabinet of files. She withdrew a small folder and sat at her desk. "Some record should exist about shifting Miss Parker from student to faculty." Her brow furrowed as she opened Percy's file. "Oh. I forgot about this." She removed an envelope, the script upon which read: *Please open upon Miss P. Parker's graduation or when she has been provided for.* It had been sent with the reverend mother's request for Percy's enrollment. Rebecca opened the letter and read aloud:

Dear Miss Thompson,

I trust you will understand the delicate nature of this missive and will share it with Miss Parker only when you deem it appropriate. Her mother died just after birth. I never mentioned a grave, but one does exist—in York. Miss Parker knows nothing of it, for it remains an unsettling sight.

I tremble as even I write this, but if there is any man who takes pity upon the poor girl, may he escort her hence to retrieve what was left at the site. This must sound nothing short of unholy, but I have prayed upon this matter so long I think it best to share it with you and have you appoint someone of upstanding mettle for the task.

I kept silent for fear of casting further pall over Miss Parker's already trying existence. She wants desperately to attend school; I couldn't shadow her adventure thus. I hope you kept her at Athens as long as you were able. Convent walls were not meant for her spirit, one meant never to be contained, not even in praise of our Lord.

If you have concerns, please contact me. The location of the grave is known here at the convent, should you never speak with me directly. I apologize for the mysterious circumstances surrounding our dear girl, but they have always been the cloak about her white shoulders. It is not her fault she was born odd. I would it were otherwise.

Sincerely,
Reverend Mother Madeliena Theresa

Alexi set his jaw and examined the paper. "That answers the question of where to reserve a honeymoon cottage: York." He rose. "May I leave the arrangements of the Bay Room to you, as I have countless other preparations to make? May I borrow Frederic to send missives?"

Rebecca nodded. After he gave thanks, the door closed behind him. She lifted hands to her forehead, wishing everything were otherwise.

* * *

Isabel came bustling into the sitting room, a silver tray in hand, and Alexandra Rychman looked up from her sewing to evaluate its contents: a small white card with rolling script. "Michael Carroll, ma'am. He apologizes for any inconvenience, but extends an invitation. He says it has to do with your brother."

"Show him in."

Alexandra, with just as striking features as Alexi but elder, wheelchair-bound, retreated from her sewing table and rolled toward the threshold, smoothing the folds of her black taffeta dress. She loved visitors—few though she saw—and more so, any news of her brother.

Isabel, once she had removed his hat and cloak, led a broad-shouldered man with unruly pepper grey hair into the sitting room. He heralded sunshine, as if his very presence could cause a shift in seasons. No one could linger in winter near his cozy hearth.

"Miss Rychman!" He bounded toward her, taking her outstretched hand and kissing it. "Do you remember me? It's been years since."

"You're part of Alexi's little . . . clique."

"A founding member, yes, indeed," Michael chortled. "You're looking well, Miss Rychman, if I may say. And I hope you're feeling up for a bit of an adventure?"

Alexandra smiled. "Who *wouldn't?*"

Michael grinned and patted the nearby sofa in a gesture of triumph. "I ask myself that question daily!"

"Well, then?"

"Your brother has instructed me to bring you to London."

Alexandra's eyes sparkled. "Has he now. And what on earth is the occasion?"

Michael beamed. "Why—he's getting married!"

Percy had fabricated a convincing enough story of the night prior, and she distracted Marianna with titillating details of

Alexi's first kiss that possible gaps in the plot were entirely forgotten. Side by side in the dining hall, their giddiness was tempered only by the unknown.

"You'll have an *estate*," Marianna murmured. "Is it far?"

"I shan't be closeted away. I'm to stay at Athens in some capacity. He promised. Though his home isn't far, and I want you to visit."

"Oh. Good then." Marianna brightened. "I've been trying to be so happy for you while ignoring how terribly sad I am at the thought of you going away."

"You have Edward."

"While I love him desperately, he's no replacement for your company."

Percy was moved. "Those are the sweetest words anyone has ever—"

"I doubt that," Marianna interrupted, grinning. "Surely you've heard sweeter things of late. From him, of all people. It does amaze. He's so cold . . . until he looks at you."

"I know, it's very disconcerting. Isn't it wonderful?"

Footsteps sounded behind them. The dormitory chaperone, Miss Jennings, a squat, unpleasant, mousy-haired woman, stood over them looking terribly uncomfortable. "Miss Parker . . . a . . . gentleman is at the door for you."

"A particular gentleman, Miss Jennings?" Percy asked.

"Er, yes. Professor Rychman, miss. But why a professor would be calling on a student in the evening—"

"Ah, yes, my fiancé. Thank you kindly, I was expecting him."

The surprise turning to horror upon the woman's face was worth a fortune, and Marianna masked a guffaw by sputtering into her teacup. Percy threw her thick cloak about her shoulders, kissed Marianna's forehead and graciously swept past the chaperone, running to open the door to her striking beloved.

He'd straightened his appearance, replacing his tattered clothes with a new, elegantly tailored black frock coat and pressed trousers, as well as a fresh crimson cravat and charcoal waistcoat. His mop of black hair was carefully combed and his arms were clasped behind his back. "Good evening," he murmured, presenting a cluster of roses. He shot a disdainful glance at Miss Jennings, who scowled from the doorway but quickly disappeared.

Percy gasped and giggled. "How beautiful," she breathed, taking them in her arms and allowing their perfume to wash over her. "Thank you."

"As we were not afforded a proper courtship, I thought there ought to be a few niceties somewhere in the midst of our mad affair. Come, take my arm, dear girl, there's something we must do."

"Of course." Percy slid her arm into his.

Roses on one arm, Alexi on the other, Percy felt like a princess as they entered Apollo Hall and ascended to his office. "A tutorial, at this hour, *Professor?*" she asked, entirely unsure of what he had planned. He was, at times, an unpredictable man, a quality that had its delights.

Alexi gave her a scorching look. "Of sorts," he purred.

He swept her into his vast office teeming with books and fine furnishings, closed the door behind him. Percy raised her eyebrow at the sound of the clicking lock. He plucked the roses from her arms, tossed them on a nearby bookshelf and waved his hand to set a fire roaring in the fireplace and his desk's candelabra ablaze. Then, scooping Percy into his arms, he carried her behind his desk and sat her upon it. She stared with wide eyes, her breath short and her body afire.

He loomed, placing one hand on either side of her, and leaned in. "You see, my dear Miss Parker," he began in a businesslike tone edged with a growl. He pressed his forehead to hers. "Until I indulge a moment or two of the fantasies that began to accost me when you first came here to call, I'll never again find this room the haven of academic productivity it once was. I'll be driven entirely to distraction until I purge a few less-than-scholarly impulses from my blood."

All Percy could manage was an odd, gleeful sound that became a gasp when he descended upon her with a rain of kisses, his teeth fumbling at the lace around her throat, his hands pawing past layers of skirts to gain the purchase against her flesh as he laid her back upon the desk's wide marble top, its contents having been suspiciously cleared sometime prior. "At last," he murmured, "the insurmountable barrier between us lies in ruin."

"Indeed. And shall I, too, soon lie in ruin?" Percy asked, not bothering to choose between a nervous or lustful tone since she felt both so strongly.

Alexi pursed his lips, staring down at her in consternation. "No, darling, I'll give you the courtesy of a proper bed. I maintain you wed a gentleman. I did, after all, control myself during our lessons here. For the most part."

"There was that kiss." Percy giggled. "You threw me against the bookshelf."

"Ah, yes, there was that." He smirked. "How did that go, again?" He lifted and spun her. Her breath fled as he pressed her against the shelves for reenactment.

"Yes, that was it," she finally gasped, as he carried her again to the desk. "Alexi, were you really thinking such things during our tutorials? You seemed so cold!"

"I began to unhinge the moment I demanded you reveal yourself, the moment you took off your scarf, your gloves, your glasses, all your shrouds, and stood bravely before me, diamond blue eyes piercing my soul."

Percy frowned. "You looked at me in surprise, then."

Alexi leaned closer. "You were a revelation."

Tears rimmed her eyes and she looked away, terrified that when he saw the whole of her on their wedding night—her whole, ghostly, naked flesh—he would be repulsed. She pulled him near, a hungry kiss to stave off her fear.

Alexi eventually pulled back, adjusting his clothes, his

breathing ragged. "Do put yourself back together, darling. Seeing you all disheveled threatens to take the gentleman right out of me. Pull your cloak tight, dear, I see I've mauled your sleeve."

"Miss Jennings will call the police." Percy chuckled, rising to sit.

He helped her to her feet, cinching her cloak. "Tomorrow you shall be mine," he promised softly. Thrills worked up Percy's spine.

"Who will marry us?"

"Michael. He's clergy, after all. Church of England. Do you mind terribly that he's not Catholic?"

"Just don't tell Reverend Mother."

Leading her to the threshold, Alexi swept his lips against her ear. "Thank you for this indulgence." When Percy brought his hand to her lips and kissed the centre of his palm, he growled, his fingertips dragging along her cheek. "You can't possibly know how I need you."

"Oh, I've some idea," she replied.

A tearing sound drew them from their clutch. They turned to the centre of the room to find a large, open black rectangle before them, a door much like the portal Percy had opened at the Van Courtland residence. In an instant, blue fire leaped from Alexi's hands. Percy still marveled at the sight. He approached the portal. Nothing came out. There was no immediate sound, other than water, but as they inched closer, Percy heard it: distant screaming. Incessant screaming. And the chant, again, chilling Percy's blood.

"Lucy-Ducy wore a nice dress, Lucy-Ducy made a great mess . . ."

"Percy, stay back."

Percy moved behind Alexi as he approached, unable to keep from poking her head around his arm to see. Deep in the darkness, a thick cluster of shadow moved. There was a flash of red eyes in the distance, and the sight triggered instinctual panic within her. Percy clamped down on a scream and felt something sizzle upon her body. As her fists balled, the door snapped shut, and Percy's eyes were drawn to her chest, where the phoenix pendant flared red against her body glowing white. Alexi turned, his eyes wide.

"Well . . ." Percy murmured, watching her light fade as the door closed. "It seems I've no control of when portals open, but Michael must be right: whatever woke in me now reacts to danger. Did you see those eyes?"

"What?" he asked.

"The red eyes. You didn't see them?"

"No."

"Oh." Percy's stomach churned. She recognized those eyes from her vision of the cave, when Phoenix burned. Oh, God, if something were to happen to Alexi . . . The very thought sent her into a furious, righteous rage, and it was only Alexi's surprise that alerted her she was radiant once again.

"Percy!"

"Oh." She looked down at her sternum, where a ball of white light again gathered. It dimmed. "See, it's defensive. I was just worrying about something happening to you, and it must have triggered my . . . light. Tell me you've some scientific term to offer, I sound utterly daft."

Alexi shook his head.

"It's comforting, I suppose, that I have a defense."

Her beloved scowled. "Perhaps, but I don't like doors simply opening up without warning or cause. Particularly not in our intimate moments. And whose were those red eyes?"

"I . . . couldn't be sure," Percy said, daring not to voice her supposition, shoving panic aside. She fully intended to revel in the throes of love, not panic. "Now, where were we?" She moved to kiss Alexi with such passion that he had to draw back lest her innocence truly be stripped.

Staring up at him, a random thought suddenly struck Percy, and she cocked her head. "If I'm indeed some part of the goddess Persephone, for I'm no *actual* deity, shouldn't I have warranted another name? Mine isn't very clever at all, then, is it? Rather obvious, really."

Alexi pursed his lips. "Perhaps to jog some ancient memory. None of us were clever about this to begin with."

"Yet we found each other in the end."

Alexi touched her cheek. "Thank heavens."

Escorting her back to Athene Hall, he murmured at her doorstep, "Until tomorrow, my darling. Try and rest."

"You do the same," she replied.

"I'll do my best," Alexi replied unconvincingly. They did not seem able to release hands, lingering until their reverie was broken by the front door being thrown wide.

"Now, I do not care if you two are engaged or not, Professor Rychman," Miss Jennings scoffed, her face flushed and pinched, "but I'll not have such an example set on my front steps. Oh, the shame! You'll have the whole faculty thinking they could have a wife of a student whenever they please."

"Calm yourself," Alexi began mildly. "Miss Parker was sent to me by Fate. You ungrateful commoners. I shall mate Prophecy, Miss Jennings, as we control the dead lest spirits wholly unseat the sanity of banal persons such as yourself. Miss Parker's a goddess of a girl, fit to make my wife, and I will do with her as I please."

Percy gasped, staring up at Alexi. His eyes, blazing with cerulean fire, mesmerized the chaperone before he turned to Percy and said, "I've always wanted to tell the truth. She won't remember a word, and it felt lovely to say. Now, then." He indulged a languorous, wholly uncivil kiss, then ushered two dazed females back into the hall.

Left at last in her room, Percy stared out her window at passing spirits. They bade her rest, but her eyes settled instead upon a hanging still life, a ripe pomegranate at its centre. She'd turned the painting to the wall when she first arrived at Athens, and she didn't remember turning it back. She flipped it to the wall one last time, needing no reminder of that mythological fruit, which once bound a goddess to an underworld fate.

Beatrice followed the Groundskeeper to the seals, keeping to the shadows, unnoticed. It was easy, considering the chaos and noise. The Whisper-world was a hissing, echoing, miserable labyrinth.

She watched as he heaved and turned each stone pin with great strain. This seal was a gritty, moist cylinder, hardly distinguishable from other rock but for the small trickle of blood that poured forth. When opened, the fissure would leak the miasma of death into a fixed point in the mortal realm. Here in the Whisper-world, distances were odd, as was time. However, expediency and progress did seem to have pace. The Groundskeeper's work was coming along; Beatrice followed behind to reroute it. After a pin was loosened, the Groundskeeper always ambled back to reconstruct his love.

Beatrice moved to the stone and kept her boot clear of pooling crimson. She thought of the faltering goddess, her divinity rotting and withering under the fist of Darkness, how the form she bore had bled as she laid down the foundations for Beatrice to now finish, coupling hers and her lover's energy toward their goal. Perhaps this pool was even her blood, refusing to dry. A relic.

She pressed the locket. Hallowed Phoenix fire sparkled in her hand, leaped onto and nestled in the wet stone, kissing the blood dry, creating a pulsing rectangle of possibility where before was only rough stone and the sour air of danger: the portal was rerouted to familiar, friendly bricks.

Beatrice took a deep breath. Though she tried to put on a brave face, her heart had not stopped pounding since she died. So much for eternal rest. She wished to feel in better hands. The current Guard . . . It wasn't that she didn't trust them, but when she'd broken into their breakfast and examined them, the table was rife with obstacles; she saw mortal frailty cloud each and every gaze. Every single one of them ached for something, was unsettled by something, felt guilty, trapped, unappreciated or unrequited. How keenly she felt their flaws. Prophecy balanced on the edge of a knife, and there was no divinity to ease her mind; that divinity died when the goddess gave herself to the world. The blue fire now held in her hand, this fractal remnant of Phoenix, was all that remained for Beatrice. It would take her someplace new, the next phase of her quest. She hoped when she opened her eyes she would see something comforting.

Beatrice found herself floating above a plot of soil in a York graveyard, a place she recognized, a place of shadows and wind. It was not what she hoped. Her lonely, weighted heart pounded harder with complex memories of grave digging. Her transparent hand grazed and swept across a familiar tombstone. A smaller, grimmer marker lay next to it.

She spoke softly to the stone, caressing it though she could not touch. "Since I've not seen your ghost, my only comfort is that you've surely found peace. May Ibrahim and I join you soon, and we'll all embrace in that Great Beyond." Sensation was an echo, yet she acted as though she could still participate in rituals of the flesh. Tears streamed down her phantom cheeks, surprising her. She missed Ibrahim. She missed her Guard. She missed sweet Iris Parker, this young mother dead before she could appreciate her unique baby. And to her surprise, she also missed the goddess, difficult as their relationship had been. Though she was a woman skeptical of prayer, Beatrice needed divinity. Thus she prayed over her friend's grave that their myriad sacrifices would not be in vain.

CHAPTER SIX

The stunning light of morning was jolting. The day would eventually bring the night, and Percy thrilled with desire and trepidation. She knew nothing of intimacy, save the kisses and caresses Alexi had shared. A new education awaited.

She glided downstairs to the dining room, where an urn of hot water was kept for the restless or studious. Readying a cup of tea, she chose the spiced blend, for it reminded her of the scent of Alexi: clove and leather-bound books.

A rustle behind her proved to be Marianna, her eyes a bit groggy but her excitement palpable. "And how doth the bride to be?"

"Nervous."

"Of course. May Edward come?"

"Of course."

The girls sipped their tea, took hands and silently watched the sunrise. Only a hasty tread behind them eventually roused their comfortable quiet, the disdainful Miss Jennings, again with news. "Miss Parker. More company for you. Two French ladies." She grimaced. "Bearing a rather large box."

"Oh, do let them in." Percy turned to Marianna. "I believe it's my wedding dress!"

The two girls hurried to the door where Josephine and a tiny woman whose black curls alone could be seen through the window. "Hello, Percy dear," Josephine called as they entered. "This is Madame Sue, a sorceress of the trade."

Percy made introductions to Marianna as they moved

the garment box upstairs and into her room, Madame Sue streaming fabrics dramatically from her own apparel.

"And how do you know Percy, Mademoiselle Belledoux?" Marianna asked, clearly admiring Josephine's gown.

"I'm a friend of the professor"—Josephine smiled—"and thus, of Miss Percy."

"And I am the hired help," Madame Sue volunteered, adjusting the corsage of pearl-tipped straight pins stuck to the lapel of her sweeping robe.

"The best seamstress on the isle, I tell you," Josephine said.

The box safely upon Percy's bed, Madame Sue did the honours. Everyone, save madame, gasped. Inside the box lay the most beautiful assemblage of light blue satin, lace and sparkling silver thread that modern fashion could imagine. Percy lovingly scooped up the thickly corseted bodice. The plunging neckline was lined across the bosom with thin, starched lace and silver-and-seed-pearl-embroidered ivy. Out tumbled three-quarters sleeves from which lengthening layers of pale blue lace fell in bells. Full skirts were doubled and cinched with a pearl-strung cord. A curl of satin had been arranged at the small of the back, like a rose, which bustled the train before sweeping downward.

"Oh, madame," Percy breathed. Marianna's hand would not leave her mouth.

"Pleased?"

"More than I can possibly express. You are an exquisite talent."

"Thank you. Step in, let us make sure it fits. I adjust, then I sleep."

"I'm terribly sorry for the rush, madame," Percy said.

"No matter, people must marry when the fit seizes them, I suppose. You aren't expecting, are you?"

"No!" Percy cried, blushing as she was helped into the dress.

"Good." Madame yanked hard upon the corset strings, and Percy felt her ribs bend and her breath fly. "Ah. Fits well, this."

"Indeed," Percy squeaked, her already slender waist further tapered and her curves made voluptuous.

Madame disappeared somewhere behind the bustle and made a few adjustments. Reemerging with a small pair of scissors, she flitted about clipping threads, stood back and clapped her hands. *"Finis."*

"Madame!" Percy could not stop staring. "How can I thank you? Do stay for the wedding!"

"No. Weddings make me anxious. Promise me only that you will come by and let me experiment with your white face in other colours. And bring that eerie man of yours. I see him always in black. I make him a cloak of bright orange."

Everyone laughed before Josephine said, "Percy, I'll return for you at half past. I must go make sure Alexi's kept his head and the chapel is presentable. *Oui. Allons-y,* madame." The two women then disappeared in rustles of fabric and French mutterings that Percy understood as Madame Sue's surprise that such a sweet, pleasant girl was to marry such a brooding man.

Percy and Marianna simply stared at each other.

"Marianna, I cannot believe this is happening."

"Nor can I. Most certainly not after your first quarter!"

They giggled. It was rather sudden, but Percy wasn't at liberty to explain.

Josephine entered Alexi's office to find him pacing. "Alexi."

"Hmm?"

"Has your suit arrived?"

"What? Suit? Oh, yes. Just now."

"May I see?"

Alexi pointed to the alcove where a long, exquisite suit coat hung beside a silk cravat of pale blue.

"Oh, Alexi, how lovely—and you even got the blue correct!"

"Give me a bit of credit."

"Constant black aside, you're always well-appointed, yet I'm impressed. Now, you'd better—Alexi!"

"Yes?"

"Stop pacing, you're driving me mad."

Alexi moved to his desk and sat with unusual obedience that came only from distraction. "What were you about to tell me?"

"Dress yourself. You never know what strange delays may occur. You had better tune the chapel, too. Heaven only knows what might erupt."

"Ah, yes. I suppose none of us has any idea." He tapped a quill incessantly upon the desk. Josephine had never seen him fidget.

"Alexi, I am sure this must be overwhelming for you."

"Yes." His low voice was slightly strained. "It is, a bit."

"You needn't be nervous. Besides that this has been foretold nearly all our lives, I daresay you can do no wrong. The girl's absolutely mad for you."

Alexi stared straight into Josephine's eyes, and then she saw the strangest of all sights, a foreign image to which they would all have to grow accustomed: his wide and genuine smile. "Yes. She is, isn't she?"

Josephine returned his smile and masked the ache within.

Jane was clad in her finest dress, still relatively plain but it would have to do. She found the headmistress staring out her office window, Frederic upon the inner sill, absently stroking his feathers. Quite smartly, in a bit more colour than her usual custom, Rebecca was dressed in a fitted purple jacket and mauve skirts. A cameo at her throat, lace cascaded between the double-breasted folds of her jacket. It was clear she had taken great care.

"Good morning, m'dear," Jane said at the open office door. "You look stunning."

"Hello, Jane." Rebecca beckoned her in, her smile strained. "May I offer you tea?" She placed Frederic outside the window with a piece of bread and closed the casement.

During the business of preparation, the two women were silent. Cup in hand, Jane asked, "Has he been by at all this morning?"

"No. That's best, isn't it?" Rebecca's gaze was particularly sharp.

"It will grow easier. We've had such a shock. We all must mend. But she's a sweet, dear presence—"

"Of course she is," Rebecca snapped. "And I will care for her, as we all must. I trust you to leave me to that; trust me in that."

"I didn't mean to suggest otherwise."

"I knew that none of this would be easy," Rebecca murmured, and a strained pause followed. "Only, I wish he wouldn't have—"

"What?"

"I shouldn't speak of it."

"To me, you may."

Rebecca looked up, surprised. Her friend wasn't one to speak volumes or make overtures; she had always been detached, and Rebecca loved her for it. This admission could be made to no one else: "When Alexi first admitted feelings for Miss Parker, I . . . pressed him on it, made my own confession, like a fool. He told me if we'd been born to another fate that he might have made me his wife." Bitterness drew down the corner of her lips.

Jane granted the statement a necessary, gracious few moments. "And I'm sure he meant it. He cares for you. You're close—"

"*Were* close," Rebecca muttered. "I cannot imagine the tenor of our acquaintance will continue."

"Of course it will; don't be absurd. There is no threat imposed upon the betrothed by your presence. You are Alexi's dearest friend."

"He has a new confidant."

"We all do. I have this strange feeling she'll take all our confessions before the year is through," Jane stated. "I'm sure she'll know my secrets soon."

"Your secrets, Jane?"

Her friend grinned. "Certainly. But, Rebecca, think of it: you've always been in Alexi's shadow, the both of you scowling away the hours. Now you must come into your own. You're too powerful to allow this to weaken you. You've had years to prepare."

Rebecca exhaled a long breath. "I'm glad you came this morning, Jane. Thank you. I suppose we'd better survey the chapel. Surely Josephine has thoughts on the arrangements."

"I must confess," Jane murmured, "I am looking forward to the few days Our Lord and Master will be out of town."

Rebecca raised an eyebrow, and saw a most mischievous light in her friend's green eyes. "Why do you say such a thing, Miss O'Shannon Connor?"

Jane escorted Rebecca out the door with a mysterious smile. "A bit of work to be done, Headmistress."

The chapel was a small white wonder of light and warmth, the stained-glass angels ablaze from within. Rebecca and Jane found Josephine in a flurry of movement, singing a French ballad and telling Elijah where to place several bouquets far larger than his head. Lord Withersby followed orders, grumbling and sneezing as she said a few pointed words about weddings.

"I don't suppose you'd like to do this madwoman's bidding, would you?" he asked pathetically at the door.

"No, watching you is far more entertaining," Jane replied.

Michael emerged from the sacristy in a white robe and a

cleric's collar, a Bible in his hands. Rebecca moved down the aisle and declared, "Well, aren't you the picture of priestliness, Vicar Carroll."

He chuckled, flushing, opening his arms to gaze down at himself. "We ought to have some measure of formality and godliness, shouldn't we?" He flashed his winning smile.

"With Elijah Withersby present in a chapel?" Josephine called, having disappeared behind the altar. "We must take all precautions."

"A stroke of lightning might as easily smite you, my darling," Elijah called from behind an armful of lilies.

Josephine reemerged, candles in her hands. "Please elucidate, Lord Withersby. Do."

Elijah balked.

"Might we set discussion of sin aside for the moment, for Miss Percy's sake?" Michael begged wearily.

Every sill bore a candle and every pedestal a bouquet of lilies, the scent pervasive and welcoming. Once all was in place, as if on cue the chapel door was flung open and all candles burst immediately into flame. Alexi strode down the aisle, more compelling than ever, particularly elegant in his wedding attire. His hair was as neat as could be and his eyes were particularly stirring. When his companions remembered to breathe, they greeted him warmly.

"The man of the hour," Elijah said with good cheer and a sneeze.

"Hello, my friends." Alexi eyed the chapel. "Marvelous. Simply marvelous. Thank you." He offered Rebecca a lingering glance. She returned it with a smile. Jane squeezed her hand in silent encouragement.

"While you tune, Alexi, I'll be off to prepare your bride," Josephine said, and she darted down the aisle, shimmering and rustling golden taffeta. Elijah could not help but watch. When he saw Jane smirking at him from the pew across the aisle, however, he scowled.

Alexi drew a meaningful relic from his breast pocket—a

thick, pale feather—and, with the powerful grace unique to him, moved to each window and tapped its stained-glass angel. Each glass seemed to vibrate, a soft hum rose, an invisible choir: the chapel would now allow no unwanted visitors.

Michael had disappeared but returned, opening wide the door for a woman in dark green. She advanced her wheelchair into the aisle, and Alexi darted forward, sweeping his sister up in his arms and carrying her up the aisle to seat her in a front pew. "Alexandra, my dear!"

The woman observed the room with wonder, knowing there was something inexplicable, craning her neck as if to hear with better ears. "What news, and so sudden!" she exclaimed. "You made no hint of it a few days past, when the two of you visited. Surely this surprised Miss Percy as much as I!"

"Yes, indeed. But it couldn't be helped," Alexi replied, his eyes glittering. "I'm very glad you're here."

"I wouldn't miss it for the world."

Alexi kissed his sister upon the temple and took her hand, sitting to anxiously await his bride. He noticed his favourite librarian, Miss Mina Wilberforce, duck into the chapel with an amazed smile, a bright white flash against dark brown skin. She'd long ago curried his favour by boldly having taken on the name of an emancipator rather than a master, and by proving she knew every book in the Athens catalogue. He hadn't thought to invite her, so he supposed Percy must have, of which he was frightfully glad. He had a host of friends here after all, to share in his sudden happiness.

Michael gestured to Jane, who fumbled beneath her pew for a fiddle and moved to sit with it in a chair at the altar.

"Ah, good. Music," Alexi stated.

Marianna opened the door to Josephine, who found Percy sitting wide-eyed upon her bed as if she had not blinked in an hour. The German girl had swept up Percy's hair into artful spirals.

"Come, dear, it's nearly time." Josephine rustled in the garment box to reveal a pearl tiara, set with blue glass flowers, and a veil of pale blue. Percy gasped, as if it were the final touch of absolute reality. "Yes, my dear, he really is going to marry you," the Frenchwoman promised softly. "He really is." Marianna was quiet but smiled.

The train hooked and the crowning veil set, Percy stared in the mirror and her eyes watered. She had applied just the faintest hint of rouge to her cheeks and lips, and had lined her white eyelids with the thinnest grey, which caused the ice blue slivers of her irises to jump forth. Feeling beautiful, she plucked her phoenix pendant out to hang not against her skin but proudly in the open, a mark of the fate-forged bond of long ago.

The journey across the Athens courtyard was a spectacle of whispers and gaping mouths. Josephine and Marianna looked like proud family, escorting her. Percy could hear faint strains of a stringed instrument from inside the chapel, and fainter still, the ghostly trace of what she could only liken to an angelic choir.

If The Guard wondered why none of the harmless, gamesome spirits of Athens had wafted into the chapel, it was because they were all clustered at the outside door, awaiting the bride. A living gentleman stood among them, a handsome youth with wild, curly hair and a dimpled grin, blissfully unaware of the floating dead nearby.

"Oh, Percy, you are incredible!" said Edward Page, the young lad smitten with Marianna, who slid her arm onto his with unconscious ease. "Congratulations! As surprising as this is, congratulations on this most auspicious day!"

"Go on, you two." As Percy stepped away from view, Josephine ushered the young couple through the doors. Marianna turned to blow her friend a kiss, and they shared a familiar giggle—the last of their maidenhood.

There was a box at the door, and Josephine opened it to place a cluster of perfect white lilies wrapped in blue satin in Percy's trembling hands. Percy smiled at the bouquet, and at the misty-eyed Josephine, before returning her attention to the dead who'd come to see her wed.

"Leave this to us, Percy," said the boy with the soft brogue who usually kept to the main foyer chandelier. "We know you've no father to give you away, and so we wish to walk you down the aisle."

"Thank you all," Percy murmured, her eyes glimmering with tears. "That's very kind of you." She turned to Josephine. "You may go on, thank you. The spirits wish to present me." The Frenchwoman sighed in appreciation and slipped into the chapel.

The spirits encircled Percy. While she felt the air around her grow freezing, she was lost in the excitement on their faces. Their entire spectral strength amassed, they were just able to manipulate the door. Percy came in full view, and the crowd was rendered breathless. A ghostly radiant goddess, she moved forward, floating in loving and spectral procession to the haunting sound of Jane's strings.

Percy and Alexi were stunned by the sight of each other, overwhelmed by the magnetism that seized their hearts. He stood awaiting her at the base of the altar, and energy surged between them as they took hands. Percy took her place opposite him and, to her, the rest of the chapel disappeared.

They did not hear Michael's Bible verses; they heard only the beat of each other's hearts. They responded to the liturgy and made their vows, but it was as if their lips had not moved; they were each drowning deliriously in the sea of the other. They exchanged simple silver bands, and the gentle pressure of sliding rings onto each other's fingers was an inimitable delight.

When pronounced man and wife, Alexi lifted the veil to kiss her and she fell against him. Their kiss was of such fusion that they felt the ground tremble. The slight sound of angels grew into a bursting chorus. Rising from the candles and met by an aura of light from their bodies, white flame began to pool, merge and expand into a hazy, egglike form that grew as their kiss sustained. As it ended, the form burst into a great, bird-shaped sun. The avian form threw open expansive wings, and a wave of heat and deafening music blew through the chapel.

The Guard cried out. A phoenix bathed in light, rising from the indomitable love within two mortal hearts—this was raw, divine power, their purpose and origin made manifest. Marianna and Edward squealed. Mina Wilberforce's hands went to her face. Alexandra gaped, tears streaming down her cheeks. Many of the attendant ghosts breathed sighs and vanished, at last sent to their rest.

Elijah turned to Marianna, Edward and Mina. He pointed a finger toward each set of eyes. "As beautiful as this is," he began nonchalantly, "I'm terribly sorry, we'll have to pretend that never happened." Their gazes clouded, and soon only selective memories of a more mundane nature remained.

When Withersby turned his fingers in the direction of Alexandra, Alexi stopped him. "No, Elijah. Let my sister keep this sight."

Alexandra eyed her brother with deepening wonder. "Thank you," she murmured desperately.

"Are we married now?" Percy breathed, amazed by the blue-coloured flame wreathing her beloved's eyes and her own. A thin line of the same traced The Guard's hearts, each to the other, a cord of light binding them fast. The phoenix pendant was a tiny sun around Percy's neck.

"By the gods themselves, it would seem," Alexi replied.

The couple walked down the aisle, arm in arm, unable to take their eyes from each other. Jane broke into a jig, and the assembled company bounced out of the chapel, Rebecca taking care to wheel Alexandra to safety as everyone embraced. Jane was lost to her music, a new spirit floating behind her. Aodhan's hard, deeply masculine features wore affection, and his ghostly hand hovered just above her shoulder. Beside him floated Beatrice Tipton.

Beatrice's expression was almost threatening. Her voice was kinder. "Go on, my lady," she said to Percy. "Enjoy what you've worked so very long to attain. Enjoy your mortal love and a bit of celebration. There's time soon enough for the rest. But please take care. Remember all I've said."

Percy swallowed and nodded. She turned to behold Alexi, who was ignorant of all but her. She delighted in his thirsty gaze before turning back to find Beatrice and Aodhan gone.

Michael, unable to contain his overflowing heart, swept Rebecca into a jig. She at first refused, but it was impossible to deny his joy for long and so she acquiesced with a chuckling sigh. It was Josephine's giggle that alerted them all to the host of gawking professors and students eyeing first their dancing headmistress and second their most mysterious, brooding professor, clearly wedded to and infatuated with their strangest student. Rebecca simply laughed; there was nothing else to be done. Jane continued to play, relocating beside Alexandra, who from her wheelchair watched as if the world had been made far more beautiful.

Alexi kissed Percy's hands and moved to kneel at his sister's side. "There is an ancient magic within us, Alexandra. I've never wished to keep secrets from you—"

She placed her hand on Alexi's shoulder and shook her head. "Thank you for what you allowed me to see. Oh, Percy. Goodness—Mrs. Rychman." Alexandra beamed as Percy knelt at her feet in a rustling pool of blue satin. "You look incredible. The both of you . . . Alexi, what on earth made you finally allow someone close?"

Alexi tucked Percy's arm in his. "There was no way around this woman's radiance. Now, we must be off. You shall dine at our estate soon. Michael has instructions to escort you home."

"Good, then, Brother. Thank you."

A huge smile approached, a white crescent against brown skin, and Percy jumped up to welcome Mina. Her friend reached out to take her ivory hand in a darker one, murmuring, "Congratulations, Mrs. Rychman. I never doubted your husband's mind. What I doubted was that he could ever smile. How dear it is that you are the one to unearth such a miracle. Come find me after your honeymoon, I'll give you presents—books!"

Alexi bowed his head. "Hello, Miss Wilberforce, thank you for being a part of this special day."

"No—thank you, Professor, for proving love presses past barriers." The librarian lifted Percy's hand in hers, showcasing the contrast that had brought them together, triumphant. Both ladies were quietly overcome.

"I'm so glad to share this with you, Mina. It's been quite a quarter," Percy whispered.

"I should say."

Headmistress Thompson approached, and Mina stepped aside. Alexi stepped aside, too, watching with feigned disinterest as Rebecca said, "Allow me to congratulate you." She opened her arms, and Percy eagerly stepped into them.

"How can I thank you, Headmistress—?"

"Rebecca."

"Thank you for everything you've done in granting me a home here at Athens, before any of us knew this fate. You have been so kind to me from the first—"

Rebecca looked pained. "No, child, I—"

Percy gushed, undeterred, "I love Athens so deeply. I have a family now, a home, meaning, and suddenly life is glorious. You allowed these blessings to unfold. I am so grateful that you have granted me a place on the staff. Thank you for everything you have done, and will do, for Alexi and me."

The headmistress's face was unreadable, but when Percy took her hands to relinquish her wedding bouquet, Rebecca shook her head and refused. "Oh, no—" But Percy would not accept it back. "Ah, all right then." The woman chuckled, masking unease. "I believe your husband wishes to depart."

"Oh, Percy!" Elijah cried, as Alexi took her by the arm and the glowing couple walked off to cheers. "My dear, beware His Royal Eeriness! Heed my warnings! He has *terrible* designs on you! He'll take you to some desolate place, force you into black robes to recite mathematics! You know not what you do! O, poor youth, sacrificed on the altar of the Constant Sneer!"

Percy laughed delightedly and turned to her love, who pursed his lips and arched an eyebrow at Elijah. She grinned. "Is that so, husband?"

"Oh, I've designs on you, my dear," he said, fixing her with a smoldering gaze. "Hardly terrible."

Percy shivered in anticipation.

A footman waited atop the front steps of Athens, holding a cloak for Percy; an ivy-bedecked carriage stood below. As the door of the cab closed her inside, Percy lifted the curtain to look back at the crowd. Rebecca's lips were thin, and her colour wan; the bouquet hung limply from her hand. Michael was studying her. Elijah was still spouting dire warnings, and Josephine was pulling affectionately at his arm, begging him to desist. Alexandra was waving. In the portico shadow, Marianna and Edward were stealing a kiss. Aodhan again hovered over Jane. Beatrice seemed to be inspecting the foundations of Athens, tapping at the flagstones in an unsettling manner.

Percy chose to set all concern aside. "Thank you," she murmured to the heavens. "Let me live with this loving, mad family forever. I could never have dreamed such treasures mine."

She turned and reached a hand out the window, aching for her new husband, who was speaking to the driver and sliding tickets into his breast pocket. Alexi climbed in and relaxed across from her, and Percy gave one final wave out the window before the driver had them jostling off to the northeast. A questioning look crossed Percy's face.

"York, my love. I thought we would spend a couple of evenings in York."

"How lovely! We'll see Reverend Mother, then?"

"I thought it might be nice to see where you spent your earliest years—but first I've some dreary, eerie nook where I intend to cloister you away and set upon you with black robes and endless theorems."

Percy giggled, her hands reaching for him. He shifted to sit beside her, and she burrowed close. She gasped with a sudden thought. "Are we to take a train, Alexi?"

"Certainly the most efficient way to travel."

"Oh! I've never been on a train!"

Alexi chuckled. "Even our simple adventures will be full of wonder. You'll make my whole world new." He leaned close to brush her lips with his.

"Careful, Alexi, these hints of romance could ruin Elijah's image of you."

"You'll have tales, indeed. I promise."

The other train passengers stared, of course, at the white-skinned girl dressed like a princess. Percy, however, was so joyful and unaware, their looks grew more captivated than rude. Alexi found his defensive edge softening, for his bride remained wholly unruffled. The only eyes she noticed were his, which he kept fixed upon her. The day's light was so diffuse she was eventually able to stare out the window of their well-appointed car, eagerly watching the English countryside until she dozed on his shoulder.

They disembarked at York at twilight, the last of the sun fading in a final gasp of rich purple. Alexi helped Percy into the carriage procured at the station. Drawing her into his arm, he noticed how the lace around her neck quaked. "Darling, are you cold?"

"No, my dear. Why do you ask?"

"You're shivering. Please tell me you're not frightened." •

"What would I be frightened of?" she murmured with a smile. Alexi's awkwardness was not assuaged. "I know you will be gentle with me," she added.

"Of course I will be gentle."

"Though the breadth of our emotions may . . . tax our capacity for restraint."

"So I am not alone in feeling . . ."

"More than a mortal can contain?" Percy finished.

"Precisely." Alexi choked and turned away, hardly able to look at her until the carriage pulled up outside a small cottage far from civilization, waves crashing in the distance. Then he leaned in like a thrilled schoolboy and said, "You wait here a moment, I have to make sure everything is as I instructed."

He hopped out of the cab, unlashed a case and darted up the walk, disappearing into a dark building where a single lamp burned in the window. In the several minutes that followed, Percy bit her lip and forgot to breathe.

She was startled by the carriage door swinging open. Alexi held out his hand for her, bidding the driver bring their remaining cases. The man did so, running ahead to place the bags inside the door and hurrying back to the carriage so as not to be an unwelcome presence, but Percy and Alexi didn't notice him in the slightest; Alexi swept her up in his arms and strode her to the cottage.

The main room was dark inside. Her husband placed her just beyond the threshold, removed her cloak and made a small gesture with his hand. Instantly, the room was alight. Countless candles on sills, end tables, mantel, all across the wide bay window that looked out upon the glittering, final sunset-sea—all burst into spontaneous flame at his command. Percy exclaimed in amazement. Alexi grinned.

The room was also interspersed with bundles of heather. It smelled like a rolling heath. They both took in the scent, and Percy asked, "Alexi, did you arrange all this? Oh, wait until I tell Lord Withersby, he'll faint!" He only bowed his head in reply. She ran to the window where the moon had risen to wash the sea with luminous silver. "Oh, the view!"

Waves crashed against the rocks. The water sparkled with moonlight, and reflected flames danced in the window-panes. A fire roared in the fireplace, the cool room becoming cozy. Behind Percy, Alexi opened the door to a bedroom and gestured, igniting fires in a tall hearth and atop candles all around the fine little room. Percy gasped again, Alexi's inexplicable power over fire a seduction of its own.

A four-poster bed was hung with velvet curtains and trimmed with clusters of heather. Alexi breathed deep. "When you and I shared that moonlit dance at the academy ball, the floral crown woven into your hair—that scent would not leave my nostrils. I imagined you lying beside me, in a field of it. It was the first time I allowed myself to find you intoxicating. And the scent of it here, now, unlocks everything . . ."

Moving to open a narrow wooden door, he revealed a tiled washroom and a fresh array of candles that sprang to life with a wave of his hand. Within, steam poured from a copper tub. Moving to the threshold of the bedroom, he motioned to lower the fires in the main room, making those in the bedroom all the brighter. He walked then to the bed, mostly drawing the curtains. He sat in that opening, at the foot, and Percy was enthralled by the roaring fire reflected in his eyes.

He loosened his cravat, not blinking. "My dear," he purred, and the sound of his voice made her steady herself upon the door frame. "A scented bath awaits you, as does a bit of fin-ery. I'll wait here."

Percy nodded, dazed. "Will you . . . unfasten me?" She turned her back to him and indicated her garment's clasps.

"Yes, love," he whispered.

She felt the lace around her shoulders release. His finger lingered there, tracing her nape and tugging gently on a lock of falling hair. He unclasped her necklace and drew the pendant aside. Bending over her shoulder, he stared down at the scar that was revealed where the pendant had once burned her, a mark of Prophecy. He traced it gently before his finger strayed to the swell of her bosom. Percy's breath hitched.

"That scar has beautiful memories," she murmured, smiling over her shoulder at him. "You kissed me for the first and most glorious time after seeing it. There is pain in this Great Work; I see that. But you are my reward . . ."

"My reward, indeed," he said, shuddering with pleasure to be so near her.

Unhooking an embroidered panel of her dress, his palm slid down the revealed laces of her corset. The ties loosened and expanded with his sharp tug, allowing Percy a deep breath and a gasp. Then Alexi knelt, both hands at the small of her back. He fumbled with the layers of her bustle, opening a space where the thin muslin of her camisole was the only barrier between his fingertips and her flesh. She felt both his hands encircle her waist as he led her back a step.

He bent his head, lifted the bottom edge of her camisole and kissed the bare skin at the small of her back. A sharp breath and accompanying shiver worked up her spine. He unfastened the skirt along her side, one hook and eye after another. The satin hung down, the muslin against her skin fluttering as a small draft tickled the backs of her legs. Percy stood paralyzed, aching to know where his hands would travel next. But he simply took her hands, placed in them the bunched fabric of her skirt and patted her on the rear, sending her lurching forward.

"Oh. Thank you." Percy choked, turning to face him at the washroom, her loose dress starting to slip from her shoulders.

"Do you require further aid?" Alexi rasped, staring at the line of her collarbone.

"I won't be but a moment," she replied, biting her lip.

Shifting her skirts and closing the washroom door, she learned a sumptuous lace gown awaited her upon the back of the door, with ribbon closures from neck to toe. Percy blushed. It was nearly transparent light blue lace without lining. The note attached to the first ribbon said, *Tie every bow. I have waited all my life for this night, and it must not go quickly.*

Mind hazy and heart pounding, she slipped her wedding dress from her body, hung the layers on a peg and lifted her muslin undergarments over her head. She stared down at her white flesh and trembled as she stepped into the bathwater. It was lightly scented and perfectly warm, greeting Percy's calves, then caressing her entire body, but its warmth could not stem her trembles. She drew soap along her arms and legs, and everything inside her prickled. In mere moments, it was the right of powerful male hands to trespass every inch of her, and that would be her every pleasure.

She could not stay long in the water. Drying herself, she stared at her new gown. The lace felt incredible against her skin as she slid it onto her arm. Her shaking hands had trouble, but she tied each tie and unpinned her snow-white hair, glancing in the mirror to see that her blue-white irises had somehow grown as luminescent as those dark eyes awaiting her just outside. Never in her wildest dreams could she have imagined this scene. She longed to fling open the door and fly at him with passionate joy, but a fear lingered: what if the sight of her—the unmitigated, complete *whiteness* of her flesh—was too much?

There was no turning back. She opened the door.

Alexi gasped. There in the door frame, steam pouring out around her, an angel appeared through misty clouds. Her body was perfectly alabaster, its contours visible beneath the sheen of soft blue, and a waterfall of pearlescent hair tumbled over thin, delicate shoulders. Her eyes gleamed, tiny moons ringed in blue. Her cheeks had gained an even flush, and her pale lips were parted to allow quick, irregular intakes of breath. The shadows of her white skin were nearly the blue of the gown that clung to her thin body, every bow tied. She glided to him as if magnetized. The tips of each candle flame in the room rose, as if wishing a better view.

While Percy was preparing herself, Alexi had removed his fine dress, replacing his wedding attire with a black silk robe that buttoned down the chest. He rose now as she moved to him. Their eyes locked, and their shaking hands found each other. Alexi cupped her face and slid an arm around her waist.

"I love you," Percy blurted.

He swept her into his arms, parted the bed curtains and laid her gently down. Her hair was a gleaming mass upon the pillow, and blue lace spread about her like a pool of water. He stood there a moment as she gazed up at him. Slowly, he knelt. Billowing black silk slid over pale blue lace. He flicked the bed curtain shut behind him, the foot of the bed open only to the crackling fire.

"Percy," he whispered. "Before words fail us, as I know they will . . ." He lifted her so that she reclined upon his knees. "I need you to know that, Prophecy aside, no matter what divine remnants have taken up in us, I, as a mortal man, am desperate for you. I'd have loved you no matter my fate."

Grateful tears fell from her eyes. "How is it, Alexi, that you know what I crave to hear?"

Alexi smirked. "The benefits of marrying a man of genius. Now, Mrs. Rychman . . ." He slipped the first tie of her gown open at the neck while simultaneously undoing the first button of his robe, and she gasped. "I must kiss you and cease discussion"—another tie fell open—"as my senses flee." And another. Their subsequent kiss was nearly violent. He lowered himself to lie beside her, first pinning her down with a hand upon her shoulder, then scooping her tightly to him. When he at long last drew back, the phantom image of wispy blue wings folding in around Percy caught the corner of his eye, a spirit remnant, perhaps, of the force that guided their work and destiny.

He guided her hand to the buttons of his robe and was patient as her hands shook; he wanted her to do her part. One by one each tie was loosed, each button undone in slow, beautiful torture. A thin line of flesh could be traced down both their bodies, but that was not enough. Alexi parted the lace of her gown and it fell to the bed. He took in the full sight of her blinding white, sculpted body. Her eerily breathtaking gaze filled with fearful tears. Those brought forth his own.

"Oh, Percy, don't be frightened," he murmured, a tear falling from his eye to her stomach, causing a tiny shiver.

"M-my love," she stammered. "I'm only frightened you may not like what you see."

Alexi moaned. "How I can convince you that I am *enslaved* by what I see?"

"I . . . suppose you shall show me," Percy replied with meek hope.

"My God, shall I. You are the epitome of beauty."

Slowly, reverently, he ran hands down the length of her colourless body. Percy arched upward with a soft cry. Alexi climbed above her and his robe parted. They stared at each other.

His tall body was well-defined with such musculature as would befit a man of letters. Percy's eyes devoured each hard plane and angle. Everything about this man was impressive. Absolutely everything.

Alexi proceeded to prove to Percy that nothing about her unique flesh did anything but excite him, blessing every inch of her trembling skin with lingering, questing, exploratory kisses. In these delicate moments, if there were divine beings housed within them and drawing on ancient passion, Percy could not tell, for she was lost entirely within her own.

When Alexi could no longer bear delay, he joined their bodies with a frisson of pain and cries of pleasure. Their limbs wrapped tighter during the progressing stages of passion, and they only took their eyes from each other when kisses so required. Perhaps, Percy thought deliriously, they did see gods in each other's gazes.

They loved like music: each touch garnered a soft sound, each shift of a body was underscored by an acute reaction, their breath kept time. The tempo of their connection progressed and relaxed, largo to allegro and again to largo, gasps spurring allegretto. Movements were repeated, a prolonged symphony with digressing interludes and desperate refrains, each with a gradual build. The orchestral duet at last grew too hot for their blood to contain, and the candles and hearth in the room erupted higher in an explosion of light, mirroring the indescribable ecstasy of the entwined before extinguishing their flame. Shuddering sighs mixed with deep kisses and tears. Percy heard her heart hammering in her ears, and Alexi's pounding where she laid her head, his ragged breath a rough breeze on her neck.

They remained locked together with wide, amazed eyes and clutching hands. Words would only diminish the power of what had just occurred, and so they sealed their good night with a languorous kiss. Alexi held Percy as close as he possibly could, and they drifted into blissful, well-earned sleep.

CHAPTER SEVEN

Because of the Whisper-world's ongoing chaos, the Grounds-keeper did not trust the pieces of his dear one not to be trampled upon, stolen or digested. For safekeeping he moved her ashes and parts into a makeshift laboratory, a little gardening shed he'd long ago fashioned out of skeletons and gravestones. Upon a stone dais, right in the shed's centre, lay a metal coffin. Glass jars were nearby, having been filled with meticulous care, lining a shelf just above his head and labeled for fingers, toes, elbows, breasts . . .

"Piece by piece, love," he murmured, continuing with his chatter.

To his great pleasure, at times the ash would seem to scream and roar, proving there was fight in his lady yet. He was off to unfasten another seal, but he would return soon.

With the good professor absent for an unprecedented few days, the remaining Guard felt giddily unsupervised. This sense of wanton freedom manifested itself each in very different ways.

Elijah Withersby made it very clear to Josephine Belledoux that she was to draw every shade and lock every door in Café La Belle et La Bête. He demanded she remove any potentially breakable object from the tables, floor or bar, because he intended to utilize every possible surface to their amorous advantage. There would, subsequently, be discussion of marriage, and when that may or may not be appropriate . . . which would likely start a fight, which would likely end in lovemaking. They had their rituals, and fresh titillation came from the fact that their rites needn't be contained solely to the walls and surfaces found in the flat they secretly shared.

Jane had studied plans of how to quietly break into a children's hospital. She could only hope none of the rest of The Guard read the papers in the morning.

Headmistress Rebecca Thompson was experiencing a different, far less entertaining sort of abandon. From the moment Alexi left Athens, the fissure inside her had grown to cavernous proportions. She wandered to a nearby dim and empty pub for a less-than-savory meal. Returning to her office, she lit a gas lamp atop one of her file cabinets and kept it trimmed low. From her desk she pulled something she had never before used but had prepared for this day: a flask of potent liquor.

When she let Frederic in the window, the bird hopped about, inspecting his mistress from various angles. She removed her jacket, loosened the ties of her collar and took a draught. The sensation that burned her throat was welcome; it would help numb what was breaking apart.

She leaned upon the desk and a strange growl emerged from her lips. Why couldn't she have a prophecy of her own? Was she not as swift, decisive, strong-willed and suited for leadership? Why were she and the other four resigned to a lonely fate while Alexi alone might reap a life almost average? Could not all of The Guard be granted complementary companions as Percy was meant to augment Alexi?

But, Rebecca didn't want just any companion. She wanted *him*—compelling, arrogant, difficult, honourable, inscrutable, magnetic, haughty, inimitable him. The man who was wed after the whirlwind course of a school quarter. The man who had never been and would never be hers.

The stinging draughts she took increased in both frequency and effect. Prickling numbness drifted down her limbs and blurred her unmatched mind. Her elbow brushed

Percy's bridal bouquet. Scowling, she picked it up and began wresting the lily blossoms one from another. "He loves me not." She tossed a lily to the floor. "He loves me not." Another. "He loves me not." Soon all the blossoms lay mutilated upon the floor, the stalks cast aside as headless stumps.

Frederic noticed the change. She did not respond to his squawk nor his nibble upon her ear; she only folded in upon her body and there were soft, strangled sounds of sorrow. The raven flew out the window.

There had been a time, long ago, when she contemplated how easy it would be to jump from Westminster Bridge, to fall lightly from that precipice, to sink heavily and leave the weight of her lonely heart at the bottom of the Thames. But her strong will—one that cherished the greater good of the Grand Work—hadn't allowed for serious consideration. When she turned away from that bridge at the age of twenty, a cluster of spirits had gathered at the crest, and one came close enough to mouth the words, "Thank you." The dead needed The Guard to keep order. They needed *her*. She had to keep order inside herself and out.

This had been enough to sustain Rebecca for a long while, but today the ache was too much to feel her life had any reward. Anger, too, was close at hand. She had never understood the burden of her heart, as she'd known from an early age that Alexi cared for her in friendship not passion. Her love was an inane trap, and not a day passed when she did not curse her womanly weakness.

"Cheers," she mumbled, raising her flask, her words thick and fumbling. She kicked a lily blossom. "Cheers to the newly wedded couple. May they find eternal bliss. May they tell me how in hell I might find just a *hint* of it. Just a bit of something." She felt the flask slip from her hand and tumble onto her desk, soaking a few scattered papers with a strong scent—a hazy realization as she collapsed onto her arms, weary and bitter and slipped into unconsciousness.

She had no concept of the time when a soft knock at the

door roused her. Sitting up with a jolt, she watched the room spin. "Who is it?" she called, her words slurred.

After a moment, a familiar voice replied. "Don't you know the soft rap of your friend?"

"Carroll? I'm busy. What do you want?"

"A not-so-little bird told me you were not well."

"I'm . . . fine."

"You do not sound so." There came the sound of him trying the knob. "Rebecca, open the door."

"Told you, I'm busy. I've . . . institution to run, you know."

"Of course you do. But it's well past the hours of business, even for a worker such as yourself. Rebecca, please unlock the door."

"I'm not in the mood for company," Rebecca replied.

"You leave me no choice, then, Headmistress." Rebecca heard an otherworldly sound familiar from their Work, and the door of her office swung open to reveal a well-dressed, cautious Michael Carroll, whose ever-untamed hair was in a state of relative calm. Barely able to lift her head, Rebecca had to take a moment before her eyes would focus.

The vicar's rosy cheeks flushed darker when he saw her. "Ho-ho," he breathed, entering and closing the door behind him. "What have we here, my dear headmistress?"

It took Rebecca a moment to realize that she was slumped in a puddle of liquor, the scent of which had filled the room and that soaked the sleeves of her blouse. An alarm sounded—she was not a woman to be seen like this—but she was too incapacitated and vulnerable to make any show of rectification.

And, Michael knew her. When her eyes could focus, she recognized such a softness in him, such frightening concern and understanding. It was as if he could see right into her soul, because she'd inadvertently allowed it. She was furiously ashamed and knew he saw this, too.

"Michael, I . . ."

"You needn't explain." He walked around to her.

"But Michael, this isn't—"

"Like you? I know it isn't, dear." His arms were lifting her to her feet.

"What are you—?"

"I'm taking you upstairs."

"Oh, that isn't necessary. I'm just a bit . . . under the weather," Rebecca said curtly, taking a step and swaying. She sputtered, chuckling suddenly as he swept her into his arms. "I suppose I'm not well at all, actually." Frederic the raven had returned to perch upon the sill. Once he saw his mistress being attended, he flew off again into the darkness.

The vicar carried her out of her office and began to ascend the two flights of stairs to Rebecca's apartments. En route, a staff member came upon them and gasped. "Not to worry, not to worry," Michael was quick to respond. "The headmistress is quite under the weather, and I am a doctor as well as her friend, so she will be well managed." He wasn't a doctor but he forgave himself the lie. Anything to protect Rebecca's reputation.

Her apartments had a wide sitting room laid with Persian rugs and chairs covered in dark fabric, an adjoining bedroom, boudoir and water closet. Michael sat Rebecca in her high-backed Queen Anne, and her head lolled to the side.

"Michael, what are you doing?" she mumbled as he left her to rummage in a pantry set apart from the sitting room by carved wooden doors.

"We must tidy you up a bit, my dear."

"I'm . . . fine. Come here. Come back."

"Yes, dear?" Michael had returned with water, handed her the glass and bade her drink.

"Why did you come?" she asked slowly, her words almost an accusation.

"Because I felt the weight of your heart, my dear. I was already en route when Frederic found me. Such knowledge is my job, you know."

There was a long pause as Rebecca's face twisted. "But you didn't go to Alexi when his heart was heavy, did you? Not when we turned against him and made him forsake Miss Park—his bride."

"No, I didn't go to him then," Michael replied slowly. "And that was a mistake. I tried to gauge the damage, but I felt nothing. He kept it too well hid."

"Not from me," Rebecca said. "He didn't hide it from me. I saw him broken. We broke him. He loves her that much. *So much.*"

"Is that what this is about?"

"What?" Rebecca eyed him sharply before her eyes unfocused and she took a sip of water.

"About Alexi's love for his wife?"

Rebecca grimaced. "No. I just wonder why you're here. Save your talents for our Work, not me. This has nothing to do with The Guard."

"Oh, but it does."

"No," Rebecca said. "My . . . I am . . . capable. I can well handle myself without meddling."

"Is that so? All of us have hearts, my dear. And what goes on within them affects us—and those around us. *Deeply.* But, come now. We must get you out of this soaked chemise." As if happy to change the subject, the vicar stalked off to rummage through her boudoir closets.

"Michael, what are you doing? I can certainly dress myself!"

"Here, then." He returned with a crimson quilted velvet robe and took Rebecca by the arm, leading her into the water closet, hanging the robe on the back of the door, which he then slid closed behind her. "I am standing right by this door until you dress in something that does not reek of whiskey."

"Don't be a pest."

"You are very welcome, my dear."

It took some time before Rebecca's hand fumbled upon the handle, but when the door slid back, Michael smiled. The bleary-eyed, tousle-haired woman was changed into the robe and Michael wasn't sure he'd ever found her so lovely. Brown hair streaked with strands of silver; high, noble features . . . The awkwardness of the moment caused them both to colour slightly, before Rebecca again swayed on her feet.

Michael chuckled as she leaned against the door frame. "Come now, my dear headmistress, off to bed with you." He refilled her water, then led her by the shoulders into her bedroom. He placed the glass and two white tablets upon her bedside table, allowing her to lean upon him as he did. When he turned again to face her, in the light of the low-trimmed lamp, she appeared soft and youthfully frightened. "Michael, please don't . . ."

"Speak of this? You know me well enough to know better."

"Thank you." She fell against him in a clumsy embrace.

Michael closed his eyes and slowly allowed his arms to encircle her. Gently he eased her down to the bed, pulled back the covers and tucked her in, bending to gently brush from her drained face a waving lock of dark hair. She looked up at him but could not hold his stare.

"Forgive this old spinster, Michael. I don't know what's gotten into me." Tears leaked from her downcast eyes.

Michael knelt by her bedside. "Don't apologize to me, Rebecca. I only wish I could heal your heart."

"I . . . I love him so," she murmured, her voice cracking. Michael turned away. "I know. I know."

Rebecca, quietly crying, reached for his hand. After a long moment, Michael turned to face her. Dimly, through her tears, part of her realized there was something he wanted to say but was struggling against it. She could see it in his face: something sad and desperate, something lonely and furious, something startlingly familiar. But, she recalled, she was drunk. Nothing could be trusted, for she was a broken old woman.

He took a deep breath, and his usual smile returned to his face. "Shall I bring you breakfast tomorrow, dear head-mistress? Methinks you might not feel keen to wander down to the kitchens in the morning."

Rebecca gave a little moan and covered her face with her hands. "Oh, what you must think of me!"

"I think nothing but that I like eggs in the morning. You?"

Rebecca chuckled wearily. "Yes, yes."

"Good, then." Michael paused. "Shall . . . I leave you?"

"Yes, yes, you'd better," she hastily replied. The thought of company in her bedchamber, however innocent, was vaguely appealing yet entirely foreign and off-putting.

"Good night then, Rebecca."

When the vicar rose, she looked up, meeting his eyes. "Thank you, Michael. And . . . yes, company will be nice in the morning, indeed." Her still-incapacitated brain working slowly, she suddenly reached out. "Wait, I've a confession." Michael sat, ever attentive, and words tumbled clumsily forth: "I knew it was her. Somewhere within me, instinct told me Percy was our Prophecy from the start. I . . . I just didn't trust it. Whether that was because I was honestly concerned with her being a student, concerned about the traps of which we were warned, or if it was instead my own blind jealousy, I'll never know. I could have cost us everything."

Michael shook his head. "No, no, Rebecca. Nothing is up to just one of us. We have all been blinded differently. Alexi needed to be questioned. We hardly recognized him for his passion and vehemence. It was cause for discussion, then, as were the gifts we honestly noted in Miss Linden."

"Betrayal was a part of Prophecy, and I—"

"So it was," Michael interrupted. "But we've all scored little betrayals here and there, unwittingly, over the course of our work. We're mortal, and if the gods wanted something different, they shouldn't have sent us to do the job."

Rebecca nearly smiled. "You are so sensible."

"It's about time you thought so," he chided playfully. But he meant it. "Sweet dreams," he said, rising again. Rebecca sighed slightly as he slid her bedroom door closed behind him. On the other side, Michael sighed as well, aching keenly for all that remained unsaid.

CHAPTER EIGHT

The black door hissed open again. Beyond, a shape. He not often took form, but when he did he wore that beautiful face. Tick . . . tock. Flesh . . . and bone. The beautiful face, looking about for something lost. Those terrible, burning red coals in the sockets of a skull. A burst of righteous fury. Those burning eyes blinked out, and soon afterward the hiss of the door closing. Peaceful darkness returned. For now. He couldn't know her. Not like this. It wasn't her anymore. But would he seek her nonetheless?

Percy stirred, her eyelids fluttering as she began to wake. She released the dream, refusing to give nightmares importance. Instead, she focused on the fact that her beloved lay naked against her. She heard the lull of the waves and opened her eyes enough to glimpse bright morning light play upon the curtains.

At the sound of her husband's breathing, she blushed and recounted each exotic moment of the night. How beautiful he looked while sleeping—and he stirred in turn, his eyes

slowly opening. He emitted a soft, purring groan. The press
of his warm, bare body sent a pulse of longing through hers.

"Good morning, love," he said.

"Good morning, indeed," Percy breathed, sighing and
shivering as he kissed his way down her neck and back. The
previous night hadn't merely whetted their appetite for
each other, it had illuminated starvation.

As the next morning saw Michael arrive in the front hall of
Athens Academy, he looked up into the transparent face of
a young boy. The harmless haunt of the foyer chandelier, a
particular favourite of Rebecca's who had floated in the crystals for as long as Michael could remember, was gesturing
worriedly up the stairs. It took a moment for Michael to
realize the boy must have seen him carry Rebecca to her
rooms.

He looked around to assure himself the foyer was entirely
empty before he dared answer. "The headmistress is fine.
Don't worry. She's simply tired."

The boy's brow furrowed in disbelief. He then pointed
down the hall toward the headmistress's office, bobbing a
bit for emphasis.

Michael walked under an arch into the hall beyond, his
footsteps echoing across the polished marble. A few students ducked into doors here and there, late to classes, as normal. But . . . something wasn't quite right. And as he stood
before the formidable door marked HEADMISTRESS, he recognized what it was: a narrow, unmarked door, subtle, and
of the same wooden paneling as the walls, had appeared beside Rebecca's office, which Michael would swear was never
there before.

Suddenly, a spirit burst through and nearly right through
Michael, had she not floated back with an irritated bobbing,
folding her arms over her chest. She was tall, and Michael
recognized her from just before the wedding.

"Mrs. Tipton, isn't it? Hello. What are you doing?"

The ghost gave Michael a knowing, unsettling look. She opened her mouth and began speaking. He tried to follow the movements of her mouth, but it was no use; only Percy could hear the dead. The spirit batted her hand and, as she did, a bit of familiar blue fire leaped to life in her palm. Then she vanished.

The middle of the new doorway sizzled, and a flash of blue fire emblazoned upon it the number seven.

"Can you feel them—your friends?" Percy asked softly, attempting to translate the expression on Alexi's face. They lounged side by side, sipping tea by the sitting-room hearth of their honeymoon cottage. "You have not often been away."

"True, duty requires us close. But there is no danger, if that concerns you. A few spectral rumblings, but nothing they can't handle."

"You would be able to sense if there was pressing danger?"

"Yes."

She wondered about mentioning Beatrice's hint of betrayal, wanting to know what her husband thought of it, but she was afraid it would sound like she was questioning his friends, the people he knew, loved, trusted and led—or worse, questioning him. Until she had reason to doubt, she simply could not. Instead she would stay alert, as advised.

"Can you sense other things? You cannot . . . read the mind, can you?" Percy asked, blushing, suddenly wondering if he'd known all the scandalous things she thought while sitting across from him at his office desk.

"Not exactly, no. Though I never had to read your mind, my sweet. Of your many talents, hiding your enraptured gaze was not one of them."

"Well, then," Percy chuckled. "It's best that you married me. While my eyes may have betrayed my feelings, the rest of me surely would soon have followed," she said, tucking herself under his arm.

"Oh?" he said, trailing a finger down her body. "Do share such a bodily demonstration of your feelings."

Their day had been spent lazing about, sipping tea and a bit of champagne, kissing, caressing, and then always tumbling entwined onto a soft surface. It was the divan presently being put to good use. They had not bothered to dress since they arrived, and they still wore only gowns, though Alexi had allowed Percy to replace her nearly transparent robe with a lined one. There were, after all, drafts. Not that this kept him from every now and then loosening her strings, at which Percy giggled but did not protest. Throughout her life she had been forced to hide her skin. With Alexi she—the whole of her—could exist without shame, in celebration.

He traced the line of her jaw, clearly still amazed by her. But Percy could see clouds covering his wonder and pulling darkly at his mood.

"What is it, love?" she asked.

"I cannot stop thinking about those red eyes. The ones you saw in the corridor."

Percy gulped. They'd been in her dream, too. "Yes?"

"Were they the eyes of that hellhound?"

"I . . . don't think they were."

"Hades, then?"

Percy made a face. "Must we use these names? It's absurd. How can I now treat them as anything more than myth?"

"What—the devil, then?" Alexi's eyes blazed with jealous fury. She'd never seen that look before, and it stole her breath with its oppressive intensity. "I don't care what that thing's name is, but no one will ever lay a hand on you. Is that clear? I don't care who or what might be seeking you out, but I have you now. You are mine."

"Yes, yes, love. There's no contest, Alexi. I want to be

nowhere but with you. If something were to beckon me elsewhere . . . why, I wouldn't want to go. Tell me you don't question me!"

Alexi sighed. "I don't question your love. I just don't trust the forces that wish to tear everything apart, the ancient vendetta that began this in the first place. The goddess warned of a war when she lay the Grand Work at our feet. If it's true that we've only begun the fight . . . well, as Beatrice Tipton said, we are only pawns. But I don't want a war. And I don't want you to be anything other than mine."

Percy furrowed her brow. "What do you mean?"

Alexi looked away.

Percy moved to catch his eye. "Truly, Alexi. Do you not trust me? Do you not trust who or what I am?"

He stared out at the sea, his jaw clenched. "I just . . . I don't know what you are."

Percy rose to her feet, agitated. "I was born flesh and blood. I am now your wife. Don't tell me this has something to do with how I look—"

"Not in the slightest! It has to do with what comes out of you, where it comes from and who you may have been, the question of your status, whether goddess and immortal, or—"

"Alexi, I'm no goddess. I'm mortal."

"How do we know for sure?"

"I nearly died in your arms, Alexi. Shall we *further* test the theory of my mortality?" She shook her head. "I still have trouble accepting my own skin, all my queer qualities. I fell in love with you because you were the first man to ever make me think I could belong, that I was accept—"

"Percy, please don't upset yourself," Alexi demanded, rising and placing hands upon her arms. He guided her back to the sofa, held her covetously. "That's not what I wanted."

She sighed, turning to him with tears in her eyes. "I am too fragile to be questioned by a man such as you, by someone so important to me. Please just accept me for anything I am and might be. I've no machinations, no knowledge beyond your own. *Please.* The world does not accept me. I had hoped you . . ."

Alexi's jaw worked as she trailed off. He wiped the tears from her cheeks. "I do accept you, Percy. No matter if you have to watch me age and die before you, or I have to hold the Whisper-world off forever so it can't steal—"

"Is that what this is about?" Percy breathed. "Aging, and *possession* of me?"

"In part. Watching you sleep—a perfect angel at my side, I envisioned you twenty years from now, entirely unchanged, and me haggard—"

"We both shall age. And I am yours, forever, no matter what," she said.

"Yes," he murmured, accepting her words. "And I am yours."

They watched the sea. The sky was darkening.

Alexi finally waved a hand, and all the candles in the sitting room burst into flame. He plucked a thin, freshly bound book from the console table and said, "I read something that made me think of you. A new poet, an Irishman named Yeats." He launched into a recitation, and Percy was rendered helpless by it:

I bring you with reverent hands
The books of my numberless dreams,
White woman that passion has worn
As the tide wears the dove-grey sands,
And with heart more old than the horn
That is brimmed from the pale fire of time:
White woman with numberless dreams,
I bring you my passionate rhyme.

He dropped the book. Percy had melted into his lap like a puddle of moonlight, drunk upon the tones of his voice, staring up at him in adoration. "My white woman, indeed," he murmured. When there was such wonder, beauty and passion in the world, what on earth could there possibly be to fear?

CHAPTER NINE

The Groundskeeper scowled. "Be gone, I'm hard at work!"

To his irritation, one particular wraith kept hanging about his makeshift laboratory on the riverbank, a chiseled-faced man with an intense look, dressed in cloth and metal bands, and whose hand at times faintly glowed. The Groundskeeper batted at him with his broom before focusing again on the rows of glass jars labeled with body parts. "I'll make you whole again, my sweetie-snaky-lassie. We'll sort out what happened, and what great punishments will be dealt! Lucy-Ducy had a nice dress, Lucy-Ducy made a great mess . . ."

After a long moment he hit himself on the head and muttered, "Seal number twelve." Turning back to the coffin, he gently patted the edge. "I'll be back, my lovely, but the Undoing continues without you. Soon you'll see your hard work come to fruition!"

As he ambled down a diagonal concourse of grey mist, mumbling and singing, a shape slipped out of the shadows behind him, following but keeping closed in a fist the blue fire that occasionally sparked from her palm and locket.

Rebecca Thompson's first notion of daylight came in a pounding headache. She moaned and refused to open her eyes. Why on earth was she in such a state? She threw off her covers and steadied herself with a hand on the bedside table.

Something small and round had been left there, and she squinted, picking up two tablets. She wondered how they'd gotten there but was thankful, and she downed them with a similarly provided glass of water.

Her eyes widened as she stumbled into her washroom. The blouse she'd worn the night prior was soaking in a pail of water. It took some time before she vaguely remembered having put it there, and when she gazed into the mirror she groaned. She looked as though she had awoken from death.

"Oh, no," she murmured, and her face fell into her hands. "Oh, Michael, I am so sorry."

But soon came a soft rap at the door and a voice calling, "Hallo! Eggs, as promised! Shall you welcome your breakfast, Headmistress?"

Rebecca opened the door, and Michael Carroll entered in a rush of bluster, good cheer and anarchic hair. He carried a steaming tray. Rebecca stared at the floor and gestured him farther into the room, closing the door behind him. "Morning, Michael, please forgive—"

"I told you, no apologies—and I'm starving," he said, breezing past to place the tray upon a small table near the window overlooking the Athens courtyard. A newspaper sliding under the door spared her any more pleasantries; Michael, always eager for news, bounded to fetch it. "Well, what do we have here this fine morning? What news of common mortal—? Oh. Oh dear."

Rebecca looked over to find him agape. A gurgling laugh began at the back of his throat. "What? What is it?"

"Could this be what I think?"

He brought the paper to Rebecca. She rubbed her eyes and focused on the blaring headline:

WARD OF TERMINALLY ILL CHILDREN CURED BY
UNKNOWN MIRACLE!

A shining toddler was sketched mouthing a thank-you to a winged angel who looked awfully familiar. After reading a bit, Rebecca looked up at Michael, who only shrugged. Glancing back down at the paper, her face showed a mixture of awe and anger.

"Alexi is gone for a mere day, and look what happens."

"Shameful. Shameful! None of us can behave," Michael said. Rebecca looked up, flushing with guilt, only to see that he was laughing, his cheeks rosier than usual. "Heehee! Can you just imagine the nurses entering their ward to find their invalids throwing pillows and bouncing on mattresses?"

Michael's glee could not be contained, though Rebecca tried to fight its contagion. This would not please Alexi in the least; they were not supposed to make their work evident in any capacity, no matter how wonderful the consequences. She frowned. "How on earth did she do it?"

"I don't know, but we'll go and ask after we eat! Before we do, though, did you happen to notice there's a new door by your door?"

"What?" Rebecca said.

"Beatrice Tipton is adding doors."

Lucretia Marie O'Shannon Connor, known simply as Jane, sat near the window of her flat with her embroidery, humming an old highland tune as a cool breeze trickled in from the slightly opened casement in her study. She'd had a glorious night, and Aodhan had been there. She wished he were with her now. She knew she had become too dependent upon his spectral company, but the older she grew, the more she pined for him. Regardless, it had been one of the very best nights of her life. And she knew his name, thanks to Miss Percy. A small but significant treasure when you could not hear or touch the man you loved.

A loud pounding upon the door made her prick her thumb. The plump white cat at her feet gave an annoyed growl before stalking downstairs and toward the door.

Michael Carroll bounded up the staircase, nearly trampling the beast. "Oh—careful there, Marlowe. My dear Lady Jane, how on earth did you do it?"

Jane blinked innocent eyes at him, but guilt heightened her Irish accent. "What in the name of Saint Hugh do y'mean?"

"The children's ward! Don't even think to deny it, you delightfully devilish gal. Oh—ha! Saint Hugh, patron to sick children, eh? Clever! Bloody brilliant!"

Jane noticed that Rebecca stood behind Michael, lacking his excitement. In fact, the headmistress looked peeved, even a bit ill. Jane's heart sank. She'd hoped no one would mind. They were sick children, for Mary and Joseph's sake! Alexi was the only one who should reprimand her. But then again, Rebecca might, too. She was, after all, second-in-command.

"I want to know everything!" Michael persisted.

"Michael, m'dear, there's nothing to tell. Rebecca, what is this raving all about?"

"Quite the sensation," Rebecca responded, pulling the paper from behind her back. "While I deeply respect the act, and though Elijah can daze anyone who pries . . . really, Jane, if Alexi were to hear—"

"Please don't tell him," Jane interrupted, urging Rebecca and Michael to sit. "You mustn't think I meant to create such a scene, but the light just spread. It was all around me and *in* me. It grew like sprouting flowers. Those sleeping bodies just radiated vines of that light that kept on growin'! One of the children stirred. She said the angels had come, just as she'd prayed. Oh, Rebecca, then the light spread to all of them. The whole room was thick with light, curing, wrapping, healing . . ." Her tears ran as freely, and Rebecca had to clear her throat and fight the onslaught.

Jane continued. "Once that glorious web started spinning, I couldn't stop it. It would have broken my heart. You don't know how much more I want to—"

When she choked, Rebecca leaned forward and placed a hand upon her knee. "Yes, love, I do. I cannot imagine having the depth of your gift and being so constrained. But you know why we must be judicious."

"I know. I do know. And I am sorry."

"Don't you dare apologize," Rebecca snapped. When Jane looked up, startled, she smiled. "I only wish I could have been there to see."

Michael spoke up. "How did you get in?"

"A handy bit of lock-picking," Jane replied, careful not to incriminate accessory forces. "I've gotten rather good at it," she added hastily.

Her friends knew better than to pry, but Rebecca rolled her eyes. "I'm sure."

"We're taking you to tea! Our treat!" Michael declared, grabbing Jane by the arm and marching her downstairs. Rebecca followed.

Jane grinned, feeling better than she ever had, save for one nagging worry: before the miracle last night, Aodhan had somehow managed to trickle a bit of ash onto her hand and mouthed the word "Beware." She tried to ascertain more, but Aodhan was gone.

Beatrice Tipton was preparing one of the doors between Athens Academy and the Whisper-world, following after the Groundskeeper to undo his work with cerulean fire, but a putrid smell washed over her, heralding a powerful presence. Bile rose in her throat and she turned, every hair rising on her transparent flesh.

Funny, how her body still felt like a solid mass. She wondered if all corporeal sensations would one day go numb, hollow; but she felt so like herself, still felt the flame of desire for Ibrahim, still ached to feel his firm hand upon her hip, his lips upon—But these were distracting and ill-timed thoughts.

She had the advantage of being cloaked in deep shadow.

The goddess had done well in hiding these portal thresholds deep in the murk, frightening and taxing as it must have been for a soul of such light to do so. From this location Beatrice could watch a huge and hulking shadow, a human form hidden deep within—Darkness himself—hold out something raw and bloody. His voice was coaxing, but like stone on stone.

"Come, come, we must put you back together. Just as the Groundskeeper reassembles the Gorgon, you must become whole again, my pet. I'll not have you bested, splintered by silly mortals."

"Oh, good God," Beatrice murmured, watching the shadow of a hound whimper and slide into view.

Not that true light shone here. Just the ghost of sunlight, the spirit of a candle, the wraith of gas lamp. The Whisperworld was just that: a whisper of all that was real. But its power was formidable, as were its army and its beasts. She would have to quicken her pace. As much as she'd like to give the poor girl a rest, Persephone would yet be called out, whether she liked it or not. The "puppy" now knew whom he hunted, and when it became whole again, God help her. Beatrice wondered if there was a way to bury a part of that splintered creature, vanquished by the great light inherent to the goddess, to keep it from wholly reassembling.

The portion of Phoenix fire she controlled—an entity that had always had a life of its own—seemed to react to this thought. A tendril flared, a snaking trail of flame that dripped down from her locket, making a circle in the air and tightening it, sparkling as if in joy. Beatrice grinned. A leash? That might indeed do the trick. But for now her job remained the doors.

Alexi would have spent weeks with his beloved by the sea, but the tasks of The Guard could not go untended so long. One bit of marital business remained, however, at the Institute of the Blessed Virgin Mary, where Percy was raised.

"I was expecting a dank, dark ruin," he said with slight disappointment, staring at the Georgian edifice as they arrived. The abbey's classic brick and woodwork facade was not wholly uninviting.

"Something more eerily romantic, perhaps?" Percy smiled, peering out the carriage window. "I lived here mere months ago, trapped like a ghost, beloved by Reverend Mother but desperately lonely. How life has changed!" She embraced him.

Drawn by the sound of their carriage, a novice poked her head out from a plain wooden door. Percy alighted, and the novice nearly shrieked. "Miss Percy! I did not expect to see you again so soon!"

"I've a . . . break in term, Mary Caroline." When the sister stared at her companion, clearly baffled, Percy hurried to explain. "And this is my husband, Professor Alexi Rychman."

The novice gasped before remembering herself. "Well, then. My regards! Surprises, indeed! Does the reverend mother know?"

Percy opened her mouth to reply, but Alexi spoke first. "I sent a telegram informing her of our arrival—and, yes, of our happy news."

"Good, then she'll be expecting you. I'll show you right in."

The novice escorted them through the front foyer and down a long and unadorned hall to a modest office, bobbed once and quickly disappeared into another wing. Outside the reverend mother's door, another sister, a willowy woman in a white dress, greeted the couple.

"Hello, Percy," she murmured. "Congratulations."

Percy nodded. "Thank you, Sister Mary Therese. This is my husband, Professor Alexi Rychman."

Alexi nodded. "A pleasure."

"The young Miss Percy never required my tutelage," the sister said with a strained smile.

"Indeed." Percy grinned. "I shan't forget the look on her face the day I was reading a book aloud in the courtyard in a language none of us had yet learned. What was it?"

"Greek," Sister Mary Therese answered immediately— and, Alexi noted, uncomfortably. She opened the door behind her, and the room beyond was lit by a great fire in a hearth, casting everything in yellow light against cool shadows. The reverend mother's voice boomed out.

"My dear Percy! Come embrace me before you introduce this husband of yours." She came around the desk, a wrinkled, round woman whose mousy brown and grey hair poked insubordinately from her white coif, opening her arms. Percy ran to embrace her.

"So quickly, Percy," the woman murmured with an amazed laugh. "So quickly. This incredible news."

"Yes, Reverend Mother," Percy exclaimed joyfully. "I'm as shocked as you."

Alexi approached and bowed in deference. "Reverend Mother, it is an honour to finally meet you. I owe you tremendous thanks, for I cannot imagine my life had you not sent Percy to Athens."

Percy blushed furiously, but while the reverend mother's smile was warm, the look in her eyes was far from trusting. "Indeed. Well, these convent walls could not contain such a woman as she, Professor, as I'm sure you understand."

"Percy, will you walk with me for a bit?" Mary Therese spoke up.

"Yes, go," the reverend mother said. "I wouldn't mind a moment to consult Professor Rychman on a few . . . *fiscal* matters."

Percy looked to Alexi for permission, and he nodded as if she needn't ask. With a wave and a tiny smile she disappeared into the hall.

"Professor," the reverend mother said as the door closed. "There are many reasons why I wish to speak with you alone."

Alexi pursed his lips. "I imagine finance ranks among the least important."

"Indeed."

"Well, if it is any concern at all, I am descended of a wealthy family and have many vested interests and a comfortable estate. Percy shall not lack."

"While I am pleased to hear that, money is not my focus."

"What is?"

"Your intentions."

Alexi raised an eyebrow. He had assumed he would be welcomed with relief, not questioned as a possible threat. "Why, my intention was to make Miss Parker my wife, which I have done."

"While Percy is admittedly unique, and older than the rest of your students, she was still your pupil. Is it not forbidden for there to be relations between—"

"Of course. And after Miss Parker and I confessed our mutual sentiments to each other, we were quick to withdraw her as a student and make our union complete."

"Before her schooling was finished?"

Alexi shook his head. "Reverend Mother. With all due respect, you surely know that—proud as I am of the academy—Percy was suited for Oxford not Athens. The only class that gave her any trouble was mine, and I'd like to think that was due at least in part to distraction."

Levity infused his last comment, but there was none to be found on the reverend mother's face. "Professor, forgive my bold statements, but I am concerned that your interest in Percy may be of a fleeting, novel nature, and not one of lasting devotion. Perhaps you hastened into marriage due to . . . improprieties."

"I did not ruin the girl and marry her out of duty, if that is what you are insinuating, Reverend Mother," Alexi stated. "I maintain I am a gentleman."

The woman winced. "Of course."

"Of what else must I assure you?" Alexi asked.

"The girl is not merely an oddity, Professor, not something to be shown off at parlour séances. Her heart is vast with love but incredibly delicate. If you should abandon her to take up perhaps with another student . . ." She shuddered. "The effect upon her would be cataclysmic. Irreparable."

Alexi sighed. "Reverend Mother. True, you know nothing about me, and one might fear a lover making some sort of curious trophy of Percy. This is hardly the case. You surely know the transformative power of my wife's radiant soul; I merely became the fortuitous recipient of her affections. I would have preferred not to marry a student, but the fact remained that Persephone was a heaven-sent angel and I wished to do right by her as soon as possible."

"I want to like you, Professor," said the reverend mother, frowning. "In fact, I want to rejoice in you."

Alexi shrugged. "If you are concerned about Percy's lasting presence in my life, perhaps the announcement that she has become a permanent member of our Athens staff will help."

"Really? *Staff?*"

"Yes, we'll be keeping her busy with literary translation. Fitting, don't you think?"

When Alexi offered a slight smile, the reverend mother at long last returned it. "Perfect."

"So. Your strange, dear little charge has become mistress of a fine estate, gained a husband and employment in a matter of months. She has not done poorly for herself, has she?"

"No." The reverend mother laughed. "It's far more than I could possibly have dreamed. Thank you, Professor."

"The pleasure is mine, I assure you."

After a moment of pleased reflection, the old woman spoke. "There is yet another sobering matter."

"The grave of her mother," Alexi guessed.

The reverend mother moved to a cabinet and unlocked a

drawer. She pulled out an envelope marked with a simple Celtic cross. "Here is a map."

"Thank you." Alexi regarded her. "Percy has been strange business for you, hasn't she?"

The reverend mother nodded. "Yes. I always knew I had to take . . . special precautions."

"If I might ask, what have you done? You've not closed her off from the strange portents of her life; you have allowed them."

"You're a man of science and will scoff at my reasoning, I'm sure."

"As I once told Percy, Reverend Mother, you'd be surprised how little I find strange. Percy was hesitant to tell me of her visions, of her interactions with the dead, and I love her all the more for them. There's much about the universe that defies our explanation."

The old woman smiled. "Oh, my. A man of science with an open mind. What a treasure! I wish the rest of your kind were as forgiving to us clergy . . . In a dream, precisely nine months before the infant Percy arrived, the Holy Virgin proclaimed that unto us a strange child would come, but not to fear her, and whatever would be asked of her care, to do it. She proclaimed the girl would bring light and love to those lives she touched. How could I not obey? I sought to serve this prophesied child, and with you here now . . . Well, I rest easier knowing she has someone to love and protect her."

"That she has," Alexi said. "Now, you said 'whatever would be asked of her care' . . . ?"

"To attend to the burial of the mother as you will find. And then I was told of Athens. I made inquiries. Your school is not easy to find, you know."

Alexi smiled wryly. "Indeed, it is part of our . . . charm."

"Once examined, I saw the school was precisely suited for her. The Lord provided."

"Indeed," Alexi repeated. "Rest assured, my dear woman, I care for Percy more than I can express. I pledge my life for her safety."

The reverend mother moved to Alexi and embraced him. "I am grateful for you, Professor."

"That pleases me greatly."

A knock came upon the door, and, grinning, the old woman called, "Come collect your husband, Percy."

Percy entered, moving as if she had to keep herself from running to him. "Business all attended?"

"Yes, love," Alexi replied. "It seems I've married a pale pauper. Not a penny to her name."

Percy looked mortified. "But—"

"And I don't mind a bit," Alexi stated, sliding his arm around her waist. It took Percy a moment to realize he'd been teasing. "Shall we take a turn round your old haunts?"

"Oh, yes," Percy blurted, flustered. "May I, Reverend Mother?"

"Of course, dear." The woman chuckled. "But be sure to come back and bid me farewell."

Percy led Alexi about the cloister, from the courtyard garden where she had named every flower and staged her own version of a faerie play at age six, to the small grey confines of her old room with its one narrow window and within which she and her Elizabethan spirit friend Gregory had recited *Hamlet* in the dead of night. She explained the haunts of each of her spirit friends, only a few of whom still lingered against her uncanny knack for setting them to rest.

"Oh, Alexi," she exclaimed when the tour was finished. They sat on a courtyard bench. "Thank you for listening to tales of a weird childhood. I led a magical but desperately lonely life, knowing no one would ever understand or believe. How wondrous to have someone who understands, a lover who—" She bit her lip, shivering. The word "lover" was still such a deliciously fresh concept.

"Indeed," Alexi replied, kissing her blushing cheek. "You're a tonic of youth for an old man."

"Old man. Hardly," she scoffed. She drew near, looking furtively around to be sure they were alone. "You've proven otherwise," she murmured, brushing his lips with hers.

The sound he made, and the way his hands tightened upon her, were signs that his control was being tested. "My God, Mrs. Rychman, you lure a professor into marrying you, then drive him mad with desire inside your old convent walls? You were never meant for sisterhood."

Percy blushed, giggling. "Is this where my melancholy prince tells me to 'get thee *from* a nunnery'?"

Alexi grinned. "Indeed. And we've turned tragedy into a happy ending. We are products of our fool romantic age in the end," he murmured, running a finger along her collarbone. "Now, what did Sister Mary ask?"

"If our hasty marriage was because you'd ruined me."

Alexi chuckled. "Your abbess wondered the same. Come then," he said, rising. "Onward."

After making their good-byes, they were escorted out the massive front doors by the reverend mother and a parade of the abbey's ghostly denizens, their numbers greatly diminished since Percy's birth. Percy waved one last time to those who remained while Alexi spoke with the carriage driver; then she settled in for yet another long journey.

Alexi took a deep breath. "Before we return to London, my love, we've one last appointment. We must pay our respects at the foot of your mother's grave."

Percy's brow furrowed. "My mother's grave? Why didn't I know about a grave?"

"I think we'll see soon enough," Alexi replied.

They traveled down a road thick with brush. Percy noted the quaint York surroundings growing wilder and increasingly unkempt. At last came an unmarked iron gate and a narrow, deep patch of flat ground interspersed with white stones. As Alexi helped Percy from the cab, she took in a full view of their destination.

Alexi was sure to keep her arm tightly in his as he opened the squealing hinges of the cemetery's rusting gate. Percy stared at old, untended graves, sandstone eroded beyond recognition, moss over the epitaphs. There were no spirits that lingered here; those interred had either found peace or their lingering wraiths had managed to flee.

In a corner plot lined with thin-branched evergreens, two small stones lay apart from the rest. Alexi crossed directly toward them, and Percy felt her blood grow cooler with each step. Then she realized it wasn't just her blood; the air was drastically colder here, as if she were standing in the wake of a spirit. But she saw none.

The flat grey stone they sought was not nearly as worn as its neighbors, and the moment Alexi saw it, he pressed Percy closer, holding her as she gasped and nearly fainted. The larger stone was inscribed: I. PARKER, MOTHER. The stone to its left: PERCY PARKER, INFANT.

Percy choked, turning in to his firm embrace. "How cruel. To feel such a ghost already, and then to see this? Shouldn't it unhinge my very senses?"

"You're flesh and blood, Percy," Alexi assured her. "There's another reason for this grim landmark. Be strong, love, and wait here a moment."

Percy watched him turn and walk away, his black cloak billowing. He returned to the carriage and unlashed something from its rear: a shovel. The very sight of it made Percy ill.

"Oh God, Alexi," she called across the graves. "What are you doing?"

He calmly approached and drove the shovel into the earth beneath the smaller stone. Percy cried out. "Alexi!"

"Your infant body is not within this grave, Percy. What is?"

The question could not stay unanswered. It did not take long to unearth a small, rotting wooden box the size of a dead child. Alexi pried open the lid. Inside was a metal container, its contents a clump of folded paper bound by twine and an odd silver key. Alexi lifted both, brushed a few specks of dirt away from each and handed them over.

Percy accepted the items gingerly, her gloved hands shaking. She was scared to open the twine, and she hadn't the slightest idea about the key. She had lived without any knowledge of her mother and had become accustomed to that mystery. But, looking into Alexi's eyes, she found strength.

He picked up the shovel and began refilling the grave. Replacing the patches of grass, he stepped upon the ground to make it level. The disturbance of the earth would not be readily apparent. Then, their purpose complete, he took her arm again. "Shall we linger?"

"Allow me a moment, if you would," Percy replied quietly. Alexi promptly obeyed, walking away without question.

Percy stared down at the larger tombstone. This lonely grave was all that remained of a true family. "Mother. So much has happened to me in such a short time, and I did not expect to see this. All I can think to do is offer thanks and pray for your peace. I'm sure I owe you more than my life. I've a husband! And, isn't it incredible that an oddity such as me should have one so grand? I wish we both could have known you. I only hope heaven grants you such comforts as he has given me." Her hand closed around her phoenix pendant, her only inheritance. Out of the corner of her eye she saw Alexi standing just beyond the iron gate, patient, his arms folded in his cloak. She allowed his magnetism to draw her back. He was her family now. As were The Guard.

He loosened his arms for her to fall into. She lingered there, in his warm, comforting darkness, breathing in his subtle spices before she drew back. "Well," she murmured, "shall we journey on?"

"Yes, my dear, I can hardly wait to bring you home."

This roused an eager smile, and in that moment all surprises and sorrows were forgotten.

In the carriage, Alexi knew better than to sit opposite her. He shifted to allow her specific place in the crook of his arm. When she looked up, he nodded at the folded paper. "I'll not look, if you would rather—"

"No, Alexi, I wish to hide nothing from you. What do you suppose this key might be?"

Alexi examined it. "I once found a tiny keyhole at the centre of the floor of our sacred space below the chapel, and I always wondered of it. Perhaps we shall try it there, though I hesitate to guess what we may unlock."

Frowning, Percy ran her finger across the peculiar knots and grooves of the key. Unclasping her necklace, she slid the key onto it. Lifting the silver phoenix on the chain she asked, "Why would Mother have given me this and withheld the rest?"

The open patch at her breast revealed the perfect imprint of the silver bird, the scar that had both alarmed and excited him. "This sign branded you, brought you to us, but apparently the prophecy required you shouldn't have that key until we were united."

Percy nodded and took a deep breath. She opened the accompanying letter and read: "'My dear child, while I'll never know you, I know about you. Much like the Lord, your coming was foretold. Do not be afraid. I am not. I was delivered from death to deliver you. I wish I were clever enough to devise a more delicate beginning, but there is only the strange wonder of your birth these words stand witness to.'"

Folding the papers with slightly trembling fingertips, Percy reached to caress Alexi's hand, leaned into him with her full weight and shut her eyes. "I . . . I'm too overwhelmed," she murmured. So the letter was left untouched for the remainder of the journey home.

"So, again, beloved, I'm left to wonder," Alexi murmured as she slept on his shoulder. "What, exactly, are you?"

CHAPTER TEN

If the balance between the mortal and the spirit worlds was a tapestry, now and then a thread of that tapestry would begin to tug, perhaps tear. It was in response to this disruption that The Guard acted, to smooth each snag in the fabric. Rebecca's awareness of this phenomenon was unmatched; it was as if the whole of London were a map written in her blood, and though she was haunted by a lingering guilt that hung over her like a guillotine, the Pull at this moment was a rustle of leaves under Rebecca's skin that tumbled into a cluster. Two familiar problems were brewing due east: one on Rosebury, the other down Fleet. Perhaps the occupation would do her good.

As she had a horse brought to the Athens portico, a broad-shouldered silhouette trotted up the alley. "Hallo, my dear. Feel the Pull, do you?"

"Yes, Michael," she replied, having hoisted herself side-saddle onto the mare. "And while I appreciate your diligence, I believe I can disassemble these fools alone." She grimaced. "Seems to be the night for severed heads."

Michael chuckled. "Ah, Goldsmith and Grimaldi. Of course you can handle them. Still, I thought I would offer."

Rebecca shrugged. "I'm only fit for my own company."

"While I don't agree, I do believe you must prove to

yourself why we turn to you as well as Alexi. Now that he has his . . . preoccupations, you'll need to step fully forward."

She stared down at him a moment before her face softened. "You are right."

Michael grinned. "I could smugly say 'I know,' but that sounds too much like Alexi and we can't have that. I'll just thank you for agreeing."

"No. Thank *you,* my dear. I need someone to tell me sensible things," Rebecca murmured. Then she rode off, before he could add anything else.

In transit, her horse moving at a slow plod, Rebecca heard a familiar voice call her name and the sound of running footsteps. The Pull gave The Guard a sense of one another, and of the task at hand. Michael wasn't the only one to seek out her and her destination.

"Elijah Withersby," Rebecca replied, halting her horse. "I can handle these heads perfectly w—"

"I d–didn't want you to have a go of tonight's work all alone because you thought none of us was available," Elijah stammered.

Rebecca looked down from the saddle, offering a look of irritation that rivaled Alexi's. She took a moment to evaluate her friend's disheveled appearance, and with mild disgust noted his half-tucked shirttails and badly buttoned breeches.

"Why, thank you, Elijah," Rebecca began. "How thoughtful to be available in our moment of need."

"What can I say? I am a veritable icon of responsibility."

"So it would seem."

Elijah cursed as he caught the direction of Rebecca's eyes. He had rushed out of Josephine's amorous clutches and toward his higher calling, only to be betrayed by his pants. Josephine, at least, would remain without implication. Nor would the gaffe further tarnish his reputation, as he was erroneously assumed a libertine. Though—especially with Josephine's pointed behaviour of late—did any of them truly believe the charade anymore? Surely The Guard had long since guessed they two knew each other in ways more intimate than friendship.

Not that he could admit it. What on earth would Alexi say, after all the ribbing, upon discovering Elijah's loyal, loving nature? The revelation would be a disaster. That's what would happen, when he honoured his promise to marry Josephine: everything would fall to pieces. Not just Alexi either. His peers. His family. *Everything*. And yet he'd promised upon the prophesied addition of The Guard's seventh member . . .

"Shall I press on to business and leave you standing there staring?" Rebecca asked, interrupting his thoughts and shooing her hand at a young spirit taking the time to levitate apples from a nearby cart, to the owner's great dismay.

Elijah bowed. "By all means, my lady. By all means."

"I suppose you might as well make yourself useful. Since you're here," she allowed.

"As you wish!" Elijah said cheerfully, and promptly wiped the minds of all those who'd seen the flying fruit. Passersby dispersed, oblivious. Disappointed, the spirit gave up and sank through the cobblestones, but not before offering the headmistress an impertinent gesture.

"Busy night," Rebecca stated conversationally. "I was just on my way to Ye Olde Cock Tavern. Then to Sadler's Wells."

Elijah made a face. "Oliver Goldsmith's head? Again? And that *clown?* They must have a cranial rivalry; they're always out in tandem."

"Each won't take but a minute, especially if we work together. We'll begin up Fleet Street."

Rebecca kicked her horse into a slow walk, and Elijah strolled along beside her. "Damn writers," he opined, "loath to leave anything, frightened of fading into obscurity; it isn't Goldsmith's body haunting Fleet Street, it's merely his pride. Damn them all. There isn't a single noble profession in the world."

"Nobility comes only through *lack* of work, then?"

"My class is constituted entirely of sniveling idiots," he replied.

"What, then?" Rebecca laughed. "There must be some worthwhile task—"

"Yes," Elijah said firmly. "Ours. We're the world's only nobility, Rebecca. Though our rewards seem paltry." He eyed her. "How are you faring these days?"

Rebecca snorted. "What's come over you?"

"I was asking the questions, my dear." He grinned. "I was just wondering how it feels to be free of His Highness, if only for a bit."

Rebecca thought a moment. "Not bad, I suppose. Not bad."

"Good, then. Our leader Alexi may be, but you of all people oughtn't be kept at heel."

"He did not put me at heel." Her voice was cold.

"No, he didn't." Elijah's gaze was uncomfortably direct. "You did. He respects you the most of all of us. But you've never done yourself that honour, have you?"

A discomfited clearing of her throat was Rebecca's only response, and they walked in silence to the tavern.

"Hold on to your head, Oliver!" Elijah cried upon their arrival. "We come for it again, you witless sot! I never did like a single one of your tired phrases!"

He threw open the tavern door and burst inside with a raucous yell, drawing a pretend sword and crossing the entire first floor in a few bounds. Rebecca couldn't hold back a laugh. The burly man behind the bar had come out to tackle him, but Elijah raised his arms in a swift, grand gesture like a conductor halting a symphony. All was immediately quiet, the tavern's assemblage staring suddenly off into space. Unable to help himself, Elijah waved his arms about a bit, seeing how the entire company moved their heads in response like marionettes on strings. This caused him limitless glee, and

Rebecca had to take his arms and gently lower them, lest he play giggling puppeteer all night.

"You allow me no fun," he pouted, a stray finger still making one slovenly drunkard's gaze turn loops.

Rebecca confiscated both his hands in hers and nearly pressed her nose to his. "Fun? What about Jane's recent lark? We cannot all be allowed to misbehave."

"I thought I saw something about a children's ward . . ." he began.

"And?"

"Brilliant." Elijah grinned.

"You picked the locks, didn't you?"

"What, and let Michael steal my mischief? He lets her into the parish wards all the time. It was my turn."

The two of them walked onto the tavern's back stoop in tandem. Sure enough, Oliver Goldsmith's disembodied head bobbed at eye level in the back courtyard, his transparent features looking entirely offended.

"Stop scaring the barmaids with your corpse, Goldsmith . . . let your prose do it for you!" Elijah's magic pinned the writer by his century-dead eyes while Rebecca's incantations of banishment settled into a hush. The spirit was soon dispatched, and they crossed back through the quiet, lazing pub, Elijah relinquishing his control of the inhabitants with a flick of his wrist as the front door clicked shut behind them. He admitted, "I don't sense Grimaldi anymore, do you?"

Rebecca thought a moment and shook her head. The Pull was gone. "He must know that his colleague has been dispatched. Performers hate taking direction, especially from us."

"Fancy a drink?" Elijah offered.

Rebecca's stomach roiled, thinking of the night before. "Tea."

"Tea it is," he agreed. "To headquarters! La Belle et La Bête!"

The pair made their way to the small café and found that something had pulled all five of the remaining Guard together. Rebecca's raven had come, too, Jane's cat Marlowe entwined at her feet, and they partook of beverages, tall tales and laughter, playful derision all directed at the absent Alexi. When Percy was spoken of, which was infrequent, it was with apprehensive reverence. Shop talk, as it were, was avoided completely. Rebecca debated mentioning the strange new doors at Athens, and she decided to ignore them for the moment. Lifting her tea to her lips, she enjoyed its warmth and simply cherished her scrap of contentment.

The hour growing late, Michael was gentleman enough to see her safely back to the academy. He was always looking after her. She wasn't sure she'd ever acknowledged it, and only when he vanished back into the shadows did it occur to her that she ought to have thanked him more heartily.

She went to her office. It was an hour past when anyone should work, but there was paperwork to attend, for which she was grateful. There was a budget to be balanced, a staff to compensate, a board to please, sponsors to court, supplies to order. The work was solid, dependable; there was a science to running an institution, and Rebecca was master of it, grateful that some part of her life made sense. Her occupation was like running a household, only magnified exponentially. This partly filled the ache of not having an estate of her own, partly made up for a lack of a husband and progeny. Partly. Her students were her children and The Guard her family. The Grand Work was her husband. An ache remained.

She was deep into the ledgers when a sensation hit her so sharply it knocked her forward, her fountain pen scratching out and bleeding darkly over the corner of the lined book and onto the blotter. Her breath was swiftly cut from her, as if by a knife. Her gift was sounding a raucous alarm.

Miss Parker—Mrs. *Rychman,* she amended bitterly—would be compromised. Endangered. Before there was even a chance for Beatrice's predicted war, somehow, by someone, she would be cut to the quick. And it would be someone close to her.

Rebecca's blood chilled. Never before had the pique of her gift felt so violent or so raw. She placed her fountain pen to the side, having held it clutched tightly in her fist, and she saw her hand was smeared black. She slid her elbows onto the desk, hoping that the action would still the sudden trembles coursing up and down her spine. But, no.

Rebecca shook her head. "No, none of us. It cannot be. We wouldn't." None of them wished ill upon the girl, and so—

A cool and thorough moisture broke over her flesh. She stared up at the ceiling of her office—a beautifully crafted, wooden-paneled affair, with its centre scalloped fixture emitting soft gaslight and needing, to Rebecca's chagrin, a bit of dusting—and she prayed. "I don't know what it means," she said, wrestling with her gift, hoping that it would clarify itself once it heard her soft plea. "If I don't know how, or by whose hand harm will come to her, how am I to prevent it?"

The gift would not see reason. Only one thing remained clear: the dread certainty that Percy would be severely endangered by someone she knew. Rebecca steepled her ink-stained fingertips and slid her forehead down onto their point. She heard a small choking sound come from her throat, something strangled and defiant. The words that broke free were half a plea, half a refusal:

"Not me. It shall not be me."

As the carriage slowed, Percy gasped. A great mansion of deep brown sandstone, with a gothic facade and arching windows latticed with wrought iron, the Rychman estate was nothing if not intimidating, a magical fortress. A thrill worked up her spine to call it home.

Alexi drank in her every expression. "I want to offer everything I can to please you," he murmured.

"Oh, how you do," she cried, fumbling to take his hands in hers.

The driver unloaded their trunks at the side portico and pulled them to the front eaves where a huge brass bird with outstretched wings held the ring of the door knocker in its talons. Alexi climbed out, swept Percy into his arms and allowed the driver to open the front door. Percy's delicate fingers danced at the nape of his neck.

"Welcome home, Mrs. Rychman," he said, kissing her softly, and he carried her into the house.

Everything was dark as he set her down inside the threshold, but not for long. He waved his hand and a chandelier above their heads glittered to life. An open foyer with vaulted ceilings was illuminated, a winding banister rising to the second floor where a balustrade jutted over the foyer. The wooden floor of the main hall led into rooms at either end of the estate with glass doors open to reveal a sitting room and a library, both doorways accented by sconces of firebirds whose wings cradled glass cups of sparkling flame.

The windows at the front of the house belonged to an elegant dining room where sliding doors led into a sitting room and steps presumably descended to a kitchen. There were several vases of towering roses set upon the cream cloth covering the banquet table. Another chandelier, vast and circular, was the focal point of the room, draped with crystals that sparkled like diamonds.

"Oh, Alexi."

Wide-eyed at the elegant splendour of the home, Percy dragged her husband by the hand as she toured the first floor. She took in the open sitting room, which was replete with grand piano, divan and impressive high-backed chairs near the hearth whose mantel bore the same rich grey marble that topped the end tables. Paintings of Josephine's particular style mixed alongside pastoral scenes in classical style, all with a deep colour scheme that lent all the more richness to the cherry and mahogany wall panels. Spires of candelabra offered inviting, diffuse light.

Alexi only smirked as she tugged him next to his library, a room of dark green walls, cherry bookcases and innumerable leather spines. Percy, lost in the sights and smells, recognized his scent—clove tea and leather-bound books—and leaned close to breathe him further.

Rococo writing desks and random laboratory equipment were arranged throughout the room, interspersed with worn chairs. A large phonograph took up one corner. The moment Percy's eyes fell upon the large, fluted bell, Alexi was quick to go and turn the handle. With a sputtering hiss, out flowed a dark, tumbling Chopin étude. Alexi returned, and Percy found herself intoxicated anew by the way dim candlelight played on his features.

She pulled him again into the foyer, rejoicing in how music permeated this house. She ran to the windows and unlatched the shutters, one by one exposing the entire house to a wash of moonlight. A wild, unkempt rose garden came into view, with a winding path to a grove of birch trees.

Alexi took in an awed breath. "My God, you become the very moonlight," he breathed. Percy looked down to see how bright her skin glowed, and her husband extinguished all other light with a wave of his hand. Her body and the moon itself were the only sources of illumination.

He swept her into his arms and began to dance her around the foyer, pausing every now and then to steal a kiss. All through the house they spun, in and out of every room, a deeper kiss in each, finally waltzing up the stairs, swirling about the balcony and through each of the elegantly appointed bedrooms. Their laughing sighs whirled them into the master bedroom, which was furnished with a lavish four-poster bed thickly draped by burgundy curtains, an armoire, a wide hearth and a leather-topped writing desk. A great, arched window looked down onto the wild garden, and strands of ivy could be seen sneaking onto the panes of glass.

Arms around each other, they gazed down at their estate. Alexi softly kissed the crown of his wife's head. "Percy," he whispered. "I used to hate this lonely place, shuttered and collecting dust. The whole of it now brightens with your radiance. It is the first time it is truly home."

"How could I not shine, Alexi, with such blessings as these, as you——?" Her voice broke as she pressed her cheek to his breast.

The sentiment encouraged his covetous passion. She had assumed she would live her life entirely without such intimacies, but she'd been wrong. And Alexi held her afterward, all through the night. Percy, overwhelmed with the magnitude of her blessings, knew she'd never tire of their wonder.

Jane sat alone in her study, eyes closed. Marlowe, her white cat, was curled around her leg. She was waiting, listening for the soft chime of the clock that would bring both night and *him,* and as it did, the air around her grew cold and she shuddered with delight. A chill pressed upon her lips like a feather made of ice. She opened her eyes to Aodhan's phantom kiss.

He drew back, the chill of his lips a lingering mist. He gestured for her to open her hand.

"You've brought me something?" she asked, but the look on his face stilled her pleasure. She reached out, and into her palm he trickled a stream of ash. As Jane furrowed her brow, wondering what he meant, he pointed emphatically to the clock. "What? What is this?" she breathed.

He grimaced and tried gesticulating. Jane shook her head, baffled. The light of his shade flickered. Time was not on his side these days, the Whisper-world weighed heavy and he faded before he could offer warning.

* * *

The next morning, before breakfast, Alexi offered Percy a tour of the immediate grounds, and her excitement nearly had him skipping with her toward the rear garden. Braced by the brisk air, they strolled about the twisting, overgrown, cobbled path through thickets of what, to Alexi, was indiscernible foliage. Percy joyfully pointed out to him the names, blossoming seasons and general particulars of each.

Returning, they found the Wentworths, housekeepers to the Rychman estate. The pair did not live directly at the house, but in a nearby cottage, as Alexi wanted to keep his immediate home clear of anyone not involved in the Grand Work. The servant couple had recovered from the shock of the professor's letter announcing that he would be returning from a honeymoon with a new mistress of the house; Alexi had taken pains to describe his dear young wife and champion her sweet nature, lest they show surprise at her singular pallor. The Wentworths were clearly not prone to gossip, suppositions or much conversation for that matter, but to Percy's great relief, she no longer feared her lack of domestic savvy; Mrs. Wentworth would take care of everything.

The woman showed Percy to her boudoir, where a single trunk containing her meager possessions from Athens had been unpacked, and an entire wardrobe had been filled, via Josephine's instructions, with stylish dresses in various shades of blue and purple. The Frenchwoman had written she'd only seen Percy in these colours, and so they must be her favourite. At this, Percy burst into tears.

"Oh, madame, there's no need to cry," the round and rosy Mrs. Wentworth clucked. "The professor can send for a seamstress should these not be to your liking."

Percy laughed. "Oh, Mrs. Wentworth, I shed only grateful tears! Please understand that I was raised an orphan pauper in a convent. Living at Athens was palace enough, but now the riches of this household . . . I don't possibly deserve such immense good fortune."

"And why on earth not, Mrs. Rychman? Dear creatures who, as you do, take nothing for granted, you deserve every comfort, for you are of the mind to appreciate it. The master's a shrewd man who's kept his lamps trimmed low and his costs negligible. I've long thought it a shame, him being as well provided for, as intelligent and not altogether bad-looking as he is, that he had no wife to dote upon. I believe he's only too happy to spend money on you, that it's a pleasure for you both."

"Why, Mrs. Wentworth, you are a domestic savant, indeed." Alexi's low, rich voice slid into the room with his person following close behind.

The woman coloured. "Forgive me, Professor, if I speak well past my place, it's just that your wife—"

"I overheard her gracious tears, and I think, Mrs. Wentworth, that you spoke perfectly to the point."

The woman straightened herself proudly.

"Darling," Alexi said, pursing his lips, offering Percy his breast-pocket handkerchief. "Do grow accustomed to being provided for, will you?"

Percy stared up at him, stricken that his comment was a reproof, but his eyes sparkled with humour.

Though the dining room was large, they sat close and ate a leisurely breakfast. Percy's face was warmly lit beneath the low and magnificent chandelier, but her gaze clouded as she set down her silverware. "I ought not keep you waiting, Alexi," she said suddenly.

Her husband offered her a quizzical look.

"Mother's note," she clarified. "If you light a fire and sit beside me, I can face anything."

Alexi nodded and led her into the study. Procuring the papers, he bade her sit on a soft leather sofa. The flick of his hand provided light and warmth from the room's hearth. Percy grinned, nestled into Alexi's arm and resumed.

"'My name is Iris Parker, and I was brought from sin to deliver you, whom divine mystery surrounds. I was born into a wicked life, but Mother told me of the Lord, and the Holy Spirit was my only solace. Born with a heavy heart and wont to lapse into profound melancholy, I had clouds of darkness all about me.

"'The night my life changed, I'd been left for dead by a horde of drunken thieves after falling from high balcony rails, down onto the courtyard stones of an inn—I was always roaming. Here, I was sure, was my final stand. There was so much blood around me, I was destined for death. The fall seemed to have broken everything, and as I prayed to God to end my pain, there was a great light. I was shocked to wake, alive, in a stone room. A convent room. A bright star fell before me. In the light stood the Blessed Virgin. She was dressed in and full of light, bringing the music of angels. She kept shifting colours—'"

Alexi started, and Percy glanced at him. "Our goddess," he breathed, "who proclaimed Prophecy to us. Your reverend mother was granted a similar vision, surely by this same herald"—he stared at Percy, his expression complex— "assuring you would come to Athens. To me."

"And thank heavens for it," Percy murmured, turning again to the letter.

"'The Blessed Virgin proclaimed you like the Christ child, said that you would offer hearts peace and triumph despite all obstacles and iniquity. She said you were escaping a prison to reunite your soul, escaping an old vengeance, seeking to be reborn in love. She said you would do everything to make a life of pain into the life of love you were denied.

"'This heavenly creature wept as she spoke, and I was humbled. Each tear was silver and sang with sorrow. She caught the droplets in her hand. She proclaimed I would henceforth be with child, and when she opened her hand the silver tears had formed a necklace—a bird. I wish I could leave you more than a talisman as inheritance, but this is no ordinary pendant. It is from the divine.'"

Percy plucked the phoenix pendant from her breast and brought it to her lips before continuing.

"'I do not know if you are a messiah, Persephone. That is the name I have been told to call you. Our Lady said so with such blushing fondness that I could not resist. I cannot question the goodness of her bidding, nor can I question that you of all creatures were not born of natural cause.

"'The Virgin vanished, but a woman in the room remained. I started, but she told me not to be afraid, just like the shepherds in the field. Her name is Beatrice, and she pens these words, as I never learned to write.'"

Percy and Alexi took a moment to stare at each other.

"'Beatrice understands pain and loss, is a sister in this journey. She confirmed my vision. I do not know why I trusted this stranger, but she leads me on, unfailingly quiet and kind. We've descended the eastern English coast, always moving. We are en route to York, where the Institute of the Blessed Virgin shall surely take you. I shall leave these pages for you there and cover all traces of your birth from intrusive eyes.

"'Sprits are now visible to me, Persephone. I see them everywhere. Perhaps you will, too. Beatrice hushes them when they come too near, lest they kindle fires of madness in my mind. But . . . to have a purpose, Persephone, to become part of something greater than ourselves, to serve something lovely and mysteriously divine—this is the greatest validation of life itself.

"'I will make sure the sisters know to send you to find 'The Power and the Light' at a school in London. That was my instruction. The Power and the Light. Whatever that is, Persephone, it sounds stately and grand.'"

"It is our benediction," Alexi spoke up. "And the motto of Athens. It seems that the power of The Guard is somehow tied to that building. But . . . I still don't understand. If all of this was carefully orchestrated, why wasn't I simply alerted to you from the first?"

Percy shrugged. "Beatrice said destiny could not hold our hands. I daresay falling in love with you of my own volition was far better than being told to do so."

Alexi stared at her, his eyes soft. "Indeed, Percy. You are correct and very wise."

They turned their eyes one last time to the scrawling script.

"'We've begun to fondly call you Percy. Forgive me your nickname, as I don't believe I shall know you long as a child. Still, let me indulge in such motherly contrivances. You're my last gift to give before I join the Lord. I'll cradle you, Percy my girl, and then be off. I sit without sadness as Beatrice writes this. I once begged for my constant darkness to end. You made my ending sweet and filled it with light.

"'I know the world awaits you. Who knows what strange gifts you may acquire, what pharisees will attempt to denounce you. You were not born like a common mortal. You shall not live like one. There are dark forces that defy light. Some might search for you. I trust you'll see things, the light or the dark of them. I pray you find your way through.

"'If for some reason you've not been, go straightaway to Athens. In London. You're awaited there, fated for a great love. But a storm comes. All the spirits are murmuring. The very air is filled with excitement. The clouds are swirling, and all the dogs are barking. You must be a very special girl, indeed, my miracle. God bless, my child. I'll hold you soon, and I'll speak to you in heaven.'"

Percy set the papers aside. Tears streamed down her face. Alexi lifted her chin and wiped her eyes. She leaned against him, and he folded her close.

"I need you," she murmured, blurting the first thing she could think to say.

"Good," he replied. After an awkward moment, he kissed her cheek. "I love you," he whispered. Then, rising, he left the room.

Percy blinked after him. She wondered if she should feel

hurt by his departure. Instead, she exhaled slowly and felt comforting familiarity in solitude. Moments of distance and awkward silences couldn't be avoided with two such solitary creatures as they had always been. She had seen a brief moment of fear in his eyes, perhaps of losing control. Love could be overwhelming, and perhaps it was sometimes best to walk away, lest the tempest lose its wondrous beauty for its dizzying effect.

CHAPTER ELEVEN

The Rychmans' first estate dinner party was comprised of an average group of middle- to upper-class English citizens, well-assembled and appointed, or so said appearances to any of the uninitiated. Not that anyone outside of The Guard was invited.

Percy played excited hostess at the door. Alexi had retained no house staff beyond those needed for dinner preparation, and so it was he who took their coats and cloaks to the wardrobe near the door. He allowed his more congenial half to comment upon his guests' formal attire and bid them enter the dining room.

Rebecca lingered at the entrance, keeping Michael behind and out in the chill a moment as she pressed Percy's hand in hers. Holding on for a bit too long, an odd light in her eyes, she spoke softly. "Welcome back. I trust you had an enjoyable time. Now that you've returned, please take care of yourself. You've wedded a dangerous fate. Please, *please* take care and be alert."

Recalling Beatrice's words, Percy felt her blood chill at this warning. Perhaps Rebecca's intuition sensed something her own visionary nature could not anticipate.

Alexi's sharp ears picked up on every word, and he fixed Rebecca with a curious, concerned stare, but before anything further could be said, Lord Withersby brought up the rear of the entourage, nearly shoving Michael inside, whisking Josephine hastily across the threshold so that he could enter.

Stumbling into the foyer, he cried incredulously, "The light, Alexi!" He flung his arms before his face as if blinded. "The sheer light of the place!" Taking Percy's face in his hands, he kissed both cheeks. "Why, I never knew this place so grand! I've never seen it lit! This husband of yours, madame, if you'll know, always prowled about here in the dark."

"So I've heard." Percy cast a smirk in Alexi's direction, and Elijah gurgled in protest.

"You've got her smirking now, Alexi! Come, you oughtn't have affected such a change upon this sweet face. Soon, heaven forefend, you'll have her sneering. Who knows what disasters may yet befall her in this house, and you'll douse all the lamps again—"

"Does he leave it any wonder why I was desperate to go on holiday?" Alexi asked Percy, offering only a sneer as response to Lord Withersby.

"How was your time away?" Michael asked. "The sea is lovely no matter the clime, I imagine."

"Indeed, Michael, indeed," Percy assured him, leading Elijah toward the dining room. He was trailing behind her, staring about the estate as if he were attempting to compare its grandeur to his own. Every now and then she noticed his gaze shift nervously. His mouth was pinched, his laugh a higher pitch than usual. Perhaps none of her new companions had a particularly relaxing time in their absence but instead were more tightly wound. This did not help Percy's hope for trust among her new peers, but she chided herself for being haughty enough to think it had anything to do with her. Surely personal dramas were afoot, nothing more.

A hearty course sat open and ready for the guests on their plates, though Mrs. Wentworth hadn't understood why Alexi didn't mind if their dinners went cold. The company took seats, leaving Percy and Alexi the ends of the table. Michael's fork poised over his dish.

"Percy dear," Alexi began, "the roses you provided are lovely, but would you mind moving them to the hutch?"

"Of course."

As she did so, Alexi waved a hand and a huge ball of fire flashed over the table, warming all plates and only slightly singeing napkin edges.

"I daresay I'll never tire of that!" Percy exclaimed. Alexi flickered a proud smile.

Michael and Jane were both immediately lost to the raptures of well-seasoned potatoes. The rest began to pick like birds at their meals.

"So, *mes amis*. York, was it? Did you see any of the town?" Josephine asked.

Percy ducked behind her napkin, unfolding it slowly as her face had acquired mottled patches of rose. Indeed, they had not explored one acre of the town, as there were far more pressing personal explorations taking place.

"I procured a quaint cottage and it was quite relaxing," Alexi replied calmly. "Directly over the sea, away from the village. Thankfully no disturbances, ghostly or otherwise, befell us. I hope your time here was similarly quiet."

"A few admonishments here and there—" Rebecca began.

"Goldsmith's reprobate head again," Elijah interrupted.

"I hope you all behaved yourselves," Alexi intoned.

Jane took a swift drink of wine.

"Model citizens, we were," Josephine declared. Elijah, seated beside her, threw an odd glance over his shoulder, making Percy wonder what adolescent behaviour they had been up to.

"I'm sure," her husband offered.

"You'd best return to Athens as soon as possible, Alexi," Rebecca said hesitantly. "There have been . . . changes. I cannot explain it. Beatrice Tipton is doing something. She's been seen coming in and out of doors. Actual, physical doors. New ones. It's odd."

Alexi furrowed his brow and was silent for a moment. Percy wasn't fond of the idea of doors, especially not portals to the Whisper-world, and she was sure he agreed. "First thing in the morning," he declared.

"It was lovely to see Reverend Mother again," Percy offered, eager to bring normality again to the table. "It was quite clear everyone was shocked by my marriage. While I enjoyed showing Alexi my old haunts, so to speak, I confess that Athens felt more my home after a few days than years inside that brick institute."

"And Reverend Mother," Alexi added, "quite approved of me."

"But I daresay, old chap, there must have been a bit of convincing the mum that you weren't some cad academic with a passing fancy for the young and studious."

Percy choked on her potatoes, but Alexi set his jaw. "My proper intentions and the advantages of my position were made quite clear, thank you."

"'Advantages of your position.' I'm sure."

Michael spoke up. "Elijah, wouldn't you like to introduce Mrs. Rychman more gradually to the insults and injury lobbed at her husband, or have you fully armed the battery this evening, this but the warning volley across her gentle bow?"

"Perhaps it's best I learn to pick my offenses, as it appears I shall have many from which to choose," Percy replied, amused and a bit dazed, and everyone chuckled.

"To the wedded couple, their well-deserved holiday, and their safe and happy return to this fine estate," Michael said grandly, raising a glass. Everyone followed suit.

"Thank you, my friends," Alexi declared. "I think it hardly in need of announcement, but we would be well-advised to hold a meeting tomorrow night in our chapel."

"Agreed," Rebecca seconded. "And, you are aware of tomorrow's staff meeting at Athens, are you not?"

"Indeed. Percy and I shall both be in attendance," Alexi replied.

Percy shrank in her chair. She'd forgotten about her new role as staff. She wondered if she was too shy for such an office, sure the faculty would regard her with curious disdain.

"Do come early," Rebecca said sharply. "To see the . . . changes. And take care." She stared at Percy a moment before picking up her drink.

Alexi nodded, then launched upon a surprising subject. "We were given a letter from my wife's late mother. It seems she knew Beatrice and was visited by our goddess. A prophecy this was, indeed, and she left items for future examination."

Percy busied herself with her tea. Her life had never been of interest to a group, and the openness with which Alexi initiated discussion of such odd and yet intimate portions was jarring. Feeling as pale as her flesh ever was, she was thankful he did not further mention the singular circumstance of her conception, lest Lord Withersby jokingly proclaim her the world's next messiah.

"I've much to ask Beatrice, but we ought not have her trying to speak to any of you directly," she said. "It seemed my mother went a bit mad from hearing spirits."

"Why, then, Mrs. Rychman, have you not?" Michael asked.

"I must be special," she replied, giving a small grin, knowing he meant no implication. "Or I'm completely mad already."

"You did marry Alexi," Elijah offered. When Josephine groaned, he added, "Come now, she nearly begged for that!"

"Whatever you might do to avoid baiting him, *ma chérie,*

may aid in keeping this irredeemable predator at bay—for which we shall all be grateful," Josephine instructed tiredly. Percy simply nodded.

"We hoped he would give you a bit of respite, at least in your own home," Rebecca muttered. "Next time, you may have to accidentally forget to send his invitation."

"And the event would die a prompt and quiet death," Elijah assured her.

"Only peace and quiet—blessed peace and quiet—would survive," Rebecca replied, removing a cutlet from Elijah's plate and planting it on her own. "How splendid the thought."

After dinner and wine softened the jousts and eased all tensions, the gentlemen of The Guard retreated to the study for sherry and cigars, while the ladies sat in the parlour with coffee and a plate of small pastries that Josephine was loath to relinquish. After a long moment, Percy finally voiced her concern. "They won't be . . . talking about me over there, will they?" she asked meekly.

"Of course," Jane replied, shrugging. "I'm sorry, Percy, but it's the truth."

Josephine leaned in to add her opinion. "I have no doubt Elijah has by now made at least one inappropriate comment."

"If not five," Rebecca said.

Indeed, across the hall, in the suitably masculine den that had so delighted Percy earlier, Lord Withersby placed one thin hand upon Alexi's shoulder while the other jauntily swirled the liquor in his crystal snifter. "So, old chap, let's get right to the point. Tell me. Was your Persephone suitably divine?"

Michael, cigar in his mouth, gasped and sputtered smoke out his nostrils, and could only watch in choking horror to see if Alexi would promptly throw Elijah from the premises. Their leader turned very slowly to peer down his nose at Elijah with a face that Lord Withersby had never seen. Relish glittering in his dark eyes, his look of triumph was nearly frightening.

"Exquisite beyond words."

Elijah held up his hands in reverence, and in the silence that followed only Michael could be heard, still forcing out his improperly inhaled smoke.

The ladies were engrossed in a pleasant discussion of what was to be done with the rear garden and other estate improvements when Rebecca shot from her perch upon the divan and strode toward the closed glass doors, a hand at her forehead. In the room opposite, Alexi had done the same. They each flung wide the doors at the precise instant.

"Highgate," the two chorused. All eyes were upon them.

"Again?" Josephine pouted. "Why always in my finest dresses?"

The Guard gathered into Alexi's two carriages. Mr. Wentworth hardly raised an eyebrow as Alexi helped ready the second team of horses, but Percy was inspired to murmur to Josephine, "Heaven only knows what that family must think." They stood in the rear garden watching the conveyances being brought out.

Josephine smiled. "I daresay they're quite accustomed to seeing us on impromptu jaunts. Elijah now and then tickles their minds so that they don't ask too many questions. They know we're out of the ordinary, and I secretly think they like us for it."

"What's Highgate?"

"The great graveyard, where London's most fashionable dead are interred. Quite a place to see," Josephine replied.

They set off, and soon tips of obelisks and angels in the distance heralded Highgate's approach. Alexi's hand was pressed firmly over Percy's, and he stared ahead with fastidious concentration. A congregation of ghosts glowed just inside the fast-approaching gate.

Alexi helped her down once the carriage pulled to a halt. Visiting hours had long since passed, but Michael held out his hand and the enormous locked gate swung wide. A ring of dead children coiled at the centre, but there was an additional flank of unrest. Adult spirits lined the tall iron gates of Highgate, waiting. Swaying. And speaking. For Percy, there was no bugle call to arms, there was only a torrent of whispers. A dreadful singsong accosted her ears. "Lucy-Ducy wore a nice dress, Lucy-Ducy made a great mess . . ." The children's voices filled the air. Percy felt her stomach roil, and she wondered if the head of a cavalry charge felt the same.

"You hear something, don't you?" Alexi asked.

"They're all speaking, Alexi, the children, in some sickening rhyme, and the others . . . Well, the others think you have brought me as an offering. As one of them. But I don't know what they want."

"My attention. I've been away. These spectral delinquents require the firm hand of a master." And with that he gestured to The Guard, who darted forward among the grand monuments.

Surrounded by graceful angels, carved mausoleums and fine crosses, a bright, full moon illuminating the scene, Percy couldn't help but be taken with the eerie light particular to a graveyard; the luminosity of an eternal crossroads.

Her husband lifted a hand toward the children, who suddenly seemed as curious as the adults to see Percy. Tendrils of blue flame snaked forth like ivy from his palm, and he became the great conductor. The transparent adult phantoms squealed and giggled or wailed like banshees, one by one realizing Percy was indeed living flesh. Before they could comment further, Alexi wrapped glowing cords of light around wrists, waists and necks, attaching them in fiery shackles.

The cantus was begun, Alexi insisting Percy join the circle. The Guard's voices lifted, focusing their power and whipping a wind around them, coalescing their ancient force. Alexi cried out a word in the ancient Guard tongue: the simple call to peace Percy had heard before. The spectres reacted. Some drifted on, some simply faded, some sank into the ground, perhaps still too attached to their rotting coil to abandon it fully.

The hovering children watched the adult spirits around them fade and pouted, their fun cut short. They again took up their nursery rhyme. "Lucy-Ducy wore a nice dress, Lucy-Ducy made a great mess . . ."

The Guard's power rose again, the blue fire crackling forth from their circular conduit, reaching upward in tall flames that tickled the feet of the bobbing young spirits, who sobered, their small eyes angry. "Beware the wrath!" one little girl in a white nightgown called, wagging a finger at Alexi. "He'll lock you away, he will!" The other children picked up the new taunt. "He'll lock you all away!"

The girl in the nightgown floated close, getting louder. "She's coming. She's coming. She is coming!"

Long ago Percy realized the calls of the dead often meant nothing at all. She hoped that was so now.

"What?" Alexi asked.

Percy winced. "'She is coming,' the girl screams."

Rebecca turned to Alexi. "Remember little Emily, the Luminous case months prior—?"

"I don't think this one means Prophecy," Alexi retorted. "Someone else."

Percy shuddered. The Guard turned back to the remaining ghosts.

"Children, I demand that you go to bed this instant!" Rebecca cried, using her best headmistress tone. Alexi followed the admonishment with a renewed burst of blue fire. The spirits screwed up their faces and descended, sinking again into the earth beneath the small gravestones marked with lambs and flowers, floating onward to where Percy did not know. The sight saddened her, but at least the job was done.

Returning to their carriages, Rebecca addressed only Alexi, but made no effort to hide her anxious question from

Percy, whom he instinctively kept locked by his side. "Athens?"

Alexi raised an eyebrow. "Now?"

"I don't mean to alarm you, Alexi, but what's happening on the grounds is so . . . strange. Oughtn't you come? There are matters—"

"Rebecca, dear, it's near midnight. Fresh phantasms can await the dawn."

"Indeed," said the headmistress, her mouth thinning. She straightened her shoulders and marched off.

Percy watched her retreat. A few paces behind her was Michael, attempting to be noticed. Rebecca deigned to allow him to ride back in the same carriage, and they vanished into its interior. A thought occurred. "You would have gone, wouldn't you? Before?" she asked Alexi.

"What do you mean?"

"Before our marriage. You would have gone to Athens. Rebecca seemed surprised. Disappointed. I'm all right, Alexi. If you should go, please don't hold back on my account."

"I'm taking you home, and that's final," he said. The look in his eyes made Percy's body flood with heat. "We must dole out your supernatural excitement in pieces. I'll not subject you to more, no matter what may lie in wait at Athens."

As the children foretold, she was nearly complete. The Groundskeeper hummed as he peered over the coffin lid. The shape of a female body lay in the coffin. His sweetie-snaky lass. Not much could be said for her condition, being that she was entirely ash, a headless body of congealed grey soot that registered tiny, hitching breaths from a quivering sternum. He had catalogued her requisite parts and mostly put them back. There were a few pieces missing, to his dismay, and he wasn't sure she'd come together exactly whole. Or what the effect would be. But something still lived and stirred in those ashes, angry.

Her head was the last of the large jars to be uncorked. He lifted it gently, ash inevitably flaking off for him to collect and return. The fragile head made rattling, hissing sounds, its mask of an open mouth frozen in a moment of rage and defeat. He attempted to soothe it. The body trembled as he poised the head above the crumbling neck. "That's it, my Dussa-do. Soon my pretty girl lives again."

He set the head atop the neck and massaged the ash together. The body hitched and seized, ash flaking off as a hideous growl sounded in the room like a growing storm. The ashen body sat up, slamming flaking hands on the side of the coffin. Its open mouth roared, and the entire Whisper-world shuddered the echo.

"WHERE IS SHE?"

"Mrs. Rychman, you ought to establish calling hours, in the interest of becoming better acquainted with your husband's baffling bohemian set," Mrs. Wentworth said after break-fast. Preparations were being made to return to Athens.

Percy blinked. She turned to Alexi, who also appeared confused.

Mrs. Wentworth sighed. "Honestly, Professor. You ought to attempt the civility your station requires, and encourage your wife to do the same."

Alexi wrinkled his nose. "Calling hours. Headmistress Thompson always said ladies should have offices for those sorts of things. And really, Mrs. Wentworth, I'd never have thought you cared one whit for my civility—or for my 'baffling set.'"

"While I've had no cause to disapprove, mystery does not breed utter indifference, sir," the woman replied with a slight smile.

Alexi chuckled then allowed, "Calling hours, eh? Only when I'm in class. Otherwise she'll be with me at Athens. I can't spare her more," he added, grazing Percy's hand with his own.

Seeing the warm expression he caused, Mrs. Wentworth importuned, "Mrs. Rychman, please give me an invitation list and I'll take the cards out promptly."

"Thank you very much," Percy said with a shrug. When it came to matters of society or the house, she vowed to simply smile and agree, still thinking it mad that she should be mistress of a fine estate at all.

She dressed for the meeting at Athens in dark blue, in a dress finer than that of any student yet suited for her new profession. She stared into her wardrobe mirror for a long moment, then dove into a drawer to pull a soft scarf of pale blue. She'd once wrapped herself daily in it. The familiar shield, along with her dark, tinted glasses, she would keep close at hand. She placed both items in her reticule.

Wandering into Alexi's study, she found him deep in a pile of notes, attempting to decipher which marks he had given to which student. A week of exams had been over-taken by grave prophecy, peril and marriage.

"Alexi, will my old professors be in attendance?"

"Hmm? Yes, some of them will be there. Not everyone attends the meetings, however . . ." Alexi trailed off, raising his hand in triumph as he found what he sought. "Why?"

Percy drifted to a leather chair, staring out the window at the sky.

"Alexi, I disappeared. What will they think? What of my final tests? Will I not have to answer to them?"

"You fell ill. And then we were married," Alexi replied. "The staff has already been warned of our union. Our vows will appear sudden, perhaps even lecherous on my part, yet marriages have been made over less. There was every ru-mour about the headmistress and me, and I'm sure this out-does anything they may have assumed of me prior. But there isn't a thing to be done for opinion," Alexi replied with a nonchalance Percy envied.

She grimaced, not wishing to recall her own assumptions of the closeness between him and the headmistress. "You're such a help." Then another thought made Percy gasp. "They'll think I'm with child."

"What?"

"They'll think that's why we had to marry so suddenly."

Alexi's brow furrowed a moment before he shrugged. "Perhaps."

"But, Alexi. What if I . . . what if we . . . ? I mean, could . . . ? *Can* I? Can we? Is that part of Prophecy? I . . ." Percy worked herself into breathless shock. "There's so much, Alexi, so much in this new life of ours, I'm . . . Forgive me my ignorance and frailty."

"Hush," Alexi said. He moved to kneel before her and took her hands. "I don't care a whit what staff may think, Percy, and I hope you'll soon feel the same. As to your question, my dear: of course I've wondered. I don't know if we may conceive. While child-rearing hasn't been part of The Guard's expectations so far, things with you and me may be different. And, of course, we are mortals, so there is no reason to assume it an impossibility. Yet we mustn't expect it. We must take our lives one day at a time. Can you pledge to do so with me?"

When Alexi cupped her cheek, she stared into his dark eyes and could breathe again. "You calm me so," she murmured. But the thought was there, and she was not sure she could contain the raptures of her sudden sentiment.

"The idea of a little one does have its delights, though, does it not?" he murmured, making her wonder if he had the ability to read her mind. The two of them gazed quietly at each other before finally turning away from the powerful subject.

Mr. Wentworth was on hand to drive them to London in the good professor's finest carriage. As Alexi settled opposite Percy, he watched her rustle in her reticule and withdraw her scarf. Winding it through her hands, she then pinned up her braid in ritualistic fashion, wrapped the scarf about her head and slid her dark glasses upon her nose.

"I thought we discussed this," Alexi spoke up. "Shall my wife hide herself?"

Percy bit her lip. He stared at her with that same unsentimental acceptance that had bolstered her from their first private meeting, the look that allowed her to believe she could escape the personal limitations of her ghostly appearance. She smiled. "I suppose if I was able to go without this in a ballroom, I might do so in a meeting. I derive such fortitude from you."

He almost smiled. "I've stubborn pride enough for us both."

CHAPTER TWELVE

Outside her office, Rebecca pointed across the wood-paneled hall. Alexi and Percy turned to behold a narrow door, a soft light emanating from beneath. The door hadn't been there before, and it was marked with a seven.

Alexi folded his arms and peered close. "There's a draft. I don't suppose you've opened it?"

"Not while you were away, no. I thought it best to have our whole group present."

Alexi pursed his lips and turned the knob. Locked. He raised an eyebrow. "Skeletons in your closet?" When Rebecca scowled he suggested wryly, "I suppose haunts have keys and guest rooms now."

"I've a key," Percy spoke up, pulling her mother's key and phoenix pendant into view.

Rebecca furrowed her brow, squinting. "And that came from . . . ?"

"My grave."

Rebecca looked in alarm at Alexi, who merely shook his

head. "I believe your key is meant for our sacred space, Percy. We'll try it tonight."

"Speaking of meetings, ours is about to start," the headmistress stated, glancing at the watch on her waist-pocket chain. "I suppose we'll have to see if any of the faculty have noticed our little . . . renovations. Where do you think this leads, Alexi?"

"The spirit world—cold draft, eerie light and all," Alexi replied, and walked away toward the grand staircase. Rebecca and Percy hurried to catch up.

"But Alexi," the headmistress said. She leaned close and spoke softly, and Percy had to strain to hear as they walked. "Doors that open from the spirit world into ours—actual physical doors like we've never seen, and that are locked from this side? Don't we want to keep them shut?"

"I didn't say I was fond of the idea," he replied. Looking around for Percy, he drew her forward and tucked her arm into his so that they all three strode side by side. The act made Percy's heart swell: she would not be left out. She was privy to this madness, too, and her powerful, mysterious professor wanted her on his arm.

Rebecca moved ahead. Percy found herself wishing Michael were there; he always seemed ready to take the headmistress's arm. But Michael wasn't employed by the school, so there seemed no remedy.

As they ascended the stairs, Marianna rounded the corner, espied Percy and ran to throw her arms around her neck. Alexi moved out of the way as if dodging something dangerous and braced for a squeal.

"How was the honeymoon?" the blonde girl crowed.

Percy blushed as a few staff turned with raised eyebrows. Marianna bit her lip and tried to drag her into private. Alexi had moved down the hall a few paces but was staring back at her expectantly, so she extricated herself from Marianna's grasp and said, "It was wondrous, darling, but I must go. I cannot be late to the staff meeting. I hope to see you soon!"

Her friend withdrew as if ashamed, stared at her as if she were something different. It was true that she was. Things were altered—yet Percy wanted to lose none of the warmth and delight of her friend, exchange it for distance and cold formality, so she grasped Marianna's hands in hers. "We'll make time to talk, I promise. You simply must visit the estate."

Her friend nodded. "Of course, Mrs. Rychman," she replied.

Percy blushed. "While that title yet thrills me, you mustn't call me it. To you of all people I will always be Percy."

Alexi inclined his head, still waiting. Percy nodded nervously, kissed Marianna on the cheek and rushed off to take his outstretched hand. Glancing back she saw the blonde smile, buoyant and seemingly unruffled, but a slight melancholy tinged her lovely green eyes as she turned and descended the staircase, off to the classes from which Percy had been removed.

This shift between them was only natural, Percy supposed. She was older than the other girl, and her relationships must unfold as they would. Her new responsibilities were adult ones. *Prophesied* ones. Particularly those of The Guard. And she wished to be nowhere else but at this school and by the side of her formidable husband.

The Athens staff meeting was held in a small lecture space on the second floor of Promethe Hall. The conversation was quiet and mostly polite, if a bit strained as Percy and Alexi first entered. Utterly unruffled, her beloved went about business with enough indifferent arrogance as to confound any possible critics. Still, as Percy could feel eyes upon her and an impending wave of speculative gossip, it became more and more apparent that Alexi, while claiming no care for public opinion, seemed to be enjoying the idea of their scandal. A mischievous sparkle lurked in the corners of his sharp eyes as he boldly kept hold of her hand. She couldn't help but be amused.

Headmistress Thompson ran the meeting with brisk efficiency, stating that attendance was holding and that there had been no notable infamy among their modest student body. Everything was well in hand. When a teacher inquired about her recent health, Rebecca coughed and dismissed the notion with embarrassment.

Occasionally Alexi and the headmistress would glance at each other, surely wondering if the subject of architectural changes to Athens would arise. But it seemed these were doors only visible to The Guard. This relieved them both, Percy could tell, though the lines relaxed only around her husband's mouth, not Rebecca's.

There was a brief welcome given her, the new linguistic appointment, and Percy was grateful for the utter lack of ceremony. Her former dormitory chaperone, Miss Jennings, kept a scowl on her face, stewing over the unexpected couple. If she had only done her job, her thickly knitted brows seemed to say, that haughty Rychman would never have been so bold.

Meeting adjourned, Percy released a breath and was the first to glide into the open foyer beyond. Alexi moved behind her. "Come, my dear, let me show you to your office."

"I've an office?"

At the end of a long hallway there was a paneled wooden door with freshly painted gold script that read: *Translation Services, Mrs. A. Rychman.* Alexi opened the heavy door, and the sight beyond garnered Percy's gasp. The room was a fair size, with a bay window that took up nearly an entire wall and looked down onto the school courtyard. Light shone brilliantly through its Bavarian-style glass and the smooth panes at the centre. Every furniture cushion was a royal purple. The walls held books, floor to ceiling. Percy was agape.

"Mrs. Rychman," her husband began grandly. "Our Athens translator and envy of all faculty as resident of the Bay Room."

"Oh, Alexi, I don't deserve this. How was this beautiful room not occupied?"

"Because it is most assuredly, and most constantly, haunted." He grinned. "I didn't think you'd mind."

A few books floated from a bookshelf and opened their covers to settle gently on the leather-topped desk. The room dropped a number of degrees and a greyscale, square-jawed, professorial gentleman came through the bookcase to fix Percy with a transparent stare. His hair was long and bound behind him. Percy glanced at the books on the desk: poetry in several languages.

The ghost held out his hand, and a lovely woman with windswept hair slipped through the bookcase and into the room. Alexi nodded in greeting. "Professors, may I introduce your new tenant, our new linguistic administrator and my wife Persephone? Percy, Professors Michael and Katherine Hart."

Percy smiled. She recognized them. Every year on their anniversary, these wraiths were known to waltz in the tiny graveyard behind Apollo Hall. She'd watched them, enraptured. The deceased academics eyed her appraisingly.

"Hello, Professors Hart." She made a small curtsey. "Pleasure to meet you. I see you have placed a book of sonnets on my desk. I do hope you'll do me the pleasure of reciting your favourites. I, unlike others, am able to hear your ghostly voices."

The floating forms turned to each other and smiled. Katherine said in a sweet voice like the wind, "You'll do fine then. Perfect, in fact. Welcome." She took her husband's arm and remarked absently, "Lovely couple. Wonderful how those with gifts find one another." The two vanished back through the bookshelves.

"I remember them, you know," Percy said.

Alexi took a seat upon the bay window and gestured for her to join him. "The waltz in the graveyard?" He gave a slight smile. "I saw you from my office window that night, your arms open to them, starved for such a thing. I didn't know what else was to be done but teach you how."

"Our waltzes . . ." Percy breathed, remembering his lesson, then the academy ball, when the blooming flower of their affection could at last be denied no longer.

The sound of her breathless recollection compelled Alexi to kiss her. He drew back after a languorous moment to see Percy's eyes remained dreamily half open. "While I could easily busy myself with you in all manner of ways, I've a bit of business," he admitted. "As for your new position, I've a book for the Russian consulate. Your work will fund a scholarship for young girls in need of education. Shall I fetch it so you may begin?"

"Wonderful!"

"I'll be back again in a moment."

She watched him go and bit her lip, indulging a bit of a swoon against the bay window cushions.

"Oh, how you love him!" declared a strong female voice. "I admit it's a balm to my weary soul. I've worked so hard."

Having thought herself alone, Percy jumped to her feet and whirled to find a ghost floating near her desk. "Hello, Mrs. Tipton," she said.

The spirit straightened to greet Percy properly. Her presence in life must have been very potent, as intimidating as Alexi and the headmistress had been to Percy at first, as her shade lingered on in a form very nearly solid. "My lady!" She floated forward. "You look so much the spirit. I wonder how you managed that particular trick."

"Excuse me?"

"Your colour. I wondered how on earth you managed it."

Percy flushed. "No trick, madam. I certainly would not

have chosen this colouration had it been within my power to affect."

"Well, it shall come in quite useful on the Whispering side."

Percy hoped Beatrice didn't mean what she assumed. "Would you . . . care to sit down?" She was trying to be, as Mrs. Wentworth suggested, a civilized lady. But etiquette with the dead wasn't in any ladies' handbook.

"No, no, you sit. I suppose you've questions for me."

"Indeed."

"Lovely wedding," Beatrice murmured. "Made me think of the rite Ibrahim and I had. Intimate. Powerful." Her eyes hardened. "But that was long ago. Where shall we begin?"

Percy sat again at her bay window, a sliver of sunlight falling across her lap. She wished she could busy her trembling hands with a cup of tea. "Please, tell me of my mother."

Beatrice stared at her a moment, impassive. "For the brief span I knew Iris, she was a good woman. Kind, generous." The ghost looked away. "Full of a faith I never understood, giving herself to her fate in a way that I admired. Because, damn it if I didn't fight my own fate." She turned again to Percy, her expression pained. "Remind me that you remember nothing of the old times, of the other side, of the life prior to your current flesh."

"All I know are the simple visions that led me to Alexi. Tiny flashes. Should I remember more?"

"No, it's just as well." Beatrice sighed. "You've begun again, a clean slate. I just have to remember not to lay any lingering resentments at your feet, my lady, for it isn't your fault."

"I'm Percy, please."

"Indeed. You're not my lady. You're Mrs. Alexi Rychman, and all is as it should be."

"Is it?" Percy asked. When Beatrice looked up she added, "Why did you fight your fate?"

"We've not the time for my lengthy answer. I both loved

and hated the Grand Work, what it took from me. In life I was a mortal pawn for an ancient vendetta, preparing for a prophecy of strangers, and I remain servile to it here in death. I resented the powerful force that was Our Lady, and yet I loved her, for while she was not mortal she loved like one, wished to live as one, and loved The Guard like family. But she couldn't know the burdens she brought onto us by this calling. She had so many burdens of her own, her poor form faltering after so many years in that dark Whisper-world for which she was never meant. And so she never truly knew how it was for us."

Percy sat silent, feeling a bit helpless, regarding Beatrice with open empathy.

The spirit wafted closer, her edges softening. "But we must finish what we started. What began eons ago with a murder."

Percy shuddered in sudden recollection. "I relived a horrific death by fire, more vision than memory. There was a great, winged angel of a man, reminiscent of Alexi—"

"Yes. That was terrible history. Phoenix splintered under Darkness's fist, but he could not be quenched. He and his attendant Muses lived on in what became The Guard, using mortals to fight Darkness's viler whims. The goddess Persephone deteriorated without her true love, quite literally rotting in the Whisper-world. She awaited the day she could finally give over, could choose this side for good and be close to the pieces of that life she cherished. She brought remnants of Phoenix to this school. Eventually she was brave enough to choose this life. To become you, something immortal made flesh. Much like they say of Je—"

Percy's hands flew up. "No, you mustn't."

"Ah, yes, you're Catholic." Beatrice chuckled. "Theologically confusing, I'm sure. Will be interesting when you next pray your rosary. You could choose not to believe in anything, like me, and then be surprised by moments of supreme divinity. Tell me: are you happy?"

Percy, reeling, took a moment, thought of Alexi and all that had changed. "Yes. I would say I am most blessed."

"Good." Beatrice nodded and stared out the window.

"Why the gift of language?" Percy asked suddenly. "Why can I hear, know and speak each tongue I encounter?"

Beatrice stared at her. "Because death speaks every language." When Percy shuddered, Beatrice added, "The goddess spoke to all the dead. She was beloved for it. It seemed she passed on that gift to you. Oh, it taxed her immensely, but she tried to set as many to rest as she could. Sometimes it only takes one word of kindness, you know, to set a soul at ease."

Percy's eyes watered. "That's lovely," she murmured, feeling a sudden pride in her heritage, confident in her endeavour to carry on that noble work in this life.

Beatrice grinned suddenly, a bit wickedly. "I wonder if your husband remembers you stealing to his bedside as a youth, making him a man . . ."

"I beg your pardon?!" Percy flushed.

The ghost batted her hand. "Don't be jealous. He only ever loved you. Divine, mortal, she who became you. As a divinity you—"

"*She.* I'm not—"

"She came to The Guard on their annunciation day. She proclaimed Prophecy. You may ask them about it."

Percy tried to calm herself. "Yes, Alexi mentioned her, and that some part of her might be guiding me—or inside me."

Beatrice nodded. "Desperate, she came to him in dreams. In Alexi she found the closest match to her beloved as ever was incarnate. She wiped his memory to make him fresh for what she would become, but not until afterward. She wanted to be with him as a bride, and was scared she would not find him in whatever she became. But here you sit."

Percy grimaced. While she had no right to be jealous, exactly, she was more confused than ever about her identity, and was suddenly afraid Alexi loved someone from his past.

A knock sounded at her door. "It is I, dear. Kindly open the door for me," called a low, rich, unmistakable voice.

"Such a striking boy. What a fierce and imperious man Rychman has grown to be. And how love transforms that stern face." Beatrice sat, hovering, on the desk while Percy scurried to open the door.

Alexi swept in with an armful of books. "Your first assignment, my dear—Shelley's work to be translated into Russian as a gift to the czarina. A grand beginning, eh, gifts to royals funding the education of the disadvantaged?" It was as he placed the stack through Beatrice that he noticed her on the desk. Jumping back, he straightened his robe and held his head high. "Percy, my dear, you didn't tell me you were receiving company."

She rushed forward. "My apologies, love, it was rather sudden."

"Hello, Mrs. Tipton." Alexi narrowed his eyes. "So, you arranged our lives, did you? Percy's mother—"

"Alexi," Percy admonished. A long moment passed as spirit and professor stared at each other.

"It's all right, Percy," Beatrice chuckled. "I knew he'd waste no time." She floated about the room, Percy and Alexi watching, Percy ready to repeat her every word. "What shall I tell you, and what must I leave to discovery? I, of all souls," Beatrice murmured evenly, "know the importance of being left to fend for oneself. It is the only way one learns. Survival in the face of uncertain terror makes one keen. You, Professor, are very keen."

Alexi was immediate in his reply. "Keen to know a few answers."

"I have no answers for you, Professor. I simply bear tidings of war."

Alexi set his jaw. He had begun to look not at Percy, even though it was her voice that brought Beatrice's words to his ear. Instead, he focused on the spirit. "You've relayed your message, then. Oughtn't you return to whatever sort of elysian fields lie beyond if you've nothing more to offer?"

Beatrice narrowed her eyes. "No sentiment to offer me? No respect or accolades for your predecessor? How cool you are, Professor, in this mechanized, sooty and melancholy age." Her transparent hands clenched. "We've no fields, Professor, they're burned and gone. An eternal prison fashioned by Darkness is all I've heard awaits our kind. We must yet earn the Great Beyond." The spirit turned to Percy and said, "I'm sorry, my dear, but you do realize what's ahead, don't you? Why all those portals open? You do realize, don't you, that you'll have to go back."

"Go back?" Percy asked meekly.

"The hell you will." Alexi whirled on Percy before whirling on Beatrice. "The hell she will!"

"You blend in with the spirits, my dear, it's brilliant. And it's the only way. You have to turn the keys to start the war. He won't know it's you. He won't have guessed what you've become."

Percy sat, reeling again. "Who . . . ?"

"Darkness."

"Darkness." Percy shuddered.

"What. What are you saying?" Alexi demanded, the last exchange not having been translated. He stood over her, mad with rage.

Beatrice floated beside them. "He isn't going to take to this kindly, Percy. But it's the only way. Do not fear, you're not alone. Soon, I pray, we'll all finally be free from Darkness's shadow. But it will take a battle."

Percy related this last, attempting to strengthen her own voice, but it felt weak and young.

Alexi faced Beatrice, his eyes like fire. "I'm not letting her go there."

Percy seized his hand and brought it to her lips, not knowing what to say but yearning to touch him. His fingers twitched and he yanked them away.

"There's no other choice," Beatrice stated. "The doors have already begun linking the worlds for our vendetta's grand battle. If the doors open into *here,* into our territory, they won't open everywhere. This war must stay contained and corralled to our advantage."

"So that's what that's about," Percy said instead of translating.

"What?" Alexi barked.

"The doors," Percy explained, trying not to let his agitation panic her. "The new doors that the headmistress showed us. Linking the mortal and spirit worlds. Here. What you guessed is true."

"Athens shall be the epicentre of spiritual upheaval, then?" Alexi spat. "Isn't that what we've been trying to avoid all these years? Bringing spirits *to* us is antithetical to the very nature of our work!"

"It's precisely why we seized these stones, why Phoenix fire runs through them. Here is the only place that's safe. Our Lady and I made sure of it," Beatrice replied. Percy repeated her words.

"I'll not let the spirit world have this school, and certainly not my wife!" Alexi growled, pointing a threatening finger. But Beatrice calmly returned his gaze. "If I have to keep her under lock and key, I shall. I nearly lost her once in this life, I won't make that same mistake twice." He clenched his fists and stormed out of the room, slamming the door behind him.

Percy and Beatrice stared after him for a long moment. "He does that sometimes," Percy murmured.

"Storm out of a room?"

"Yes," Percy said, trying to excuse him. "When he doesn't know what else to say, or when it seems he cannot control the situation, you mustn't mind—"

"Come now. Of course I don't mind, I've a hell of a temper. Alexi feels just as I did; used, angry, confused. I understand. But we're still part of a fate that will take us under if we don't fight back."

Percy sighed. She stared out the window down at the courtyard where a few students and staff milled. "I've no concept of a life other than this. I will fight for it alone, no matter that I cannot remember my past."

"I fight for love, too," Beatrice murmured. Percy looked up and met her intent gaze. "He's trapped inside the Whisperworld by the hand of Darkness. We died to make this right. Whether you remember your debt or not, it's your turn to help me. No matter what."

Percy's throat dried. "I've no wish to go against Alexi."

"You may have to, at first." Beatrice shrugged. "He'll come around."

"I won't lie—"

"I'm not asking you to," the spirit interrupted. "But when you're called, you'll come, and we'll finally settle the score. From what I've observed, there are powers within you when you need them."

Percy grimaced. "It would seem."

"Darkness will never stop looking for you. You might as well start learning the map."

Percy stared at her, confounded. "Map? What map?"

"In The Guard's private chambers. A key unlocks it. The one your mother and I planted."

Percy fumbled around her neck and brought up the key on her pendant. "This?"

"Yes, that. There's another key you'll have to find to make the merger complete. That one's a bit more difficult. You'll see soon enough. I have to go—more doors need knitting. The pins are loosening again, and when they're all nearly open, we'll be forced to make our move. Stay alert and be well, Percy."

"What about the betrayal of which you spoke? I've seen no hint of such, and I refuse to make my new family suspect for no cause."

Beatrice thought a moment. "That is likely best. I wish I could say, but the situation is no clearer to me. The Guard senses when one of their number is in danger. I can only hope that now extends to you, and that they'll rally to you when you need them." And with that, she vanished out the bay window.

Percy sighed heavily and supposed she ought to find and reassure her husband, but she found she didn't really want to speak to anyone. She just wanted some silence. Of course, when one heard the dead, peace and quiet was hard to come by. Her world would never be silent. Perhaps she would just sit with a cup of tea.

Having cleaned and organized her office with meticulous obsession, Rebecca sat stiffly pressed against the back of her chair. The wool of her snug collar grazed her throat as she swallowed. How should she tell Alexi what her gift had proffered? While information should flow freely between leader and second, would Alexi not be maddened more by a vague threat than by confronting the truth in its time? Would she be granted enough foresight to keep everyone safe? Or was she stalling, perhaps out of fear, or guilt . . . or out of some deeper, secret, terrible thought that if she just let things go Percy would simply end up out of the equation?

She shook her head in defiance, demanding better of herself. "No. I will fight for the girl. Not against her." But could she ever trust herself in matters concerning the woman Alexi Rychman loved? Worse: if she told him, wouldn't he secretly assume her to be the betrayer?

Just then, the man in question burst through her door and slammed it angrily behind him. "Beatrice says Percy will have to go back into the spirit world, where none of us dare go, to bring about the war to end it all."

Rebecca furrowed her brow. "Percy has to go back? But she just got here."

"Precisely my point. Why did we fight so hard for Prophecy if we're sending her right back into the abyss? I won't let her go."

"So the doors—"

"The dark portals that open around her are beckoning her to walk right in, to pick up where she left off—I don't know exactly," he growled. "The new doors in this building have something to do with the final battle. After they are joined, Athens will be the field of conflict between the mortal and spirit worlds."

"But we don't want the worlds joined, we've spent our lives trying to keep them separate!" Rebecca cried.

"I know," Alexi spat, having a friend in frustration fueling his ire. "Spirits say things to Percy I can't hear, the ramifications of which I don't understand, and I feel like a pawn in some farce."

"We've enough doors for one," Rebecca agreed. "I just noticed a new one down the humanities hall."

"We need a meeting. I'm not going to let one ghost determine our future after decades of work." He flung wide the door and nearly crashed into Percy, hesitating outside, her hand raised to knock.

She had heard his angry voice from within and now flinched as he glowered down at her. Seeing it was her, his gaze softened slightly. He hung in the doorway. "Have a nice tête-à-tête?" he asked.

Percy sighed, staring at him with the helplessness she felt. "I've no more of an idea what to think than you."

Alexi said nothing and remained staring down at her. Behind him, Percy glimpsed Rebecca watching impassively from her desk. She said, "I . . . thought maybe Miss Thompson would like a cup of tea. And you, of course. Would you like a cup of tea?"

"No thank you," her husband said, storming into the hallway and leaving the door open behind him. "But perhaps the headmistress will indulge you. We've early dinner plans. Do be ready when I call."

"Yes," Percy breathed. *"Professor,"* she added, her throat constricting as she watched him go.

The headmistress glanced out into the hall, then at Percy, her hard mouth and furrowed brow no more forgiving than Alexi's. Percy hesitated before turning to walk away.

"Good God, girl, you look like a lost sheep." Rebecca grimaced. "Come and sit. I'll call for tea."

"Th-thank you, Headmistress."

"You may do away with that formality."

"Oh, I'm not sure that I can," Percy said.

Rebecca stared at her, scrutinizing her like the day Percy first sat in that chair, not terribly long ago. She shook her head. "You're just a girl," she muttered, turning away and pulling on the golden cord that rang for amenities a flight below.

"And by that, should I be relieved or offended?" Percy asked.

Rebecca's lips twitched. "You know, you've gotten a bit more spine than you came here with."

"I had no choice." Percy shrugged. "I married Alexi."

"I wish I could tell you that your lot would be an easy one. But then again, surely even for a smitten schoolgirl you foresaw ahead of you a lifetime with a . . . difficult man."

Percy would most certainly find no great help in this line of conversation and was exceedingly grateful for the knock at the door. A moment later, the plump and pleasant butler Percy often saw bringing professors afternoon refreshments wheeled in a tray and made a bowing exit, giving Percy only one second glance.

Percy rose and prepared a cup of tea. "Sugar?"

"No. Thank you."

Percy passed a plain cup to Rebecca, then sat with her own, a little sugar softening the rich Darjeeling. They sat in awkward quiet made bearable by the business of tea.

"Do come for my calling hours," Percy blurted.

"I've a school to run, Mrs. Rychman," Rebecca said. "I've no time for such niceties, however generous the offer."

"Alexi said as much, that women should have offices for

those sorts of things. And so you and I do." Percy shrugged. "But I suppose we'll never be quite the model citizens Her Majesty would expect."

Rebecca sighed. "Do you remember what I said to you the first day you sat across this desk from me?"

Percy nodded. "Every word. You said we must acknowledge the limitations of our world."

"That is the only philosophy by which I can survive."

"I remember being particularly heartened to hear you say you chose to run an institution rather than a household."

"And yet you ended up with one," Rebecca replied, her lips thin.

Percy stared. "The greatest wonder of my weird life," she murmured finally, breaking away to gaze into her tea.

Rebecca went to the window and let Frederic inside. The bird made a squawk and strutted about the headmistress's desk, shifting papers as he did. They both watched him, glad of the distraction while they sipped the remains of their tea.

"Thank you for the company, Headmistress," Percy murmured as they finished. "You're always welcome in my office for the same."

Rebecca simply nodded.

Feeling worse for having wanted a friend, Percy left the room. The Guard were more business associates; the initial warmth of their welcome came from gratitude that she had unwittingly saved their lives, not that she would fit into their established social fabric.

Perhaps heaven was listening, as she was almost immediately provided for: amid a rustle of skirts, a petite figure was suddenly in stride with her. "And how is the new lady of Athens?"

The familiar German accent made Percy. "Hallo, *meine liebe*. I'm exceedingly glad to see you. It's all been rather much, and I'm afraid I'm still reeling. They've even given me an office!"

Marianna made a mocking face, then grinned and

dragged her to a bench by a window at the centre of the hall. She leaned in, her eyes bright. "Do tell, how is life with Herr Rychman?"

Percy blushed, sure Marianna was curious about their intimacy—which was the easiest and most glorious part of their union. Everything else was . . . "Complicated."

"Trouble so soon?" Marianna gasped.

"No," Percy assured her, glancing toward Rebecca's closed door, not so very distant from their location.

Marianna watched, and understood. "The headmistress's jealousy is driving you mad—" she blurted.

"No!" Percy batted her hand before her friend's mouth. "If I were to describe our situation you'd hardly believe it. It is the stuff of ghosts and visions."

"Ah. Your mysteries have something to do with him, after all? I'd have thought a man of science—"

"It isn't easy for him. Or me." Percy's mood clouded. How to speak of her heart without revealing more? "It's impossible to live solely for love when there are odd forces upon our lives we don't entirely understand."

Marianna reflected. "He worries for you, then, which makes its own trouble."

"Quite wise. Yes, I do believe that's so."

"But strange forces aside, think of the miracles, Percy. Think how shocking that a man as cold as he could look so warmly at you. It's staggering."

"Truly?" Percy asked.

Marianna rolled her eyes. "You doubt it? After the rush of marrying him, do you still not see how he stares at you?"

Percy blushed, realizing how her confidence had been faltering, wilting slowly under Beatrice's vague threat, these new proclamations of future struggles and tasks, and Alexi's anger at the possibilities.

"Or . . . you had to marry him so quickly because he ruined you!" Marianna whispered. Percy's blush increased, and she shook her head. "He would have if you hadn't run immediately to that chapel!"

Percy leaned in, smiling. "That, perhaps, is true."

"So all of that smothering intensity of his, in the end, is worth something."

Percy bit her lip and stared at Marianna, the answer clear. They both blushed and sighed.

"Persephone, I've been looking for you," came a sharp voice. Percy looked up to find Alexi, her cloak on his arm, stern and stoic as if he were still her teacher.

"Hello, husband," she replied, choking off her giggles and rising to her feet.

"Hello, Professor," Marianna said.

Alexi glanced at the blonde girl and bowed his head. "If you'll forgive me, Fräulein Farelei, I'm always taking your friend from your side."

"You've every right. Just so long as you give her back, occasionally," came the reply, along with a wide smile.

Alexi held out his arm and Percy took it. When she glanced back, Marianna gestured toward Alexi's eyes, encouraging her to really see what her husband felt. Percy beamed and hoped her expression gave appropriate thanks.

"You've a guilty look of gossip about you," Alexi muttered.

Percy looked up at him and grinned. "Oh, *Professor.* I'm still your smitten, pining schoolgirl. These things cause blushes. And the occasional giggle. You mustn't take offense, as I can't promise it won't happen again."

A smile tugged at his mouth. He placed her cloak around her at the door. "I assumed you'd like a spot of dinner before our meeting. A restaurant. Unless a dormitory dining room pleases you more? Would I be allowed in?"

Percy giggled. "Hardly. Besides, I'm quite ignorant of London outside of Athens. Do educate me, husband."

Again, Alexi seemed pleased.

A few streets south sat a fine little establishment decorated with dark wood and sparkling glass. Two Athens staff at a corner table fell to murmuring the moment they arrived, but Alexi's haughty smirk bolstered Percy. She wished she cared as little as he, but they were both soon eating soup and speaking pleasantly of Athens trivialities. Percy was grateful for the distraction. Alexi's ire and talk of returning to a world and a life she did not remember would come soon enough.

Rebecca rose from the café table at La Belle et La Bête, coming to a realization. "I doubt Alexi will collect us here—he'll prefer private dining these days," she muttered, her lips thinning. "Come. Time for meeting."

"You're heavy laden," Josephine said quietly, taking her hand.

"I've been laden for years, you're only now noticing?"

Michael had procured her coat from the hooks at the door and was holding it out. "There's something you're not telling us," he said. Elijah and Jane glanced at each other, watching in silence as they dressed for the chill air outside.

"You mustn't get weary, darlings, the best is yet to come!" Rebecca declared with a hollow smile. "Poor Athens will bear the brunt of it. Come, let's hear it from Alexi. He's none too fond of the recent revelations."

"And dear Percy?" Jane spoke up.

Rebecca grimaced. "Poor girl doesn't understand a whit about what awaits. My instincts are unusually muddied, but they're clear on one thing."

"What?" Josephine asked.

"Doom."

Alexi and Percy sat in the anterior of the Athens chapel. He'd hardly let go of her hand all evening, as if he dared not. Percy didn't mind; his desire to hold her, any part of her, made her feel secure.

The rest of The Guard arrived as one, suggesting they had all been together prior; Rebecca still wore the grim mask she'd taken since first mentioning that Athens was changing. Seeing them, Alexi sent a bolt of blue fire toward the plain altar, and a black dot grew into a two-dimensional door that somehow led to a world where their power reigned.

The Guard descended into the place. Alexi waited at the portal edge, his hand out. Percy remembered: this was the path she'd trod to save them. She went through, and Alexi descended behind her, the portal door closing after them.

It was here in this colonnaded room at the edge of two worlds that he had pledged his love and revived Percy's flagging life. Hesitant, she stood just outside the circle of The Guard until Alexi drew her next to him. A wind coursed the room. Percy heard the familiar song rise, still unsure who had begun singing or if the music was always quietly there on the wind. It was The Guard's call to order, their affirmation of ancient power. A circle of blue flame leaped around their ankles, linking them.

"The Power and the Light!" Alexi cried. An enormous shaft of brilliant azure fire wreathed in white beams erupted from the centre of the floor and connected with the great stained-glass firebird hanging above. The room hummed with power, recharging and fortifying them. They all blinked, the power of the light too bright to stare into directly. "You are welcome here, Percy," Alexi murmured. "The light has never been so powerful." The rest nodded, impressed.

"I feel at home," Percy murmured, blushing. The light was like a drug, making the world wonderful and all her worries vanish, leaving only boundless love. She beamed at Alexi, who seemed dazzled by the sight.

"Are you going to stare moonbeams at each other all night, or is this a meeting?" Elijah drawled. Alexi pursed his lips as the rest giggled, Rebecca the only one clearly not amused.

Staring down his friends, Alexi donned his natural

authority. "I assume Rebecca has alerted you to the curious changes to our centre of operations." When The Guard nodded, he added, "Our battle has only just begun. Doors to the spirit world will continue to open, beckoning Percy in. The spirit Beatrice, who claims she was one of us once, has boldly declared my wife will have to go into the spirit world."

The group began to murmur, and to eye Percy in alarm.

"This cannot be," Alexi continued, quieting them. "There must be another way. I do not know if this spirit can be trusted."

"There's no reason she shouldn't be," Percy said softly.

Alexi's eyes flashed. "No reason? It would seem that, rather than separating the mortal and spirit worlds by the great walls we have tried to keep intact all these years, Beatrice is connecting them. Those walls are increasingly thin. That ghost is creating new doors. The truth is, at any moment the Whisper-world might pour right in upon us."

More murmuring rose among the group before Elijah asked, "If she was one of us and is now reversing our work, what has been our purpose all these years? Has our service in London been some sort of a joke—a charade?"

Percy wanted to calm the six. These new and vague circumstances entirely turned their world on end. But she had no news with which to reassure them, and her own dread at the idea of further battle with spirits tied her tongue.

"Our future is unknown, our very purpose questioned by these suggestions," Alexi agreed. "Unfortunately, Prophecy has left us no map."

The last word jarred Percy. She hadn't thought to mention Beatrice's map reference to Alexi; it was too much all at once. Her mind was swimming with questions of divinity versus mortality, and with fear that Alexi loved a divine image more than her own flesh. Yet, perhaps she ought to offer up the key around her neck. Or would that disrupt the proceedings, bringing a new riot to the table? It was her key, found in her grave, so perhaps it was more related to her than the current conflict. She would see to it on her own rather than distract her friends; she would study it as Beatrice suggested.

"We must watch as Athens changes," her husband was saying, "perhaps exorcise these doors back from whence they came. We must first assure ourselves these troubles do not affect our students, who are innocent of dealings with our Work."

"And we must, dear fellows, renew ourselves," Michael breathed, turning his face toward the fountain of light.

The Guard took time to do just that, breathing deeply, aware of each other soul in the circle and the preciousness of life. Their blood rushed in their veins.

"Until duty brings us next to your mercy," Alexi murmured to the sacred space.

The light faded but did not vanish. The bird above glittered as if subtly alive. Percy stared at it to the last, drinking in its replenishing warmth, as The Guard filed upward. Alexi lingered to collect her. For comfort as much as out of habit, she crossed herself and traversed the impossible threshold back into the more traditional church.

The hired carriage turned into their drive, and Alexi offered Percy a key to their darkened, empty home. With a kiss upon the cheek, he helped her down the step and onto the flagstone. "I'll be a moment," he explained, and was off behind the house, perhaps to take his beloved Prospero for a gallop.

Percy wandered into the shadows inside, turning gas lamps low and ascending to the second floor. In and out of rooms she glided, searching like a ghost in a haunt it could not quit, and arrived finally at a back chamber furnished only with a dusty harpsichord. Eager for the twinkling, antique sound to sort her mind, she rushed to the bench. The instrument was out of tune and its notes had a dull, distant quality, as if the thick fog outside had suddenly infiltrated the room—or the fog of her own doubt, from which her rich Mozart étude, melancholy in its winding chords, could not untangle her. Alexi's embrace, she knew, might cure all, but she also respected their two solitary natures. Not every hardship could be met and resolved simply by touch.

After a bit of Beethoven, then Alexi's favourite, Chopin, Percy leaned against the top keyboard, causing a lingering, dissonant noise, when she heard, "My sentiments precisely."

Percy turned with a smile. Leaning against the frame, his cloak and frock coat removed, the sleeves of his charcoal shirt rolled up his forearms, his cravat open along the lines of his unbuttoned collar and a snifter of a dark liquid in hand, was her husband. Would she always be as struck by him as the day he first burst into her classroom and soul? It seemed so, especially with him in partial undress, in the comfort of his home. The sight of him now was a wish fulfilled. Her dear professor had come to her, to bid her relax and undress, to join and lie beside him.

"How you stare, Percy. Do I look that much a fright?" Alexi chuckled warily. His rakish look flushed her cheeks with longing.

"No! I . . ." Percy giggled. "To see you a bit undone utterly undoes me."

His chiseled lips curved and perfected the rakish picture. "You play beautifully, my dear. You must impress our guests when next we entertain." He held out a hand. "Come. Are you tired?"

Percy nodded and rose to meet him at the door. He offered her a sip from his snifter, sliding his other arm around her waist. One potent whiff, and the look on her face caused Alexi to withdraw it with an amused snort. The liquor, however, tasted sweet and heady in the clutch of his subsequent kiss. To the latter intoxicant they gave themselves eagerly, rather than ruminate upon the danger yet to come.

CHAPTER THIRTEEN

The gruesome face of ash growled, jaws grinding in anger, stony snakes on her cracked scalp slithering, hissing, flaking ash onto the ground. "I'm going to find her." The voice was coarse, wet gravestone. "She'll pay."

The Groundskeeper fussed. "You're hardly in a state—"

"Taking matters into my own hands. I'll prove to him I ought to have been queen all along!"

One by one, her fingers crumbled into heaps of ash. The rest of her body gracefully followed suit, like hourglass sands spilling uniformly down onto the cool stone floor. "Noooo!" the Groundskeeper howled as she again slipped away, particle by particle. "I've spent so much time puttin' you back, you can't come undone again!"

"Leave off, and leave me be," the ash hissed, congealing and trailing away in the shape of a long snake. "I've business on the other side. To see who's the greater power . . ."

The routine of breakfast and readying for Athens, Percy realized, would establish itself pleasantly. But there was an anxiety beneath her every move. The key against her bosom was growing warm, and she couldn't ignore it anymore.

Seeing Alexi to his classroom, weathering the stares of students who still could not get used to the idea of her ghost-pale flesh or her marital situation, she murmured that she would be in her office, translating—which she did, for a bit, hoping Beatrice would breeze in and recall her to her task, and reassure her myriad fears or tell her pleasant things about her mother. The ghostly professors Hart swept in to talk poetry, which was a delightful distraction, but she didn't feel she could allow herself the luxury for long.

Walking down and into the Athens chapel, she lifted her mother's key from her neck and held it tightly. Moving to the altar, she wondered how to get below. She sighed, shrugged and threw her arm forward. A similar motion had vanquished an enemy once, and it did not disappoint now. A black spot appeared in midair, grew into a square, then lengthened into a door-size rectangle.

"Well . . . that was simple."

She wasn't fond of how simple it was. She didn't like the ability to do impossible things if she didn't understand how. But, perhaps it wasn't her at all. Perhaps it was the very stones of Athens, built to respond when she came calling.

Percy descended the steps into The Guard's sanctuary. She glanced up at the bird, its prismatic beauty calming her. The fortifying pillar of power and light was absent, but she assumed only Alexi struck that particular fire.

Searching the edges of the feather carved into the dusty floor, she found what she sought on the tip, as Alexi had recalled. Her shaking hands fumbled with her necklace clasps, and the key slid to the floor with a clatter. A moment later, before she could think twice, she picked it up and jammed it into the hole. There was an enormous grating sound, and the room was suddenly awash in flame.

Percy screamed and threw up her arms, ducking, panicking of being burned alive. It took her a moment to see that the fire was blue and contained no heat, was harmful only to the dead. It was the now-familiar force and odd friend, Alexi's personal weapon: Phoenix fire.

Percy dropped her arms, and the flames lowered. They maintained a gently licking pattern on the floor: lines and angles opening into round spaces. A floor plan. A map laid out in fire upon the floor. The map revealed a building. Familiar in it shapes. Athens, but not quite.

There was a circular space off to the side, separate. There was a dot in its centre. Percy moved closer. The dot moved, too.

"Me?" she murmured. As she retreated a step, the dot adjusted.

Two other blue spots showed in a small room off a great open space. If this were the main foyer of Athens, the small offshoot would be in the approximate place of Headmistress Thompson's office. "Rebecca. And . . . Alexi?" Percy looked for other such spots.

At the top of the map, on a hazy outer perimeter, there was a red ruby of flame, bright, burning red, like a glistening eye. Behind the mark was a swath of solid, sparkling blue.

The red spot was too familiar for Percy to ignore its possible meaning. It moved. Back and forth. As if pacing to and fro. There was a wispy shape that floated above its red flame: a key. A second key in the hands of an ancient enemy . . . Beatrice had said there would be another.

Dread filled Percy's body and she yanked her key from the hole. The fiery map vanished into mist. The Guard's space was so quiet, her ragged breathing and heart roared in her ears. She ran up the stairs, out into Athens chapel and into the wing of Promethe Hall, about to run across to Alexi's office when she recalled his likely location on the map.

The map was correct. Alexi was inside Rebecca's office, barking about how he could not find his wife. His voice carried into the hall. Grimacing, Percy knocked on the door.

Alexi threw it open. "There you are. Where have you—?"

"There's something you must see. In the chapel. Below."

"What were you doing there?" he asked, aghast.

"There's a map. The key from my grave went into the keyhole just like you said. It makes a map."

"You went there without me? A map of what?"

"I can't be sure," Percy replied, shrinking away from his harshness.

Alexi sighed. "Show me. Now. Rebecca," he called over his shoulder, "gather another meeting tonight."

"Yes, Alexi," Rebecca replied.

Alexi slammed the door, grabbed Percy by the arm and began walking briskly down the hall. Percy couldn't help but ask, "Why are you angry with me?"

"You entered an unpredictable realm without aid or supervision! It isn't a place one goes alone—none of us do!"

"I never thought I was crossing you, Alexi. I was examining my mother's gift. How was I to know—?"

"What if portals open again and you're somewhere unbeknownst to me, unprotected?"

"I didn't want to trouble you—"

"I will *always* be troubled when you put yourself in harm's way."

"That isn't a harmful place—"

He snarled. "It can be. You've seen it so."

There was a strained, angry pause. Percy shook her head. "Alexi, you're acting like these new occurrences are somehow my fault. I want nothing but to be your loving wife. I want no portals, no war, no spirit world. I haven't come to you withholding knowledge. I'm at no advantage here," she pleaded against his seething silence. "It's my fate, too, you know!"

He continued to drag her forward, his gaze angry, his grip tight.

"Alexi?" she gasped.

"Yes?"

"You're hurting my arm."

He looked down, his hand a vise around her. He let go as if scalded and stared at her, his eyes wide. A flicker of shame crossed his face. "I'd never mean to hurt you," he whispered earnestly, his voice catching before his usual mask of stoicism returned.

"I know, love."

His brow furrowed in anxiety, Alexi stormed ahead.

Percy let him go. He threw the chapel doors open roughly, and Percy reached the threshold just as blue fire shot from his hand, hurtling toward the altar. A dark doorway responded, which Alexi paused before, his hand held out. Percy took it. He met her gaze, and they descended.

"It seems so long ago that I was here, shivering in your arms," she breathed.

"We were all shivering. Frightened, despairing, helpless without you," Alexi murmured, staring at the floor, at the carven feather symbol. His eyes narrowed, as if searching. "It feels like years ago, but it's hardly been a fortnight."

"Has it?"

"A great deal has happened," Alexi added with a partial smile. It faded. "And more will come."

Percy handed him her key. "The hole's where you said it would be."

Alexi bent, brushing grit from the grooves of the feather. "Let's hope Beatrice hasn't set a trap for us and it's indeed a map, not a door direct to hell."

"You may not like what she has to say, but we've no reason not to trust her," Percy repeated. "It's a map, I assure you."

Alexi set his jaw, slammed the key inside, turned the lock and rose to stand beside her. Grating stone sounded, and the room was again afire. Percy reflexively ducked, but Alexi remained still. "Do grow accustomed to this, Percy; the fire is the one consistent measure of our power."

Percy lowered her arms and nodded. "It takes a bit of getting used to."

Alexi watched as the flames became a map.

"You see, it's very much like Athens," Percy pointed out.

"Not quite," Alexi said, gesturing to small areas that trailed away from the Athens grid. "These spots don't match our floor plan. Perhaps this is two places superimposed."

"The spirit world and Athens?" Percy breathed.

"Both." Alexi nodded. "What else could it be?"

"I believe this is our sacred space here." Percy pointed to the circle at the side. She walked him around, the fire licking at the hem of her skirts and his robes, harmless. "And the patches, us. Look here. Two spots in a circular room that move as we move. And one right where the office of the headmistress might be."

"And the patch of red, near that ocean of blue? It appears to be moving. Is it a destination? It appears another key is connected . . ." Alexi squinted at the dot, the transparent, flickering icon of the key hovering above. He moved closer.

Percy cringed, reaching out and clutching the edge of his cloak. "It must be Darkness. Red. I've had visions of eyes that colour, searching . . ."

Growling, Alexi yanked her key from the lock. The fire vanished and the map was gone.

"Alexi!" She reached for him, her heart seizing with sudden fear. "Hold me, please."

"I'll not have some constant reminder of a life you never remember living. Of a creature who has no claim over you." He paced, his boots echoing on the stone, his robe whipping about his ankles. Percy could only continue to reach for him, straining for reassurance. "I'll not have a map leading the way to you. You're here in the Queen's beloved England, with me. You are my wife, whose virgin body I claimed, free from whatever literal hell your powers may have . . ."

He finally saw past his rage and noticed her outstretched hands. He darted to her, scooped her into a smothering embrace, and she kissed him hungrily, hoping passion could shove aside her deepening dread.

"Alexi, I'm yours," she gasped. "This heart, soul and body has never been anyone else's—nor will it!" She tore at her blouse and pointed to the mark of the phoenix. "That is the mark of our destiny, burned there when you prayed to find me. I've no other destiny but you."

He pressed his lips to her scar. His hands roved mercilessly, his clutch weakening her knees. She soon found herself on the cool stone floor, his dark robes engulfing her, his fingertips raking her body as he pinned her beneath him.

"You would wish for no other? You would forsake whatever divinity you may yet possess to remain with me? No matter what you learn, you are still mine?"

Percy's eyes widened as she stared up at him, wounded. "Truly, Alexi. Did my vow mean nothing? Don't you pledge the same?"

Her husband's eyes were fierce, and Percy couldn't tell if he was seething with passion or fear. Perhaps both.

"We're operating under uncommon circumstances," he hissed. "We have forces against us, pressuring, straining our vows so freshly made. Who knows what powers might break them—?"

Percy placed one of her hands on her scar and the other around her wedding band. "You're the only power that could break me, Alexi," she murmured in his ear. Craving a vow made tangible, she gratefully offered him acquiescence, hoping that passion in a place such as this sealed a further compact. "All of me rests wholly entrusted to your hands."

Concentric circles of blue fire erupted around their entwined bodies. Alexi cried out in The Guard tongue Percy had been born to understand, "My beloved is mine!"

They soon lay crumpled in a heap together upon the floor, dazed by their furious and exhausting bout of passion. Stirring, Percy heard whispers dangerously close to her face, and imagined red eyes burning down upon her.

Her eyes snapped open. The fiery gaze vanished, and she saw only the luminous bird overhead. This replacement image was so unbelievably comforting, Percy wondered what sort of innate magic it possessed.

She turned to look at her husband. Alexi had drifted off to sleep, strings of black hair stuck to the moisture on his prominent cheekbones, his long nose pressed against the thick fabric of his cloak. She hadn't seen his face as peaceful since their honeymoon—which, she reminded herself, hadn't been very long ago. Would this mysterious fate of theirs make every week seem an eternity?

A terrible thought forced its way into her mind: When her husband slept, was he dreaming of a goddess? Was he dreaming of someone not her? Perhaps the jealousy he felt was a remnant from another life, another love . . .

Without moving the arm slung possessively around her middle, she lifted her head, her neck stiff from the stone floor, to examine the state of her clothing. Alexi would never have had the foresight to bring them extra clothing. Blushing, she wondered if their disheveled appearances would make their spontaneous activity entirely obvious. Thankfully, save for the collar she herself had dramatically ripped, the only real damage to her clothing was in the layers beneath her petticoats, which she assumed she could tie and tuck to hide the evidence.

She turned to find Alexi staring at her. He snickered. "They'll think you've married a wild animal."

"I wonder." Percy grinned.

"There's a shop with fine and frivolous things just down Bloomsbury." He lifted her effortlessly to her feet. "Let me buy you something to mask our pastime."

"Otherwise Lord Withersby will never keep quiet."

"I daresay he'd flush with jealousy."

"Hardly. He only has eyes for Josephine. But answer me this," Percy blurted, suddenly set on learning the truth.

Alexi raised an eyebrow.

"Beatrice said that I . . . that your goddess came to you after your annunciation as The Guard, in dreams. Do you remember? Am I only something you love because . . . ?" She bit her lip and fought tears.

"Darling! First you worry I'll not love you for your skin. Now you worry I'll not love you if you're *not* that goddess?"

Percy blushed. "I don't know. I'm so confused."

"Well, we both have wondered who and what you are.

But that doesn't change our vows. As for the past . . . I can say that the goddess, your predecessor, was my first love. I do recall hazy dreams, but I never imagined that she really—"

"But she did," Percy snapped, jealousy thundering in her heart.

"Those dreams stopped at sixteen. Around the time you were born. That cannot be coincidence." He smirked suddenly. "Do you remember me at sixteen?"

Percy blushed. "Of course not."

"I lived life believing I'd marry whomever Prophecy directed. Love was never expressly stated, and Rebecca vehemently denied it had anything to do with our task."

"Because *she's* in love with you!"

"I can't help that, or my instincts. When I met you I feared I might be doomed, for I loved you, regardless of Prophecy. If my words now can't reassure you, then I'm afraid nothing will."

Percy sighed. "It would seem we're both jealous of the intangible. Part of the burden of such strange lives."

He lifted her chin with a finger. "But a lifetime of jealousy will surely never do for either of us. Agreed?"

"Agreed."

Percy gazed into the darkness beyond the room's pillars. "What is out there, beyond the light? If I were to walk into that darkness, what would I find?"

Alexi held up his right hand and tilted it toward the light. Percy had never noticed the slight scar furrowing the skin. "I once walked to where the light fades. I reached out. I did not hold it there long. Afterward, I always made sure to keep to this side."

Percy shuddered. Perhaps he was right to be angry that she had come into this space alone.

The winds of the Whisper-world were howling. The hell-hounds were eating their own tails and whining, wishing to sharpen their teeth on real flesh again, but their canine forms remained partly scattered, unable to come together. To Darkness's ongoing chagrin, his amalgamous pet could not be recreated.

The winds blew across the river and battered a massive tower, wailing against its walls like a grieving widow. Inside, thousands of spirits floated silently imprisoned, awaiting a call they despaired they'd never hear.

A trickle of ash snaked around its base, hissing and mocking those inside. "I'm going to make her pay. And when I do, when I tear her stupid mortal body to pieces, all of you will rot here. Rot, rot, rot . . ."

"A new dilemma," Alexi declared once everyone was reassembled in their sacred space. Percy fiddled with the scarf draped strategically over the torn neck of her dress as he moved to insert her key. The blue fire again burst to great heights, then settled. The red dot still paced in another space and time. The encircled Guard broke apart, examining and murmuring.

"What's this?" Josephine breathed, fascinated. She began walking the lines as if traveling the corridors herself.

"Looks like Athens, but . . ." Elijah traced the perimeters behind her.

"There we are, yes?" Michael pointed to the circle to the side. "Seven dots."

"And the red one?" Jane gulped. Alexi sighed.

"The enemy," Rebecca murmured.

Alexi nodded. "We can only guess. And the enemy, it would seem, is clearly marked. This map is very nearly Athens, as you see, but not quite. The spirit and our Athens worlds, nearly identical. And they are likely merging closer every moment."

There was instant uproar among The Guard, a jumble of questions, frustrations, fears.

"What is this sea of blue?" Percy murmured, interrupting. She pointed beyond the red dot.

"If it were simply a room, would it not look like an empty frame like the others? What fills this space?" Michael peered close.

Alexi's eyes widened. "We must have a host of comrades."

The Guard fell to nearly shouting. The idea that there was a space in which countless others of their kind existed was world shattering, them having spent their lives a meagre, proud six; it was just as shocking as merging worlds they'd vowed to keep separate. Percy used the opportunity to reach down and pluck out the key, and no one seemed to notice. She fumbled beneath her scarf, returning the key to its former place.

"Silence!" Alexi cried. "I don't like this any more than you, to say the least. But another confrontation on a far larger scale than we have seen or imagined will surely make its way to us. Perhaps we may now take some consolation in the idea that we might not fight alone."

"That Gorgon was just the prologue," Rebecca stated.

There came a familiar tearing sound. The Guard circled at the ready, Alexi stepping in front of his wife as a shield. Percy illuminated, her power beginning to burn bright, reactive and preparing for a battle. The Whisper-world through the portal roared in Percy's ears, its blackness total.

Aodhan popped into view, first bowing his head subtly to Jane, who blushed fiercely and looked away. He turned to Percy and said in Gaelic, "My lady."

Percy stepped forward. Alexi took her hand, held it tightly, limiting her movement.

"Careful," Aodhan warned. "She may have escaped. As soon as I saw her being reassembled, I stole a bit of her remains. I assumed then that she couldn't be reformed . . . but I may have been wrong. I'm so sorry . . . I would have come to you sooner, but these portals aren't always predictable."

Percy was baffled. "Who are you talking about?"

"The Gorgon."

The rest of The Guard looked on, unable to hear. Percy could hear Alexi's teeth grinding. She turned to him, begging patience. He looked away, glowering, but did not release her hand.

"Lucille Linden?" Percy clarified. Everyone shuddered.

"Be on the lookout."

Suddenly Beatrice appeared in the portal. "The troops eagerly await freedom," she stated.

"Troops?" Percy asked.

"Guards gone by. I told you it's your turn, they must be freed. Study that map, girl, you'll need it soon. But not yet. I've a last few doors to knit up behind these Whisper-world fools. You'll know when—you'll receive a sign. Go on, now, I'm sure your husband's had quite enough—"

"Percy, I've had enough of this," Alexi said, dragging her backward by the arm.

She turned to stare at her husband, and her white face flushed with frustration. "Alexi, let her speak to me! It concerns me and my fate, which then concerns all of you. Unless you'd like us to betray one another out of fear for the truth!"

The Guard raised eyebrows at a tone stronger than they'd ever heard her use. Alexi set his jaw and held her firm.

"Indeed. Let's get on with it, shall we?" Beatrice declared. "Leave you to it."

Percy stared at the spirit. "Leave me to what?"

"To study the map, and then at some point, when a portal opens before you and you are beckoned, you'll have to go through. Didn't I already tell you that? How many times must I tell you that you'll know when?"

"What is she saying?" Alexi hissed.

"At some point I'll have to go through," Percy replied.

Her husband growled, turning to Beatrice. "I tell you, I'll not see her jeopardized."

"It isn't up to you, leader dear! Now, if you don't mind, I'm going to return to ensuring your survival when the battle comes—which I now see is a thankless job," the spirit growled in return. The portal narrowed.

"I'll be there for you—for all of you," Aodhan assured Percy softly. "All of us will. You'll not be alone." The portal snapped shut.

"Beatrice says they're both here to help, we'll not be alone," Percy repeated hollowly. "And that we ought to thank her." The grip on her arm tightened, which she hadn't thought possible. When she breathed his name, grimacing, he remembered himself, gave her a look of apology and eased his hold but did not let go.

The group was silent.

"Well?" Elijah finally asked.

"Well, what?" Alexi spat. "If there is to be a war, we need not seek it out. It will come. When it comes, I'm sure we'll all know. Shall I send a telegram?"

"But don't we want to . . . prepare?"

"This isn't a cavalry exercise! We stand in our circle and use what magic we have, as we always do. Prophecy, fate and destiny have given us no other weapons. We'll meet what comes when it comes. That's all there is."

No one said a word.

Percy yearned to ask Alexi to recall the Power and Light, to bask in that ceremonial surge of heaven that made all troubles small and insignificant. But The Guard was filing out of the sanctuary, and the opportunity was lost.

At the Athens portico, Alexi nearly tossed her into their carriage. She winced and rubbed her arm. He sat next to her in silence, his hand clenching upon the folds of her skirts.

"You might take a moment, Professor," Percy said quietly,

a firm edge to her voice that only surviving incredible events had been able to fashion, "to think that your wife might be just as frustrated, confused and frightened by these possibilities as you, and that she may be forced to interact with them all the more directly. I would appreciate support, not misdirected anger. Second-guessing almost had you failing Prophecy once. Let's not test it again."

Alexi's silence shifted from brooding to stunned. He stared at her. Over his face crossed shame, then terror. She glimpsed a boyish, wounded horror, a complex mess of intentions that Percy understood, however infuriating and awkward their byproducts. In this aching, naked, helpless moment when his stoic mask was let slip for her alone, when The Guard's mighty leader allowed her to see his fear, she was able to let her own hurt go.

Her clenching heart eased, love swelling like an overflowing cup. She kissed his lips softly, running a hand through his hair. His furrowed brow smoothed as he clutched her hands in his, his eyes speaking volumes his lips would have fumbled over. Silence still remained between them, but at last it was not strained.

He went directly to his study, Percy to her boudoir. There were no words. Percy wasn't sure if he would join her in their bed or take the whole night pacing. She wanted only to sit, in that silence, and breathe. There were times in the convent when she had done that for hours, hearing only the occasional whisper of a passing ghost, the comforting low drone of a Mass bell where she was expected but often absent. She held her own Mass, privately, the murmur of the breeze her rosary, and she knew that God was there.

"Our Lady," she muttered, glancing at her first confirmation rosary hung on her armoire, a string of pearls as white as she. "Leave divinity to someone else. If I must see ghosts, I must. Let me help put them to rest and then let me be. But must there be some grand finale? Can't something more powerful than I fight it?"

As she undressed, she was not ashamed to linger in the wicked thrill that unlacing her torn undergarments provided, for that fierce, mutual passion needed no apology. But looking up again, she paused at the mirror and could do nothing but stare at her arm. A nasty, burgeoning red and purple bruise covered it, Alexi's firm grip. It needed apology. But now was not the time.

Slipping into the comfort of a luxurious white robe, she ignored how much a ghost she appeared and instead fancied that she was a votaress of the moon. Lighting and stoking a fire, she gathered her filmy white robes, perched on the window seat of their bedroom and pretended that she was part of the moonlight.

A long while passed before she heard his foot on the stair. He paused at the doorway. She turned.

He was in that delicious disarray of undone buttons and shirtsleeves, a nearly empty snifter in hand. "Hello, my north star," he murmured. She moved to rise and greet him, but he entered and set the snifter on the dresser. "No, no. Stay there in the moonlight. You're positively magical." He sat across from her on the window seat.

"Are you all right, love?" she asked.

"I will sometimes . . ."

"Need quiet. Yes, as will I."

He nodded, and his eyes flashed suddenly. "I'll fight to the death for you."

Percy's brow furrowed. "Let's hope it won't come to that."

He reached for her. Percy kept a hand on the ribbon that clasped her outer robe closed.

"Let me touch your skin," he murmured, taking her hands in his. "It calms me," he explained, sliding his fingertips under the robe to slip it from her shoulders.

Percy grabbed, but she was too late. She'd hoped to keep the damning mark from his view, or at least spare it for another day, but his eyes widened and there was no distracting him. The mark was garish in the moonlight. His fingertips reached toward the bruise, trembling. "How did this . . . ?" He looked up at Percy in confusion, and back to the bruise.

"It doesn't hurt. Much," she said meekly.

Alexi's eyes were an emotional maelstrom. He jumped to his feet, unable to meet her gaze again.

"Alexi, please." Percy reached out.

His cloak was around his shoulders and he was out the door. His footsteps bounded down the grand staircase and the front door slammed. The pound of Prospero's hooves down the lane carried away into the night.

Percy was chilled by the utter silence of her house, blinking as the shaft of moonlight widened through the window. Rising, she went to her armoire and plucked free her string of rosary beads. Gliding to the bed, she slid back the velvet drapes and turned down the covers.

Yet another tempest. Storm and calm, storm again. She sat against the headboard and tucked her knees up under her chin. The only sound was the click of her rosary beads, one by one, as she sought simply to breathe.

Michael could feel a weight approaching like a swinging pendulum. He anticipated Alexi. He brewed a hot cup of mulled wine: one of their favourites to share, good for the darkest nights of the year, and for the darkest hours of the soul. Alexi tried his door and found it open, and he soon appeared at the threshold—haunted, powerful, a strange creature that didn't quite know himself anymore.

"Hullo, friend," Michael said. "Shall I take your cloak or do you plan to pace about a bit and run back out the door?"

Alexi furrowed his brow, stepped into Michael's modest living room in the small and simple quarters the Anglican Church bestowed upon him for his modest services as parochial vicar to local parishes. He sat. Then he stood, removed his cloak, hung it on a wooden peg and sat again. Michael held out a mug. Alexi took it and sipped. He set the tankard down unevenly, a drop spilling out and down the side onto the rough wooden table stained with years of hard use.

"There's a bruise on her arm," he said finally. "A large, ugly bruise."

Michael sipped his wine and said thoughtfully, "When we try and protect those we love, we sometimes use unintentional force. I daresay we've all been bruised by one another at some point."

"I was a man of measured control once. I prided myself on the quality."

"Do you now wish to be violent?"

"Only against those forces who seek her out. But I dragged her away from Rebecca's office and down to the chapel, and she . . . said I was hurting her. And there I went again tonight, seizing her just the same and dragging her back from the portal. I only saw the effect when I tried to touch her skin, when I . . ." He trailed off, sure Michael understood.

"You don't recognize these things now inside you," the vicar stated. "These baser urges of jealousy and lust, the ravages of fear and the compulsion for control. Well . . ." Michael smiled wryly. "You understand control, Alexi, but not in relation to someone you adore. Your courtship was strange and harried, your lives hanging in the balance. You're both practically children in terms of love, and children are often scared. We react with improper force when we are scared."

Alexi took a long drink and was silent. Michael knew, from conversations past, mostly in their youth, before Alexi had as fashioned the many walls of his adulthood, that his own role was to clarify the maelstrom of the heart, not to expect an easy flow of conversation.

"While I believe she intuits all these things," he continued, "you cannot take it for granted. While I'm sure you apologized . . ." He halted as Alexi's eyes flashed with frustration. "While I'm sure you will apologize, and while I'm sure she knows you'd never mean to hurt her—"

"I told her that," Alexi snapped.

"Then why are you here?"

Alexi's knuckles were white on the table. His breathing was slow and deep. "Because I'd let the spirit world take, seize and *rule* this world if it meant she'd be left alone. This directly conflicts with my duty as mortal protector. In fulfilling Prophecy, have I lost my will to maintain it?"

"If that's the question, who should take your place as leader?"

Alexi's eyes widened and flashed with repugnance as he pounded the table.

Michael leaned in. "I thought so. Then you'd best get this under control. You'd best trust her, no matter what the fates may have to do. She's no one's pet. Not some mythical god's former bride, nor your toy—"

"Of course she's not a toy."

"Then let her approach the spirit world without making her feel she's betraying you. Let her do her job on the edge of danger, and you may do what you must. She isn't plotting, Alexi. She's not full of memories she'll not share, or powers yet to reveal. She's a sweet girl overwhelmed by life, who only wants to love and be loved by you. Duty and fate will take their course. They must. But, 'Worry not for tomorrow. Sufficient for the day is its own trouble.' Don't make more."

"She . . . she has reassured me as well."

"Then why come to me? Don't you trust her words? Oh, Alexi. Mend thy ways."

"I do! I don't trust *me*. I don't . . . know where to relegate this fear. My power is all that I've had, and my duty—and now she is all that I care about. And I seem to be hurting her. Where do I put all this instead . . . ?"

"Put your fire into your fire, your love into your wife and your fear unto the Lord. Times like these are good for prayer."

Alexi rolled his eyes. "Dear One True God," he muttered, "please protect the mortal coil of a pagan goddess. Amen."

Michael chuckled and stroked his mustache. "'Persephone' is just a name for a spirit of beauty at a certain time in history. I'm sure we could argue a biblical place for her if it matters. Your wife has the name of that pagan goddess, but the fact remains that she's your mortal bride in the Year of Our Lord 1888—and she's Catholic, so pray for her, damn it. I don't care how confusing it is. And pray for us, to anyone. If the dead are about to flood Athens, divine goodwill couldn't hurt. Your prayers can be in Hindu, if you like. Now, go home. And apologize."

"Yes, Father," Alexi said wearily. Rising, he threw his cloak over his arm. "Thank you." Bowing, he saw himself out.

Michael hoped the Lord would grace Alexi with peace. He also allowed himself one moment to wonder if he himself would ever find it. Sipping his wine, he stared into the fire and simply breathed.

Alexi found Percy tucked in their bed, rosary in hand. She gazed upon him calmly as he entered the room and removed his suit coat.

"Where did you go?" she asked quietly, not an accusation.

"To confess," he said. "Now I seek forgiveness."

Percy held out her arms, and he fell gladly into them.

Josephine was particularly ill at ease as she absently tended to her fellows, well aware personal frustrations were to blame, the Grand Work aside. At an hour too late for common company and yet too rattled to be alone, several of The Guard found themselves at La Belle et La Bête, a bottle of wine between them.

It was Elijah who broke the silence with classic inelegance. "He does push her about a great deal, doesn't he?"

Josephine noticed that the women in the room, even

Jane, bristled. Michael, who had just showed up, furrowed his brow. "What did you expect?" she asked honestly.

"Elijah, he *smiles*," Michael offered. "That's quite a change."

"I . . . I fear for them," Rebecca said softly and winced.

Josephine's heart went out to her. Surely everything Rebecca said would be tinged by her particular closeness to the matter. The slight flush on the headmistress's high cheekbones was a bloom of shame atop her cool and efficient exterior.

She continued, "While they are"—she swallowed—"*besotted* with each other, that does not erase character difficulties. She so timid, he adamant. For us to succeed, I fear they must become the true partnership destiny demands. We all need to become one, else we court failure—betrayal, even."

The group looked at one another warily.

"There are forces keeping our hearts closed," Michael said. "These confound us. I'm as guilty of it as any." His eyes flickered to the object of his adoration.

Rebecca studied the room. Jane turned away, her knee jostling the table and making brown-tinged flowers tremble in a vase. Josephine's bosom burned with a thousand things she wanted to say, but instead she felt her face twist into a grimace. Looking at the fading posies, she plucked the wilting stems free and moved to toss them in the basin behind the bar, ruing that she was behind on the most simple tasks of her café duties. That spoke to her own faltering heart, which was similarly tinged brown on the edges.

"Two people can love each other dearly," she said, storming around to pluck fading bouquets from other tables. "But anxiety, fear and silence can keep them apart. Percy and Alexi, of all people, cannot afford distance. None of us can." She dared glance at Elijah before looking away, feeling ill. This was not the time to speak of broken promises, but her patience waned. Elijah surely knew. At the table he'd grown nearly as fidgety as Jane, whose reason for anxiety was anyone's guess.

"We must support them," Michael rallied, "and stand up for Percy if she needs it. And ease the tempest that is our leader, if *he* needs it. We're all Alexi has; she's all he has, and he's constantly aware of that. Think how close he's come to losing her. Considering its Alexi Rychman we're talking about—"

Elijah snorted. "Dear Percy's all the more of a saint."

"It isn't our business to discuss their marital dynamics," Rebecca hissed, absently dissecting a biscuit with her fork. "We must be sure we're no longer at odds like we once were in this very room. No more of that!" she said. "Our circle will never have faced such strain as I feel is to come. We need to be whole."

Josephine set her jaw. If the men they loved couldn't help their hearts be whole, what could be done? The women in the party couldn't just be whole on their own with a snap of one's finger. They were humans, with needs, and those needs were not without labour.

Her grimace must have showed, for Elijah's eyes widened with boyish helplessness. Squaring her shoulders, Josephine brought wine to the table for everyone but him. He could fend for himself.

It was not long before they dispersed. Elijah led the charge, darting out the door with such swiftness that it was a dagger into Josephine's heart. Left alone with the café's frequent haunts, she wept freely as she rinsed wineglasses clean, fancying she was rinsing away the blood of a broken heart. But when she turned, she started. She would have dropped the glass in her hand had not the General, a ghost dressed in century-old military regalia, managed to shift it to settle dangerously but unbroken upon the bar.

Lord Elijah Withersby stood frozen, a box on one arm, a corsage of fresh roses in an outstretched hand.

Josephine glanced around the tables. While she'd been

crying behind the bar, he'd quietly replaced all the faded posies she'd so angrily discarded. Fresh red rosebuds elegantly filled each vase. She swallowed. Elijah did small deeds of incredible beauty. He always had, for her. Damn him, for those small acts kept her heart cloven to him.

He set down the empty box, and his oft-harsh features were soothed by the golden glow of the gaslight. She let him approach and pin the corsage upon the broad lapel of her blouse, but did not offer him a look of apology when, with a yelp, he pricked his finger and sucked upon it.

She folded her arms and stared at him. He began speaking with his index finger in his mouth. "Thith damned Work hath kept uth from leading anything rethembling a normal life," he began. She reached up and impatiently withdrew his finger. While she'd long ago fallen in love with his antics, this wasn't the time. He began to pace the room. "Josie. You know why I'm hesitating."

"Dis moi," she said.

He sighed. "I find most of my class disgusting, and I've said so numerous times. Still, I resent that I've never been able to . . . be a part of it. I've used my gifts to hide for the majority of my life. I am a stranger to my family, to my class—one that none of the rest of you would have been welcome in, but rightly mine. I float between, a ghost."

"There are worse things than to be a wealthy man with no responsibility."

Elijah's eyes flashed. "No responsibility? Do you and I lead such different lives?"

Josephine thought about saying that he was plain lazy, unable to handle the least responsibility, and that's why he'd gone off and abandoned The Guard ten years prior, but he had paid dearly for that time; only Josephine knew how dearly. No matter her feelings of anger or betrayal, she could not pick at that particular scab.

"The name Withersby means nothing to me," Elijah continued with a pleading tone, "but for the rest of my family it means everything. Identity is a strange beast. I suppose I just want to know who and what I am before I make another sacrifice."

"Oh, *je suis un sacrifice*," Josephine said through clenched teeth. "Years of exhausting farce keeping our tryst a secret and now I'm a sacrifice."

"Josie, we agreed long ago that to be the lone couple amid this damned group would be bloody awkward and more miserable than our exhausting farce."

"It was just an excuse."

"No, it wasn't! We truly acted for the sake of balance, considering our delicate group dynamics. Josie, you always agreed with me. If you've been resenting it all these years, you needed to have told me."

"I assumed you'd keep your promise."

"And I . . . want to." He stopped pacing, his coat of many layers and frills stilling as his body did. "Josie. You know how much I love you. And I know I'm being selfish. But life isn't fair, and while I resent society for its impositions, I cannot change the fact that if I marry you, I'll be shunning it for good without ever truly having known it. That isn't fair."

"Staring at Rebecca, who has always loved the man who just married another, I'm yet reminded of what is and is not fair. You ought to consider yourself lucky." She fought back tears, her nostrils flared, her head tilted back, defiant. "Once you told me I could charm the royal family itself, that society would love me and forget my station in an instant. *Mon Dieu*. That it wouldn't matter! When did that sentiment vanish—with age? I've faded, perhaps. That's it. Not the flower of youth anymore, am I?" She wrested his corsage off her blouse, tearing the lace, and threw the small buds across the bar where they slid through the General's drooping, transparent head.

"Josie, good God! You're still our Helen of Troy—"

"Indeed? Well, if I've still the face that could launch a

thousand ships, would you bloody set sail already? Haven't you heard a war's coming? That's what people do: they marry the ones they love before they go off to maybe die. Your exclusive invitations to seasons, balls and fetes be damned, you're a superficial coward and I'm a fool!"

She tossed her apron behind the bar and stormed upstairs, slamming the door behind her. Elijah sighed, rubbed his face with his hands and locked the café door behind him. Then he went off to be an empty, unremarkable stranger in his vast estate, no closer to feeling at peace.

If someone had been praying in the Athens chapel at midnight, they might have noticed the thin trail of ash trickling from behind the white altar, a misty line snaking up and out through the chapel doors. The smoky particles slid inconspicuously out of Promethe Hall, gliding down the steps to the courtyard more like an unending insect than a snake, now, tumbling forward inch by inch on millipede legs, finding the shadows and lingering. It slithered on, across the cobbles, paying no heed or reverence to the angel fountain; it was sniffing something out.

Up to and under the door of Athene Hall, the ladies' quarters, and past the drowsy matron at the desk, silently the ashes sniffed one way and then the next, beginning an ascent up the wooden stairs. It stopped at door number seven, at a familiar scent. An enemy scent. She was here . . .

No, she *had been* here. Now, she was in their protection. But there was still a way. The ash trickled on, continuing its hunt.

CHAPTER FOURTEEN

Percy's calling hours at the Rychman estate began with a visit from a man of the cloth.

"Hullo, Percy!" Michael said at the door, sweeping his cap off his head.

"Hello, Vicar! Pleasure to see you! I assume you're here for Alexi? He's just gone into Athens."

"Ah, but it's a vicar's duty to call upon the ladies of his congregation, and while I know you're not a member of my Anglican parish, you're a member of my far more exclusive assembly."

Percy smiled. "Do come in. I daresay Mrs. Wentworth cooked up enough treats for an army."

"And I always have the appetite of one!"

Once settled in the sitting room and plied with the afore-mentioned delights, the clergyman was quick to the point. "I don't suppose it's a surprise your husband is fraught with worry. It isn't easy, you know, for a man to deal honestly with the heart."

Percy eyed the vicar, daring to turn the tables. "Oh?"

Michael waggled his mustache. "You'll not get gossip out of me, young lady."

"Fine," she retorted. "But I'm not used to talking about my own particulars. It's unsettling."

"You're the centre of a maelstrom, bound to cause discussion."

"But . . . what if I really do have to go into the spirit

world because duty demands it? I don't want to go. Alexi doesn't want me to. But what if I must go without his permission? He'll never forgive me, never trust me . . ."

"If indeed you must go, we will be there to support you—and to support him when the appropriate time comes. But the both of you must not worry about tomorrow—"

"'Sufficient for the day is its own trouble,'" Percy murmured, finishing the scripture. "Now, I rightly knew what I was getting into with him, Michael. I knew he was a brooding man. But I've never known him to be mercurial."

Michael shrugged. "Love makes a man mad."

Percy narrowed her eyes, curious. "How have *you* managed to keep your wits?"

He raised an eyebrow but remained unruffled. "Secrets of the trade. Alchemy of the heart—most profound magic of all. But I'm not here for my sake." He leaned in. "I beg you realize Alexi's absolute adoration for you has turned everything on end, so have patience. If I know him, you'll need a lifetime supply."

Percy chuckled. After a moment, however, she was again bold: "When, Vicar, will you set patience aside and tell her?"

Michael made to act innocent.

"A war is coming," Percy continued. "We shall need all the love we have."

The vicar rose, giving her a dawning look. "Why, that's a most sensible thing to say, Mrs. Rychman. Most sensible." He kissed Percy on the cheek and allowed her to see him quietly out the door.

While Percy assumed she'd see Josephine before anyone, it was a surprise that Jane was next. The Irishwoman sat alone and uneasy in the parlour that afternoon, and Percy donned her tinted glasses to protect her eyes and opened every shade; the full light seemed a more inviting environment for company.

"Aodhan," they chorused after a tense silence.

Jane sighed. "I suppose I'd best tell you about him."

"I don't mean to press you, but it may—"

"Help, yes. Thank you for telling me his name."

"My pleasure."

Jane took again to the tea she'd been brought, but could delay no longer. She entered an almost trancelike state as she related her past. "Our Work was a gift. I was a girl caught out of time, thrust into a world advancin' too quickly, growin' too broadly and losin' all magic. I understood why I was chosen, but . . . there was somethin' more.

"Useless to my family, I was turned out at eighteen. Your husband bought me my Aldgate flat, and I was never so lonely. I know The Guard loves me, but I've not the beauty of Josephine, the efficiency of Rebecca, the confidence of Alexi, the wit of Elijah or the joy of Michael. It didn't help that it took time for my talents to manifest. Initial victims suffered more than they should. I needed help, but no one knew how. Then, one night, there came a terrible sound on my doorstep.

"Outside lay a mass of white and red—a cat, terribly mauled. I can't bear to see a creature in pain. A cold draft came in as I took the creature to lie upon my table. The cat looked at something, fixed-like. It was a man floating by my side, his hand upheld. Nameless to me, but beautiful. So beautiful. I pressed my palm to his cold mist and felt newfound strength. My hand glowed, and I suddenly understood why others' pain causes me such misery.

"I laid healing hands on the creature, and the skin beneath the fur began to mend, the spilled blood rolling away like mercury. Aodhan . . . touched my face and took the tears from my cheeks. I gained both love and Marlowe that evening."

She stopped, and Percy took the cue to refill her tea, patient with the silence and not looking twice at Jane's fierce blush. Finally Percy said, "It's an incredible story. Thank you for sharing it with me."

Jane smiled, pleased. "Feels good to tell it. When we could spare it," she volunteered after another silence, "we went healing. I practiced with him, in alleys where the sick and dying lay untended, in sad, dim wards where the only light was our combined illumination."

"And The Guard never knew?"

"Elijah, having once accidentally brushed me with his touch, saw what I'd been up to the night prior. He pledged to say nothing if I'd now and then take him along. We never said a word, only smiled at each other when all was said and done, enjoying our secret. Now and then Michael would let me into his parish children's ward, too."

"Brilliant." Percy grinned.

"Aodhan keeps me company, see. Now and then I'll play fiddle and we'll dance a reel—a piece of common heritage. I never told the group, for fear they'd think it 'fraternizing' with the opposition. Not a single word. Gentle spirits are no enemies, but are we to *love* them?" Jane asked, blushing. "And I do love him."

A popping noise resounded through the room and a black portal appeared over the tea table. Both ladies' hands went up and they jumped to their feet. Their visitor was the very spirit in question. His palms were outstretched in a gesture of peace, and his broad shoulders took up the portal's full width. Jane went red, but Percy smiled.

"I cannot help it," Aodhan explained to Percy. "Now that she knows my name, I must come when she calls. Do tell her how much I love her, my lady, will you?"

Percy beamed at the ghost and then Jane. She related the man's message, and watched tears flow down Jane's cheeks. Jane didn't bother to dry them.

"And I you," she said to Aodhan. "Though you've heard me say it before. It's good to hear the same from you. Thank you," she added, turning to Percy.

"My honour."

Jane's tear-stained face became thoughtful. "Loneliness has long been my burden. Before I ever saw a ghost I felt them—felt like one, myself. I'm sure you must understand."

Percy nodded but said nothing.

"I've never spoken about my names," Jane confessed. "The rest of The Guard assume it's some Catholic trapping. My Christian name is Jane. When I was very little, before we came to England, we lived beside a graveyard outside Dublin. I'd go there every day and visit two graves—two ill-kept graves separate from the others and on opposite sides, entirely isolated. Alone. Lucretia Connor, Marie O'Shannon . . . barely thirty years alive. The father of the parish must've given them a marker out of pity, a small comfort of little use in death . . ."

Jane shifted her gaze between Percy and Aodhan, who floated, rapt, at the portal. She went on. "I wondered if those young women had ever had a love. Surely they'd no family. Even in death they'd no one around them, even in the cold ground. My heart hurt for them, so separate, shunned, failures. I was terrified I'd turn out just the same—or worse, never have a marker, like so many families, perhaps even mine. I don't even know what happened to them," the Irishwoman murmured, her tearful eyes wide. Percy thought about her own mother's grave, similarly sorrowful, and took Jane's hand.

"My family disowned me, like what surely happened with these lonely women. But those lasses live on in me through their names, and I pray I share some of my blessings with them. Because I do feel blessed. If not for The Guard, I'd have turned out the same as them. Without Aodhan, I'd have gone into the ground never having loved. Even though my family is this inexplicable ragtag force against the restless dead, and my love is one that can never be requited, both things are a blessing. I fancy taking their names brought these two souls peace."

"Never requited?" Aodhan whispered. "We are two beings of one heart. A heart so big it can hold a grander family than she possibly knows, and all the great mysteries of the universe. What more is there?"

As Percy relayed his words, Beatrice suddenly popped into view behind him. "You could join him, you know," the ghost said to Jane. "End your fleshly existence, follow your lover into this undiscovered country . . ."

Aodhan turned in horror, but Percy nonetheless relayed what the female spirit said. Jane went red, flustered, her accent never so thick. "It's a sin to do so! To take yer life by yer own hand?" she cried. "Don'tcha think I've thought of it? I'd have done it already, to be with him, but . . . And there's work to do. I've The Guard, I've a duty—"

"And I'd never want such a thing!" Aodhan exclaimed.

Beatrice folded her arms, looking coldly furious. "A *sin*. The Grand Work sounded my death knell and I stepped forward to meet its chimes. If Ibrahim and I hadn't gone in when we did, none of you would likely be alive. Sacrifices are sometimes necessary." She vanished back into the darkness, the portal flickering as she did.

Aodhan sighed. "I'll see you soon, Jane, my love. I'll wait for you ever and always. Don't rush to be with me." He bowed, and just as Percy echoed his last word, the portal snapped shut. Jane stared, and her fingers absently caressed the air where the portal's edge had wavered.

"My first friend was a spirit. Who is to say whom we mustn't love?" Percy asked. "Why, for that matter, Alexi suspects I may not be human."

Jane wiped her eyes and stared. "Why would that matter?"

Lifting her teacup, Percy swirled her spoon around a few stray leaves. "What might it mean for our future? Am I really free to be here, to be Alexi's, or am I still bound elsewhere—in the spirit world? He's quite worried about fate."

"Then perhaps he should enjoy you while he has you. We're being too quiet, too careful—all of us." Jane straightened, her cheeks flushed. Her tone was suddenly righteous. "Josephine and Elijah should've married years ago. Michael, for the love of the Holy Saints, should bloody tell Rebecca how he feels. Rebecca needs to stop pining over your husband, and your husband shouldn't give your past a second thought. And I should be able to love my blessed Aodhan!" Her face was scarlet but proud. "There. I said everything, and I haven't even had a drink."

Percy grinned. "Cheers." She raised her teacup. "Thank you."

"What would calling hours be without gossip? The real task is up to you. Since you're new, sweet and unassuming, you must convince us to stop worrying and love what we have. Otherwise we'll end up with nothing."

The following day Percy was deep in translation, happily busy in her office at Athens, when she heard a knock at her door. "Percy!" came a familiar call.

"Marianna, do come in!"

The door swung wide and her friend, blonde hair slightly askew, came flouncing into the room. "Oooh, what a palace!" Percy rose from behind her desk to give the German girl a hearty hug, but Marianna pulled away with a pouting lip. "I knew it would be different. I knew I'd hardly see you."

It was true; she'd seen her best friend so little since the wedding. She'd hardly had a chance to catch her breath. "Are you all right, my dear?" she asked. Marianna looked more tired than usual, her eyes a bit sunken.

"Quite well, thank you. A bit fatigued, I confess. And you?" The girl drew back and whirled about the polished floor of the office, her eyes devouring every detail. "Life as Mrs. Rychman?"

Percy blushed. "Still incredible."

"How close does he look after you?"

Percy paused, surprised. She considered the bruise on her arm and told the truth. "He's very protective."

"And his estate . . . ?" Marianna offered a baiting grin.

"Not to be believed," Percy said. The two shared a familiar, girlish squeal. How many times had they shared fantastic dreams of marital bliss, dreams Percy never expected to come true? "Oh, Marianna, come tomorrow for a visit. You received a card, didn't you?"

"Ah, yes, so I did."

"Now that I'm staff . . . I'll excuse you from class." Percy grinned, sitting at her desk and scribbling a note. She tucked a bill in the paper. "There's fare for the driver. Alexi makes sure I always have money; just this morning he pressed it into my hand and said, 'I'll have you want for nothing.' And it's true—I want for nothing more than him." She was eager to share the happiness of her good fortune rather than dreadful portals and ghosts.

"Just so long as he doesn't leave you alone," Marianna replied. When Percy furrowed her brow, her friend explained. "He broke your heart once, remember? That other woman in the courtyard?"

Percy blinked. She wasn't sure what she'd told Marianna at her infirmary bedside in the haze of that fever just before all hell broke loose. She must have mentioned seeing Alexi strolling with that monstrous woman Lucille Linden. Shaking the memory from her mind, she said, "Yes, but that was all explained. There's nothing but confidence between us now." She handed Marianna the note.

Her friend's eyes, while sparkling with the usual mischief, held something else as well—an odd, detached distance. She said, "Of course. Now I'm off to torment Edward; your marriage has inspired me. Tomorrow, then! Your estate! I cannot wait to see where he keeps you!"

Percy frowned as Marianna gave a giggle and trotted out of the room, but before she could wonder if the tenor of their friendship had indeed changed forever, there came a shimmering dark portal in the centre of the room. There was an odd silence within. Percy had prepared herself for the infernal nursery rhyme, but this silence was more frightening.

Beatrice stuck her head out. Percy started. "Dear God, Beatrice, this business is increasingly unnerving!"

"Only the beginning, princess. My. It's coming along nicely. Any day now, really."

"What?" Percy asked with dread.

Beatrice hopped out of the portal, and it closed behind her. Shaking her head she said with forced patience, as if addressing a child, "I've told you before: the worlds will become one and the real fight will begin. It's almost joined." She patted at the air where the portal had been. "I'm grateful for these paths the goddess created, otherwise I'd never be able to get around. He's got everything locked down, now."

"What—?"

"Of course, to bring things to their inevitable head, there's still the key you'll have to get from Darkness. That's what we really ought to be training you for."

"But I . . ." Percy trailed off. Beatrice concentrated fiercely on the wall.

"Come on," the ghost encouraged the wooden panels. As if in response, suddenly there was a new wooden door, narrow and thin, next to the one into the hallway from Percy's office. A faint blue light pulsed around its slender width. Beatrice snorted in triumph.

"I don't understand, Beatrice. How do these new doors differ from the dark portals? Are we to open them?"

"Not yet. But when the time is right, they'll need to be flung wide so that reinforcements can fly directly to your aid. There will be a great swarm, like water through a tiny hole. We can't be congested, the floodgates must rise!"

"Reinforcements . . . ?"

"Darling, you put the key in the chapel lock. You saw the map. There's another key. It's there, inside." Beatrice gestured toward the Whisper-world. When Percy grimaced, noticing a few stray bones cluttering the corridor beyond, the ghost added, "Oh, don't mind those, he's dredging the river to make things exceedingly unpleasant."

Percy shuddered.

"The second key you'll bring back to Athens, take it to the second lock upstairs, and the merger will begin. The chapel map is there so that The Guard can watch you while you're in there." Beatrice pointed again behind her.

Percy shook her head. "Not only am I not sure what you mean, I'm terrified to go."

"Darling." The ghost clucked her tongue. "You'll find this will make sense once you just trust your instincts. It was your plan, after all."

Percy balled her fists. "I'm not—!"

"The goddess. I know, I know. It's true, you're mortal flesh." The spirit looked at her gravely. "But you're also more. You'd do well to believe it." A moment later saw Beatrice's departure.

Percy sighed, baffled. Thankfully, Alexi's instincts hadn't been piqued and he hadn't come running. How she was to relay this latest exchange, she didn't know. Some time to determine a course of action was welcome.

She turned to her desk. In one last attempt at being a diligent professor, Alexi had left a book upon it with a note: *I ought to have tried this before. Indulge me, will you?* Percy opened it. The book was a Grecian tome on mathematics. Perusing it, a flood of disparate pieces fell into place in her mind, and she sat stunned as her barriers and blockades fell away amid the Greek characters and explanations. She chuckled. Thank goodness they hadn't tried this successful combination; otherwise the private tutorials that brought them together might never have forced their hand! Maybe her failures, too, had been somehow designed to bring them together. She had to tell him.

Traversing the familiar path to Apollo Hall, a familiar, titillating thrill worked through her body. She'd felt it on many a walk toward his classroom, that place she'd always both anticipated and dreaded. Strangely, Percy found her feelings unchanged; though her love had grown, so, too, had her fear of proving a fool.

Outside, she peered past those familiar Gothic arches and into his classroom. He paced to and fro, in the midst of some maelstrom of algebraic explanations, and she grinned, watching his beautiful and fearsome presence rule the room. His emphatic points caused some of the younger students to jump. She was sure she'd jumped just the same.

A rustling noise made her turn. "Hello," Percy said to the flustered boy who approached, books for Alexi's class under his arm.

"Late. Again. I suppose he'll have my head for it."

"It's all right," Percy reassured him. "He's not always terrible."

The boy peered at her. "That's right. You married him, didn't you?"

Percy blushed. "Yes."

"Hmm." He stared at her a moment, and Percy braced herself for an insult. Instead: "Can he be kind, then?"

Percy smiled. "Quite."

"Proof," the boy said, raising a finger, "that no one is to be underestimated." And with that, he held his breath and entered the classroom.

Alexi whirled at the sound of the opening door. "Mr. Andrews, you are late again, making it four times within . . ." He trailed off, staring through the door.

Percy waved, allowing herself a rushing thrill that she'd derailed this fearsome academic's train of thought. She blew him a kiss, then withdrew, lest she prove a further distraction. A few students fell to gossip, and she could only imagine what they had to say. Perhaps the moment alleviated Mr. Andrews's punishment. But soon the class was silenced with a fearsome clap upon the podium that could be heard down the hall, and Percy giggled again. She'd await him in his office and practice how to both inform and reassure him of the tasks ahead. But how could she reassure him when she herself was terrified? She'd toss in the conversation with Beatrice amid a few correct geometric problems and hope he'd be too shocked and thrilled to care.

Ascending to his office, she noticed more strange panels that hadn't been present before, more doors fit smoothly into these wooden panels. The few students she saw wandering the halls seemed oblivious to their existence; but as only select people could see ghosts, she wondered if this was the same. Not many saw spirits. Of those, only a select few became The Guard. What would her poor friends have to withstand? And Athens? What was the plan of her divine predecessor? There was more guesswork to Prophecy than seemed fair.

Having been left a key to Alexi's office, Percy let herself in. She stared fondly at the innumerable bookshelves, the open room with its vaulted ceiling and Gothic arched windows, the moody and intense gilt-framed canvasses on the wall, the fireplace behind the lavish marble desk topped with candelabra, and Alexi's huge leather chair. Memories washed over her: The time Mozart's "Requiem" beckoned all the ghosts of Athens to dance. The time he taught her to waltz. Their first kiss. Wonderful things had happened here, but then frightening things, too. That spectral dog sniffing her out. The time he cast her aside, thinking there'd been a mistake in destiny . . .

Ghosts wafted in and out through the walls of bookshelves. Moving to the chair opposite Alexi's, she had to remind herself of her purpose. A desire struck her that she should send for tea, but it seemed this office, however fine, was not equipped with a bellpull. Yet, there was a service on a fine, wheeled tray, near the lilylike bell of his phonograph. Tea sat at the ready, the diffusers full beside the saucers, water in the cups. But how would it be heated?

Percy laughed at her silliness. "Of course. My husband is magical!" Despite the unknown terrors that lay ahead, there were simple yet awesome comforts to their odd world.

Just as she was smiling over this, she heard Alexi's step on the threshold. She turned and ran to him, offering her husband a brief but adoring kiss. "Hello, love. I was about to ready tea." She moved to set the diffusers to steep.

"Step back, dear," he instructed. Waving his hand, he summoned a burst of fire above the kettle and cups.

As they settled in their chairs and Percy was about to launch into her news, there came a knock at the door. "Come in," Alexi called.

"Would you like me to—?"

"Just stay and sip your tea, Percy. We've nothing to hide. Not anymore."

The door opened and the Apollo Hall librarian, Mina Wilberforce, glided in, her beige frock a contrast to her dark skin. She nodded to them both. "Professor, Mrs. Rychman."

Alexi stood. "Hello, Miss Wilberforce."

Percy jumped up. "It's so good to see you, Mina! Would you like some tea?"

"Hello, Percy, and yes, thank you. I daresay I've never seen either of you with such a glow. This new life certainly agrees with you."

"Indeed." Alexi smiled, pulling another chair to the desk as Percy brought over full teacups. Alexi bade them all sit. "To what do we owe the honour of your visit, Miss Wilberforce?"

Mina stared at the floor as if counting the boards. "I wish I came with nothing but friendship on my mind, but I've been noticing things."

Percy withheld a shudder. Alexi's face was blank.

"Heavens forgive me for saying so," the librarian continued awkwardly, "but, Professor, you're not the average gentleman. There's something special about you; I've always thought so. And, Percy, you're hardly ordinary yourself. I'll hope you'll not deem me mad when I say that the building and grounds of Athens are changing. Subtly, but I'm sure of it."

Alexi and Percy glanced at each other, then at Mina.

"For instance, the cobblestones," she continued. "They've always been laid in triplicate. Not in septuplet."

"The stones now sit in patterns of seven?" Alexi clarified.

"Yes, Professor. Athens has gone entirely to sevens. Wall panels and cut-glass windows—there were five diamond panes and now seven. The classroom numbers are different, as if we've suddenly more rooms. All in multiples of seven. Is there something that confounds science at work here?" It was more consternation than concern in her expression, as if a supernatural answer would be an irritation rather than a fright.

Alexi set his jaw. "So it would seem, and I cannot offer explanation. Thank you, Miss Wilberforce, for bringing this to my attention. I shall look into it. Is there much gossip among the students?"

Percy wondered how much Elijah would have to clean up.

Mina gave a small smile. "I doubt a soul loves this building more than I, save, perhaps, the headmistress. Athens is sacred to me, and I notice everything about it. I doubt the student body at large would catalogue such details. But, thank you for confirming that I'm not mad."

"No, you're not mad," Alexi replied. "But if you'd mind not causing any uproar, the headmistress and I would greatly appreciate it."

Percy glanced at her husband, surprised he would be so forthcoming.

The librarian nodded and set her tea on the desk. "Tell me what's magical about the two of you," she said. "And about Athens. Please?"

Percy bit her lip, wondering what Alexi would do.

"I beg your pardon?" he said.

Mina sighed. "When I met you, Professor, and then you, Percy . . . I thought you might be one of those persons with a sense beyond what is immediately knowable."

"Indeed," Alexi said, not a confirmation, not a denial. "Is there some way I can help?"

Alexi's face remained blank. "Pray, Miss Wilberforce."

"That I do." Mina wrung her hands. "Every day."

Alexi stared at her. Surely some mesmerism was employed. Percy thought she glimpsed blue fire in his eyes, and Mina rose, calmed. "Thank you for tea. Do tell me if you determine the cause of transformation," she murmured. "I'd like to know if God—or the devil, for that matter—is a mathematician." She went out.

As the door closed behind their visitor, Percy stared at Alexi, who went to the window to gaze down at the cobblestones. He said, "Well, it seems we do have friends on that other side." Turning to Percy, the stained-glass window behind him giving him a halo, he added, "At least it's seven. That's our number. Not his. Beatrice did say something about troops, yes?"

"Yes. Troops we're to set free."

"Troops. That swath of blue on the map." His eyes lit, and he gave her a hopeful smile. "Thinking on it, that's the best news I've heard since you first said you love me."

Percy grinned. "And how about this news? That book you gave me?" She reached for a paper on his desk and scribbled out a few theorems she now knew to be correct. She looked up at him and giggled, Shakespeare ever the best retort; "In the end it would seem it was 'all Greek to me.' "

Alexi laughed loudly and spun her about. "Come, let's

have a meal, and then on to a drink with the others. I must toast to the fact I'm not a failed professor after all."

La Belle et La Bête was well-worn with loving use, and Percy drank in every detail of the place Alexi had oft mentioned but that she had yet to visit. He led her through the front door, where the paint of some hundred years had chipped in ringed layers. She glimpsed several familiar faces of The Guard already inside.

Thinking of Jane, she paid special attention to the spirits. One at the bar wore an antiquated military uniform, toasting glory the empire had long forgotten. Two Restoration-clad ladies in the corner were murmuring brazen things about the mistress of the establishment and Lord Withersby—and while it was no terrible shock to Percy, given what she'd sensed between them, the language was more colourful than she required. A former actor floated in from nearby Covent Garden, trailing a lavish costume and greyscale greasepaint, offering recreations of his finest theatrical moments to the windows and oblivious passersby. The Guard had long ignored these harmless haunts, but Percy couldn't help but take them in, her ability to hear their eternal and oft repetitive chatter adding to the café's colourful atmosphere.

The Guard gathered around a circular table, likely appearing loud and inappropriate to any outsider: fraternizing across class lines, myriad buttons undone, familiarity between unmarried men and women—all with a vicar presiding. But the few other patrons here didn't seem to notice, likely suspecting the seven of them to be a resident theatre troupe and thus excused. Empty bottles on tables, complements of the gracious hostess, also might explain the relative obliviousness.

Alexi enjoyed watching Percy take in the scene. He leaned in and murmured richly in her ear. "This is a second home to me, Percy, and while it's hard to believe I've never brought you here, I've enjoyed bringing you home far better."

"*Bienvenue,* Percy!" Josephine rushed to kiss Percy on both blushing cheeks. "As you see, I keep the wine French, cheap and flowing—a bit like my morals." She snorted and darted behind the bar to procure Alexi a spot of sherry.

Percy giggled, blushing. She had to remind herself that she was now a married adult and no longer a convent girl. Her skin might not have any colour, but the world did, and she enjoyed it.

"What may I offer you?" the Frenchwoman asked, shoving the snifter into Alexi's hand.

"Well . . . a glass of red wine?"

Josephine pursed her lips. "Now, I'm no enemy of red wine, but I'm guessing that's the only drink a convent girl knows."

"Champagne then," Percy said.

"*Oui!*" Josephine clapped and darted off.

Alexi took Percy by the arm and sat her down beside Jane, who was insisting to Michael that Margaret Pole's incessant execution inside the Tower of London was getting ridiculous. "The poor woman's not only runnin' round the scaffold, but she's nearly acrobatic. I went to quiet her last night and she'd floated up the lancet windows, taunting her executioner to follow. It's been since 1541, and she was seventy-two—shouldn't she be tired by now? Vicar Carroll, go remind her martyrdom's no sport."

"I daresay watching would be sport." Michael grinned. "If more people saw ghosts, why, cricket would be supplanted in a heartbeat."

"Nil!" Elijah protested.

Jane waved a hand. "You're welcome to her. Charge admission." Everyone chortled at the thought.

Josephine set a bubbling glass of champagne before Percy and took a seat. Alexi launched right into business. "Athens is changing more than we thought," he stated, swirling his snifter.

"Back there with you then," Elijah said. "You're spoiling our fun."

Alexi continued, unperturbed. "All in multiples of seven. Windowpanes, floorboards, cobblestones—I daresay I've been so preoccupied I'd not noticed," he admitted, grazing Percy's hand with his own. "Our perceptive librarian did. This has, unfortunately, gone beyond our little coterie."

"The war. We can't ignore it," Rebecca said. "Truly, friends, it will be like nothing we've ever known."

"You said that about that hellhound. Jack the bloody Ripper," Elijah muttered.

Percy froze, suddenly stunned. It was because of her that those women in Whitechapel were dead. That dog, that *thing* had been looking for her. She'd had no time to process the fact, but now that she did, tears sprang to her eyes.

"Yes, well, Prophecy continues, and each of its myriad parts is something we've never known," Alexi retorted. This didn't comfort Percy.

"Ah-ah, I feel where your mind is going, young lady, and it will do no good," Michael cautioned.

"It's my fault," she gasped, a huge and terrible pain seizing her.

Michael moved to place a thumb on her sternum, and a jolt of light followed, chasing her sorrow and overtaking it with numbing calm. Percy eyed the vicar with renewed wonder.

"They will do you no good, Percy, those incapacitating thoughts. You need your heart, your energy, for the trials ahead." He turned to the others. "We all do. Hold on to joy. To happiness. To love." He made an effort not to let his eyes linger on Rebecca but failed; Percy noticed. "Hold to light, for darkness seeks to steal our breath."

The Guard all sat in uncomfortable silence. Josephine rose and brought back two more bottles of wine.

"But the number seven is *our* number, friends," Alexi rallied quietly. "There are indeed troops, spiritual friends who will fight on our side. I believe that now. No matter how strange it is to realize this . . . I feel a bit less left to the wolves."

This eased things enough for them to speak of trivialities for a bit, to tease Alexi, to act like all was as it should be. But while Percy didn't know The Guard perfectly well, she could tell it was a bit of a show. The underlying tension wouldn't go away so easily. Those doors had to open, and the mysteries to reveal themselves.

CHAPTER FIFTEEN

The next day began in peaceful, solitary quiet once Alexi kissed her and left for Athens, this being her agreed-upon time for calling hours. Percy dressed in gauzy layers, indulging the habit that whenever she was alone at home she would wander like a resident ghost. She was still amazed by the estate's size, and that it was all, in part, hers.

For the lady of the house's pleasure, the Wentworths had stocked the small ground-floor kitchen with treasures for high tea. Percy made light sandwiches on small breads with delicate ingredients she'd never dreamed of eating at the convent; soup and gruel had been her constant fare. She couldn't wait to share exploration of the grounds with Marianna, to youthfully revel in these delights.

The knocker's loud clatter sent her running to usher in her beaming friend, whose eyes appeared glassy and grey, but whose smile was so welcome and familiar Percy overlooked for the moment whatever weariness plagued her.

"Oh, Percy!" Marianna had worn her finest dress, and

she swept into the entrance foyer with appropriate appreciation.

"Wait until you see it all," Percy giggled, taking the
blonde girl's traveling cloak and stowing it.

In a tall hallway mirror, Marianna caught her reflection
and paused to tuck a stubborn curl into the pile of locks that
threatened to spill down her shoulders. She absently brushed
her fingers on her bustle before turning to Percy with a
girlish bounce. "So, a tour?"

Percy was only too happy to oblige. She swept Marianna
about the estate, room by room, everywhere save the ex-
tremities, and her friend cooed in delight. Percy swelled with
pride. When she opened the master bedroom and Marianna
glimpsed the sumptuous furnishings and four-poster bed, a
devilish grin was offered that made Percy blush fiercely.

"And does the master of the house show you every comfort in the privacy of these quarters?" the German girl
asked huskily.

"Verily," Percy breathed, placing cool hands on her
warm cheeks. "Oh, goodness—tea! I'm to offer you tea and
confections as the lady of the estate," she added with theatrical grandeur, before giggling. "Alas, I'm a royal disaster at
this. No one ever taught me fine manners at the convent,
never thinking I'd have the good fortune to use them. I'm
so very out of my depth."

Marianna hummed, amused.

Percy led her friend into the parlour, where she'd drawn
the curtains on one side to let light pour in, though the
other side fell in shadow. Percy seated Marianna in the light
and herself in the shade. "Enough about me and my ab-
surdly grand house! How is your Edward?"

"Oh, he's fine. I've not seen much of him, though. He
thinks I'm sad because I've lost you." Marianna cocked her
head before righting it again. There was something almost
marionette-like about the movement, and Percy found her-

self wondering if she'd always had such quirks. Had she always been daydreaming of Alexi and never seen how her best friend was a bit odd? Or was something wrong?

"You've not lost me, dear. I'll be here and at Athens for you. You may visit anytime."

"Well, I have been dying to see more of you, darling, so he's not entirely wrong." Marianna abruptly rapped her hand on the round marble table, rattling the teacups on their saucers. She leaned forward. Her green eyes, tinged with grey, sparkled. "Tell me. How does it feel to be truly powerful?"

"What do you mean?" Percy asked. Her pulse quickened. Surely her friend meant the house, Alexi's wealth, her sudden station . . . "I'm not powerful, Marianna. Or, at least, if these trappings do improve one's station, I'm no different than I was before. Being deeply in love is the only change to my heart. The rest are simply blessings."

Marianna rose listlessly, squinting at the sculptures on the mantel. "Did you ever find out who you were? You were so preoccupied with visions, I was curious if that professor of yours told you who you are. Searching for answers, some powerless young lady who could be so much more . . ."

Percy laughed nervously. "I'm no one but myself. Percy Parker . . . Rychman." She moved to the tea tray, disturbed.

"Persephone," Marianna said.

"Yes."

"We're all wondering what our place is in this little farce, aren't we, and who will win in the end."

"Win what? What on earth are you—?" Percy, having busied herself with a plate of scones and clotted cream, turned to find herself alone in the parlour. "Marianna?" she asked. Silence.

She shook her head, assuming her friend had gone for the water closet or was off mischievously searching the estate's drawers. Giving Marianna some moments to declare herself, putting away the tea service, Percy then poked her head back in the parlour, but Marianna still hadn't returned. She called out with a laugh, "What, are you off to procure some souvenir to take to school, some trinket of the fearsome Professor Rychman to dangle before his frightened students?" No answer.

Percy wandered the first, second, then third floors of her home. Standing at the base of the attic stairs, she promised herself that, the first moment back at Athens, she would demand a doctor examine Marianna. Her friend looked a bit unwell, and her mind was clearly off, too. She'd have to ask Edward.

"Marianna?" she called, her worry echoing up the stairs ahead of her. Just that morning she had explored the attic, peeking under dusty cloths at lavish furniture for parties that had not been held for decades, gazing out the tiny dormer window onto the struggling garden far below. And it was there that Percy finally found Marianna, staring out that small window, her blonde hair undone and spilling in a cascade down her back.

"Marianna." This time, it was not a question but a demand. "What are you doing up here?"

"Indeed, a lovely house," the girl murmured. "A lovely life."

"Marianna . . . what's troubling you? You're not quite yourself." Percy approached her, boots creaking across the wooden boards.

Reaching a hand back, as if urging Percy forward, Marianna did not turn around and look. Percy approached, eager to discover the source of her friend's melancholy, her faraway gaze, her hollow voice . . .

Marianna seized her hand. Her grip was ice-cold. "Can you trust a man who leaves you all alone in a huge estate, far from all your precious friends? It's true that I'm not myself." The blonde girl chuckled. "But I'm so very glad to see you again, Persephone."

Her body did not move, yet Marianna's head turned entirely backward on her spine—a sickening, unnatural swivel. A scream leaped to Percy's throat. Tears of grey ash poured from her friend's vacantly staring eyes.

It was certainly no longer Marianna who stood before her, broken and horrible, ash spilling from her mouth, spewing onto Marianna's fine silk garments and spattering Percy's face. Marianna's fallen hair now stirred to life, ashen snake skulls suddenly swarming over her scalp. It was the betrayal of which Beatrice warned. Perhaps a fatal oversight.

"Hello again!" A voice gurgled from deep inside Marianna's throat. It was the voice of Lucille Linden. The Gorgon who had once nearly killed The Guard had returned.

"Oh, God. Percy!"

Inside her Athens office, fear and despair overtook Rebecca like a bolt of lightning from above. The betrayal. It was happening. Her veins felt the pull of spectral activity, the pulsing pain a distinct sensation of something untoward coming upon one of The Guard. She gasped, jumped to her feet and flew out the door.

Flinging open the Bay Room door, startling the professors Hart, who were silently reading to each other while floating above the window seat, she found Percy's office otherwise empty. Rebecca didn't take time to ponder the girl's whereabouts, she was out and across the courtyard in a rush, lifting her prim skirts and running toward Apollo Hall.

Alexi paced at the front of his room, menacing students with a verbal onslaught of mathematical theorems. Rebecca saw him through the outside window and threw wide his door without a thought to caution, deference or protocol. Upon seeing the look on her face, he dropped the chalk he'd been using to hastily scrawl equations on the board behind him.

"Your wife," she choked.

Alexi ran up the aisle, had her by the elbow and out the

door in an instant. Behind them, the students fell to chattering. Neither of them cared.

Their questions came at each other in chorus:

"—Where is she?" Rebecca breathed.

"—What's wrong?" Alexi barked. "Home," he answered. "Calling hours."

"Damn!" Rebecca cried. Why hadn't she thought of Percy's calling hours? It was her fault for not thinking about the ways of a lady, a civilian particular she was foolish for not having considered. What if they were too late?

Alexi was beside himself as they ran to the rear stables. "What is it?" he demanded.

"A Pull. Pain, like I felt with Jane. I'm afraid something's got Percy," Rebecca panted.

Alexi shot ahead to the stalls. Prospero anticipated his master, pawing the ground, wide black eyes fiercely alert and ready. A moment later, a blur of swirling black swept past Rebecca, a clatter of horse hooves and a deep cry for swift speed.

Rebecca procured one of the trusted mares kept at the school for emergency, used most often in service of The Guard. No amateur when it came to riding, she managed to keep Alexi in sight.

A mile from the school his hand flew to his head, his tall form shuddered and she knew he felt the discord now that she had earlier. She prayed her warning had been in time.

Josephine and Elijah rounded the corner in one of the Withersby carriages, heading as if to the academy. It wheeled round to follow Rebecca's cry as she flagged her hand in a northerly direction. Jane's worried face peeked out from one window, and Michael appeared on horseback close behind. The grim looks on their faces made it clear they felt the Pull as well.

Rebecca cursed herself. If she'd told Alexi the moment she'd had the first shudder of concern, the first fear of betrayal, perhaps he'd have kept Percy always in the school. This delay could cost them everything, and it would be her fault. At least in part.

But if all The Guard were accounted for, who was responsible? Who was the betrayer?

Percy shrieked again. Lucille laughed, and Marianna's hand seized Percy's throat. Her other arm struck the window, breaking the glass into dangerous shards. Marianna's delicate hand came away bloody.

"You didn't really think I was so easily defeated, did you? Don't you realize that nothing is safe? No one is safe? You're a liability to all involved! Give up now before everyone you love suffers."

"No!" Percy choked. Her flesh started to burn with light.

"Yes, yes, you and that blasted magic of yours. I was unprepared for it before. But I'm invincible now."

"You don't even have your own body," Percy gasped. "You're hardly—"

"Shut up! Damn your mortal words, I want blood. I always hated her. From the moment Darkness dragged her down there, mewling and weeping and retching fruit. I hated her light and colours and the noxious life sprouting in her sickening wake. I should have been a goddess, not a monster. Now you're mortal, and I'm a goddess. How stupid of you." Lucille drew Percy's cheek close to the jagged glass. Percy struggled, but the supernatural strength flowing through her friend's body was besting her.

She tried to focus her light like a retaliating blow. But truth be told, she still wasn't sure how to use it. She was, after all, just a mortal, and perhaps helpless if left alone. Her heart begged Alexi to somehow hear her cry. Her face neared the jagged glass.

"Let's see. How did our puppy treat those victims? Just

how did the Ripper cut their faces? Before I send you out this window, you'll look like all those girls who had to die before your stupid Guard understood. Even then they were helpless! Pathetic, all of you. Pieces of dead gods. I'll take all your lives with me, and *I* shall reign in shadow's seat—a place I adore, and a beautiful place you wish to destroy. I'll turn your world Whisper instead!"

A surge of righteous anger bolstered Percy, and her light expanded, edging Marianna's body back, loosening the grip on her neck. Lucille growled, and Marianna's true voice cried out in pain.

"Marianna, darling, it's Percy," Percy choked, wedging her hand between her own throat and the preternatural grip around it. "Fight the demon that has you. Fight her!"

Marianna whimpered, sounding like her friend again before her eyes clouded and she gagged, an ashen serpent crawling from her mouth.

Thunder sounded on the stairs. Outside, friends' voices.

"Percy!" Alexi cried, bounding into the room and stunning Marianna's body with a dizzying jolt of blue fire. The blast forced Percy's release, causing her to fall forward. Her hand slid against the broken glass. Scarlet blood poured garish from her white skin, but Alexi dove to catch her as she collapsed. Snakes flaking grey ash slithered to lap Percy's blood from the sill.

The ashen serpent hanging from Marianna's mouth retracted into her throat and Lucille spoke with a gurgling hiss. "You again? Still failing your little sweetheart, Rychman?"

Another bolt aimed right for the mouth reeled Marianna's body backward, ash and spittle flying everywhere. Percy was woozy from pain and loss of blood, but Jane's lit hand was suddenly upon her, mending her deep gash with a tingling light.

"Our only failure is that we didn't cast your ashes to the

four corners," Alexi roared, rushing forward and roughly grabbing the possessed body by the throat. Perhaps he couldn't see who it was through his rage, and past the layer of ash covering Marianna's face.

"Alexi, please," Percy begged. "Look. It's Marianna! She's taken over Marianna. Take care!"

Alexi stared at his quarry and scowled. "Damn it. *Bind!*"

The rest of The Guard hurried into their circle.

Bound by blue fire, Lucille Linden screamed within Marianna's body, the fact that she was now a possessor giving Alexi's fire some advantage. But Lucille was doing what she could, spitting hot ash to scald them, snakes lashing out like fanged whips. Marianna's eyes, ears, nose and mouth were fountains of clotted ashen fluid, a horrific sight Percy forced herself to watch because it was her fault.

"Cantus of Extinction!" Alexi cried. Notes of music rose beautiful and fearsome as The Guard encircled Marianna's body, Jane at her side. Wind whipped their clothes, and the music of the Grand Work crested in the air.

Percy forced herself to stand and give them energy, trying to siphon off her light, which still felt unwieldy in her body, offering it into the torrent of blue fire that Alexi wreathed around Marianna's body, trying to suffocate the possessor. Michael breathed loudly, forcing them all to remember to do the same.

"Extinct? I'll never go extinct," Lucille shrieked, flapping Marianna's jaw like a grotesque puppet. The blonde girl's eyes rolled back in her head, ashen tears still streaming.

Josephine stepped forward, holding an image on a locket before Marianna's shifting, gritty eyes. "Dear girl—"

Marianna's mouth twisted and Lucille gurgled from within. "Your pictures are meaningless to me. I'll kill this girl. And your dear girl, finally, finally dead."

"Hush!" Alexi bellowed, a crackling bolt of fire sizzling Marianna's body, causing her to lurch violently and vomit more ash. It was good, perhaps, to see the offending substance purged, but Percy feared they were killing her in the process.

"We're losing her," Jane cried.

Percy panicked, her chest suddenly a white blaze.

A familiar ripping noise announced a portal. Aodhan came rushing out, either sensing danger from beyond or summoned by Percy's reactive light. "It's the Gorgon, Aodhan, taken over my friend!" Percy cried in his Gaelic tongue.

Jane eyed her beloved. "I don't know that I can do this all m'self," she admitted. "Please help if ye can."

Aodhan floated close, brushing a transparent hand over the Irishwoman's shoulder, staring grimly down at Marianna. He passed his other hand—glowing, healing—over Marianna's eyes, which fluttered. She moaned but remained unresponsive. To Percy he admitted, "Alas, spirits such as these will take revenge at all costs. The body will die."

"No!" Percy sobbed.

"Unless . . ." Aodhan's expression darkened.

"Unless what?"

"I take her in. Into the Whisper-world."

"Then she'll certainly die!"

"Not exactly. For a hapless mortal, not a Guard, there's time before damage is irreparable. Beatrice can help me. But you must come, my lady."

"I could rescue her from there once healed, and return her to the living here?" Percy asked, speaking still in Gaelic.

"Translate!" Alexi demanded.

One of his hands clamped upon Percy's shoulder, the other tightened around Marianna's blonde-turned-serpentine curls. The Guard struggled to keep her possessed body still. It kept seizing up and going limp, ash snakes champing at whomever was closest.

Beatrice sidled into view at the threshold of the portal, gazing grimly down upon the situation. "So, it was her. I'm sorry, dear. We didn't know. But like Orpheus came for

Eurydice, you may come, a god disguised. It's nearly all in place. They won't stop, things such as these," the ghost explained, gesturing disdainfully to Marianna's messy body. "Not until you settle it once and for all. Let the Healer and I deal with this. You and The Guard use the map and the doors. Knock, and the door will be opened.

"The time is upon you," Beatrice said, addressing them all. Percy murmured the translation. "Your beloved Athens changes. There's no stopping it. If you want to blame someone, blame a goddess and her hapless guard, but do not punish yourselves by doing nothing. Percy, you are the key. You must attend the destiny that awaits you."

When Alexi heard, he roared. "I told you, I'll not allow her in! Take me." A bolt of blue fire hurtled from his hand toward Beatrice, his intent unclear. But she held up a hand and the fire congealed, clearly now hers to command.

The rest of The Guard gasped.

"It isn't your choice, leader! You can't go in or you'll fall to pieces! Allow for the fact your wife is built for things you are not," Beatrice bellowed, Percy fumbling the translation in choking murmurs. "Possessed as you are, a living Guard *cannot* step across—shall I regale you of ugly tales the goddess told me of those who tested this? It isn't a matter for discussion! Your stubbornness, however massive, cannot stop fate!"

Marianna's body convulsed, giving a horrific sound and a pathetic cry. The life was being choked out of her, the monster within desperate for someone to die. What was left of Percy's friend was begging for mercy, her eyes still spewing ash—and now a new horror: blood. Jane wiped her cheeks only to see them wetted again. Percy wept, clutching her fists at her breast as if she could hold the light there and cast some spell of salvation.

"Cantus of Extinction," Alexi growled, showering blue fire upon the mane of snakes, which squealed and spat. "Resume it."

The Guard joined hands, but Aodhan voiced caution.

"Such a cantus may kill the girl. This is no ordinary possession."

"It may *kill* her, Alexi. Please," Percy spoke up, seizing his hand. The blue fire tingled up her wrist.

"Well, then, what do the spirits advise?"

"Tell Jane to give me a lock of her hair," Aodhan stated, and floated back to the threshold of the Whisper-world, where his transparent body darkened to grey solidity. Percy furrowed her brow and repeated the request.

"This isn't the time for romance," Alexi growled.

"I'm not being romantic. I need a tether. Do as I say," Aodhan insisted. Percy translated.

Jane stared at her beloved. A practical woman who thought to carry practical things, she pulled a penknife from her jacket pocket and without hesitation cut a long lock. Aodhan gestured for her to bring it close. She moved toward the portal, offering the lock in her open hand, and Aodhan's hand became transparent across the threshold as it reached toward hers. A draft drew the hair across to where his hand was able to clutch and raise it. Both the lock and his hand glowed with healing light.

"We lost our gifts long ago, but they live on in Athens, and in you." Jane was visibly moved as Aodhan kissed the lock and wound it about the leather band over his shoulder. The locket around Beatrice's throat pulsed with Phoenix fire.

"Now the girl," Beatrice murmured, gesturing to bring the victim closer.

"Take good care of her," Percy said.

"Take good care of yourself," Beatrice countered. "And wear grey. We can't have mortal colour giving you away. Don't forget." She pointed a finger at Percy.

As The Guard encircled and gingerly lifted the body, Alexi placed himself between his wife and Marianna. "Percy, stay back."

They got the body unsteadily onto its feet, ashen snakes snapping at them, catching a strand of Josephine's hair and a corner of Elijah's fine suit. A burst of fire flew from Alexi's hands, flinging Marianna's body toward the portal. Aodhan and Beatrice stood with waiting arms. They caught Marianna, their forms solid in the Whisper-world. Snakes flailing and sputtering, they dragged the body in. The portal closed.

Percy loosed a sob. The Guard's shoulders sagged in a group sigh, failure threatening to consume their spirits. Backing away, Percy slid down the wall into a heap on the floor, shaking her head. "This is all my fault! I'm a disaster," she cried, tears flowing. "I'm a danger to all who come near, to all who are close to me, to all whom I lo—"

"I'll not hear another word," Michael barked, immediately on his knees at her side. "This is beyond any fault of yours, and you must accept that or we cannot move forward with power—only fear, which is what the enemy would want!" He placed a firm hand on her collar, and she felt a gust of peace.

"Friends, thank you," Alexi said quietly. "Give me leave to calm her. Don't go far. Make yourselves at home."

The Guard nodded and filed downstairs, Rebecca at the rear. Alexi moved to grab her arm. "Bless you, Rebecca. If you hadn't felt the call when you did . . ." He faltered. Overcome with emotion neither of them did well expressing, she nodded curtly and exited.

Alexi eased Percy into his arms from the floor. Supporting her, he led her down into the parlour, where he swept a roaring fire into the hearth. He heated tea with another gesture, and forced a cup into his wife's shaking hands.

"I am a danger to those I love," Percy stated, guilt threatening to undo her sanity.

Alexi stared at her with both consternation and adoration. "This work means danger."

"But I—"

"What, shall you go and leave us? Try and lure the danger elsewhere? It follows us, Percy, and you were sent to us. This is our lot."

"I . . ." Percy's mouth moved to protest, but she had no words.

Her husband's face was grim. "The day I was chosen to lead The Guard, an ill force swept through this house, paralyzing my sister and frightening my grandmother to death. It was, perhaps, a warning, an early taste of the trials that would come. My parents left me this house and a bit of money at the age of sixteen. They never said why, but I know it was because I frightened them. They thought I was ill luck. That I doomed the family name." He eyed her, his expression as tortured as she'd ever seen. "This work will make you question everything, Percy, and make you despair. But you must persevere."

She nodded. They both had been dealt shares of pain, and she better understood his zealous protection. She'd chosen to take that doomed name, she was choosing him, this house, this life; and with her vow of marriage she'd promised never to abandon him.

He pressed her against him, stilling her shaking body with the embrace. "We must persevere," he insisted. "I am at your side."

"Thank God," Percy said. "Yet . . . don't be angry for what may be asked of me, what I cannot control. What must happen."

Alexi stared at the fire and held her tighter.

CHAPTER SIXTEEN

Inside the Whisper-world, Aodhan and Beatrice were hard at work saving the body and soul of an innocent victim.

They ferreted Marianna away to a dim chamber where Beatrice mustered their hallowed fire, grateful her time at Athens had given her a store of power; otherwise she'd be useless.

At any other time, Beatrice admitted, brushing ash out of Marianna's curls with a comb, her actions would have caught the attention of this entire spectral world. The molten, ashen liquid seeping from the girl's facial orifices was a truly grue-some sight. But she and Aodhan went oddly undisturbed, for the whole arrangement of the Whisper-world was like a door hanging on one hinge. Beatrice didn't blame the current Guard for their hesitation. Their new task went against everything they'd all fought for, their whole, thankless lives. She herself had fought destiny to only in the end acquiesce. Bleeding the Whisper-world onto Athens was dangerous, but it was the only way to regain balance.

Mortal and Whisper-world edges rubbed with freshly combustible friction. Long-sealed walls had cracked open, forgotten vaults now spewed fresh venom. Spirits never be-fore mixed were now fighting and cursing along the river. All that remained a fortress unbroken was, unfortunately, the prison room where Darkness had corralled his sworn enemies. But that, too, was scheduled to soon crack open. So long as Mrs. Rychman kept her head.

Only a pile of restless ash evidenced their painstaking

work, oozing grimly from Marianna's mouth with every healing burst Aodhan managed. He continually brushed the offending substance into a ceramic jar. Other jars lined the edge of a yawning hole like the stacked skulls of an ancient crypt.

It was bound to happen, Beatrice realized as she heard his distinctive howl. It would seem he'd been the monster's lackey from time immemorial and he proved her champion yet.

"What're you doing?" the Groundskeeper cried, shuffling into their grim workplace. "That's my Lucy in there. You let her go. You let her out. That host is alive! What are you doing? You're breaking every rule—"

"Be my guest and please retract your Lucy. We're just trying to return her," Beatrice offered graciously.

The Groundskeeper pointed. "You're the troublemaker."

"Why, so I am." Beatrice bowed. "Are you going to help your beloved or not? We could make sure she never leaves this body."

The Groundskeeper's face twisted, staring at the fire that sparked around Beatrice's neck and had leaped into her hand. He was clearly wary of her power. "No!"

"Then allow us to take care of this. Here are some of her parts—by all means, take them away." Beatrice gestured to the arched hole in the stone behind them and all the jars.

"I'll expect more," he threatened, counting.

"Indeed." Beatrice nodded, standing aside as he rushed to scoop Lucille's remains into his arms. He soon scurried away, singing. "Lucy-Ducy wore a nice dress . . . Lucy-Ducy made a great mess!" His voice faded down the hall.

The two Guard went back to work. When the next jar was half full of ash, Beatrice lifted a rock, placed it inside and sealed the lid with twine and a burst of blue fire for good measure. She handed the hissing contents to Aodhan, who vanished, well aware of what do to with it.

* * *

From the moment the sun broke across the horizon, a heavy dread rose within those of The Guard who'd spent the night at the Rychman estate. Alexi was gentle, taking his wife into his arms, but the weight of failure was there between them as they woke, like a cold chill.

"All I can think of is Marianna," Percy murmured. She nestled into his shoulder, his nearness her only comfort. "Let the world pass us by, Alexi, just stay and hold me."

"Would it were that easy. I'd love nothing more. But the call is strong in my blood. There's work to be done at Athens; our safe house no longer safe. We put our students at risk if we tarry." He kissed her temple, then commanded, "Stay close to me today."

Percy nodded. But, what if there were a door? Would she take it at a run, to speed this inevitable dirge onward? Uncertainty must drive her mad. She had to trust Beatrice: she'd know when it was time.

Josephine had prepared cold breakfast and tea, and the others sat quietly in the parlour, eyeing Percy with funereal expressions. She graciously accepted the tea Jane hurried to offer as she entered.

Alexi broke the dreadful silence. "Friends, you feel the weight of Athens as I do, do you not?"

Everyone nodded.

"The storm gathers," Rebecca agreed. "We've a war to weather, friends. We must go and save those beloved bricks."

Michael nodded. "May the congregation say amen."

Their anchor of a building was on a fault line ready for a fearsome quake, a shifting mystery. Athens was proving to have a character of its own, and none of The Guard could be sure whose side it was taking, its changes taking their sacred number or no. A luminosity grew about the stately bricks that gave students pause, as if they could not trust their own eyes. The sad truth was that they couldn't.

Staff and students were not sleeping, and many stated

they were seeing things like ghosts. The Guard could not disagree: the Athens spectres were plentiful and particularly active. Percy heard them babbling as if only recently dead, jarred into a new awareness of themselves.

Elijah was most taxed by the trying morning, adjusting the minds of the academy's residents, who understood only that neither themselves nor the hairs on the backs of their necks could rest. All seven of The Guard crowded into Rebecca's office. She handed Elijah her flask and no one even raised an eyebrow. "We can't run a school like this," she said.

Percy stared at the carpeting—a sensible and ordinary grey, like most of the headmistress's wardrobe, grey like what she'd don in the Whisper-world—nightmares coursing her mind like a grim carousel. She'd stood silently at Alexi's side all morning, and they'd examined each new door Beatrice had erected about the grounds, each emblazoned with some variant of the number seven.

"We have no choice but to close the school," Alexi replied.

"I've done my best—a thorough wipe of every mind, but their fears will grow again. I can't be everywhere at once," Elijah said.

Rebecca shook her head. "I'll gather them into the auditorium. I'll tell them . . ."

"That you're giving them an extra bit of holiday," Michael said. "For being smashing students. I realize you never allow yourself holidays, Miss Thompson, but the world loves them. So do students. We're not too terribly far from Christmas. It's soon the season of love." He pounded his fist on a bookcase and smiled, and the others couldn't help but feel the stale air of the office seemed a bit easier to breathe.

Rebecca began to deliver sharp orders. "Alexi, have house wardens gather staff and students immediately into the auditorium. I'll need everyone's help to keep order. We must use whatever means necessary—all our usual tricks—to convince students and staff that Athens is granting them an enjoyable respite, nothing more. Then, my friends, we will shut ourselves within these walls for a siege."

Percy realized there was no specific task for her. She had no usual place in The Guard's work, had no established methodology to aid them. Yet, she had work of her own.

The others walked ahead, falling in behind Rebecca's brisk tread. Alexi led Percy to the side of the hallway and said, "Percy, I'll meet you in your office."

"No. Meet me in the sacred space. I must study that map."

"Percy, I'll not have you in there a—"

"Come for me when you've dispatched everyone," she interrupted.

"I told you: you must stay by my side today."

"Sitting alone and useless in my office isn't by your side. Alexi, if the great maw of the Whisper-world is to open and bear down on us, I'd like to be prepared. That map is the only clue we have."

Alexi sighed. He lifted his hand to touch her face, but he was stopped by the passing students glancing at them out of the corners of their eyes. "My desperation in wanting to see you safe trumps all," he murmured. "But, go. I'll come once staff and students are on their way. Just . . . don't go in."

"We've time yet," she replied. It was a reassurance but no promise. Alexi clenched his jaw and his fists and stalked away.

Her tread was weary as she walked to the Athens chapel. She tried to think of how beautiful her wedding had been, of how much she loved Alexi and was lucky to have found him, and thoughts of how she had indeed been provided for brought some consolation. In a rear pew she found Mina Wilberforce staring in consternation at the windows.

The librarian glanced up as she approached, and pointed down the line of amber-glass angels. "There are seven. There were six. How can one explain that? I pray its God's work here, but I fear . . ." She trailed off, shaking her head.

"Have faith," Percy murmured. "Staff and students gather in the auditorium as we speak. Perhaps you'd like to join them."

"And you?"

Percy eyed the chapel. "If the devil's at work here, I think I'd best pray." She couldn't assure others of their sanity and have any remaining for herself.

"Indeed. Well, then. Bless you, dear girl."

"And you."

Left alone, Percy took a deep breath.

Darting up the aisle, she threw her arm forward, opening the dark doorway and descending the stairs into the centre of The Guard's mysterious space, which she'd never entirely comprehend. Pulling the key from her chain, she bent at the centre of the floor and turned it in the feather. There came the usual grating sound, and the rush of blue fire to which she was now accustomed. She almost pressed her face down into it as the patterns again formed themselves on the floor; their tingling power was an intoxicant.

Instead, she rose and paced the perimeter of the map, determining the precise, rectangular lines of Athens; the courtyard in the middle, Promethe and Apollo halls, the girls' and boys' dormitories. Beyond that familiar floor plan, the flames were taller in some places, and she murmured, "Perhaps those are spaces of spirit world import? And surely this cannot be the whole of that realm. Surely there are parts to defy mortal sensibilities." The red dot slowly traversed a circular space, the mark of a key still above it. Inside, the swath filled with blue.

Despite her better judgment, Percy moved closer. She bent to examine the circular area of blue—a space she hoped was filled with friends—and noticed that just outside its delineated lines of fire, there was moisture . . . and a murmur. A faint sound of rushing water. A river? Surely. Of course there would be a river. *The* river.

Alexi's footfall on the stair made her jump. "Well?" It was quite obvious he disapproved of her initiative.

"I've determined what is Athens and what may be what you call the Whisper-world. The flame has different heights there; the spaces are more circular. Of course, the more my eyes get used to the map, the more I believe that we only see those spaces of the Whisper-world that extend off from Athens, only those spaces that are meaningful to our fight. I cannot believe such a thing as the spirit realm would be an addition to an academy." She smiled wryly.

Alexi hummed. "The red mark circles that same sea of blue, perhaps patrolling our troops. And, look. Did you notice these?" He pointed to places on the Athens perimeter that bled outward. At each juncture, a brighter horizontal line floated. On the scale of the map, each was about the height of a door.

"Beatrice's doors. We can see where they lead," Percy exclaimed.

"We've no idea where they'll lead," Alexi argued. "Or what's waiting on the other side."

"We should leave the map open. We've no idea when any one of these doors might burst open. This map surely can't be seen from the other side, else Beatrice would have warned us, and who knows when the information will be helpful."

Alexi set his jaw but said nothing.

Percy didn't bother to ask if he heard the ticking of a clock. She assumed he didn't. But she did—ticking away the seconds of her life, or the seconds until battle. It was by far the most maddening development yet. She held out her hand, and Alexi took it, reluctantly leaving the key in the floor. They exited the sacred space, the flames licking low and steady behind them.

"Shall you pass time with me in my office?" Alexi asked. As they stepped out into the chapel, the dark doorway snapped shut behind them.

"Yes. A fire and tea would be lovely. And to think about—"

Alexi took and lifted her arm, indicated how badly her hands were shaking. When she just chuckled in response, he secured his arm around her waist and walked her toward his office. Neither said anything, simply nodded to passing students looking deliriously drugged as they carried their bags home for early holiday. Percy hoped these ghostly trials would be done by Christmas and that, as in Dickens's *Carol*, they'd all be granted their due blessings.

In his office, Alexi lit candelabra and a fire in the hearth with a wave of his hand. He turned on his ornate phonograph, a bit of soothing Bach. Percy readied tea and held it out. He warmed it with a flick of his hand, and they sat, worlds away from the simple time when their biggest mystery was her visions—and the pleasant revelation that they *both* could see ghosts.

It would seem his office was a catalyst for visions. This time, Percy saw a portal. Beatrice stood within, seeming to indicate that it would soon be time. A bright blue transparent feather of flame floated before her face.

Alexi didn't seem to notice Percy's distraction; he was busy adding drops of alcohol into his tea from the flask Rebecca had given Elijah. "Were you always so fond of sherry?" she asked.

"Not nearly as much as I am of late."

Percy nodded. She couldn't blame him. Listlessly, she rose and went to the alcove that served as a makeshift room behind a protruding bookshelf. She lifted the lid of a small trunk Alexi had packed for them, and brought out their garments to hang on the adjacent coat tree. If they were going to wait out this war, at least they'd have some fresh clothing. She had, as Beatrice directed, brought a soft slate-coloured dress.

Peering inside the chest, Percy noticed her pearl rosary.

Like a long-lost treasure, she picked it up and brought it to her lips, thankful to have something with which to busy her fingers. Then she returned to Alexi at his desk and sat upon his knee.

He perused a diary. "My first thoughts of you," he murmured, staring at the pages.

Percy smiled. "And?"

"Clinical. I wrote clinical thoughts. I couldn't admit how much I loved you until you were nearly dead in my arms. And you hang on the precipice of danger now, Percy, making me realize it all the more. I . . ." He looked away, strangled by emotion. "I swear, if you take chances with your life, I'll never . . ."

Percy kissed his face.

He jumped up, setting her on her feet before him. "Let me go instead," he said desperately. "Let me set this in motion. Let me go rather than you, Percy. I'm meant to protect you! I cannot simply let you go; it's against every principle I . . . I cannot bear to lose you."

"Alexi, my love. My dear champion." Percy put her hand on his lips. "You'll go mad if you so much as step across. None of us can take that risk. The Guard, London and I—we all need you whole."

"And what ensures you *your* mind will fare better?"

She shrugged. "Because I am not like you. Because they tell me it was once home."

Alexi pounded his desk, tears in his eyes. "Your home is here with me!"

"I've never doubted that, and I never will, husband," she said. "Please be sure to never doubt my love."

"I don't. I simply cannot bear that something might happen. I cannot . . ." His voice broke again.

"When The Guard convinced you fate was not on our side, you parted ways with me and saw fit to make me suffer," she stated. The pain on Alexi's face worsened, and he opened his mouth to refute her. She put her hands lovingly to his cheeks. "We survived. Our love survived. And we shall again."

He stared at her in wonder. "How did my dear girl grow so brave?"

Percy grinned. "Didn't you hear? The meek shall inherit the earth." Alexi couldn't help but chuckle, a tear rolling down his cheek. She kissed him passionately and retreated. "But now I need Michael. I'd like him to pray with me."

As Percy suspected, she found the vicar not far from Rebecca's office. Around them, the school was emptying, obedient and dazed students following The Guard's instruction. Elijah slumped near the main door, clearly exhausted. Josephine stood beside him, shifting on her feet. Michael sat on a bench nearby, reading. Percy fiddled with the beads in her hand.

The vicar looked up and unleashed one of those winning smiles that could brighten any day. "Hullo, Mrs. Rychman. Shocked to see Alexi let you out of his sight, but glad we have the honour of your company."

Percy smiled wanly and sat beside him. She glanced at his book. "*The Castle of Otranto*?"

"It's positively dreadful." He nodded and laughed. "I adore it. But you're not here to discuss literature with me," he stated, waggling his mustache as she smirked. "I'd say you're looking pale, but that's a ridiculous redundancy."

She nodded, turning the beads in her fingertips, unable to find the words she needed.

She didn't need any. He glanced at her hands and clasped them in his, lowering his head. "'In the beginning was the Word. And the Word was with God and the Word was God. He was in the beginning with God. All things were made through him, and without him was not anything made. That which has been made was life in him and the life was the light of mankind. The Light shines in the Darkness and the Darkness has not overcome it.'"

Percy's hands warmed and pulsed with power. Michael sent something soft and wonderful through their fingers, as if a dove of blessed assurance were cupped gently in her hands, as if hope now infused each pearl rosary bead. He moved her hands upward and said, "Keep it close to you."

She nodded. Reaching under the ribbon trim of her dress, Percy tucked the rosary inside her corset, directly against her bosom. The beads seemed to pick up her heartbeat and magnify it. "Thank you, Vicar, for knowing just what I needed."

"Of course."

Percy rose and walked away, but she bit her lip, realizing there was something else. She rushed back and fell to her knees before him, their hands again clasped. "There are times when we must make sure all things left unsaid might be said. If something should happen to me, please impress my unfailing love upon Alexi, my greatest treasure, his love worth a thousand deaths. And you'd best make sure you leave nothing unsaid either. None of us should."

Michael stared up at her. "I should tell her," he murmured. The concept was clearly more terrifying to him than spiritual warfare.

"Yes." Percy smiled meekly. "I think you should."

Michael nodded, blushed and returned to his book.

The day had darkened swiftly. Percy was about to wander back to Alexi's office when he jumped out from behind a pillar and startled the very wits out of her. Gasping, she batted a hand at him as he scooped her up into his arms.

"W-why on earth?" she stammered.

"You've seen ghosts and Gorgons. You're willing to stare down the whole of the Whisper-world. I thought nothing could frighten you." His tone was teasing, but a mournful truth lay beneath.

She reached a hand to his face. "Losing you. That is a terror from which I could never recover."

Alexi pursed his lips. Percy thought she saw a glimmer of a tear. He set her on her feet and swept her up the grand staircase.

"Alexi, what are you—?"

"Recalling my fondest memory," he murmured, taking her hand and spinning her across Promethe Hall's upper floor. They were in a stately foyer bathed in a soft purple dusk shifting toward moonlight—similar to when Alexi once discovered Percy when she thought no one would miss her if she stole away at the academy ball, awkward and unloved, to this very floor. But her dear professor had found her, had waltzed her through starlight and shadows that became chaperone to burgeoning adoration.

Percy heard a bow strike a string, and a note of music rose like steam into the air. She turned to see Jane with her fiddle, winking. Another note came, then another, a lilting little waltz to recall them to that moment they first dared dream.

"May I have this dance, Persephone?"

Percy beamed. "Oh, please, Professor."

He lifted her gracefully into the dance he'd once taught her in his office. She now seamlessly followed Alexi's lead, and they spun in and out of widening silver moonlit shafts, the sparkle in his dark eyes and the press of his hand giving her thrills that would keep her forever blushing for love of him.

She giggled as he spun her beneath his arm and snapped her back in an artful turn. "Ah, for more innocent times, Alexi."

He almost smiled. "I hate to ruin your reminiscence, but I abandoned you that night to deal with our canine friend who almost cleaved poor Jane in two. Hardly more innocent. And not long ago."

Percy winced. "How funny the mind, and memory. I feel ages older!"

"We all are, I suppose. Responsibilities weight wisdom."

"I was so eager for answers to my strange portents."

"After a longer life than yours, I'd say to be careful what you wish."

Percy chuckled. "Yes, yes, I should've never left the convent."

Alexi clutched her passionately, hands roaming free. "I daresay you can't go back." She squealed and laughed, feeling blessedly at ease.

They danced, and Jane played. Breaking every rule the Whisper-world sought to impose upon him, Aodhan appeared at Jane's side, his love its own portal. He didn't stay long, nodding to Percy as he disappeared, but his solemn gaze was a promise that he didn't take his responsibility for granted, his raised hand a reassurance that her friend still lived.

The trio's mood grew lighter as the moon rose higher. More of The Guard appeared, and Percy was delighted as Elijah and Josephine joined them in their impromptu ball. Michael stood beaming, leaning against the balustrade and taking in his fellows, offering an occasional, beautifully delivered verse.

For a little while the dread of death lifted from the halls of Athens.

Distant music lured Rebecca from her office. A keening fiddle, she assumed it was Jane's work.

She crept up the staircase, hearing murmurs and the occasional laugh. Hanging to the shadows a few steps from the landing, she took in the scene. Elijah and Josephine were arm in arm, swaying beside Jane as she played. Michael sang a soft and tender verse. Had she never realized the lovely timbre of his voice? They used their voices all the time. But that was the Work. This was their life. Their life was capable of simple, wondrous delights, perhaps, if she ever let herself enjoy them. He turned to look upon her at the words, "I'll be your paramour . . ."

Rebecca's throat closed and she turned away from Michael to stare at the couple before her. Alexi and Percy waltzed slowly through shafts of moonlight. They clearly delighted in their languorous steps, having lost all unmarried formality and strict upright carriage to press confidently close. A moonlit Percy was nothing short of an angel, graceful and blinding white, radiating love as pure as her skin was pale. Alexi, her stalwart protector, stared as if he couldn't bear to blink and lose sight of her for a moment. Rebecca silently retreated, letting tears come as they would.

She glided to the corner of the downstairs foyer, looking out over the courtyard awash with bright silver, the starkness of the moonlight matched the dawning realization in her soul: the pain of seeing them together would never lessen. Her little group faced more danger than they'd ever known, and all Rebecca could think about was how much she wished her life were otherwise, that all their lives were otherwise, that Alexi would finally realize she was the only woman for him. She had been with him all along, loving him from the very start, twenty years prior.

Shame on such thoughts. He and Percy were so stirringly beautiful, waltzing together. Only a villain would think otherwise. Pressing her forehead to the window, she welcomed the cool glass on her skin and felt the bright moon on her face, wondering how the creases of worry and loneliness must show like scars of battle.

"I know that certain things do not unfold according to our desires."

She hadn't heard the tread behind her, but the soft voice made Rebecca whirl. Michael stood partly in shadow, his bushy grey-peppered hair smoothed from its usual chaos. His entrancing blue eyes danced with an unusually bright light, and he continued. "I know we cannot always choose whom we love. And I know how it hurts to see the one we love looking adoringly at someone else. I *know*. I've been watching you watch Alexi for years."

Rebecca registered his words, gaped, flushed and turned again to face the window, attempting to hide the transparency of her heart from Michael's unmatched scrutiny.

"I cannot replace him," Michael began again, and waited patiently for her to turn. She did, and saw the same look on his face that she was sure she gave Alexi when he wasn't looking, the look that Alexi and Percy shared. Rebecca had never thought to see someone turn such adoring warmth in her direction.

Michael continued with a bravery that surprised them both. "I do not fault you your emotions, though I must admit a certain jealousy as to their bent. I do not expect to change anything with these words. I know I am bold, and perhaps a fool. But I will remain silent no longer." His fortitude flickered, and he dropped his gaze. "I shall now return to a glass of wine. Or two. But as we're too old to play games, I felt it my duty to speak. At long last. At long, long last."

He offered her a smile that could warm the most inhuman of hearts, bowed slightly and retreated, leaving the thunderstruck Miss Thompson to stand alone once more, illuminated.

Percy lay tucked beneath the arm of her husband on the alcove cot in his office. They could've danced all evening, forgetting the press of a looming battle and the doors that threatened to burst open to begin it. She wished she could have lost herself forever in music and company, with friends, wine and promises of tomorrow, burrowing finally at the end of the night into her husband's embrace so deeply that no mythic force could ever pry her free. Instead she found herself staring at Alexi's face, stern even in the deepest of sleep, shaking with nerves.

Surely Alexi only slumbered out of supreme force of will. Perhaps it was the sherry. She couldn't have slept if she'd drank the whole bottle, though; the building was alive, as restless as she. Her blood and stomach churned. She thought

she should go study the map to see if it had changed, to see
if some miracle had made the red blazing mark fade blessedly away, but she feared the answer would be no.

She thought about the moment, so recent, when she had
stared at her wedding dress and been so purely, incredulously happy. She recalled first glimpsing Alexi at the altar,
tall and awaiting her with those glowing jet eyes, pledging
his love, the burst of heavenly light that exploded from
their vows . . . Where had that simple yet utter happiness
gone? Where was that burst of powerful light to ease the
sting of darkness?

Silently, at her sleeping husband's side, Percy wept.

While there were many rooms amid the individual buildings of Athens in which one might sleep, each felt too far
removed. Instead, The Guard tossed mattresses on the floor
in locations they deemed strategic.

Elijah stationed himself in the small foyer just outside
Alexi's second-floor office, Josephine near the ground-floor
entrance of Apollo Hall. Michael was to monitor the chapel.
Rebecca wanted to be nowhere else but in the heart of her
beloved Promethe Hall, and so she placed herself in the middle of that entrance foyer, staring up at the youthful ghost in
the chandelier who kept tinkling the crystals in agitation.
Jane was in the hall between Michael and Rebecca, very near
to a few new Whisper-world doors that visibly unnerved her.

After fixing his mattress directly in the centre of the chapel aisle, Michael made rounds. Leaving Alexi and Percy
their privacy, he first went to Josephine, who had found
paper and charcoal and was furiously sketching. He knelt
at her side, kissed her temple and placed his hand over her
heart, streaming a flood of relaxation and peace through her.
"On this night, make sure you say everything best not left
unsaid." Rising, he was surprised to see Elijah enter the
room's low-trimmed gaslight. "Lord Withersby, I was just
about to come and give you a bit of a benediction."

"One last plea for my mortal soul?" the man asked with a smirk. "No use, Vicar. But it's a night where certain things must not go without saying. And while I do love you, you weren't my intended recipient."

Michael grinned. "Why, Elijah Withersby, I *have* taught you a thing or two through the years. I'm impressed. Shocked, really."

Josephine smiled up from her pile of skirts and halo of charcoal dust, but Elijah shooed the clergyman in the direction of the headmistress's office. "Go shock us in turn and take a bit of your own damned medicine."

Michael cleared his throat and straightened his ascot. "I'll have you know, I already did."

Elijah turned to Josephine with eyes she'd never seen so wide. He knelt beside her and said, "Well, Josie, that settles it—we're getting married."

She burst into happy tears and buried her face in his arm. And that's about the time they noticed the trickle of blue fire snaking about the floor and twining around their ankles, but Alexi was nowhere to be found and they didn't remember much after that. As if sleepwalking, The Guard shifted, moving where their unconscious minds led, all of them adrift in a sound sleep.

CHAPTER SEVENTEEN

In the middle of the night, as Percy lay attempting sleep, she was roused by a warm tickle on her cheek, what felt like a feather's kiss. Her eyes opened to find that it was exactly that: a sparkling, floating feather made of blue fire hovered at eye level.

It was a familiar portent. She sat up, knowing she was

meant to follow. It had been just such a talisman that once led her from a hospital bed to save The Guard from danger. But Alexi was sleeping soundly by her side. Not in danger. Not yet. Tears prickled her eyes. She didn't want to go.

The feather became a sacred heart—a strong, pounding heart aflame with power, the same image offered her the last time she was reticent—then sparkled and returned to the shape of a feather. Wafting toward her, it kissed her cheek again and caught one of her tears on its shimmering surface. The drop trickled a moment later onto the floor: it knew her pain but remained on task.

She turned to Alexi, whose powerful presence seemed so terribly vulnerable in sleep. A luminous blue mist hung about his head. Likely this was what kept him sleeping.

"I love you so. I love you so," she repeated, bending close to kiss him but thinking better of it. He might shift and curl his arm around her, trapping her with his affection. "Not even a kiss?" she murmured to the feather.

It bobbed, impatient. Sparkling. It moved forward and pressed itself to her lips.

"Thank you, I suppose," she muttered.

Blue fire was a symbol of their Work, an element that Alexi controlled. It came from a mysterious source, the remnant of some splintered god, joined now as one with the bricks of Athens. The force had been a guide to her once before, and she felt she had no choice but to trust it again. Rising barefoot, she slipped from its hanger what she prayed would not become her burial dress—grey, as instructed—and plucked her boots from the end of the bed; she would not be seen in such unfit attire as the last time she was called into this strange service, dashing off in an infirmary gown.

Leaving the alcove, a ghost waltz in her ears, she took a last look around the office, a roomful of books, grandeur, unspoken promises and unfulfilled mysteries, where she'd so often swooned over Alexi. The ghosts, they were waiting. Still. Oddly silent. They hovered in the room, looking at her, and at the feather and the office door, alternately, as anxious as she to see what would happen next.

The feather floated toward the door. The portal wasn't here, in this office; it awaited her elsewhere.

She fumbled with the buttons of her dress. Taking one last wistful look around, she folded her cloak over her arm and slipped silently from the office. The feather bobbed away down the hall.

She was prepared to meet any number of The Guard along her path. Elijah was there on the second floor, at his station, but with Josephine tucked up in his arms, both of them sound asleep. A bit of blue-lit haze, a softly musical cloud hovered about them. Percy smiled, tearful, wishing she could remain just as peacefully by Alexi's side, but the feather bounced, moved close and retreated, telling her not to linger.

Stately yet peculiar, Athens at night was eerie. It had always been a magical place for Percy, but she now had a feeling the grounds were an entity itself. The air had that particular quality, which preceded a great storm, distantly rumbling, charged and ready for lightning to strike. The moonlight managed to cut wide and sweeping swaths in contradiction to the angles of windows.

The feather vanished out the front door of Apollo Hall. Sliding her cloak around her shoulders, she carefully opened and shut the creaking front door as she slipped out, her breath clouding before her in the chill air of the courtyard. Academy ghosts glided there, and each gave her a second glance, always at first fooled that she wasn't actually one of them. If they spoke, it was in hushed murmurs to one another. Perhaps they were scared of her. More likely they were scared for her.

The angel of the courtyard stood at upright attention as always, a thin layer of ice crusting her fountain basin. But there was something different. Percy's blood chilled as she noticed that the position of the book in those bronze fingers was now face out for all to see.

The feather halted in front of the statue, and Percy saw the book was inscribed. She almost didn't want to look, for fear her doom was writ there, but part caught her eye and she eased. The words were familiar:

In darkness, a door. In bound souls, a circle of fire. Immortal force in mortal hearts.

It was The Guard's incantation, carved into their chapel, writ in their liturgy. Percy was fortified as she turned to the feather, which patiently waited. It wanted her to see this proclamation. It wanted her to know that she and The Guard were not alone, that a powerful magic surpassing their mortal bodies saturated even the mortar here, that the very stones she stood upon could cry out in support.

The feather sparkled, enlarging with pride, then it moved on.

The main foyer of Promethe Hall was lit with its own growing light, an ethereal luminosity most often seen in the body of spirits—or in the particular glow of a graveyard—but now a veritable mist hanging in the air. The fog seemed to favour the main hall, casting a supernatural sheen on the newest doors, giving them glowing auras. The feather let her look a moment before floating down to tickle her fingers, nudging her on.

She looked around for Rebecca, who was supposed to have taken a place at the centre of the foyer. The headmistress was asleep against the side of a huge wing-back chair, her hands pressed primly in her lap. Frederic perched upon a philosopher's bust nearby, his head tucked into his breast feathers, the dozing picture of Poe's eternal companion, and Michael sat on an adjacent bench, slouched against the window frame. A book of poetry lay on his lap. Perhaps he'd been reading to the headmistress. His outstretched hand rested on the arm of her chair, reaching for her even in slumber.

The feather drew close and again kissed her tears as Percy's heart once more swelled. A mist of luminous blue hung over each of The Guard, and she hoped their forced slumber was pleasant. Jane, farther down the hall, seemed peaceful, her white cat Marlowe curled against her shoulder, a bit of blue flame around his tail.

"Will no one wait awake with me?" Percy murmured.

The feather paused at the open door of the chapel, bobbing before the eerily glowing inner white walls. Of course. But this sacred place wasn't anywhere to be alone. Not now. She agreed with Alexi, wanted to run back across Athens and wake him, force him to stand at the door and wait there for her, but she knew he'd never let her go into the undiscovered country. That was where she was being led. Alone.

"Beatrice, I need you," she begged. "Come tell me everything to expect."

The dark portal at the altar was already awaiting her descent. Percy made her inexorable approach down the aisle, scared that this solemn and private ceremony would negate her marriage so a new fate could claim her as its own. But—she recalled the glorious vision accompanying her wedding vows—nothing could undo what had been done by such great light.

She reminded herself that Marianna was somewhere across a further threshold. It was her fault that her friend was there. For these reasons, she stepped through the portal and down the narrow stairs, the stones echoing softly as she entered the sacred space.

No second portal stood open inside, but as Percy stared into the impenetrable darkness beyond the stone column perimeter, she could have sworn the shadows moved and hissed. *Snakes.* Percy's blood roared with alarm.

There was a tearing sound, and a familiar form leaped from a fresh portal. "Ah, ah, careful with that light of yours," Beatrice scolded, her grey eyes feverish. "We can't give you away now that your disguise is so perfect." The spirit wafted to Percy's side, cooling her skin with a ghostly draft. Beatrice poked at her grey skirts. "Good. You'll fit right in."

Percy noticed the reactive light burning at her bosom, and made to calm herself. The light receded. "I heard snakes, and that Gorgon—"

"None of that now, it was just your imagination. That thing is still in pieces on the Whisper side."

"And Marianna?"

"Fading but alive. She can't stay much longer in our world before losing what colour she has and becoming a shade. I'm glad you're here. I take it the feather brought you?"

"Yes. What is it, exactly?"

"Part of great Phoenix himself. Part of his spirit, giving us the signs we need when we need them. Our Lady said how much it comforted her when she despaired that she'd never escape. The fire I and Alexi wield isn't ours, exactly. It is his spirit, and he lends it to us."

Percy nodded. The portal to the Whisper-world, appropriate to its name, whispered in invitation.

"Ready?" Beatrice asked.

Percy envied the spirit's efficiency, her unwavering determination. She stepped forward, but what was she doing? Why was she always—all her life—moving blindly toward an unknown end? She hesitated at the portal, heart in her throat.

She turned to Beatrice. "No, it's too vague. I can no longer live with scraps of prophetic knowledge." She shook her head, retreating back into the heart of the chapel, her feet firm on the stone feather in the flagstones. "Not until I understand more. Not until you prepare me."

Beatrice sighed. "We've no time—"

"Expediency won't help us if I'm utterly unprepared!" Percy hissed. "Darkness. I, unlike whatever chose to take this fleshly form, don't know or remember him."

The ghost eyed her, and her visible frustration softened. "Of course not. I expect too much of you, continue to consider you her. I am sorry."

Percy opened her arms, gesturing for Beatrice to go on.

"Our Lady," Beatrice began, "once explained Darkness as a sad, lonely, misguided force, neither man nor god, neither flesh nor air. The embodiment of disappointment, anger, terror and bitterness, he presides over listless purgatory. While she pitied this creature made from the wastes of man, it was never her intent to keep him company. Her heart chose otherwise, and he had no right to steal her. The imbalance of keeping such a pure, buoyant energy in such a cesspool has done more damage to the worlds than anything."

Percy took this in. Her Catholic sensibilities sought to gain purchase, clung to the idea that there might be many different names and forms for divine spirits. "But he's not the devil, exactly . . . ?"

"I don't know your devil, child. I know that there are evil forces, and there are forces that are not evil. All forces cross into the Whisper-world. Not all of them stay."

"Where does Darkness fall on the spectrum?"

Beatrice shrugged. "He's Darkness. Unpleasant. I wouldn't trust him. Nor do I trust every mortal I meet. I don't know where evil comes from, and frankly it doesn't matter. Not right now. Histories and myths are renamed and reinvented eternally across the world. I can't speak to that. What I do *know?* This is your story. We must settle the old score between Persephone, her Phoenix and their lineage of mortal friends, and the one that upset it all in the first place."

Beatrice bowed as Percy stared at the portal again, stepped toward it. This was her story. However improbable, it was hers. She knew the ending she wanted: for her husband and friends to live in peace. She sighed, closed her eyes, loosed a prayer and lifted her foot.

The threshold was cold as she stepped across. Shivers coursed down her spine, and her eyes snapped open to see spirits careening down a number of different corridors.

Indeed, she blended right in. Here, a spirit's feet remained on the ground, and while white as shrouds, they were solid. It was good her white body wore grey, else the colours of her dress, however muted this world might make them, would make her like a painted daguerreotype, a shock against the monochrome. She was grateful for Beatrice's order.

The sights and sounds of purgatory were dulled, whispery, liquid. Soft greyscale. Nothing was sharp, everything a bit delayed, slow, eternal. And it smelled stale. Not a foul smell, like rotting flesh, but a dusty moldiness with an oddly sweet undercurrent like an exotic fruit. Percy forced herself to linger no longer identifying that scent, lest she once more retch phantom pomegranate. The air hung weighty with moisture. The floor was wet. The river. She picked up her skirts, not wanting to drag the fine fabric along the muck of mortal misery.

The temperature was a pervasive chill that threatened to worm its way into her. When you finally felt that frost on your bone, Percy mused, you perhaps were here to stay. She wondered how cold poor Marianna felt, and where she was kept in this endless grey-stone labyrinth, and if any number of hearths would ever be able to reverse the damage.

Beatrice placed a solid hand on her shoulder. "Now, I won't be with you when you meet him—"

Percy whirled. "What? You said you'd be my constant guide!"

Beatrice stepped backward. "Darling, he knows me now, and I must be ready at the doors. Remember the path. Aodhan will be with you; he knows not to leave you entirely unattended."

"Do other dangers await? What about the hellhound, guardian of these sideways shadows? If I fight it, as my light did once before, will I not give myself away?"

Beatrice nodded. "Aodhan and I have discussed this. We need to throw off your scent, to make you undetected to the beast. The abomination is still in pieces, but it might congeal at any time. Your nearly dead friend can help."

Percy groaned in sorrow. "Can I see her?"

"I'm taking you there now. You mustn't wake her, however, or she is lost. This way. Remember these turns. Think of the map. Have you studied it?"

"As best I can."

"These paths will help you when the worlds combine. Once her feet again touch the stones of your world, keeping your friend alive will be easier. However, you will need to remain focused on Darkness. He will go after Alexi and your living Guard first and foremost, I'm sure."

Percy felt inner forces growl.

"Do control yourself"—Beatrice scowled, glancing at Percy's growing luminescence—"or we'll not get far. Tell me you've got some Catholic trick that can calm you."

Percy murmured a few prayers so rote that it was like her muscles alone spoke them, the first words she'd learned in her convent youth, the first words taught for when ghosts and visions overwhelmed her young eyes. She breathed easier, and the telling light of her power eased to a faint glow.

"Indeed," Beatrice murmured, clearly lost in a memory. "The prayers of our youth, like rosaries in our blood."

This recalled Percy to her beads, and she felt Michael's calming gift against her skin. She began moving again, stepping carefully.

Movement below caught her eye. As she stepped, there were tiny green sprouts that burst around her boots. Tiny spots of colour amid the dreary grey; buds, blooms, red, pink and purple; colour—spring and life. "Oh," she breathed, quite taken aback. "I'm making flowers."

Beatrice glanced down. "Ah. It seems this place is bringing out your predecessor's most charming qualities." Her face fell. "Pity they don't last."

Percy looked. Where there had been life an instant prior,

now only dead husks remained. Grey curled petals and wilted black leaves.

"Not here," Beatrice added.

Percy frowned, terribly sad. She tugged on the laces of her skirts, and the fabric hung a bit lower. The fabric kissed the ground, now hiding all traces of beautiful life created but then choked out by shadow.

They turned a corner, and Beatrice tapped on an iron gate. Aodhan peered out, beckoning them forward under the jagged arch of a crypt. Percy's hand went to her mouth. Marianna lay atop a stone tomb beneath a pale winding sheet to hide the fading green of her dress, her once-vibrant colouring blanched, shifting to grey. Ash still trickled around her eyes and dribbled from the corners of her lips. Her hands lay outside the sheet, revealing crusted grit deep under her fingernails, faint crimson blood from gashes pooled in her cupped palms, and bruises shaded the hollows of her fair skin. The damage looked all the more severe in the half-light.

Aodhan held the long lock of hair, Jane's gift, tightly, its touchstone of power allowing a healing glow to hover over her. Ash rose to the surface below the German girl's skin and worked out her pores with a tiny hiss.

Percy felt bile churn in her stomach. "How is she?" she asked in Gaelic.

"Alive for now," he replied in kind. "She dreams heavily. Your mentalist will have to heal her. Come close, I've a gruesome task to mask your scent."

Percy nodded and approached.

Aodhan pressed his hands to Marianna's cupped palms, dipping his fingertips in her pooled blood, dragging fluid black as pitch and thick as tar onto his fingertips. "Pull back your sleeves." When Percy did so, grimacing, he rubbed blood and ash onto her wrists, up her arms.

"Forgive me," he said, and lifted his fingers behind her ears. Viscous liquid—an unwelcome, horrid perfume—was dabbed behind her lobes. Inhaling the coppery scent of her best friend's blood, Percy bit her lip to keep from crying out, hot tears cooling instantly upon her cheeks.

Aodhan wiped his sullied hands on the lace cuffs of Marianna's silk dress before ripping off the accents with a sound that grated in the close air. He handed Percy the soiled scraps. "Place these somewhere."

Percy closed her eyes and tucked the befouled fabric into her corset, forcing back seizures of revulsion. "I'm so sorry," she murmured to Marianna's sleeping form. She lowered her sleeves, grateful to keep the traces of gore hidden from her own eyes.

Aodhan was back at work, brushing what ash he could into a ceramic jar and adding that to a line of containers along a nearby crevasse. "Don't worry." He gestured to the vessels. "I sent some to the bottom of the river. While there's unnatural life to this infernal grit, she won't come back remotely whole."

"Come, Percy," Beatrice whispered, taking her by the elbow. "Aodhan will lead you but must remain nearby in shadow for the sake of safety."

"Where are you going?"

"To the portal's edge. Unless I'm there to stop him, I'm sure your stubborn husband will come in after you and we can't afford to lose his wits. Once you have that key, get out. Take it into Athens, to the upstairs seal. Those doors will unlock and await you to open them."

"Where exactly is the key?" Percy pleaded, her mind spinning.

"Oh, you'll see it. Off with you now. Darkness awaits," Beatrice said grimly. When Percy quaked she added, "Remember, unless you act otherwise, he'll think you just another spirit."

"Just another spirit," Percy repeated, trying to rally, stepping farther into the cold shadows.

* * *

Alexi didn't dream often, but when he did, his dreams fell into distinct categories.

For a man who had seen so much of it, he never dreamed of the ghastly, of poltergeists or rotting shades. Rather, he dreamed of personal matters, of his paralyzed sister, forever damned to a cripple's half-life, in awe and fear of him. He dreamed of his parents vanishing for fright, of his blood relatives hanging back as if he were contaminated by a disease that they never dared treat or bothered to comprehend.

He dreamed sometimes of passionate matters. There had been the "visitations" of his youth. Those vivid glimpses of an exquisite goddess were almost the only thing that kept his embittered young heart from rejecting destiny and prophecy entirely. She'd vanished, however, presumably when Percy was born, at which point his dream lover no longer had a face. The other details remained, however, as an encouragement to keep waiting . . .

His dreams had been particularly quiet of late, save those pertaining to waking to find Percy not at his side, but tonight that was no longer true. He stood at the end of a stone corridor, breathing in both mold and sorrow. A stark grey light shone at the opposite end, and sounds echoed against the dank stones. He recognized the impassioned female voice.

His stomach and fists clenched as he moved forward into the grey light, stepping onto a platform and looking down. Across a rushing river stood cracked columns and crumbling statues that stood silent sentry over a grand dais where an entwined couple writhed. Glimpses of ghost white flesh maddened him.

"No," he choked. It wasn't her. Everyone was pale in this purgatory.

The man was a young and beautiful specimen, angelic like a pre-Raphaelite painting, nearly as pale as the woman he clutched, his mouth lean and cruel. The auburn tresses down his back looked more like streaming blood than hair.

He was naked, his hands buried under immense folds of fabric.

The writhing woman's magnificent dress was a familiar light blue. Her face was hidden under masses of hair, but no other tresses were that pearlescent white, and he could have recognized anywhere those shocking white limbs and the sound of her gasps. And with the figure wearing Percy's wedding dress . . .

Alexi felt a bellowing cry of fury choke its way up his throat and a roaring rush of fire leaped to his hands. His enemy turned to look up at him with burning red eyes, flashing a lascivious smile. Alexi felt a searing pain and looked down to find that his hands were not wielding blue flame; instead, yellow-orange fire was burning his flesh. The scent of it nauseating, the agony grew unbearable.

He told himself that this was illusion, that he'd wake up and find Percy at his side. But his flesh melted, and all he could do was stare at his wife, writhing in the grasp of the Whisper-world, property of Darkness at last.

With a wretched scream Alexi shot to his feet, throwing aside the covers of his office cot, making his office candelabra roar with tall flame before again going dark. "Percy!" he cried, turning to her, resolving that he'd truly never again let her out of his sight. But she was gone.

The maddened cry that began as anguish and finished in fury roused the nearby Guard. Josephine's worried voice echoed in the hall outside: "Alexi?"

Head spinning, groggy, Alexi threw his robes over his disheveled shirtsleeves and flung wide the door, sending both Josephine and Elijah sprawling. He stormed out into the hall. "Where the bloody hell is she?"

He charged toward Promethe Hall, and they hurried in his wake. "Alexi, surely—"

"Were none of you standing guard?"

"Alexi, we tried, but sleep came heavy—too heavy," Josephine said. "As if forced."

"I don't remember drifting off," Elijah admitted, shaking his head as if clearing it. "Surely you were sedated, too."

Alexi burst into the foyer of Promethe Hall to find Rebecca stirring in a chair. Michael was stretching against the wall. Their colour drained upon sight of his expression.

"Why are none of you in place? Why do none of you realize she's gone?" he cried.

Jane came bounding from around the corner, Marlowe mewling at her feet. Frederic squawked from the chandelier above, the ghostly boy who floated there patting the bird's head.

"Gone?" Michael rushed forward. "I kept awake, reading to Rebecca, trying to pass the time, but sleep must have fallen so heavy—"

An explosion of helpless anger obliterated all else. Alexi raised his fist as if he was about to hit something, or someone. Michael boldly held out his hand to counter him. The jolt of peaceful energy Michael delivered jarred away the unfounded violence. "Caution, Alexi," Michael said. "The Whisper-world presses in, affecting our minds and hearts. It wants to tear us all apart. Just like this." With a hand to his shoulder, Rebecca led Michael out of striking range.

Alexi reeled back in shock, horrified by his clenched fist and instead pounding it against his own chest. "I was by her side!" he cried. "What a fool am I? How could I not have felt her go? How did I fail to feel her leave my arms?" His fury propelled him toward the chapel. "Where the hell are you?" he bellowed. The images from his dream still seared his eyes.

The chapel doors were open. So was the black rectangle that led to their private, sacred space. Alexi growled and charged ahead, The Guard barely able to keep up. Frayed blue lightning crackled all around his body.

Racing down the stairs and into the chapel, he cursed to

find the murmuring portal to the Whisper-world a wet, dark, open mouth floating at the centre of the room, the fiery map licking at his feet. A small blue mark, with another at its side, moved inexorably toward the red dot in the distance.

"Alexi, no! You mustn't—" Rebecca cried from atop the stairs.

Charging the portal, he was just about to throw himself in when a ball of blue fire leaped out and struck him square in the chest. Thrown backward onto the stone floor, he saw Beatrice step into view, her eyes holding the same fiery determination as his. Her hands awash with blue flame that she pulled from the power of the sacred space and into her hands, her stance wide, she eyed him sternly.

Her words floated from the edge of the Whisper-world just enough to whisper adamantly in Alexi's ear. "Oh, no you don't! This isn't the way to make yourself useful."

Percy squinted. There was a gusting wind in the Whisper-world, carrying dust and sour air, tangling her hair and invading her skirts. Spirits everywhere were squabbling, angry and violent. The farther in she went, the more of a mess she found. Her slow steps made oddly dull sounds. Every hair of her neck was on end.

"Remember this path," Aodhan said softly, ducking a random blow by an eternally drunken sailor, deflecting him with a glowing hand that warned he not try again. "You'll need to retrace it. We can't take the risk of you going out a wrong portal and ending up in some other level of this place. I've not dared to adventure the whole of it."

"I wouldn't want to," Percy replied, thinking of how her movement would be marked on the map. "We've been veering left."

She wondered how time passed here, and she prayed

Alexi was still sleeping soundly, unaware of her absence. But she could have sworn she heard a distant roar that sounded distinctly familiar. She winced.

"You mustn't worry about him," Aodhan said, watching.

"Are you worried for Jane?"

Aodhan's lips thinned and he nodded, realizing such words were pointless. They would fear for those they loved.

"I'm scared to see this Darkness. I'm scared of what might happen inside me that I can't predict," Percy murmured. The sound of rushing water grew louder in her ears.

"Just remember, there are things about him that will make you wish to flee. Stay strong. Play his little mind games if you can, it may endear you to him, but stay strong."

"I don't want to be endeared," Percy said through clenched teeth.

"Well, you also don't want him to drag you across the river and imprison you with the rest of our sorry lot. You're not here for him, Persephone. You are here for them. Don't you see?"

All the careening spirits of the Whisper-world fell away as the corridor opened onto a huge grey space, the ceiling endless shadow, the path ahead a wide circle around a tall stone dais lined with crumbling stone pillars choked with dead ivy. Aodhan fell back. "I won't be far."

A vast stone tower sat behind the circular dais, its dark and deteriorating bricks reaching up to oblivion, and between Percy and that sweeping stone platform lay a rushing river surrounding the steps up to the dais like a moat. Upon its turbulent surface, the river bore the occasional bone or piece of trash. And across the river, atop a wide and jagged stone throne, sat Darkness.

For the first time in the Whisper-world, Percy saw a bright colour. Shimmering scarlet fabric floated around his naked torso, a corner hovering tastefully between his legs like a silken fig leaf. He was beautiful and sculpted like a classical masterpiece. And then suddenly he shifted. He was a mere skeleton.

Percy had to bite her lip. She stared at him, his face alternately breathtaking and a skull, blinking between the two as if the pendulum of a clock, ticking away seconds, life spans and eternity. It mesmerized her for a while, ticking her life away.

"H-hello," Percy finally managed to choke out, surprised a word came at all.

Darkness looked up. It was so strange to think of this force of nature as a person, inhabiting a body, but it was, she supposed, just a form—something to relate to, something finite, a single illuminated point of a lightless infinity. She was grateful for this, and for her destined ability to tread these dread paths; otherwise she and her friends would be entirely outmatched. As it stood, things looked grim. She bit back the fear that threatened to consume her.

His red eyes burned at first, then cooled into sparkling rubies as fresh as the blush upon his youthful lips—when he had lips. He examined her a moment, swiveling his head to the side, his skull sockets taking her in from each angle.

Percy felt herself blush and inhaled, expanding her rib cage against her corset, which pressed her rosary beads into her flesh, calming her with the power Michael had placed in them.

"Why, hello indeed, miss. And welcome." He'd adopted her accent, her vernacular, perhaps to make her more comfortable. Perhaps to get information more easily out of her.

He rose and walked to the edge of the river, his scarlet drape like wings in eddying currents around his limbs, beckoned her forward with a graceful hand that faded into reaching bone. "What cares shall you add?" he asked. His voice was youthful and attempted to be seductive. "Feed this river your sorrow." His hand, his bones, gestured languidly to the flowing black water. "Tell me something of yourself. What did loved ones call you?"

"Pearl," Percy replied, feeling her rosary beads chill on her skin, which was moist with sweat, nerves and the river breeze.

"Pearl. Indeed. You appear quite the jewel. Did you live well?"

"I . . . lived life well. But I was young."

Darkness clucked a tongue that silenced as he became a skull. "Yes, yes, a tragedy. You, and your unborn child with you," he murmured, smiling. "Just the sort of sadness to make you linger here quite a while, if not forever."

Percy felt the room spin, and she clutched at her skirts. Her *child?*

"You must be quite freshly dead, for you're quite luminous in this place," Darkness continued casually.

Percy glanced down to see that, to this most shocking revelation, her body had responded with a glowing inner light. A prayer for survival and the rush of Michael's power made tangible in her rosary beads allowed her the necessary breath of calm, else she'd surely give away her powers and Darkness would trap her here, put her in that stone tower behind him. Her, and her child. She had to find the key and get out as soon as possible.

Her face gave her away. "Oh. You didn't know about the baby," Darkness breathed. "How delicious!" He clapped delighted skeletal hands that clicked, then resounded as flesh, then clicked again. "Cast it all to the river, dear, tell it your grief, add your sweet tears to the well from which we drink."

He seized a cup from his throne, bone against metal making a sickening scrape. He hopped down the many stairs to the water's edge, bent gracefully, dipped the cup in and lifted it. "Come here, pretty girl. Drink with me." He reached out his other hand as she closed the final few steps to the bank. From beneath the water's surface, myriad human bones rose and formed a makeshift bridge.

Percy fought the terror wishing to overtake her. Crossing the river struck her as something she ought to avoid, not to mention the horror of setting foot upon such a bridge. Also, she would avoid all fruit.

"But what if I want to go back?" she said breathlessly. "If I'm freshly dead, perhaps there's still a place for me on earth. For me, my child . . ."

"Your husband, too, I suppose. Or are you an unfortunate? Ruined, are you?"

Percy stiffened at the insult. "My husband, too."

Those sculpted then scapular shoulders shrugged. "Very well, you may wait. I suppose there's a chance you might still live. Sometimes there come rare miracles." He cleared the river in a sudden gazelle's leap to stand beside her, sliding a bony hand around her waist. He bent his head close. "You know I'll have you in the end. I always have everyone in the end."

Percy leaned away but did not jerk aside, suppressing her revulsion. She mustn't insult him, manipulation was key. "Not everyone stays here," she countered, her voice somehow calm. "This is not a final destination for all."

"True, but all pass through. And some I want to keep. I'm looking for a new wife, you know, as my old one's too much trouble. I'm looking for several, actually, in case I lose more of them."

"Oh?"

"Once my servant finally tells me where she's gone, I'll scatter her bits across the earth and end this silly drama for good. Drink up, pretty thing. Don't worry. This won't bind you. It'll make you wiser, sadder, perhaps, but it won't bind you."

Percy wasn't about to believe him; surely he had baited her predecessor with the same lie and pomegranate seeds. She turned horrified eyes into the golden cup, hoping to mask her shaking hands. Bringing it to her lips, she heard the liquid hiss within, murmur, beg, cry.

Darkness walked a step ahead of her to inspect something at the water's edge. Percy took the opportunity to set the cup upon a stone post, and moved to fall in again at his side. It was an upraised hand begging for help that had caught his eye—or eye socket. He stepped upon the risen palm and pushed it back below the surface.

Percy's heart thundered anew. "But, how is it you don't know where she is? Your wife, I mean. I'd have thought you omnipotent."

His pretty lips frowned before he had no expression but a row of teeth. "No, no, I leave omnipotence for another being who is strangely absent. You and I, my sweet, are pawns. I may be a knight or a castle to your pawn, but we remain pieces in some elaborate game whose point none of us knows."

"Then, why find her?"

"Who, my wife? Because she's mine!"

In many ways, she sensed, Darkness was an angry child. Percy wondered if she could use that against him. "Oh, I see. Of course. One must of course fight for what is theirs." He appeared placated. He grinned, and his row of teeth gnashed in delight, and unable to help herself Percy added, "Unless it never was theirs to begin with."

Darkness glowered. His bones rattled. And that's when she saw it: the key she sought hung upon his sternum, when he was bone. It was encased in flesh when he was solid. If she could grab hold when he was bone, if she could grab and run . . . It was enough to make her nauseated with panic.

As if by the grace of a higher power, her mind's eye saw a vision: The key was in her hand. She was running toward Alexi, her bright light and fierce protector. If she pretended this were a dream, another of her visions, would it help?

Her eyes blinked back to the present moment and gazed upon empty eye sockets. Her heart surged with resolve. Darkness's head was cocked at a disturbing angle and he asked, "Do you toy with me, girl?"

Percy smiled demurely. "I wouldn't dream of it. Are you toying with me?"

"I toy with everyone."

Percy nodded. "Of course. Because you're very *potent*." Giving a coy smile, though fighting an inward shudder, she glanced at the tower behind his throne. "Why do you keep your seat of power here? It's hardly decorated, all this stone. I'd have thought you'd want something more lavish." She was risking much, pressing for information about that roomful of friendly blue fire, but she had to try. Her vision had just shown her victorious.

His cruel, beautiful mouth twisted. "Curious, aren't you?"

"I was born so. I suppose I died so."

"Well, then." Darkness held out a skeletal arm. "Shall I show you?"

Percy choked back disgust, smiled and took his flesh then bone arm.

Once Alexi had gotten again to his feet, he glared at Beatrice, who held another ball of flame in her hand, her expression intent. She pointed at the floor. Alexi followed her gaze. His eyes widened, and he watched two particular dots. He had to force himself not to cry out as the red flame sidled closer to the blue.

There was a sparkling line to the side of their demarked forms. A door. One of the new doors. Beatrice gestured and pointed below.

"I might see in, and watch for her safety?" he asked.

She gestured to the perimeters of the portal in which she stood, held out her hand and made a dramatic motion that seemed to speak to his head exploding.

"Yes, yes, I'll not go in."

She widened her eyes and held up her hand, emphatic.

"Yes, I promise. But thank you for showing me the way." Glancing at the map, he counted the corridors between and deduced where he should head. "Looks like the second floor. I'll not leave you to fend for yourself, Percy, beloved fool. I will do what I can."

He tore up the stairs and out toward Promethe Hall's grand staircase.

Darkness strolled with her, but Percy was clear to remember their path. She was encouraged by the fact that Aodhan stayed in view, far behind, visible to her only at the far corners of her eyes, stepping in and out of shadow.

When her guide's feet were skeletal, they echoed oddly against the stone. There was subtle movement around his heel and toe bones. Percy didn't stare. She truly didn't want to know what sprang from Darkness's step. She assumed it wasn't spring foliage.

It wasn't difficult for her to remember their route; they essentially moved in a wide circle. Their path curved around the dais, around the vast brick tower. The moatlike river rushed to their right and onward, its tributary path unknown, perhaps farther underground, and upon closer inspection Percy noticed that the items floating on its surface were not ordinary detritus; the occasional bone or odd remembrance, a flower, locket, portrait or letter were this waterway's flotsam and jetsam.

Darkness watched her watching the items. "All the little things people think matter. None of it matters here. Trash, all of it. Human life."

"Do you hate humans?" she couldn't help but ask.

"They're the reason I'm here. Their sorrow made me at the dawn of time, their habitual discontent keeps me here, empowers me in the grey space of the freshly dead and those who live as if they were dead—and the dead who wish they lived." He giggled at his own awkward poetry. "Some dead enter here and refuse to leave. But eventually even they, who distrust balm of eternal peace, give up their ghosts and fall into the river, their bones making it more and more shallow as they pile up, year after year."

Percy shuddered.

"I frighten you," Darkness murmured.

"No, it's interesting," Percy argued.

"It's all right. I frighten people." He leaned close. She could hear his bony jaw snap against her ear. "I like it."

Percy tried not to shrink away but couldn't help it, and the subsequent chuckle was unspeakably unpleasant.

"You'll grow accustomed to it. Even my enemies are now inured to life in the Whisper-world."

"Enemies?" Percy thrilled at the path of the conversation. "You've enemies?"

Darkness gnashed his teeth. "It started with my bride—the force I took rightfully for my own. She was made of feminine joy, loyalty and youth. She was a creature of light. We were meant to be. We make the necessary pair, she, the light to my shadow!" he crowed. But then his beautiful face was pained, and his skull, too, grimaced. "She already had a lover, stupid girl, treating him like some angel, some paragon. I burned him to a crisp. But he lived on in human pawns, and her damnable heart would never surrender."

Percy didn't bother to hide her disturbed expression, for Darkness seemed to enjoy it. "What happened?"

"Muses followed what was left of him, seeing themselves as his votaries. They jumped into human flesh to form a rather troublesome cult."

"What do they do?"

"My sustenance is the sorrow and misery gathered unto me by restless minions I send to mortal earth. But the blasted Guard sends them back empty, starving me, while they live on! But in the end, all human flesh must come through here. Even they." He grinned. "They arrive in sets of six. Horrified to see me, of course."

Percy gulped. "And then?"

"I'm supposed to let any who wish move on to Peace." He waved his hand in disgust. "Not them. I've gathered them up, found them out, given them no peace. I've now collected them all into my woe." He giggled, and his jaw chattered.

They were now on the opposite side of the dais, where the rounded stone wall of the tower continued seamlessly. There was a lock, dangling down from a thick and rusty chain from the endless shadow above. Out of the corner of Percy's eye, she saw Aodhan gesture for her to ply him further.

"Where are they? Your enemies?"

Darkness scowled. His skeletal jaw clenched. "Why?"

Percy affected embarrassment. "Forgive me. All of this is so fascinating."

"They're not more interesting than me. They're not more important than *me*," Darkness growled. "She always thought that. Always coddling and entertaining them, praising them for their work against me. But I found them, tore down their precious sanctuary, ruined their haven and locked them all up! I enjoy punishing her and her hapless servants. They've become hollow, pitiful little wraiths, weak and useless. And she's gone, so they've no one now to help! They'll turn to me, they will, once they see she's abandoned them."

Percy leaned in. "I believe you. I believe in your power."

"Do you?"

"Show me."

Darkness looked wary. "Show you what?"

"I want to see what you've done to them," she said, achingly. "I'm so curious, I just might ask to stay . . ." She waited until his scapula was a shoulder and dragged a finger down his arm.

He shuddered with an uncomfortably desirous sound and grinned at her, his ruby eyes sparkling. Growling hungrily, he dragged a skeletal finger down her cheek, returning the favour. Percy forced her shudder to appear one of desire.

Darkness plucked the key from his sternum and shoved it

into the hanging lock. There was a rumbling and grating sound. "You'll see, Pearl, how pathetic they are—and how powerful, I. You'll. Want. To. Stay."

Percy's fingers itched to grab the key, but the moment had to be right. She inched surreptitiously closer to the lock.

Across the river, large bricks fell away to reveal a vast metal door, like the kind she imagined on ancient castles. The door swung open, and a bright but flickering light came from within: hundreds—thousands!—of ghosts, from every race and era of humankind. A few of them blinked, coming forward toward the opening, confused by the prospect of freedom from their cell. They were hollow forms, luminous only in flickering heartbeats. Separately their fires were all but burned out, but together they glowed. All The Guard that ever were.

Darkness made a sweeping gesture, and the river overflowed its banks toward the prisoners, lapping at the toes of those who dared come forward. The water hissed and nipped at them with predatory teeth. The Guard spirits whimpered like wounded animals, crying inhuman sounds and shuddering, staring at the water in horror, retreating as if scalded. Darkness giggled again.

Percy's heart broke for these poor mortal souls dragged innocently into a service they never wholly understood and left to rot, left off worse than dead, simply for trying to keep Darkness from harvesting his requisite horror. Her pity turned to anger. Her bosom burned with light, and several things converged at once.

A bent-shouldered man, once dark-skinned and handsome, stepped up onto a fallen rock and away from the oncoming tide of water. Staring at Percy, his dark eyes wide, he straightened, his tunic hanging less like rags and more like a priest's robe, and two words flew from his lips in what Percy recognized as Arabic: "Our Lady!"

The horde turned to stare across the water at Darkness,

then at Percy. The assemblage of spirits fell reverently to their knees.

Darkness narrowed his eyes at her. His skull's eye sockets burned even blacker.

"She's here!" crowed a horrifically familiar voice. Percy whirled to behold an ash body with a head full of snakes, dragging and scraping into the chamber, a mere torso scrabbling toward them: Lucille Linden. Still the Gorgon lived, having half assembled while Beatrice and Aodhan were otherwise occupied. She squealed, her throat gurgling molten ash and her broken serpents rattling against the stones. "Right before your face, you damn fool! Mortal! Dash her brains against the rocks!"

Percy could feel her own light burning brighter, helplessly reactive.

Just as Darkness opened his mouth in rage, there was another sound—a roaring and tearing—and a portal opened high and distant in the air above and behind them. Percy looked up to see Alexi's silhouette in it, an upper Athens foyer and The Guard behind him, chanting strengths and encouragement and she realized her world was not now as far away as she once imagined.

Darkness whirled. "You? You *live*. And. You. Dare." His fury choked him as he shot a bony hand straight for her throat, toward her gathering light.

Percy dodged his initial clawing thrust but was unable to avoid the hard upswing of his fleshy fist, mashing her lip against her teeth, strands of her hair yanked away in bony fingertips. She reeled back in pain as red blood spurted onto her grey dress. Putting her hand to her lip, through the pain she nonetheless noticed how Darkness retracted his bones from her light.

"Damn you!" bellowed Alexi from above, from behind the portal. His booming voice carried, and it stunned all inhabitants of the Whisper-world over whom it washed. Out of the wave of fire bursting from him, a great and furious bird descended, made of roaring blue light. Its great wings and fearsome claws tore and beat against the alternately beautiful and skeletal body of its enemy. "She's not yours for the taking! She never has been!" the phoenix roared, Alexi's words reverberating from its mouth.

Darkness batted at its fiery blue wings and talons in rage and irritation, if not in defeat. Lucille's remains were kept at bay by other tendrils of blue fire, her writhing coils of hair hissing and snapping. In the distance there came barking, growing louder. Percy didn't want to wait for a third monster to face, so she seized her opportunity, snatched the key from the lock and ran.

The Guard poured from their prison, clustered in sixes as they sought to cross the river, puzzled as to how to ford the dangerous waters. These legions filled the vast grey landscape with increasing hope, freshening the mildewed air, and their arms stretched out toward where Alexi stood as an angelic sentinel, a conduit for a glorious rain of cerulean flame. The leaders drank in this energy, invigorated, he their direct source to the fire of the Grand Work making them powerful once more, and with them, the other Guard. Percy felt as if she were witnessing a masterwork painting come to life, a heavenly host arming itself at the gates of hell.

It was a terrible strain on Alexi's powerful but mortal body to be the sole bearer of such power and send it forth to others. Percy's heart seized with love and concern. She had to get out and pull him away.

"Angels have no sway here!" Darkness hissed. He cast aside Phoenix's blue fire as if it were a heaping cloak, his own red shroud flaring up around him like armour. The ticktock of his skeleton to flesh now lingered more moments in bone. He growled, turning to Percy with his eyes bloody fire. The river hissed and gurgled, and a surging wave rose that would surely rush to drag her under.

Something began in Percy's mind as soft music, and a

voice not entirely her own flew from her lips—a voice that had once proclaimed great things, banished Gorgons and saved The Guard's lives. "Perhaps not angels, but *I* once did," an elder power murmured.

An arc of light burst from Percy, landing a vicious slap upon Darkness's skull. Particles of bone flaked from his cheek. The light then spread over the river, and the black water became frosted glass, which The Guard instantly poured across, swarming the opposite bank. Countless leader spirits added their power to the firebird form still harassing Darkness. Their shackles of firelight could not hold him in this realm, but they slowed him.

Darkness reeled, swatting at the blue fire all around. He stared down his empty breast, then at the empty lock, where the key had been. Flickering into the shape of a man, he gave a pathetic wail in Percy's retreating direction: "You'd tear my heart again?"

Percy turned, a comfortable distance now between them but continued moving—she didn't trust the very shadows not to seize her. "This body doesn't know you," she cried, her voice again her own. "And it seems you never had a heart to lose."

"You. Will. All. Pay." The voice of Darkness was amplified over the water, echoing, and he broke all remaining tendrils of flame with a blow. He flung an arm forward and the river gushed up, a wave of black water and morphing stone that that crested toward her.

"Oh, I'm quite sure," Percy muttered. Standing firm, she gripped his key so tightly she thought its grooves might make her hand bleed.

There came a raucous yell, a countering battle cry, and Darkness's threat was defied. A wave of ghostly forms, brightening into blinding strength and purpose, made a wall before her, taking the brunt of the river's attack. This host of firelit Guard leaders held the line against the wave of stone, water, sentimental detritus and bones; then they all turned to her and in many different tongues said, "Run."

Percy picked up her skirts and fled down the corridor through which she had come. Flowers continuously bloomed, then died at her feet. But escape was not complete. Lucille's broken, burned body awaited her at the final intersection, shrieking and crawling and flinging herself forward, her snakes at full charge, molten dust spraying everywhere.

"Do you not learn?" Percy muttered as a crumbling hand grazed her bustle, snatching at the fabric. She seized her sturdy, doubled skirts and whipped them to the side in a blow, and Lucille's ashen head full of snakes once again rolled off her body and down the corridor with renewed screaming. "Again, I prove the greater power," she stated, allowing herself a moment of pride.

But things weren't so simple. A molten snake head had affixed itself to her hem and was starting to set her garment afire.

"At your side, my lady." Aodhan appeared, his words a cool draft in her ear, his healing energy steadying her and urging her back toward the portal through which she'd come. He kicked the snake head from her skirt and crushed it under his boot. It gave a sickening hiss.

Percy ran as hard and fast as she could, a tidal wave of restless spirits and rage swelling up behind her. Aodhan and The Guard leaders stood between her and the gathering storm, but wind, dust and bone bit at her flesh and chipped away at Aodhan's grey form.

"Place the key on Athens's soil, my lady, and we may finally have a chance," he called out through the tempest.

"And Marianna?"

"The worlds will merge and you can bring her safely home. But first you have to get back yourself! Keep running. I'll take your friend!"

The light ahead was brightening. She could glimpse forms

through the portal. Who was that just on the other side? Alexi! Her hand shielded her eyes, his face all she wished to see. He had returned from his portal above, was now standing guard here, fierce and furious.

"My love!" Percy cried.

Relief flooded his features as he first caught sight of her deep in the corridor, but his eyes widened at the chaos behind her. She was sure he cried her name, but the sound was drowned by Darkness's tumult.

A blaze of blue fire reached out and surrounded her, more powerful magic than she'd ever felt. This protective barrier lifted her off her feet and drew her through the portal, her own radiant white light mixing with Alexi's blue sorcery. She floated, a blindingly illuminated bundle, directly down into his waiting arms. He whisked her behind him as the Whisper-world portal slammed shut, the wave of Darkness's horror crashing impotently on the other side.

London's Guard encircled the couple, energy pouring forth, their arms outstretched and the wind of their magic whipping their clothes. They were ready for a fight. Jane touched her hand to Percy's split lip, healing it in the instant. Thunder roared across the sky. Percy wasn't sure from which world the sound originated.

Alexi whirled upon her, seizing her by the shoulders, desperate to keep hold of her. "Persephone, if you ever go in there again, I swear to you—"

"No, no, I've no need to go in there again," Percy said, laughing, almost hysterical. Was this relief, or terror? "It's coming to us. It's all coming here."

CHAPTER EIGHTEEN

Alexi shooed The Guard out of the chapel before whirling on Percy. "What did he do to you?" he barked, raking hands through his hair, feeling his own choking desperation.

"You saw. Other than repulse and hit me, nothing."

"You were at his side—"

"Alexi, my dear husband, there'll be plenty of time for a chat about all this, but now you must protect me. My dear, you'll not only be protecting me, but the child I carry. Our child."

His eyes widened. His brow furrowed. "Our child?"

"Yes, love. It would seem the Whisper-world can reveal some of life's mysteries."

Stunned, Alexi clasped his arms tightly around Percy, but not before he angled his face down to stare her straight in the eye. "And so you not only endangered yourself, but our child as well?"

Percy's lips thinned. "I see the professor desires only to scold his student." She tried to pull away, to stare him down with balled fists, but he wouldn't let her go. Her ire forced her onward. "Whether you believe me or not, this was the only way. I knew it. You might praise me for my bravery." She wriggled an arm free to hold up the key before his face. "Thank you for that Phoenix fire. It gave me the moment I needed, and you empowered The Guard. Our troops, indeed! Well done. But now, if you'll excuse me, we've a war to commence."

Alexi's jaw twitched as he loosened his grip, but he sought

her hands and clutched them in his. He was reeling. Their *child?* "I am so proud of you, Percy. Of your extraordinary bravery. And you've no idea my relief, but I—"

"Hate it when I undertake risk without you. Yes, I'm *well* aware. Believe me, I certainly would have chosen to have my powerful protector by my side, but you need your wits, love, and those I couldn't guarantee past that threshold."

"I dreamed he was . . . ravaging you."

Percy made a face. "How utterly disgusting. Thank heavens it didn't happen." She turned away, prepared to run up the stairs.

"How can you be so nonchalant?" Alexi cried, whirling her back to face him.

Percy's eyes flashed. "If I were to ruminate upon all that's just happened—indeed, upon what's about to happen—I would fall to pieces. Timidity was for my youth, Alexi. I'm a woman now. You helped make me so; now I beg you to be the leader I require." She placed her hand on her abdomen. "That *we* require."

Alexi's veil of madness parted. What Michael had said was true: this volatility was a disease of the merging worlds, was the master of the Whisper-world's dark ploy to sow the seeds of division. It was particularly potent poison against remnants of the Phoenix, but Alexi refused to further succumb.

He nodded, trying to shake the nearly druglike effect of fear from his body. "Of course, darling. The press of the worlds affects me . . ." He broke off, realizing apologies weren't enough. Not to her.

She seemed to harbour no ill will. Instead, she took his hand and led him up the stairs. "I should have realized. Speak to me, love, and I'll separate myth from reality. You must trust me. I'd die for you, you realize. Love has given me strength my meek nature never imagined. I went in so that we might yet be free . . ."

Alexi's face contorted. "And I, an ungrateful, jealous wretch—"

"Your fire roused and saved me. We desperately needed your intervention. But let this rage, anger, fear and jealousy now be fuel for a more productive fire. I need you to tell me where there's another lock." She dangled the key once more before him. "This was used to lock up The Guards, but now it will give them freedom from Darkness at last. Fitting."

"Will they fight for us?"

Percy stared at him as if he were daft. "Did you see what was happening in there? None of us has a choice but to fight, with no weapons but our thirst for this madness to end. That, I'm sure, is ammunition they've stored up in spades."

Their friends awaited them anxiously at the centre of Promethe Hall. All of Athens was glowing a hazy sapphire colour, the air becoming a readier medium to conduct their gifts.

"The school seal," Alexi declared, his eyes wide. "My friends, our brave Percy has the second key, direct from the heart of Darkness. Come." He gestured for them to follow him up the stairs to the stately, open foyer where he and Percy had twice now shared impossibly beautiful waltzes.

"Alexi, remember the vision we saw here?" Rebecca said. "Your glorious wings?"

He nodded, bending over the seal so seemingly tied to their fate. His fingers searched out a keyhole, and there it was, in the motto, the dot over the *i* of the word "Light." Blue fire crackled around the mosaic edges.

Jamming the key into the lock caused a roar exponentially greater than the one from revealing the map below. It was as if a thousand stones rolled away, rumbling thunderously inside the walls of Athens, azure fire streaking across every tile, floorboard and sizzling in the mortar. The noise became deafening, light pouring from underneath each of the new doorways, all of which begged to open, convulsing against their hinges.

"Open the doors!" Alexi cried.

Michael and Rebecca scurried toward the first floor. As the doors shook yet harder, Elijah cried, "Josie, Jane, come— we've got to attend to Apollo Hall."

Jane's cat was nervously pacing, hackles up, a low whine in his throat, and Frederic hopped up and down on a nearby bench. The Irishwoman called out, "Marlowe, to the head-mistress's apartments! Frederic, too, take shelter!" The white cat did not need to be told twice, and the black bird followed.

"Stay close to at least one other," Alexi called to his friends. "But open them quickly." He grabbed Percy by the hand to dart with her into the corridor off the foyer.

"Beware the water!" Percy added in a shout, crossing herself as her husband gripped the first doorknob to another world.

He flung open the door, and the two of them stumbled back against the wall, blinded. "The Power and the Light!" Alexi cried.

Percy heard an earthshaking reply in a hundred tongues, "THE POWER AND THE LIGHT!"

A hundred figures in bright blue light poured over them in a welcome deluge. These Guard spirits flew in, one after another through the doorway, with hardly time to notice Percy and Alexi. The moment they crossed unto Athens and realized they could float, they careened up and away from the rushing tides of dark water that had threatened them on the Whisper side. The moisture leached toward Percy on the corridor floor, but as she backed away from it she noticed that here it seemed a harmless pool. She hoped it would stay that way.

Running to fling open the next newly created door, Percy watched the entering Guards. Once they were within Athens's walls, the newcomers could sustain their powers; some hands glowed with blue flame or soft white light; some of the visitors were reciting incantations. Some held up glyphs or runes on their palms, clothing, lockets or shields. Some were touching each other's hearts and laughing. But all of these dear spirits of light and song would be needed, Percy knew, for the rest came pouring through the doors, too: the uninvited threat.

All jumbled among the beautiful goodness of The Guard of many eras, tumbling into Athens rather than haplessly out into the world, there were just as many dark and dangerous spirits. Rotting bodies and putrefying souls, ragged clothes and the stench of misery, these were souls loath to leave earth and unsuited for heaven. These spirits were the allies of Darkness, his army he'd assembled, and they shrieked through the halls of Athens, breaking glass and upending bricks. These were the foes of the released Guard. But Beatrice had been an able general, choosing their battleground wisely. Back at work again after wasting away behind Whisper-world walls, the forces of Light immediately joined battle.

Alexi led Percy along, his precise, scientific mind innately knowing the natural location of each iteration of seven. He called their destinations out as they hurtled forward, flinging doors open one after another, with yet more Guard and the ungodly pouring through. Alexi had the good sense to shut the doors behind them when their allies were through, minimizing the standing river-water flood and limiting the number of their foes as much as possible.

Alexi's own Guard converged in the courtyard. Snow had begun to fall in strange patterns, either hanging suspended in the air or drifting at different speeds, as the air was awash with forces that muddied mortal minds. The voices had Percy's ears splitting. She envied the fact that the rest of her comrades saw this burgeoning and haphazard battlefield in utter silence.

"All are open?" Alexi asked. Everyone nodded, breathless.

"Isn't it magnificent?" Jane cried, whirling around to behold the tumult. "Look at all of them. And here we thought we'd be alone!"

Percy had a hard time rejoicing. Where was Darkness? What rooms and vaults and hideous secrets were yet to open?

The ground beneath them gurgled and shook. The angel fountain, graceful throughout all elements, seemed suddenly frail. Her basin belched, black muck oozing from her spouts, and the drain at the centre of the courtyard spewed foul water, its metal grate flying from its moorings. The stones were soon flooded with death water.

The Guard sought higher ground, knowing they didn't want to test the perilous substance as bones began vomiting from the drain. Percy gave a small cry as foul muck landed on the fold of her skirt and hung there. She shook it off, following the others up an exterior staircase to the wide balcony of Promethe Hall. It looked out over the courtyard, one door attached to the ballroom, the other the infirmary. Gazing across the clerestory windows down into the alley outside the school grounds, she noticed the drains there too regurgitated bone and dark water.

Alexi set his jaw. "I'd held hope that Athens would take the whole brunt, but perhaps a bit of collateral damage was inevitable," he murmured, holding her tightly to his side.

They gazed down over the muddied courtyard, where several individual combats had begun. From an Asian Guard at one end, Percy heard haiku directed toward a disembraiteled spirit who kept throwing his intestines everywhere. She was thankful the absurd scene was in greyscale; otherwise she'd have retched. Another set of Guard, these six in thick robes and dulcet Russian tones, were trying to return the bones back to the depths from whence they came, though they made sure they themselves floated well above.

Percy gasped, hearing a dread sound. "Barking," she whispered. "That barking. It's back, the hell—"

As she spoke, an ink black cloud snarled upward from the basin beneath the angel, a hundred bones gnashed in its hundred salivating jaws. The hellhound responsible for the Ripper murders had returned at last, its teeth bared as it again smelled its familiar Guard prey. It showed one oozing dog's head, then three, then thirty; its chimerical form gained mass and ground, leaping up a full story to snap in Percy's face.

Alexi smacked its thirty snouts with blue fire. The Guard encircled Percy and began a cantus, the hymn blending in with those of the other Guards. All were of a relative pitch and in the common Guard language, developed for this sacred purpose, and they combined now to great effect. The Russian and Asian troupes had turned their fiery songs upon the rear of the hound, which lashed out and tore edges of their cloaks and tunics, but yelped and plummeted back down onto the angel fountain to rock her on her basin.

Surprisingly, the angel retaliated. Sapphire lightning crackled around her graceful bronze body. Her wings flapped and her eyes blazed. The hound burst into a thousand acrid wisps of smoke. The other Guards seemed just as amazed by this as London's, and the Chinese and Russian Guards stared up at Percy. She thanked them for their service in their native tongues, and they smiled and rushed to join her up on the terrace, but another set of irreconcilable souls came bounding out into the courtyard. Seeing them, Alexi gestured that The Guards might wish to remain as courtyard sentinels.

Luminous tendrils of flame poured from the angel's spouts, a life-giving fount of blessing from which The Guard alone could draw. "All of Athens comes to life to fight," Josephine breathed excitedly. "Reflecting and magnifying our powers!"

"So long as her foundations don't get turned against us," Rebecca cautioned. She gestured to the south side of the

courtyard and the entrance to the ladies' dormitory. Dead
ivy had begun to wind its way up the stairs. In its wake, the
warm red sandstone of Athens's exterior bricks grew sooty,
black water lapping at the base of the portico.

She glanced into the ballroom behind her and growled.
Its glittering grandeur was kept reverently closed save for
one special gala night, but now all manner of pathetic creatures were hanging from chandeliers, overturning the furniture and attempting lewd displays upon the busts of famous
philosophers that lined the golden-trimmed hall.

"Damn all of you. This is our ballroom, not a brothel!"
Her tone was the one reserved for students found breaking
the rules of no contact, a tone that could make a mother
superior feel chastened. Flinging open the French doors, she
charged onto the polished wooden floor with a stern recitation of common propriety taken from a contemporary ladies' handbook, making the offending phantasms screw up
their faces in dismay.

Another Guard appeared in the ballroom, an elegant Af-
rican troupe. This group was leveling impressive proverbs
to stun the wits of the rabble, to confuse them away from
destruction. Their mentalist and healer were attempting to
keep several poltergeists from overturning fine divans.
They had been successful before, but here they found the
chandelier crystals raining down through their bodies.

Their leader was an incredible woman with hair covered
in a light veil but trailing long locks. Her eyes held the fire,
not her hands; and without a sound between them, only a
nod of proud recognition, she and Alexi began weaving and
dodging in an intricate dance of shockingly efficient casting.
Their magic bound each and every offender to his spot, wailing and gnashing their teeth. One by one the offending spirits began to fade away for good, their bodies flickering or
peeling away into wisps of smoke, or popping out with a
small snap and a burst of light. It was either peace or noth-

ingness for them, Percy assumed, for the power of Athens was creating Judgment Day for them, and there were no second chances. The spirits seemed to realize it, too, for they offered Percy their last words, few of which were pleasant.

Seeing that the room was sufficiently secured, Alexi and the other leader stared at each other and shared a smile. Then the woman turned to Percy.

"Thank you," Percy said in Swahili.

The leader's smile grew. "Our pleasure," she replied. Then she gestured for her Guard to move on. They darted from the room, vanishing though the walls and into the hall beyond, where only Percy could hear the sounds of their distant skirmish.

Alexi nodded to his friends. They nodded back; then the group went to open the ballroom's hefty doors. Beyond, their beautiful Athens was looking monochromatic. Dust, ash and grime coated once-polished surfaces. The Romanesque arches were graying, and the stones were rougher hewn.

Rebecca patted the walls. "Come now, dear bricks. Don't fail us now." Light sparked in the mortar, fighting the contagion.

As she passed beneath the arched ballroom doorway, Percy recalled having been once too terrified to pass through. That breathlessly exciting night of the academy ball, it had been the confidence given her by her best friend—

"Marianna!" she cried. Whirling to the others, who were rushing toward the main foyer, she called, "I don't know where Marianna is. Aodhan said he would bring her, but I haven't seen him since the Whisper-world."

"We can't have you go looking for her," Alexi replied.

Rebecca was kinder. Seeing that Percy was beginning to panic, she clamped a firm hand on the girl's shoulder, trying to snap her into focus. "Do you have any idea where they kept her? Can we access that place from Athens?"

"She was in a room off the threshold where I entered, and I entered from the sacred space below. The chapel. Is there a new door in the chapel?"

"I'll look," Rebecca stated. "We shouldn't all go, and you are most important."

Suddenly, a noise. While Percy heard it most clearly, they all felt it: the dog, of course, had regrouped. Percy opened her mouth, but it was Jane's fearful exclamation. "Alexi!"

"You'll need to go attend that." Rebecca shooed her compatriots toward the growing howls. "Let me seek out the girl."

"We shouldn't split," Alexi argued.

"Marianna Farelei is a student of Athens Academy. Our students are the only children I will ever have. Now, I am going to bring her home, and I'll not hear another word about it." So saying, Rebecca stormed off down the hallway. Michael stared at his companions for a moment before turning to dart after her.

Alexi set his jaw. "Well, friends . . ."

Percy clenched her fists, resolute. "I rebuked that dreadful canine once before. I'll do it again."

All of Athens darkened but for the light of their precious blue fire as they ran toward the chilling noises. The sound rose to an unbearable crescendo. Just inside the Athens auditorium, they stopped. The auditorium was twice its former size, its ceiling having been replaced by a dark and stormy sky. There were no seats, but instead the vast room sloped sharply down in narrow stone steps, like an ancient amphitheatre. Everything was Whisper-world grey.

The steps led to a black stone platform that crawled with movement. No, this wasn't a platform; it was water black and endless, the river of misery. Behind it fluttered a thick bloodred curtain.

Alexi muttered, "All the underworld's a stage . . ." Percy loosed a nervous snicker.

The barking peaked and then went silent, but this was its source. The London Guard pressed into the top tiers of the amphitheatre, and other Guards began to follow suit.

The silence did not bode well. Percy couldn't swallow for dread. Then, all of a sudden, the curtain was ripped asunder and the dispersed hellhounds came snapping forward, their heads numbering in the hundreds, leashes around their necks pulling something dreadful.

With a bloodcurdling scream, a pile of bones atop crimson fabric drenched in gore was pulled into view. The bones began to assemble in the air as the hounds snarled and drooled; toes built into feet, bones scrabbling upward to form legs and torso, arms and head. And then the blazing red eyes. Darkness's skull head shrieked, his red robes snapping up around him like enormous wings, liquid flying out from the unfurling mass to spatter them all. "I will drag EVERY. LAST. ONE of you back to the depths!"

The assembled Guards looked down at their clothing, now flecked with red blood.

"Listen," Alexi cried in their communal tongue. Surely the first of their group had known this day would come, that their ageless forces would need common words. He wondered where in this assembly those souls were, or if they'd somehow managed sweet respite in some Beyond. He wished to thank them, and prayed they were correct in their calculations, if this moment had been their intent. "Our Sacred Lady, now mortal, remains in our ranks! We are unbeatable in concert! *Cantus!*"

A thousand voices rose, sending both Percy and Darkness reeling. A gust of wind was created, an earsplitting force. In return, the infernal dogs howled and lunged, causing shrieks from the front battalions of Guard as pieces of their grey ghost flesh were snagged in hellish teeth.

Darkness did not tick seconds in beauty anymore; in battle he was only bone. He lifted a forearm. The stones below him shuddered, and a wave of dark water surged forward, a curling tide of hungry horror. Many Guard members screamed, some dragged suddenly forward as if the water had hands, a violent undertow yanking them back across the river, back to their prison. The sight broke Percy's heart.

Alexi's eyes had hardened, desire for vengeance pouring from his person in thunderous ferocity. In response, the mist rising from the black death water and the clouds blanketing an unseen sky attacked his mind; these tried to dissolve his will and the wills of the assembled host. The air had been souring for hours. The current atmosphere was one of pain and failure. The ceiling of hazy clouds roiled, descended, swept destructive breezes against cheeks and hands, between Guard members, whispering to each of their greatest fears, sapping strength and confidence. This wind was what kept spirits restless. They could all become so. It would be easier to give up . . . The Guards' hope plummeted.

"Hearts, we need you!" Alexi cried in The Guard tongue, giving the command for his absent Michael.

Hundreds of upraised fingers moved in fluid choreography. A warm gust of fresh air blew through the battlefield. The pitch of the clouds lightened. The grey walls flickered with shocks of blue lightning, and the cresting water receded. The Guard breathed deep; there were smiles and surges of hope, the occasional triumphant laugh.

"It's working," Percy whispered.

"Leaders, a dam against the tide!" Alexi called, and the other leaders cast forward a brilliant wall of azure fire, corralling the dark river with a barrier it could not surmount.

Percy noticed that from Alexi the Phoenix fire trailed off and away in sparkling rivulets, eddying toward the hearts and hands of the other leaders, he the great mouth of a glorious river. Jane's healing light was a thin and gauzy line from her own body, creating an intricately woven line like a luminous Celtic knot to link her fellow healers, and she imagined the other powers were the same. While Athens's bricks held and sustained Guard power, so did the living Guard remain the conduit. She prayed their strength would last beyond mortal limits.

A few more scattered Guards joined ranks, but Darkness's cry was a summons for his minions. The crimson robes flying around his skeleton became a flag, his bones the saber-rattling call for his spectres to fight with everything they had, to show no mercy. He lifted a bony fist in the air and shrieked, the angry dead and the hellhounds doing the same. Percy clapped her hands over her ears, almost overcome.

"Darkness wants us for his own!" Alexi cried to the other Guard. "But we want Peace! Whatever peace there is to be had." The academy resounded with his army's affirmative response, and the great clash began.

Flickering with blue light, the auditorium was awash in battle. Alexi's command of The Guards was lost to separate instances of chaos. Guards were torn to pieces, but they gave as well as they got, including against the dog creature of one then a hundred forms. The skull head of Darkness swiveled, his vertebrae clicking too loudly, his digits become razors. He was searching Percy out. Alexi stood before her, wondering how long he could hide her in the tumult.

Rebecca and Michael fought off countless dead to get to the chapel, where they found a stained-glass window of an angel that now happened to be a door. Blue light emanated from its sill. Climbing onto the ledge, Rebecca turned the small latch that opened the window. The glass swung inward to reveal a small crypt. Marianna lay atop a stone tomb there, like a corpse, and Beatrice and Aodhan paced to and fro.

The spectral pair turned in great relief to see Rebecca and Michael. Hoisting Marianna up, ash still clinging to bits of

her dress and hair, they practically threw her at Rebecca and
Michael, came out, closed the window behind them with a
gust of their spirit draft and flew off toward the fray, presumably to their respective Guards.

"Indeed," Rebecca muttered, readjusting Marianna's
weight in Michael's hold. "Where on earth do we take her
for safekeeping?"

"Do we bring her to the fight so we can keep an eye upon
her? Where *is* the fight? I hear only barking but I assume
poor Percy's hearing Armageddon itself."

Rebecca concentrated, using her senses to isolate the
centre of the storm. "The auditorium. But, shouldn't we
keep her outside all that mess?"

"Can we afford to stay separate?" Michael asked.

Rebecca grimly held the door as he carried Marianna
into the hall beyond.

"Come out, come out, little whore. I know you're here,"
Darkness sang, his jaw flapping. His sledge was still pulled
by hellhounds, his robes dripping a sickening precipitation
of gore. The mixture oozed everywhere, the water sapping
the will of The Guards, the blood inciting the hunger of
the unsatisfied dead.

Keeping to the rear of the auditorium, that wall of stone
behind him, Alexi remained a steady conduit, allowing the
Phoenix fire to flow through him. But as Percy feared, it
seemed it was taking a toll upon his body. But his eyes never
left her, ready in an instant to transfer every ounce of his
sorcery to protecting her.

Perhaps Darkness's senses were dulled by not having
eyes; surely, he could tell living mortals were in the room.
Or perhaps here, with the Whisper-world tied so close, his
surroundings all seemed very much the same. A few of The
Guards nearest had formed a barrier in front of the living
Guard, smashing back those enemies who dared venture
too close.

How, Percy wondered, was one to kill a god? It was a problem. Whatever she'd once been, she'd gone and gotten herself mortal. That seemed a distinct disadvantage.

It was as if Darkness read her mind. He called out, "You'll curse the day you went mortal, pet. I know a few things about you that I'm sure you can't resist, no matter what form you take," he added with a giggle. His jaw fell open. Pulpy red liquid poured forth, a vomitous fountain, its sickly sweet smell distinctively rotten fruit.

Pomegranate. Percy heaved at the odour.

"There you are, Persephone, dear. Smell is the most potent of all memories, they say, especially with a mortal nose. It never ceased to turn your stomach—you always promised I sickened you." Darkness howled with laughter, suddenly rising up nearby, red robes flapping, foul juice dripping. As he advanced, insects and worms sprouted from beneath his bony feet, their scrabbling, writhing forms wriggling forward, desperate to help decompose the living Guard.

Alexi roared and summoned a coil of blue fire. Darkness dodged. His hellhounds lunged forward, but he restrained them and lifted a hand. "Ah, ah, ah!" A slash mark appeared on Percy's white face, and then Alexi's, and both stumbled back, their faces weeping blood. Jane was immediately at their side, reversing the damage.

Alexi's next blast of fire seared Darkness's shoulder, but the god just laughed. "You're a broken little human possessed by a feather. Some weaponry," he scoffed.

"Don't I have you to thank for it?" Alexi spat. He gathered a seething force that pressed forward in huge, gusting flames, an assault that knocked Darkness back several paces, singed and gouged. The hellhounds retreated, too, echoing their master's snarl.

Aodhan drifted into view, causing Jane to look up in relief. Percy looked over, too. The ghost anticipated her inquiry, saying, "The headmistress has your friend," and he added his efforts to transmitting the winding cord of Jane's light to others across the battlefield.

Percy's protective light seared forth from her bosom, illuminating everything around her. Guards close by could partake of this bright warmth, absorbing strength and power against the onslaught. Both Jane's and Aodhan's hands changed position, to maximize and reflect her radiance.

"This will never end," Darkness whispered terribly. "You can't kill me; mankind made me out of hate and sorrow. But you can avoid this. You can give up. Admit that all these centuries of fighting were senseless. Apologize to the legions of souls you've enslaved in this pettiness. Phoenix is broken! Admit it! Return to me, and accept that the greater god wins!"

"Strike!" Alexi cried out, and many Guard who were victorious in their individual skirmishes were now able to lend hands. Roaring bolts of blue fire came from all directions, encasing their foe.

Darkness screamed, still not beaten. "I will take something you love! You keep loving, and so I must keep taking things away! I *will* break this pathetic habit! I don't love, I take! And because I do not love, I must win!" He turned his fiery eyes upon a new morsel, ever targeting the vulnerable.

Rebecca and Michael were just arriving. As they laid the still-unconscious Marianna on a shadowy ledge, her young and fragile body seized as Darkness appraised her. She shrieked in pain, her eyes opening only for a moment, then closing again in a faint. Michael placed his hands over her eyes. Elijah rushed over to wipe such nightmarish memories utterly clean. Percy's anger widened her bright light.

The enemy's army was composed of predators seeking fresh, innocent blood; Marianna was a pure and empty vessel, ripe once more for possession. Nauseating hunger burned in their eyes as they came flying at her, ten then twenty, each trying to gain purchase and seize her for possession. Percy cried out, trying to go to her, but Alexi kept her pinned within the protective circle of several Guards, her light maintaining a shield that seemed to keep the hounds of Darkness at bay. Her light also fended off his insects of decay.

"You're right," Michael cried. "We shouldn't have brought her here!" Lifting Marianna again, he and Rebecca fled back into the foyer, both enemies and spectral friends giving chase.

"To my office," Rebecca commanded.

Michael obeyed, and the two of them rushed down several corridors, Marianna still in tow. In the office they found Frederic hopping up and down on a wooden file cabinet, distressed, having shed a few black feathers onto the floor.

"Frederic, you were supposed to take refuge with Marlowe!" Rebecca scolded. The bird squawked.

Michael dumped Marianna in a chair and spun to face their pursuers, whose numbers now equaled six, three having been almost immediately dispatched by a most obliging and efficient Aztec Guard. But keeping six devilish fiends from a vulnerable body was no small task. He and Rebecca started in with a fresh cantus, but they were interrupted by a shriek. It was Percy's, and it made their blood chill. It was perhaps the most heartbreaking cry they'd ever heard. Alexi's anguished cry came swiftly after. Something was terribly wrong.

Michael and Rebecca stared at each other, ashen-faced. Thankfully, the Aztec Guard hadn't noticed, and they went on pummeling the enemy spirits.

"Go, Michael," Rebecca commanded. "We're almost done. We can spare you."

"Rebecca, I—"

"Percy needs you. I feel it. I'll be all right."

Tears rimmed Michael's eyes. "Rebecca Thompson, don't you dare be some martyr for—"

She reached out, grabbed his neck, pulled him to her and pressed her lips briefly to his. "I may yet have something to live for. I'll be no martyr. Now go."

Michael paused, breathless. He nodded and ran out the door, heartened by the battle cry Rebecca unleashed, casting a spirit out into the hall with the gust solely of her own power where it promptly disintegrated. She bellowed an impressive line of Blake, then a psalm for good measure.

Michael stopped at the edge of the auditorium. His friends stood frozen around Percy. Blood was everywhere, and a swarm of insects.

Darkness ignored the cerulean fire Alexi continued to throw, his red robes now ablaze, his eyes like burning coals. His skeletal jaw was a terrifying grin. He hovered a few yards away, held back but barely.

"Oh, you sorry girl. You never should have chosen this path. It is fraught with misery. You've so much to lose. You may think you have power over me with your little army of friends, but you see, some part of your body still remembers."

"I'm not her," Percy hissed. "You do not own me."

"Your light is hers."

Percy shook her head. "She no longer exists. Accept that she's gone, has rejected your claim once and for all. You can't now have power over this flesh, for it was never yours."

"All flesh is mine," Darkness snarled. "You are what she became, and I will have power over her remains forever." He lunged, and his frosty aura made The Guards' breaths crystallize. "All that is and all that *could be* will be mine, too."

An eviscerating pain doubled Percy over to gasp for air and clutch at Alexi's arm, causing him to send aside a stray jolt of blue fire. He caught her and cried for Jane in the same instant, pulling Jane back from where she'd been helping as a hellhound mauled a Norse mentalist. Jane's eyes widened in horror as she advanced.

Percy's lower body felt as though it were being ripped open. She clutched at her abdomen and her hands came away bloody. Red poured down from between her legs and rolled down the sloping auditorium pitch. Those insects born from the tread of Darkness frolicked in the crimson pool.

In a horrific sensation, Percy felt energy leaving her: her child, the child she'd not even had a chance to think about, to welcome, let alone cherish. Her heart and body cleaved in excruciating pain. When Alexi realized what was happening, his cry was just as unbearable.

"No!" Percy screamed, tears choking her, her hands clawing at herself with rage, her face contorting in anguish. A great wind whipped her snowy hair, her eyes ferocious suns. "You'll not have me! Not my love and not my child! DEATH WILL NOT HAVE MY CHILD!"

There were lines, apparently, even Darkness should not cross. He wholly underestimated the breadth of love's power. He always had. Blinding white light exploded from Percy's body in a thunderclap of brilliancy that made everyone wince, the rays actually dazzling shards that pierced directly through her foe and every vile spirit that happened to be near. The blast cracked the ribs around where Darkness ought to have had a heart, and it pulverized his torso, sending him hurtling into the lapping water at the bottom of the auditorium. His dogs splintered and dove into the water, howling and whining, the light too bright for their eyes. All insects and agents of decay were incinerated.

But the dual strains of the force she commanded and her loss of blood broke Percy's mortal body. She collapsed, caught by Alexi, who was barking orders for the leaders to continue striking Darkness without mercy. He lent one more blast of his own power, falling to his knees, sweat pouring off his brow, chest heaving. Remaining the sole living conduit for such a mass of eternal fire threatened to break him, too. But his fading wife needed him.

Beatrice was suddenly at his side, and a handsome dark-skinned man. "Oh, Percy," she breathed, seeing Percy's grave state. She turned to Alexi, seeing his and Percy's flesh reach their limits. She closed her eyes, and a surge of blue fire coalesced through her hands into Alexi, feeding him power to energize the gathered Guard who chanted for strength and to heal the mortal incarnation of their goddess. Alexi was a most powerful leader, but Beatrice had been one, too.

Jane directed the healing, she and Aodhan deftly gathering and cleansing her precious blood from the stones and surging it back toward her, replenishing what had been lost. A small ball of light that did not seem directly connected to Percy hovered just above Percy's abdomen, hesitant, like a fading star about to fall from the sky.

"Ah, ah," Jane said, tears falling from her eyes. "Michael," she murmured, "help!"

With exceeding care, the light of Jane's hands guided the tiny star back. It hovered as if unsure, confused. Michael dropped to his knees beside it. "'The light shines in the darkness,'" he wept at the small, sparkling orb, "'and the darkness shall not overcome it.' *The darkness shall not overcome it!*" The star of wonder dove back into the safety of its mother, and Percy's drooping eyes shot open. She gasped, a surge of pain accompanying the flood of warmth.

Michael's tears getting the better of him, he stood and looked around for Rebecca. His soul leaped to see her, ashen-faced, beyond the doorway. He nodded that the worst seemed to be passed, and she put a shaking hand to her mouth, steadying herself against the door frame.

Percy stirred. What had been an unimaginable amount of blood lost was returned again to her veins, the horror reversed.

Leaders pummeled Darkness with inexhaustible vengeance. His bones broke piece by piece; his miserable form disintegrated. The blue Phoenix fire living in the walls of Athens streamed in luminous waterfalls from the bricks, the scale having finally tipped in their favour, the grey pall reversed that had made this place the Whisper-world's domain.

Percy wanted to sit up, to see. She cleared allies from either side. Healers of The Guards, in rows around her, urged her to sit back and lie still. But she struggled to stand, feeling her strength surge back into her with the force of righteousness, unable to cope with the threat that Darkness might still hang over them.

Alexi's eyes were wolfish, his jaw clenched. One arm was back to protect Percy; his other hand continued casting fiery bolts into the shuddering pile of bones below, no matter that his magic was past spent; his fury sustained him. He would not stop until Darkness was dust.

Beatrice took the moment to present the distinguished, handsome Egyptian by her side. It was the man who first recognized Percy in the Whisper-world, and the man for whom she had fought so hard. Mr. Tipton bowed.

Percy opened her mouth to greet him, but before any pleasantries could be exchanged, her eyes were drawn to her enemy's bones, still encased in the neutralizing blue flame of Alexi and many other leaders. But, Darkness yet stirred. He would perhaps always be partly alive.

The bones jumped. Something whistled through the air. A long shard of bone hurtled directly toward her, a clear and unobstructed arrow seeking to pull her into death's arms after all. Time slowed, aching, terrible. Percy opened her mouth to cry out.

Jane stood just to the right. In that fraction of a moment, something changed on her face.

She took a step to the left.

A sickening crunch sounded as the javelin of bone struck her in the back and burst through her. Blood bubbled up from her lips, a gory shard jutting out just below her brooch.

The wailing cry Percy heard from The Guard, living and dead, would haunt her forever. Jane's body slowly pitched forward. Aodhan was at her side but unable to catch her with his incorporeal hands. Alexi released Percy and jumped forward, sweeping Jane gently to the floor, his eyes wide with shock.

The Guard healers swarmed. Jane was bathed in light, chants, words, cries. But Jane did not stir. They tried again. Stillness. The healers hung their heads and stepped back, stunned.

Rebecca, shrieking, sank to the threshold of the door-way, shaking her head and refusing to believe. Michael ran to her and cradled her, unable to look at this final unex-pected loss. Josephine had backed herself against the stone wall, tearing her hair and ripping her sacred locket from her neck, causing a gash and hurling the pendant aside.

The blue-fire mortar of Athens, still working on bring-ing the room back to its normal state, erupted in its own reaction. Alexi's fury melded with it, fire leaping from ev-ery pore of his body, tumbling Percy aside with its inten-sity. Every Guard leader gasped, for their bodies, too, gave up the borrowed ghost flame to create a roiling, gigantic flurry of winged fire and talons.

The watery traces of river reversed to again become the lip of the Athens auditorium stage. Alexi's fiery bird swept down toward the pile of bones, raging, evaporating any lingering vile spirit and enveloping the shards of Darkness in an oblivion of blue.

To Percy's ears, all went quiet. All she could hear was her own breath and her heartbeat. And fainter still, she imag-ined another heartbeat. A tiny one. Her tears flowed as she stood deathly still, but the world kept wailing silently as they stared down at Jane's body.

A glimmering, shimmering transparent form—sexless, gorgeous, its hands lit with glowing light, a pearlescent spirit unlike any ghost the London Guard had ever seen—lifted from Jane's body. The spirit had a music to it; as it wafted in the air it made a sparkling noise, a symphony of stars, the exquisite orchestration of their Grand Work.

"Her possessor," Rebecca choked from the doorway, stumbling forward into the room. "A Muse." The healing spirit looked sadly down, bent to kiss Jane's body and took flight. It soared to the front of the stage, where it swept in and among the other Guards, administering music and glory, beauty and hope, though it had lost the bodily instrument it so adored.

It suddenly dawned on Percy that something not of this world had long had hold on Jane, and that perhaps she'd wanted to give over to that embrace, as Beatrice had even suggested. Percy forced herself to look at the body. Aodhan floated nearby, kneeling at Jane's side, stroking her cheek with phantom fingertips, murmuring odes of aching love, his grey face paler than she'd ever seen it.

Jane's greyscale spirit, lacking colour not vibrancy, lifted out of her body with a laugh. She floated several feet above the melee to look down at everyone. Aodhan leaped up with a cry, reaching to touch the hem of her garment and thrilling that he finally could. He did not bother to hide his joy.

Beatrice, who'd been watching with her hands clutched around Ibrahim, moved forward. "You see? It's all right."

The spirit of Jane smiled and moved to take her outstretched hand. She turned to her fellows. "What on earth are you all wailin' about?" she insisted, her brogue thick with delight. They stared at her dumbly, so Jane turned to Percy. "Oh, that's right, Percy. Would you tell them what I'm sayin'?"

"She . . ." Percy gulped. "She wonders what on earth you all are wailing about."

"We need you," Josephine cried.

Jane looked around and shook her head. "No, you don't. It's over."

"I . . . I didn't deserve that, Jane," Percy murmured, guilt overtaking her in a feverish rush. "I didn't want you to die so that I might live."

Jane batted her hand in the air. "You and your child are desperately needed in this world. In that moment, there was no other way. Just like Beatrice said. Some sensible sacrifices have merit." Percy translated, tears coursing down her cheeks. "Now I'm needed in *this* world," Jane declared, floating to Aodhan's side and caressing his cheek. "We needed to each follow our hearts to get to the appropriate end of this journey. I finally followed mine." She glanced at Michael. "And Darkness has not overcome me."

Aodhan took her hand. Jane closed her eyes in bliss, bringing his now-tactile hand to her lips, kissing it slowly, relishing contact after a lifetime separate. Giggling, she glanced at her friends. "Don't worry, you'll see me haunting about. And Percy, tell Alexi that if he blames himself for this—as I'm sure he will—that I will swap his sherry out for Irish whiskey until the end of his days."

Percy related this information, and The Guard, while they could not laugh, at least gave a few shaky smiles. The tears returned soon enough, especially once Jane's ghost jigged out of the room with Aodhan, Beatrice and Ibrahim floating out alongside them, chatting gaily. The living Guard were left with the gruesome reality of Jane's body, which now lay in the aisle between auditorium seats, the last of the Whisperworld's dreadful amphitheatre having vanished.

Alexi bent and lifted the body, the bone that had pierced her having turned to sand. But they were not spared gore, as Jane's blood poured down his vest and dripped onto the floor in a thick trail. He laid her down upon a ledge at the back of the hall and unclasped his cloak to place over her body, his face a mask of pain.

He charged suddenly back down the aisle, his torn robes

flapping. Centre stage, the sullied red fabric that reeked of dog urine and Darkness's inanimate bones were a blaze of blue light, burning merrily like a hearth fire, and some Guards lingered on to watch and warm themselves in vengeance's glow. With a warlike bellow, a terrible sound of grief, Alexi sent the last of his power, wave after wave of lightning, magic, energy, again and again into the remains, as if the more he could just keep pummeling it, the more he could ensure it could never hurt anyone again. But he could not make it right.

Percy ran down to him, stumbling in her own weakness as she did, Michael darting in to take her by the arm. Alexi's Guard assembled but hung back, knowing they didn't dare try to stop him.

He kept striking until he fell to his knees. Percy rushed to take him in her arms, which found new strength in holding him. Her body muffled his heaving sobs. The blue bonfire of Darkness died down, its fuel gone and the conflagration having faded to flickering sapphire embers.

A wind picked up in the room, as did an ancient music, a heavenly balm. A murmur sounded, as the thick cerulean flames, entwined within every collected Guard, coalesced into enormous wings, an ephemeral and angelic form that was awesome in beauty and fearsome in masculine strength. "It is finished," the great angel whispered in all ears, hearts and veins.

The vision floated out the door, and Alexi somehow found the strength to tear off after it, breathing heavily, moving awkwardly. His Guard obediently up and followed. Upstairs to that sacred seal they ran, chasing the divine bonfire until it swirled over the motto of Athens, sparkling above the dictum of their Work before diving down into the image to rest, settling once more into the stone. With lingering licks of flame and then stillness, Athens was again mere bricks of a normal mortal school, settled solidly on foundations no longer precarious between worlds.

The six survivors turned and beheld their mass of spectral fellows, whose work was done. Each had destinations, desires, duties, and they wanted to go about them. But first they wished to pay respects. They wafted forward, filing before Percy and Alexi, bowing or nodding.

Dimly Percy registered what words she was offered. She was told by a few leaders and Hearts that her child would prove important. And while Percy's instincts told her that this was most certainly true, all Percy cared was that her husband and child were alive.

Beatrice floated forward from the crowd, her face troubled. "I did mean to tell you that I would have liked to have fought more at your side, my lady. But I needed to find and fight with my Guard—at least, the three of us who are now spirits."

"I believe you've fought at my side often enough," Percy murmured.

"True." Beatrice smiled. Her quiet, stoic husband was still present, and she took his hand and pressed it lovingly in both of hers. She gestured him forward, attempting again to present him.

"Hello, my lady. Ibrahim Tipton at your service," he said in a rich Arabian accent. "Raised by an Englishman, I learned to appreciate certain aspects of the country you've chosen as your own. I am glad to have had a part in fighting for you here, then and now." She sensed he was making peace with his past in this brief introduction.

"Hello, Mr. Tipton—and thank you," she murmured, sharing Beatrice's smile. "And where will all of you go? I pray you will go on toward Peace!"

Beatrice's lips thinned. "Some didn't make it safely onward this day. Some of us were overwhelmed, dragged back under into the despairing depths, back across the river. Some of these Guard will take to that realm again, to rescue their friends who fell. Some may choose to remain always vigilant. I cannot say. But most of us will go to Peace. Long awaited, and far from here . . . Peace. I've no idea what it will be like, but I've never anticipated anything so much as this blessed day."

Behind Beatrice, another figure broke ranks. A thin man in dark robes with skin that must have been darker in life and a face so engaging it was hard to look away floated toward Percy. In Arabic he said, "While this war is at an end, keep your heart open to the world, my lady. You never know what battles your lineage may face, in the air, in the ground . . . Don't forget us. And don't close *every* door."

While the words themselves might have an ominous cast, the man, clearly the Heart of his group, was so full of peace, assurance and love that Percy couldn't find any fear. He bowed and spun back to Ibrahim, clasping his friend's arm.

Beatrice spoke. "Don't mind Ahmed. He's always been full of tall, albeit brilliant, words. You, my lady, deserve a lifetime of peace. Please take it, for the worst is blessedly over. If Darkness is ever to manifest again, the good news is you're mortal and it won't be in your lifetime. And the cycle of the vendetta, at least, is at last broken. Good-bye, my friends. Good Work, and peace be ever with you."

"And also with you," Percy murmured. "Thank you for everything you did to bring me here. I'm sure it's been far more than I can fathom."

Beatrice paused. "Our Lady said before she took form that she hoped she'd have the good sense to thank me." She smiled. "She'd be pleased you're so sensible. And kind. She'd be most pleased by that. And by the man who adores you."

Percy turned to Alexi and took his hand. Only when staring at Percy did the pain in her husband's eyes ease. She turned back, but Beatrice and her Guard were gone. The remaining Guards bowed and filed down the stairs.

The air of Athens was sweetly restive; every hell-raising spirit was gone to oblivion or flung to the outer darkness. The press of dread was lifted from their veins, their minds clear in the stark dawn light. Only grief remained, and none of them was sure what to do.

Michael gestured toward the trail of pilgrimlike spirits leading down toward the chapel. "Come," he suggested. "Let us follow."

Alexi nodded. "I will bring Jane's body."

Carrying her, it felt like a funerary procession. The Guards directly ahead of them, some in buckskin and feathers, some in ballooning pants and curving hats, were consoling one another. Clearly one of their number had not made it to his peaceful moment. A greyish spirit that would have been a ruddy-skinned woman pressed her hands to her breast, raising high, keening notes into the air that only Percy heard. By the mourner's side, a man wearing a wolf skin placed an arm around her shoulder, the feathers in his hair fluttering with the tiniest remainders of flickering blue flame. War, no matter how unusual, had its costs.

Soft pledges were made, vengeances were declared, and above all companionship was renewed, the one constant of their Work. Only Percy heard, tears silently rolling down her cheeks. She was utterly struck by the weight of her own mortality, far from the shifting and everlasting forms of any divinity. Each moment was increasingly precious to her, and each moment urged her never to take even the slightest bit of life for granted. Her hand pressed to her abdomen, she closed her eyes and gave a thousand thanks, the rosary beads against her chest picking up the echo and flooding her soul with blessings.

As they passed Rebecca's office, en route to the chapel, the headmistress gestured Percy inside. There Percy found Marianna laid unconscious in a chair, her face peaceful. She rushed forward and kissed her friend softly on the forehead.

"We'll move her to the infirmary promptly," Rebecca promised, and held out her hand. "Now you should rejoin the others."

Percy took Rebecca's outstretched hand and brought it to her lips. "I cannot thank you enough. For everything."

Rebecca swallowed. "My duty and my pleasure."

They moved in silence to the chapel.

Alexi had laid Jane upon the tomb of Athens's founder, careful to keep her covered, as none of them would be able to see her face without breaking down. He held out his hand for Percy, his gaze sharpening upon the sight of her. Only when she moved to his side were their bodies able to stop shaking, each the other's foundation. He kissed her forehead. She murmured her love and he kissed her again, a tear dripping onto her cheek.

The procession of the spirit Guards filed down into the space sacred to them all, finally released to their private destinies. The living watched. Michael reminded his companions to breathe by moving slowly past them, one by one, putting a hand to their constricted throats.

When the last of The Guard vanished into the darkness, Elijah, Josephine, Rebecca and Michael were suddenly tugged forward, something pulling from inside their bodies and snapping out of them. Wispy, shimmering forms more angel than human floated before them, nodded, blew kisses, sparkling with song and soulful splendour. These collective possessors, these Muses they'd never faced, never known as friends or personalities, only as incumbent powers, were now separate entities. Their indescribable faces full of pride, they moved close to their instruments and touched each cheek with adoration.

"With you we are greatly pleased. Now rest, beloveds," they said. "We're all due for a nice rest." Then, in unison, the divinities flew ahead.

Percy expected them to duck inside the portal, but instead the quartet held out their hands just before it. The portal snapped shut, and the Muses sighed with weary relief. They wanted no part of the Whisper-world, it seemed.

They did not suit, Percy admitted. So it was no surprise when the four heavenly forms flew back over The Guard's heads and followed the same course as the Phoenix fire, on toward the centre of the building, divine friends intending to rest together once more, settling back into the stalwart bricks of Athens Academy.

The school chapel sat white and quiet. The amber stained-glass angels along the wall had lost their ethereal glow and looked now like average windows. The silence was, to Percy, after all the raucous spiritual noise, deafening.

Alexi waved a tired gesture toward the altar. One candle sputtered to a low flame, but that was it. He stared at his hand.

Tensing, he cast that powerful arm forward again, expecting the portal to their sacred space to open again as it always had under his command. The altar remained a plain space bathed in white cloth, nothing supernatural about it.

"They're gone. Does that mean we are finished?" Michael breathed.

"I . . ." Rebecca searched her own mind. "I don't have my library. My mind doesn't have its resources."

"Damn," Elijah muttered. "It will be so much more difficult to get away with things."

Josephine smirked, but then suddenly her eyes widened. "I wonder if the British Museum will take down my art. Will its protective charms have worn off?"

Alexi pursed his lips. "You spend your lives complaining about the Work, and now, when you're released—"

"Well, I complain about you to no end, Alexi. It doesn't mean I wouldn't miss the very hell out of you if you were gone. It is the way of love," Elijah said, his brow furrowing.

Rebecca shook her head. "We're such mortals in the end. Never satisfied. But you have your café, Josie, and your art. Michael, the church. Elijah, your . . ."

"Wealth and ill manners," he was quick to offer. "Outlasting even the very face of death. Oh, and I have Josie. That's something, I suppose."

She swatted happily at his shoulder.

"Yes." Rebecca nodded. She turned to Alexi and looked him in the eye. "And you, Alexi, have Percy, this school, and . . . your child. Congratulations."

Alexi drew Percy close. Percy opened her mouth to offer Rebecca her blessings, but something in the headmistress's expression stilled her.

"I . . ." Rebecca said. Her hand moved unconsciously toward Michael. Staring down at it, he blushed. While his gift might have vanished, his smile was still magic, and he reached out for her. Rebecca seemed to come to herself, though, as if she'd forgotten she was not alone. She cleared her throat. "I have the blessed bricks of Athens."

Her eyes flickered toward Jane's draped body. Her hand did not make contact with Michael's; instead, she moved inexorably toward the body, her face betraying more emotion than she'd ever before let show.

"And Jane has . . ." Josephine tried, her voice breaking.

"The hand of her longtime love, and the peace of eternal life," Michael spoke up. He'd followed Rebecca a few paces but respectfully kept his distance.

They all stared at the black-draped body atop the antechamber tomb. Powers or no, spirits or no, that their living circle was incomplete was an irrevocable fact. Rebecca placed a hand on either side of Jane's covered head, and her tall spine bent, weighted, and shuddered as silent tears poured down her face. "Dear God," she gasped to the body, her shaking hand hovering over the Irishwoman's head as if wanting to touch but not wanting to feel the solidity of death beneath her fingertips. "Dear God, it should have been me."

There was a terrible silence. Everyone stood stunned. Michael clenched his fists, his hopeful face stricken. He stepped toward her. "Rebecca, you mustn't—"

She snapped jarringly into her usual stiff pose, clapped her hands together and swiftly wiped her eyes. "I think we ought to clean the auditorium," she said, her head high, crossing between them and toward the door. "And then I wouldn't mind a drink."

Deep below London, a few clusters of bones still bobbed along sewer eddies, unfortunate escapees that hadn't gone unnoticed by all Londoners. Amid small remembrances and other scraps of sentiment, a few sealed jars, small and round, floated out along the Thames. Their contents hissed and rattled.

Surging onward into the estuary, the jars swept out into the North Sea and, facing the English Channel, bobbed onward toward the shores of France, gaining momentum.

Epilogue

Seven months later

Percy sat in a tall wicker chair and looked out at her lush and immaculate summer garden. She'd roused it from weeds to glory with uncanny skill, as if the plants sprouted from her very touch.

The birds in the bushes were nearly as raucous as the assembled company. Alexi was fussing by her side, arranging pillows and setting still more food upon the tray beside her. Smiling up at him, her white-blue eyes blinked from beneath her wide hat. She tried to adjust forward, but her abdomen was round and huge beneath her flowing gown and she chuckled, for she couldn't truly move with any amount of grace.

"What do you need?" Alexi asked.

"Nothing, love, I'm just trying to get a better look at our friends."

He eased her forward, and they gazed at the assembled company, hand in hand. Josephine sat on the lap of Lord Withersby in a fine dress that nearly swallowed him with its absurd poufs, eagerly sharing the ways in which she was shocking high society while cultivating their secret obsession with her. On the garden bench opposite, Michael was close at Rebecca's side as she smiled, absently fiddling with the ring on her finger.

Alexandra Rychman's wheelchair sat beside the Withersbys, and she was placing bets on which members of parlia-

ment or royalty would proposition Josephine first. Lord
Withersby was adding handsomely to the pot, delighted by
the game.

The Rychman estate had seen more activity in the past
seven months than it had in Alexi's lifetime. The entire east
wing was opened up and refreshed, and Alexandra had been
moved into it; more staff had been hired to deal with the
growing needs of a growing family, and there were weekly
dinners with friends, teachers and even students of Athens.
Marianna and Edward, of course, hadn't been left out. Thankfully, Marianna did not recall anything of what happened
prior at that estate, or of spectral war. Percy was only too
happy to assure her that her related dreams were nothing
more than nightmares.

A sturdy woman stepped from the French doors and hovered over Percy anxiously.

"Yes, Mrs. Wentworth, what's troubling you now?" Percy
looked up with a grin. "I swear, between you and Alexi, I've
no chance to fuss over myself. You've anticipated me before
I even think of a need."

"I just . . . I just don't know about all this activity," she
said, refreshing Percy's tea. "It's too much for a woman in
your condition. You realize women of your station go away
and weather their months in fine country cottages, relaxed
and quiet. They're certainly not seen in this time—"

"But she's so beautiful, everyone should see her!" Alexi
cried, kissing her slightly plumped cheeks, which blushed as
his lips touched them.

Mrs. Wentworth folded her arms. "Just when I thought
the lot of you were attempting to act civilized. After twenty
years. It does make a woman wonder. What took Lord Withersby so long to take a wife? And what on earth does his family say? Josephine is lovely, but, goodness, it couldn't be a
stranger pair to make a social call, especially considering his
station. Now Mrs. Carroll there, that was quite the shock. I'd

long given up hope for the headmistress. They're sweet, Michael and she . . ."

"Yes, that," Percy said pointedly, staring at Rebecca and Michael with a smile. Marlowe the cat lay curled at Rebecca's feet. "Those two are a story in and of themselves. Not without divine intervention. I'd say it was worthy of Dickens, wouldn't you, husband?" she asked, her eyes sparkling.

Alexi smirked. "'Twas a Christmas miracle, indeed."

Mrs. Wentworth blinked. "But why ever did you all wait so long? Of course, you, Professor, if you'll forgive me . . . You I'd written off ages ago!"

"And I didn't make the proper social match either, now, did I?" Alexi said, his hands fingering the pearlescent braid down Percy's shoulder.

"Oh! But Percy, she's—why, a king would take her as his own if he got to know her dear and precious heart! But the rest of your . . ."

"'Baffling bohemian set,' I believe you once called us," Percy offered.

"Percy was a particular inspiration," Alexi offered. "That dear, precious heart of hers allowed everyone to at last open their eyes. We saw love staring us in the face." He drew his finger down her cheek and smiled in a way that made her heart skip.

"Be all of that as it may," Mrs. Wentworth continued. Alexi rolled his eyes, but she was unperturbed. "Professor, don't you think your wife would best be somewhere quiet and restful instead of weathering those howls of Lord Withersby and Mr. Carroll? Your dear sister Alexandra and I could give Percy good quiet company just an hour north. That way she wouldn't be excitable with all this entertaining—"

"We don't make Percy excitable while entertaining. That's why we have you!" Alexi stated, blinking up at her. "I do hope you've enjoyed your raise."

"Yes, sir, thank you, sir, you were always generous and

then some. And do forgive me, Professor, I know you see things in a way that no one else I've ever met does."

"Why, thank you," Alexi said.

"And I'm not saying I know what's best for Mrs.——"

Percy chuckled. "My dearest Mrs. Wentworth. I grew up a lonely orphan in a quiet convent. All I ever wanted in life was a family filling my home with living, mortal sound. I never dreamed I'd have a husband, much less such a striking one, and I daresay I can't go without his company, or these howls of laughter, for even the length of a pregnancy." She gestured Mrs. Wentworth closer. "You see," she murmured conspiratorially, "there was a very special and very secret duty that the lot of us had to keep. Dangerous. Elite. But we've done our service well, and have been rewarded with a . . . retirement. And so we're all making up for a deal of lost time. We deserve it."

She stared up with great gravity and Mrs. Wentworth's eyes widened, putting her hands to her lips. "Oh! Surely my lady means the Crown! You've been serving Her Majesty as spies, haven't you?"

"Something of the sort." Percy smiled.

"And if you tell anyone," Alexi said, "we'll have to dispatch of you. So please keep running this estate as well as you do, and we'll live in it as we see fit."

Mrs. Wentworth straightened herself, her bosom puffed out with pride. "Indeed. Professor. My dear lady." She gave them both a salute and exited, head held high.

Percy put a hand over her mouth to keep from laughing. She turned to Alexi. "I'm sorry if I said something I oughtn't, but she would drive me mad."

Alexi grinned. "It's all right. We can say anything we like now that we're powerless. People saw bones choking out of London sewers, but what can we do? Children in hospital wards have been seeing an angel who looks suspiciously like Jane, but what can we do? Our little clan is finally living life. What else can we do?" He threw his hands jovially in the air.

She reached out to draw him into a kiss. He slid his chair closer, took one of her hands in his and placed his other hand on her womb. "You don't mind that I'm no longer filled with mysterious power?" he asked.

While his tone was disinterested, Percy knew he was desperate for reassurance. While his life had lost its previous meaning, the life of a husband and father would resonate with a joy the Grand Work could never offer.

She snickered. "You don't mind that I'm not actually a goddess?"

Alexi shook his head. "I may still call you one, though."

"And I still think you're full of power."

His chiseled lips pursed in supreme satisfaction.

Percy leaned back in her chair, breathing deeply the scent of flowers, feeling the warmth of a small patch of sun on her white face and knowing that she'd never been happier. She pressed their entwined fingers gently against her abdomen, and in response there was a movement from within, a tiny kick.

A soft gasp leaped from Alexi, and he dropped to her side. Sliding his hands around her, he laid his head upon her rounded womb and looked up at her in wonder; this fearsome, striking man brought to his knees by a tiny kick. That, Percy thought, was power enough.

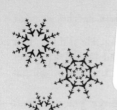

Join Rebecca and Michael for

A CHRISTMAS CARROLL

Featured in

A MIDWINTER FANTASY

Available October 2010

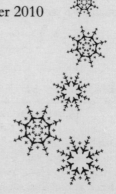